"Goodman's rendering of this true-life adventure is both captivating and riveting."

Sheldon Winston, Educator

"Wrath of the Shinai *is the ultimate story of redemption, revenge, and the meaning of love."*

Neil Kanowsky, Advertising Executive

"A smashing study of one person's courage to surmount the greatest obscenity ever endured by a child."

Larry Liguori, Pilot

AND FROM THE CHARACTERS IN *THE SHINAI* . . .

"What is mine is mine and you won't take what is mine."
"You can't beat me, because I am willing to do anything to win. I am willing to hurt you in a way that no one else has ever done."
"Let me die; I disgraced myself."
"What I did was wrong. I held him up and punished him rather than finish him like I could have. I didn't care."
"There are a lot of things you don't know about my life. If you want to leave, now would be a good time."

—Gian

"I am the only person you are ever to fear."
"The best way to understand pain is to endure it yourself. A good fighter can take pain."
"You cannot care about anybody."
"You are no better than the ground I piss on."
"I guarantee one of those men would have beaten you to death and never had a second thought about it."
"Never give him hope. Never let hope exist in your opponent. If he thinks he has a chance, you have done something wrong."
"What you do should have no feeling. Fighters limit themselves. You have to be willing to go anyplace—to do anything."

—Katsuro

"Katsuro, you made this child into a robot. He is not a man—he is a fighting machine. Scripted to fight, maim, and maybe kill. He feels no pain. He inflicts pain. You made him this way. What did you expect?"

—Michael

"It was because of your eyes. The first time I met you I knew you had a lot of pain and were so sad."

—Catherine

"Every week I'm going to come here and you will give me a piece of your money. And just so you remember me, I'm going to break the opposite hand of the hand you write with. Every time you look down at it, you'll remember me, and if you fail to pay me, I will cut it off."

—Ryuu

"They are my children. They are my blood. I could not give them what I gave you."
"That is supposed to make it better?"
"I don't have to make it better. I feel at peace with what I have done. Look at what I have given you. Good luck."

—Katsuro and Gian

The Wrath of the Shinai is inspired by the life of Gian Aaron Molina. The memory of Gian's childhood is consistent with any child's memory. These recollections are filled with challenges that could have numbed Gian's recall, controlled his focus, and yet stimulated repressive thoughts. Since Gian's memory could have been impaired by multiple factors, the author has taken literary license in telling this story of abuse, brutality, redemption, revenge, and the search for love, even though the basic story remains true to Gian's adventure.

This novel is based on the memories of a tortured human being whose very existence is due to his determination to survive and live an existence worth living. However, some episodes have been fictionalized. Characters, names, places, and incidents have been changed to protect the innocent, even though they are inspired by actual events. Therefore, any similarity to actual persons and events is coincidental.

—Don Goodman

WRATH OF THE SHINAI

SHINAI NO IKARI

竹刀の怒り

A NOVEL
by

DON GOODMAN

with

G.A. MOLINA

iUniverse, Inc.
Bloomington

Wrath of the Shinai

iUniverse books may be ordered through booksellers or by contacting:

iUniverse
1663 Liberty Drive
Bloomington, IN 47403
www.iuniverse.com
1-800-Authors (1-800-288-4677)

ISBN: 978-1-4759-5568-2 (sc)
ISBN: 978-1-4759-5569-9 (ebk)

Printed in the United States of America

iUniverse rev. date: 10/11/2012

ACKNOWLEDGMENTS

For the many who provided invaluable help, whose knowledge made my job a little easier, and who gave of their time, I thank you.

Richard Potashin, a Ranger at Manzanar National Historic Site, whom I met in the summer of 2008, gave me the insight to see where it was possible to leave Manzanar during the war even if you were a Japanese prisoner.

To my wife, Sally, whose dedication, caring, and persistent search for perfection in editing made this novel a huge part of both our lives. Besides, she may have spent more time editing than I did writing. In fact, I know she did.

To my friend, Brian Adelstein, who spent many hours combing this tome for inconsistencies, offered a positive critique, and urged me on.

To Gian Aaron Molina, who lived through an incredible, unbelievable childhood of horrific abuse and not only survived but turned his abuse into a positive force.

To Gina's wife, who went with the flow in allowing this epic to be written.

To all my grandchildren, Danya, Jack, Jason, Erika and Sam (in order of their becoming part of our family), who keep me young in thought. To my son, Ken, whose insights into Aaron's life led to such a remarkable film script. To my daughter, Lesley, who has always encouraged me to continue writing and telling stories.

A special thanks to Danya whose talent as an artist made the Shinai's cover so enticing for readers.

To Ryan Boyd my finish editor. A mysterious voice over the phone who took the final challenge and nailed it.

To Norika Keimi for her translation into Japanese.

Our friend from the top of the Tower of Pisa, Kaori Yamamoto, whose email after our brief meeting was a delightful surprise. Thank you for your translation to Japanese, also.

PROLOGUE

Two compact, muscular teenagers, fellow members of the United States Martial Arts team, competing in London for the World Martial Arts Championships, arrived late at their hotel in the Bayswater-Lancaster Gate region north of Hyde Park. They strode up the front steps of the famed White Hotel and were looking forward to a good night's sleep after an intense three-day competition and a hearty meal of American food at the Hard Rock Café.

"I couldn't believe Katsuro let you out of his sight tonight, Gian. He is the strictest guardian I have ever met. Does he ever let you train with anyone else but him?"

Gian smiled at the thought of being allowed out tonight without his usual companion and mentor. "No, never. It is his way or no way."

"He sure is a taskmaster. I don't know if I could ever train under him. He is tough." The eighteen year-old John would never realize how prophetic his words were.

Gian, trained to a code of silence about his upbringing and his childhood, just grunted and remained silent so the conversation about Katsuro would end. "I'm looking forward to a good night's sleep. I'm tired."

John held his talk for a few minutes as they entered the small, antiquated elevator and slowly ascended to their room on the third floor. "This elevator gives me the creeps. It feels like it might quit running any minute. Scares the crap out of me. Don't you get claustrophobic in these things?"

Gian didn't answer. He was anxious for the ride to end. He seldom got to room with a teammate from the American team. Katsuro was always his only companion. But for some reason the team captain and leader, Ed Riso, from the Bronx, assigned John to be his roommate, and Katsuro never said a word as far as Gian knew. Equally puzzling to Gian was that on some evenings and several afternoons, Katsuro disappeared for short and then long periods of time. Never had Katsuro let his protégé out of his sight.

But Gian didn't ask, because he had been taught not to question his mentor. Never!

The two teenagers quickly undressed and dove into their twin beds for a good night's sleep . . . A sleep that would never come.

Dressed in a full business suit, a fast-moving Katsuro, belying his eighty-seven years, burst through the front lobby of the White Hotel and raced up the stairs rather than taking the old rattle-trap elevator. He asked his attendant, who carried his wristwatch, for the time. He did not want to be late, so he hustled to the third floor and unceremoniously banged repeatedly on his protégé's door.

"*Juko*, it's time to get up and see the city. Open the door." The words were gruff and demanding.

Gian heard the voice and sprang straight up and out of bed. He bounded for the bolted door. Katsuro burst in and growled, "I want to show you something important. Get dressed and come with me."

Quivering from the loud outburst, John asked meekly, "Can I come, too?"

Katsuro wanted to say no but thought better. He would need a witness to destiny. John could be that witness. Careful planning of possible events and outcomes was always in the back of Katsuro's mind. *Never go without a design and plan. Always know what you will do in any circumstance.*

The three descended into the streets of London, followed by the two attendants who accompanied Katsuro like shadows everywhere he went. It was 23:30—just enough time to meet the inevitable. Gian strode with the old master as they crossed one intersection after another, heading for wherever the old man was taking them. As they slowed, Katsuro said, "Just follow me. It is time for you to see real life."

John was puzzled but he knew better than to ask. Besides, the old master scared him. Gian never asked. His training was to follow orders. He knew the consequences of ever asking or questioning his mentor.

Katsuro stopped at the front entrance to a pub bearing the curious name Lamb and Flag. A sign swung harmlessly over the pub's entrance: "Bucket of Blood," printed in red. Upon entering, the three hardly noticed the garish-looking interior. Over the din of drinking and carousing customers Katsuro shouted, "Follow me," as he waved his right hand in a continuous forward motion. Gian, a muscular, five-foot-nine, 165-pound fifteen-year-old, pushing his way past the ale-swigging hordes, tried to keep up with Katsuro, who simply threw aside the drinkers as a bouncer would. They edged toward a narrow door at the back of the pub.

"Come!" It was a command of impatience. Katsuro opened the door and slid inside. Gian, John, and the shadows followed. They had entered a room that resembled a massive barn. The two boys stood stunned. A crowd surrounding a series of mats sprawled across the floor roared at the chaos they were watching intently. As Gian closed in on the scene, he saw two swarthy, sweaty men of immense size battling each other in a style of fighting he had never seen. Katsuro shouted over the din, "This is street fighting. There are no rules except two: no eye gouging and no biting. The last person standing is the winner, or if one quits. It is a fight to the death."

A large black man, with muscles resembling pieces of rippling steel and a bald head glistening from the intensity of the lights hanging from the ceiling, brought his knee into the groin of a barrel-chested hairy specimen. The black man sent the ape-like creature back on his haunches. The ape, holding his crotch and screaming in pain, fell back onto the mat. The black man, his knee aiming straight for the groin again, fell on him. The ape slid to his left and the knee, aimed at his vital parts, fell on his inner thigh. The ape rolled quickly to his right, throwing the black man off balance. The ape quickly drilled an elbow into the black man's neck sending him reeling, face down, onto the mat.

The ape rose to his feet and kicked the black man in the stomach as he lay on the mat soaked in his own sweat and blood. The black man flipped to his left and tried to rise. Again and again the ape's right foot punished the black's midsection until he puked. The ape stepped back, and the black man lay on the mat, barely moving.

Gian and John stood transfixed. They had never seen anything like this street-fighting. John, terrified at this savage beating of another human being, drew back. Gian stood his ground. He wasn't disturbed by what he had seen. He wondered what he would have done had he been fighting. He watched the ape accept the crowd's congratulations and walked off the mat to collect his money.

"Only the winner gets paid." Katsuro beckoned for the two boys to follow him. He stood at the entrance to the fight room where the last fighter had entered. "*Juko*! You have often told me you don't know how good you are. Tonight, you will find out. You will fight next."

Horrified, John pulled back. "Mr. Katsuro, these grown men are twice Gian's size. He could get killed."

"Silence, you! It is time *Juko* learns if he is a man. Remember, rules are made to be broken. This is a street fight, and the person you are fighting wants his money. Let's find out just how good you are."

Gian stood silently. He closed his eyes and saw the winter landscape of his home in northern Japan. He imagined the soft white snow he once thought was heaven. His mind traveled to another time when the old man stood above him and whipped him for not following his directions, for not taking what was his, for not doing his best against all odds. His mind suddenly went blank. All thought left his being. His very soul fell into a trance, a ritual of repetitive action, of a body and mind trained to focus on only one thing.

Katsuro stood back knowing Gian was mentally preparing for his destiny. Mechanically, like a trained robot, Gian removed his shirt. Katsuro led him behind a door and handed him a pair of fighting trunks with elastic lacing. Gian's trim figure inhaled slowly. In and out. In and out. His eyes glazed with a single focus. Fear never entered his new dimension—fear was not permitted. Only the mindlessness of combat and victory ever impinged on his space. He forged an iron will. He became *metal*, with an indomitable spirit based on repetitive practice and experience. Gian had been fighting since he was three.

It was time to show he was a man.

Like the great Samurai warriors that preceded him, Gian stepped out onto the battlefield, his private battlefield of mats, without swords, without steel, but with steel resolve. No thought—just reaction.

Gian barely saw his opponent. The giant across the mat had a belly that jiggled as he walked. His legs looked like slabs of meat.

There was no referee—just the two combatants. The large surly crowd wanted blood. The betters called for their money. Pure hell surrounded the mats.

Gian focused. He saw the man, more than twice his size, breathing heavily as nearly 400 pounds of fat plodded those few steps to the center of the mats. With the speed of a jaguar and a fist of iron, Gian shot a straight jab into the big man's gut. The fat man, slow but powerful, drew a breath, stepped back, and then forged forward. Gian whipped a leg across the man's belly and drilled a knee into his solar plexus. The giant slowed again, but then moved forward. Gian took a step back, rolled to the mat and whipped his legs across the big man's leg, knocking him off balance. The fat man dropped to the mat. Like the Samurai, looking for a kill, Gian landed on the big man and drove an elbow into his windpipe. The giant wheezed trying to catch his breath.

And then the pummeling began—a jab, a punch, a roundhouse fist to the face, over and over and over. One fist shot after another, tearing the flesh from the giant's nose, his bones splintering. His cheekbone swelled from the constant pummeling and finally burst into a bloody pulp. Still, Gian saw none of this. He knew he had to keep hitting this man. He raked a backhand across the ear and the ear, too, burst into a bloody mess.

Many hands dragged Gian from the collapsed giant. Gian felt exhilarated. He had pummeled the man. He had beaten him to within an inch of breathing no more. He heard the crowd cheer him.

"Great fight, young man," a patron, holding a fistful of money, yelled at Gian.

As Katsuro came to his side, Gian waited for words of praise. Instead he heard, "Why did it take you over seven minutes to beat this fat slob? Too long. You took too long to beat him. You will fight again."

John took a deep breath before sputtering, "B . . . b . . . but . . ."

"Quiet, you! Not one word. You are a child. *Juko* needs to prove he is a man. You will fight again."

John leaned next to Gian. "You can't fight again. You could get killed!"

Gian shook off his friend without a word. He threw his head back and, like the robot he had become, grew detached from everything and everyone around him. Once again, all thought left him. The warrior was back. The warrior was back without fear.

John's eyes swept across the mats. The man stepping onto the mat was incredibly tall, at least a foot taller than Gian. His arms hung below his knees. His ears stuck out like a donkey's. His hair was matted to his forehead, probably hiding scars proving him to be a street warrior. A wide mustache covered other scars. John could only imagine the number of times he had been to war.

Gian's mind worked like a well-oiled clock. In sync with his training and experience, Gian envisioned how to fight this battler. He entered his personal phase of *Heihō*—a spiritual place in Gian's mind. There he found belief in his superiority, an awareness of his invincibility, and his understanding of what he had gone through to become indestructible.

John stepped back from the mat. His stomach was churning. His hands were cold and clammy. Would he witness the death and destruction of his friend?

Gian kept replaying Katsuro's words, *"You took too long. You took too long . . . too long . . . you . . ."*

Mustache ran to the middle of the mat and stopped. At that instant Gian knew he had him beat. The man didn't charge and attack him. He stopped short. Was he showing fear, or maybe caution? Regardless, Mustache was his.

Gian ducked under a roundhouse right from Mustache's long arms and buried a straight jab into his wishbone, just below the chest cavity. Gian's fingers dug deep into the tall man's chest. Mustache dropped his right hand to clutch the torn flesh. Gian whipped his left leg to the man's right side, burying his knee into his rib cage. He quickly dropped to the mat and slung his leg across the back of Mustache's left knee. The tall man fell to the mat clutching his leg. Gian leapt like a wildcat and dropped a knee to Mustache's head as he drove the hard bone of his elbow into the tall man's cheekbone. Mustache summoned his strength and drove a fist into *Juko's* groin.

John flinched and moaned.

Gian never felt the pain. He never touched his groin. He made no sound. He was oblivious to the blow. He was set only on one goal, beating his opponent and beating him quickly. Gian delivered a punishing blow to Mustache's neck, then clubbed his elbow into the man's face and began the pummeling until hands pulled him from the prone body.

Gian smiled inwardly. *That wasn't seven minutes.* He had beaten him quickly.

Katsuro grabbed *Juko* by the arm and pulled him back. "You didn't protect your groin. He touched you. I warned you to watch out. You got hit. Fight again."

Gian's body was pure sweat. John offered to get his friend water. "He wants you to fight again? I can't believe it."

"No water! *Juko* must learn to do without and suffer for his faults. Leave him alone!" John withdrew once more.

The crowd listened as the announcer read the names of the next two combatants. When they heard *Juko*'s name, there was a loud buzz. A well-bearded man, half drunk, holding a drink, staggered up to Gian before Katsuro could grab him. "You crazy kid. This guy you're fighting next will kill you. He has never been beaten. You're good, kid, but not that good. Duck out now, kid."

"Get away from him you old drunk. *Juko* will beat him and beat him bad."

The bulldog-like man on the other side of the mat stood without moving. His eyes never left Gian. He followed him across the mat. But Gian never saw the bulldog. John whispered to Gian. "This guy is left handed, Gian. Watch out for him."

Gian knew he had made a mistake and had temporarily lost his *Heihō*. *Heihō* must help him refocus for this encounter.

Gian knew the bulldog was intent on slicing him apart and he had to prepare. Gian had no fear. Katsuro had always told him, *"I am the only person you are ever to fear."* The instant the fight started Gian did the unexpected, charging across the ring and ramming his gloveless thumb straight and deep into bulldog's throat. The bulldog flopped to the mat gasping for air. His face turned purple. Gian, like he had done twice before, fell on the man and began pummeling him with both hands, driving his fists into the man's face. The crowd, stunned, grew silent and let the beating continue. The bulldog fell unconscious. Gian stood above the man and walked away.

The fight was over. Jericho stepped next to Katsuro. "Your fighter want to come back next week? I can get him a great fight with good money."

Katsuro said nothing as Gian dressed. Katsuro put his arm around Gian's neck and walked out into the early morning dew of London. The three sauntered back to the White Hotel. The silent shadows always there, always silent. Gian waited for Katsuro to speak but he never said a word. The three walked up to the third floor. John and Gian entered their room and Katsuro stood at the door.

Finally, Katsuro broke his silence. "Could you have killed that man? Could you have killed him?"

The fifteen-year-old stood in silence, not knowing what to say.

"Answer me! Could you have killed him?" Katsuro raised his voice.

Gian stuttered, "I . . . I don't know. I don't know." Gian's voice faded, his head bowed.

"If you couldn't have killed him, you failed. You lost. You have to want to kill him and be willing to kill him. He would have killed you. You failed! You failed! You are not yet a man!"

Katsuro shut the door. Gian stood silently. *I have failed. Failed. Failed again!*

* * *

Three Days Before . . .

the midnight mauling of the three street fighters by a fifteen-year-old, Katsuro, the martial arts master and *Juko*'s trainer, made several visits to the Bucket of Blood with his silent shadows. These visits were to a man named Jericho, who was always one step ahead of the law that sought him only when the complaints against him by the powerful who felt cheated became too many.

Katsuro, a man of immense wealth and immense power, and obsessed with perfection, needed Jericho, and so he met him in the Bucket of Blood three times.

At the end of the first day, when the American Martial Arts Team met its counterparts from England, Katsuro made a call to a telephone number he had secured from the head of the British team.

The captain of the British Team, a man in his sixties, had known Katsuro from other tournaments. "Jericho is his name. He runs fringe-street fighting events at several local establishments. He's always up against the law but has never been convicted of anything. He's the guy to see."

"Give me a contact number for him," Katsuro demanded in a businesslike tone, but still polite to a fault.

The British captain wanted to ask Katsuro why he wanted this contact, but bit his tongue, knowing Katsuro's reputation. A reputation that said, *Leave him alone, never ask questions but be polite. Things ended better that way.*

The muscular, compact British captain tore a piece of paper from a pad he carried, wrote down a number, handed the paper to Katsuro, said "Good luck," and walked away.

Katsuro had worked hard on his reputation. It got him what he wanted quickly and without any complex explanations. This detachment, he felt, was important for getting things done. The number he dialed was answered with, "Yeah?"

"I wish to speak to Jericho."

Cautious to a fault, Jericho asked, "How did you get this number and who wants to know?"

Katsuro uttered the name of the British captain.

"Okay, Jericho here. Who's this?"

"My name is Katsuro. I wish to meet with you. I have a business proposition, one you will like."

"Tell me about it." Jericho, a Welshman by birth, once a prizefighter, bore the scars of his former trade.

"When we meet, I will tell you." Katsuro raised the intensity of his voice. His tone was a demand. Katsuro always got what he wanted. "You will be well compensated for our meeting."

Jericho liked what he heard. "At the Bucket of Blood one hour from now." Jericho hung up the phone. *What does this guy Katsuro want? What is he willing to pay?* Katsuro had piqued his interest.

Within the hour, Katsuro entered the strange world of this English pub. He knew the establishment's history. It had been the meeting place for some legendary street brawlers, and apparently it still was.

Jericho was not hard to spot. He stood at the edge of the bar, wearing a bowler hat crowning the well-muscled body of a younger man. But Jericho was equally surprised to see Katsuro. The man, short in stature, was equally well-muscled but stood with an erectness that belied his eighty-seven years. His stride was full, and his bearing showed a man of pure power and agility as he brushed past the patrons in the flourishing bar. His shadows followed.

Neither shook hands. Katsuro bowed out of habit rather than respect. "Where do you hold your street fights?"

The squat, erect Japanese's perfect English surprised Jericho. "What street fights? They are illegal."

"I am not here to discuss legalities. I am not the authorities nor do I care about the authorities. Where do you hold them?"

Jericho shrugged. "Follow me."

The two entered a large room where, a few days later, *Juko* would fight. "Okay, I want to arrange a fight for my protégé. I want him to fight the toughest street fighters you have in your stable. Killers."

"You want your so-called protégé to be killed?" Jericho's curiosity had been raised even higher.

"No, I want to make sure these men will give him a fight, a real street fight."

"Who is this protégé? How many street fights has he had?"

"He is not a street fighter. He is a martial arts expert."

Jericho snickered. "Street fighters eat martial arts people for lunch and spit them out before dinner."

"I want three of these fighters. He will fight one after another."

Jericho grew angry. "Quit pulling my leg, old man. I'm wasting my good time with you. I don't have patience for this crap."

Katsuro ignored the term "old man" for the sake of business and brevity. "I will pay £1,000 per man. You do with the money as you wish. But I want to see these street fighters first."

Jericho put out his hand. "The money, now, or I'll know you're crazy. You want to pay me to have your protégé killed? I won't do it. I'll stop the fight before they kill him. Murder isn't my business."

"This isn't murder. It's survival." One of the silent shadows handed him an envelope, which he then gave to Jericho. Katsuro never carried anything on his person.

Jericho peered inside. "There's only a thousand pounds here. Where's the rest?"

"I will meet you here tomorrow and you will show me the fighters. And I will give you another thousand. The night of the fight I will give you the rest—cash, of course."

The meeting the next day was short. Five men stood in their fighting tights on the mat in the middle of the barn-like room. Katsuro ordered all but one off the mat. He removed his suit. He handed his jacket to his attendant. He put on his *gi*. "You, prepare to fight!" Katsuro pointed to a heavyset street fighter with a line of tattoos across his arms.

The tattooed fighter looked at Jericho. "He kiddin' me, mate?"

Katsuro spun on his toes like a ballet dancer and drove a devastating kick into the man's midsection. The tattooed man bent forward and the old man's fingers dug deep into his throat. The man coughed gasping for breath. Katsuro's fist smashed into the man's face, dropping him like a ton of cement. He smashed his fist into the man's face repeatedly. Jericho and two of his street fighters pulled Katsuro off his victim.

"If this is the best street fighter you have, you had better keep looking. You make sure, Mr. Jericho, the ones you select for my protégé are much tougher than this man." Katsuro's aide threw an envelope at the fallen man's feet. "This is for your pain." Katsuro felt good. He needed to beat someone. It had been a long time, and he knew his fighting days were numbered—not gone, yet numbered. He felt good.

Disappointed, Jericho stared at his fallen fighter with disdain. Begrudgingly, he admired the old man and his attacking style.

Katsuro dressed hurriedly. Jericho followed him to the door. "I shall return tomorrow to have a look at the fighters you select," Katsuro told him.

Jericho, wanted to say something but not knowing quite what, called out, "Same time tomorrow?"

Katsuro nodded.

At their next meeting, Jericho lined up the three toughest fighters he could find. Word had gotten out about the beating Katsuro had administered to the tattooed man, and about the £500 this man had been paid. Jericho found it easy to get the street fighters he wanted for £500, a price set by Katsuro. To street fighters, £500 was good money.

Katsuro looked at the three men. "They will do. What time are the fights?"

AUTHOR'S NOTE

A person's history has many life-altering occurrences. Some are easily recognized as they happen while others need the passage of time to accentuate how important they were. Gian Aaron Molina, a.k.a. Gian Michaels ('*Juko*'), had many such life-altering events that could be easily defined. Gian Aaron Molina's family and life were determined by a series of events and a medley of characters well before he was even conceived.

Other events occurred after he was born into a brutal life. Still others accentuated a life so complex they are difficult to believe. Gian's life depended on the ambitions and goals of others. Gian's life also depended on one individual's intense desire to mold him into an image he himself could never obtain.

The result of these goals for Gian led to a life that is difficult, if not impossible, to comprehend. Gian was raised by a man named Katsuro, a Japanese businessman who believed life should be lived by the tenets of *The Book of Five Rings.* The book, written by a Samurai warrior from the 12ᵗʰ century, preaches a strict philosophy of Zen. Its tenets are based on the strictest moral and ethical codes combined with a doctrine of discipline and self-denial seldom reached by any individual.

Katsuro, a Grand Master, a teacher of martial arts, a practitioner of Zen, and a sadist of unquenchable drive, saw in Gian a child he could train to follow *The Book of Five Rings.* The result, Katsuro believed, would be the ultimate fighting machine, devastating and indestructible.

CHAPTER ONE

MARCH 10, 2001

"Shit! Take me to another bar. I'm not drunk enough. I still feel the pain. Do you hear me? I still feel the pain!" The towering hulk shouted at his friend, Ted. "I still see them. They're coming after me. They're going to take me back. I can't go back. I want to die. Stop them, Ted. Stop them. I've had enough. He wins! He wins!"

The towering hulk began to sob and punch the dashboard. Ted could feel it reverberate as the powerful hand smashed it. He heard Aaron's plea. Ted had never heard or seen his friend cry. He knew it was Aaron's alcohol-infused state that caused these feelings to surface. Ted's twenty-eight-year-old martial-arts instructor's heart pounded. *What should I do with him?*

Aaron had a hard time catching his breath. He sucked air in heavy gulps. His chest heaved. "I give up, Ted. Please let me die," he whispered. "Please, please. Please let me die."

Ted hurt for his new friend. *Why does Aaron want to die? He's a world-champion fighter. Why does he want to die? What should I do?*

Ted leaned over and touched his friend's bulging arm. At a traffic light, he slid his hand to Aaron's thick neck and pressed a purple vein. His fingers sought a pulse. Ted had taken many first-aid classes. Aaron's pulse was so faint Ted could barely feel it.

Ted bolted to life. His instincts and training drew him to attention. Aaron may get his wish—he might die.

The light turned green and Ted made a sharp turn west and headed straight to Best Falls Hospital. Suddenly, Aaron's head rolled back and forth, then lurched to the window, cracking his skull against the glass. Ted turned and heard Aaron moan. Ted drove as fast as the traffic would allow. Ted glanced over at Aaron often, remembering the first time he had ever seen him. It was a dark

1

room, with only a set of spotlights illuminating two men grappling on gray mats. He saw this giant, with a tormented young boy's face, fighting a sleek well-trained pro in the middle of the ring. He had heard of the legend. A young man, with a boy's face, undefeated, a world-class fighter.

Ted had watched the face, especially the eyes with their singular focus on destroying the other man. The stare on the giant's face scared Ted. He had never seen such intensity, such fierceness, such determination to kill.

And when the cruel, destructive, bloody pummeling began, Ted shivered. The hulk's handlers pulled him from his victim. The prone victim, gasped, "You crazy, son-of-a-bitch, this is supposed to be a workout. Dumb bastard!"

Aaron stared down at his victim. He said nothing. He didn't need to speak; the stare was bone chilling.

Despite Ted's initial fear of Aaron, they became friends. Perhaps it was the first thing Ted said to Aaron when he approached him a week later. "Hey, man. It was a pleasure watching you fight. If I was in the ring with you, I'd really be afraid. You have that look."

Puzzled, Aaron asked, "What look?"

"The look you could kill the other guy."

Aaron felt hands lift him from the car. His head ached. His wrists were strapped to a gurney. His head lifted slightly as he pulled against his restraints. Even with his enormous strength he couldn't free himself. Then, just as suddenly, his mind whirled to a time gone by when he was pinned and confined and feeling hopeless. His mind raged. His body convulsed. He saw the lights penetrating the cold corridors of the strange hospital where Ted had taken him. He whispered to the shadowy figure nearest his head. "Please let me go. Please! I can't be tied like this. I must get out. Please let me out. Please!"

"Sorry, fella. You need to be held down. You're just too strong. We've got to protect you from yourself. Just relax. You'll be okay." The voice was matter-of-fact.

Aaron heard little of what the voice said. Tears formed and rolled down his cheeks. "Please let me go. I'll be good. I can't do this anymore. Just let me die."

Silence. "Sorry, buddy. We wouldn't want you to kill yourself. Can't do it."

Aaron's mind, muddled and confused, leapt to the past. "Please don't leave me here. Please. Oh, God. Not again. Please."

BURIED

His mind reeled back to when the shadowy figure of Katsuro looked down at his tiny protégé. The surroundings were familiar, too familiar. This is the yard where he played. The grass, manicured by the Tachigi family gardener and cut to a perfection only the Japanese would demand, was a place of terror. Especially to a seven-year-old boy who was forced to dig four-foot holes with a large spade and then replace the dirt in that same hole, over and over. More than a year before, Katsuro had begun what he called "strength training." *Digging the earth, lifting the soil and moving the dirt, will build your strength. You need to get stronger every day; rain or shine, snow or warm sun, you will dig. Your body will become muscular and stronger each day. So dig the holes deep and pile the dirt high, then throw that dirt back into the hole. Strength is power and power will win fights. You must always be stronger and tougher than your opponent. Remember, always stronger.*

After almost a year of this strength training, Gian grew weary of the process. He failed to see the need for making himself stronger when he felt very strong already. Unfortunately, he made a mistake only this strong-Wiled child could make by asking, "But why, Katsuro, do I have to keep digging these holes? Am I not strong enough now?"

Katsuro's face grew sinister. "You question me, boy?" Katsuro smiled. Gian had come to hate that smile. It meant he had done something Katsuro didn't like. "You question my word? Let's test that strength you say you have. You will get in this hole, and then you will dig yourself out. This will test your strength little boy."

Katsuro picked the boy up and placed him into the deep hole. He turned to his son Ryuu and his grandchildren, who were watching, "Replace the dirt into the hole up to the boy's chin and then trample the dirt so it becomes compact and hard."

Katsuro bent down and grabbed the boy by his hair, "You asked about your strength? Now let's see just how strong you are. Go on, dig yourself out, little one."

"Please, Master, don't leave me here." But the struggling creature, the tormented, abused figure would not cry. "I will get out. I will."

The child tried to lift his arms from under the cold earth. As strong as he was, only a few minuscule cracks formed in the soil. His body remained firmly encased in his dirt tomb, which had hardened like concrete.

"Come on, little man. You can make it." Ryuu laughed as he left the yard. Gian hated that laugh. It meant he would feel more pain.

The yard emptied. Only the small boy's head protruding from the soil, his soul buried in Mother Earth, distinguished this yard from any other. Gian did not call out. He did not cry. He knew better. He knew above all he could not fail, or the punishment would be worse than any he had already endured in his nearly eight years.

From the dojo she watched her grandfather make the small boy dig the hole in the middle of the yard. She heard the voices. "*Digging will make you stronger. Digging will make your muscles bigger. Dig, little one.*"

Horrified, she watched her grandfather place the boy into the pit. "*This lesson will test your strength, little boy. Now you will get to dig your way out.*"

Terrified, she watched from her seat at the side of the dojo as Ryuu stomped the ground to harden it. She winced when she heard the tiny voice asking to be freed. She bit her lip watching him struggle to escape his tomb. Only when Ryuu came toward the dojo did she run to resume her training.

Time passed, only noticed because the sun disappeared and night came in its cold fury. The cold air stung his face. He tried to pull his arms up, but to no avail.

He was trapped. His body trembled and shook like a light earthquake under the rigid soil. Night brought rumblings to his stomach. He was hungry. But Katsuro's words, ingrained in his mind, came to him: "*Any pain you feel is only in your mind—even hunger. You can go without food. You can survive that feeling by thinking through any pain and desire. Force your mind not to want and you will not want."* The earth was solid. His tiny body ached and shuddered under the terrifying thought he might be in the ground all night, or longer. His eyelids became heavy. He wished himself to sleep to escape his nightmare. Exhaustion brought a restless sleep.

The earth never gave, never moved.

The next morning she ran to her upstairs window to check on the struggling boy. She wiped away a tear. *Margaret, he's been in that hole for almost a whole day and night. Maybe you should help him.*

However, Margaret knew the consequences of being caught trying to help this white, pale-faced, slender child now living among her brothers and sisters. She felt sorry for him. She watched him often in the dojo as he underwent the wrath of her grandfather, whom she feared. She knew that she could never suffer what she had seen this Anglo child endure—the beatings, the torture. She trembled. Fear drove her to bury her thoughts, temporarily. She went about her day.

Gian watched the dirt in front of him. Nothing moved. Not even the tiniest fleck of dirt shifted. He was buried alive and a chill went through his young body. He wanted to call out and ask to be freed, but that would mean he failed. He would never admit to failure. *Maybe, Gian, it is time to die, maybe! Death doesn't mean you failed. It is just another adventure. Maybe this is your day. You have prayed often for it to happen. Maybe it will happen today.*

Katsuro came to see his protégé toward the middle of the afternoon. "You ready to quit, little man? Are you ready to admit you have failed? You can't get out, can you? You could die here. Is that what you want?"

Gian looked at his tormentor. "I don't fear death and I won't give up. I Wil get out."

"Good, little man. You get out, and when you do, be ready to resume your training. You are now missing today's training session. See you in the dojo, little man." Katsuro left, never offering Gian anything, not even water.

Good for you, Gian. You didn't ask for water. He probably would have thrown it at you and made the ground even harder. Besides, that would have meant you wanted something and couldn't stand the pain of thirst. Gian smiled through his tenseness. The smile felt good. *You will beat him, Gian. Don't ask him for anything.*

Night fell again, and the small, tormented figure fell asleep. It was dark with no moon. Darkness blanketed the yard. Only Gian's deep breathing could be heard. Margaret watched from her window. *It is dark, Margaret. Get your small shovel and dig him out. If he dies, Margaret, he willl die because you didn't help him. Help him, Margaret. Help him!*

She tiptoed down the back stairs that led into the garden. She raced to him. She plunged the small shovel into the ground. The sleeping, caged figure's head bobbed. "Shh, Gian," she whispered. "Do not speak. I will help you dig out. Just don't talk."

She dug slices of earth from around Gian's back. He could feel the earth's pressure released from his spine. She tossed the dirt away. No words were exchanged. Gian felt the dirt loosen. But he was still imprisoned.

Suddenly, she heard a sound. The voice came from the other side of the house away from her room. "Good night, little prince. Sleep well. Maybe I will see you back in the dojo, someday." Ryuu smirked.

Margaret heard Ryuu cackle and then the window closed. "I must go. Now be free," she whispered

"Thanks." He mouthed the words so no one would hear him.

Gian rested and even slept a while to restore his strength. As the stars sparkled above him, he began his final attack on his cage to move the earth. At last he felt the soil give.

At six that morning he pulled himself up and over and he fled his earthen prison. He stumbled to his room. With strength drawn from fear of Katsuro and fear of failure, he showered, slurped water, and readied himself for his morning workout in the dojo before going to school.

* * *

The attendants placed him in a bed and checked to make sure he was safely tied down. "He's a big strong one. I wonder what his problem is?" The two attendants left the room and Ted entered.

Aaron lay motionless. He spoke in a whisper. "Don't let them put me back in there. Please don't let them. They are coming to get me. Don't let them take me. Please don't let them take me!"

"I won't, Aaron. I won't let them get you." Ted knew some things about Aaron's family. On rare occasions, he had talked about his family and his problems. *But what is he talking about now?*

Silence again, but not for long. Aaron yanked at his restraints, screaming over and over, "Don't let them take me!" His cry for help could be heard up and down the hospital corridors.

The doctor on duty was a man of diminutive stature, but he was quick. As the shouts of pain were heard at his station, he grabbed a syringe and vial from his arsenal of medication and hurried down the hall. The doctor met up with two burly orderlies who burst into the tormented patient's room. Together they held Aaron firm as the doctor injected the medication that would send him to another world.

Aaron never felt the needle. Needles had been part of his life since he was nine. As quickly as he was injected, a feeling of peace came to Aaron but that feeling of freedom was too brief.

THE HANGING

Katsuro called out the instructions and his grandchildren followed them precisely, in unison and in rhythm as the moves were called. Nearing the completion of the exercises, Sam, one of the grandchildren, fell, grabbing his thigh. "Grandfather, it hurts, my leg. I have to stop."

Katsuro stopped his instructions and rushed to Sam's side. "You will be fine, Sam. You just need your leg massaged. Ryuu, take over."

Ryuu continued the drill. On his own, Gian stopped to watch Katsuro tenderly help Sam to the massage table. Seeing Gian had stopped his workout, Ryuu shouted, "*Juko!* Keep working! Do not stop until we tell you to stop."

Gian dropped his head and went back to his routine, but with much less intensity than before. After Katsuro had finished with Sam's massage, he marched over to Gian, scowling. "*Juko*, every routine, every workout must always be done with great concentration and effort. Start your routine again and do it right. You hear me?"

"Yes, sir. I heard you."

Katsuro noticed a tone of disdain. "You don't like what I am telling you?"

Knowing better, but unable to control his words, Gian said, "When I am tired or hurting, you never attend to me. How come?"

"Don't question what I do! Never! I'll show you what it means to disobey me."

"Ryuu, take down the punching bag." And turning to Gian, he said, "Be rude to me, will you!"

Ryuu disconnected the punching bag from its pulley system, then grabbed Gian by the wrist.

"What are you doing? Stop!" screamed the terrified child.

Ignoring Gian's cries, Ryuu wound tape around and around Gian's small wrists, pulling it as tight as he could.

He lifted the little one onto the bar that had held the bag in place. Eight-year-old Gian now hung, swinging back and forth like a pendulum.

Wagging his finger at the trembling boy, Katsuro screamed, "Listen to me carefully, *Juko.* "Remember this, and remember it well. Never disrespect me! Never! What you do, what you say, even the expression on your face, will always show what you are thinking, especially to your opponent. Never reveal your feelings! And, never, never show any pain!"

"I will teach you how to feel pain." Katsuro took the *Shinai*, lifted it above his head, and let the straps dig into Gian's flesh across his back. "But first you must know pain. You must learn to shake the pain from your mind; and when you do, you will never feel it when you are fighting. Pain is only in your mind, only in your mind." Again Katsuro lashed the dangling child. "Never disrespect me again. Never!"

Then the *Shinai* whipped across his legs. Gian knew that if he cried or screamed the beating would get worse. Katsuro wanted him to cry for help. That would mean Gian was a failure like his sons. Gian gritted his teeth, sucked in his breath and readied himself to absorb another day of beatings.

Gian's mind wandered from the whippings; such wandering was his personal salvation. He thought of Katsuro's sons who had been trained to be martial arts experts but had failed because they did not have Gian's resolve or heart. Katsuro's words lingered from a previous day: *None of them have your heart. None of them. You never cry. You never give up.*

Each time the *Shinai* burst onto his flesh, Gian thought about the day Katsuro had let slip what he thought of his sons. Gian smiled inwardly. The old Master looked up when his young protégé arrived for his dojo lesson after he had been buried in the backyard for two days. "You have shown your strength, young man. You escaped burial. Now you are here for your training. Good!" It was the closest Katsuro had ever come to complimenting Gian since his training began. Katsuro confided just above a whisper. "None of my other children could have withstood what you went through. You are tough. Now it is my job to make you tougher."

Katsuro had never spoken about his family. Gian had very little contact with them. He had just seen them training. He was surprised when Katsuro admitted they had failed him and he hadn't. He tucked this rare revelation into his memory and went about his routine.

These lashes, while hanging helpless, brought Gian back to the pain he was not supposed to feel. But he did feel it. However, the lashes felt a little less severe. The old man, now nearly eighty, had lost very little of his power but Gian noticed the difference. Even though Katsuro ran five miles every day and worked out to maintain his strength, age had taken its toll. His arms grew weary as he thundered the *Shinai* against the flesh of his protégé. But he would never admit that his physical strength wasn't what it used to be. That would mean he was no longer the Master, and he would always be the Master, until the day he died.

With a sadistic expression, Ryuu bowed to his father and gently took the *Shinai* from his hand. Ryuu, too, had noticed his father's diminished intensity and fervor when he whipped the boy. But Ryuu had experienced no weakening. In fact, he felt greater and greater power as his father grew older. He knew, one day, that he would be the Master. "Allow me, father, to give this child the pain he deserves. It will be my pleasure."

With the *Shinai* in Ryuu's hand, the bamboo leaves stung like they hadn't in a long time. Gian felt that pain. Gian fell into another world as the *Shinai* tore at his flesh. Finally, peacefully, Gian fell into unconsciousness.

Katsuro ordered Ryuu to stop the whipping, "Stop, he cannot feel pain when he is unconscious. Stop! Undo him! And bring him over to the bench."

* * *

Gian called out again in his drugged stupor: "No, not that stuff, it smells so bad. It really smells awful. No, not that stuff!"

* * *

Katsuro wiped the blood from Gian's body and then plastered his cuts with a substance Katsuro's grandchildren dreaded, it looked and smelled so awful. Margaret called it Dragon Vomit.

Even the grandchildren, who were in the dojo while Katsuro and Ryuu were beating Gian, gagged as they watched their grandfather, Dr. Katsuro, paste Gian's cuts with the Dragon Vomit. Katsuro then wrapped Gian with gauze that barely covered the green stuff.

Gian, who had been revived by the *Vomit,* called out to the children, "What's the matter, can't stand a little vomit? If I can stand the beatings, you can stand the smell of this."

Katsuro pulled the gauze a little tighter. "Quiet! Always endure your pain in silence so nobody will know if you are hurt."

* * *

A few weeks before the beating, Margaret had spoken to her mother as they indulged in their nightly ritual bath together. "Why does Grandfather mistreat Gian? He is so little." Her voice trembled in a hushed whisper, as she was forbidden to question her grandfather's actions.

Rita whispered back to her child with the big brown eyes, "Your grandfather is trying to teach Gian to be a great fighter and not to fear pain. You are too young to understand that my child. Never ask again. It is your grandfather's way." Rita saw the gentle tears as they formed in Margaret's eyes.

Margaret looked like her mother, slim but sturdy, with high cheekbones and a long face. Her large brown eyes had never left Gian as he hung from the system of pulleys that held him in place. Those eyes filled with tears as the *Shinai* left its mark on the body of the boy she had grown to admire. It wasn't the first time she had watched him being beaten, and it wouldn't be the last. He was so alone. He was so helpless.

Katsuro had ordered the family to leave the dojo. Margaret did as she was told and slid outside. She was the last to leave. She walked quickly around the side of the building, moving in the shadows toward a slightly open door. She slipped back into the structure through the side entrance and into the massage room. There she could see the tiny figure lying on the rubbing table.

The dojo was silent now. Everyone had returned to the main house, leaving Gian alone in the darkened room. As he rallied his strength, Gian fought the pain and slid off the table onto the floor. He tried to stand, but the cuts on his leg immobilized him. When he reached for the top of the table to pull himself to an upright position, the pain grew incredibly intense.

Margaret covered her mouth, squealing a silent scream, feeling his pain. But she never moved to help him. She, too, was immobilized by her fear of Katsuro. What if he came back and found her with Gian? She trembled and watched the pitiful figure slump to the floor. She watched him crawl slowly, in agonizing pain. She saw droplets of blood from underneath The Vomit and gauze, and watched it leave a trail smearing the floor as he moved bravely like a sloth, to the exit and eventually out toward his house.

Margaret watched the creature slide on his hands and knees at an even pace across the grass. Suddenly she felt an overwhelming love for this boy. Maybe it was her mothering instinct, maybe it was her admiration of his determination to survive, or maybe it was just her fervent hope he became the man her grandfather wanted him to become. Somehow, Margaret knew this boy would make it. Tears stained her face. *God bless you, Gian. You will need His help and He will give it to you.* She wiped away her tears as she watched him disappear into his house.

Upon seeing the beaten child, Gian's Nanny put her hand to her mouth. She tried to help him, but he whispered in pain. "No. Hurts too much." He struggled to lift himself onto the living room couch. He lay on its pillows, staining the fabric with blood.

Nanny brought him a glass of water. He could barely swallow. Only the sweet tongue of Dog made him feel better. "Will we make it, Dog? Will we?" Gian whispered. Dog didn't understand the words, only his master's pain.

Later that night Gian crept into his bed and cried. In the dark he felt more alone than he usually did, but at the same time, the darkness protected him from the beatings and the pain. Dog tried to snuggle close to him, pressing against his body. Gian pushed him away. "Too painful for me, Dog. Too painful." Then, as an afterthought, Gian said his prayer silently: *Let me die. Just let me die.*

* * *

Ted watched his friend struggle against the restraining belts. Although only semi-conscious, Aaron was mouthing words. He appeared to be swallowing his tongue; he rolled his head to dislodge it and groaned mightily. Suddenly, with unexpected violence, Aaron began to scream, "They're coming for me. Get me out of here. Don't let them take me. Don't let them hit me. Save me."

And just as suddenly, complete silence. Aaron's breathing became very shallow. A nurse burst through the door. "His vitals have gone down. His breathing is barely . . ." She checked his vital signs again. "Now his signs are normal, but just a few seconds ago, they showed little life. Strange."

Ted watched in silence. "Have you known him long?" asked the nurse. Her white uniform was a little snug around her middle.

Ted shook his head. "Off and on for a few years. Why?"

"Does he have any family?"

Ted shook his head again. "Just me and my mom. We are not his real family, but I guess we're all he has."

"Why don't you call your mom. Maybe she should be here when he wakes up."

"Okay."

Anna, Ted's mom, arrived at the hospital. *These places always smell of alcohol and disinfectant. Phew!* she thought.

She entered Aaron's room just as he was waking.

"Anna, I want to die. I really want to die. I can't do this anymore. Please let me die." He repeated those words often as the day wore on. "I just want to die. I can't do this any more." His mind whirled, confused and tortured.

Aaron slipped into semi-consciousness and into another nightmare.* * *

24 HOURS

He had been lifting rocks for well over an hour, placing them carefully in a tidy stack at one end of the yard, and then returning them to the original location. "Lifting rocks is better weight training than lifting weights. Besides, here you get the benefit of nature," said the Master.

Gian was in no mood for Katsuro's placating comments. Besides, he was tired. Katsuro had given him a thunderous beating with the *Shinai* the day before. He was so sore he couldn't sleep. Sleep-deprived and weary from a day of lifting, he said to Katsuro, "I'm tired. This is too much work. I'm so tired!" His tiny voice was raised ever so slightly.

Katsuro lashed the ever-present *Shinai* across Gian's legs. "You are tired? I'll show you what tired is." Katsuro paused for a moment, thinking of something to teach Gian what tired really felt like. "I want you to walk for the next 24 hours. No stopping. Just keep moving. If you stop, I will make you walk another 24 hours. Then you might really be tired. You understand me?"

13

Gian was stunned. Once again Katsuro had picked an arbitrary punishment and an arbitrary time, a time wholly unrelated to anything. *Why 24 hours?* He thought as he began walking around the yard in a large circle. At first walking was easy. But then weariness began to set in. As an eight-year-old, still coming to understand his lot in life and how to survive it, Gian wondered why Katsuro treated him so badly. He didn't treat the others this way.

First Katsuro sat and watched Gian. Then, one by one, Ryuu, Yukio, Teddy, and then Katsuro again watched him. There was always somebody in the yard with him. They never left him alone.

Yukio delighted in torturing Gian. Not only did he make verbal comments, but he used the *Shinai* on him often. "What's the matter, Gian, getting tired? Being tired is never an option." Just as Yukio finished taunting him, Gian's left leg cramped and he crumpled to the ground in pain.

"Don't stop, Gian. You know the rules. Stopping will only make your punishment last another 24 hours." Gian crawled over to the fence and pulled himself up. His body was stiff, the painful knot forced him back to the ground. He kicked his leg out as he crawled. Slowly, the pain subsided. He rose again.

As the twelfth hour without food or water passed, his body bent, his mouth parched, Gian took his mind to another world. *Who is that child walking? He looks familiar, but he isn't. Why would anybody be walking around a yard for such a long time?*

Finally, his legs gave out. He fell to the grass and started to slide on his belly. As soon as he could, he lifted himself to his knees and continued to crawl. Seconds seemed like minutes. Minutes seemed like hours. Hours seemed like days. And the day never ended.

His knees became bloody. His hands stung from the blades of grass. "Get up, *Juko*. Walk! Show me you are not tired." Katsuro taunted him, just as Yukio had done.

Gian gathered his strength, what little he had left, and stood. He shuffled his feet slowly. He could barely move them from the weeds they were trampling. Gian fell again. Like the snails that infested Katsuro's garden, Gian slid his body across the grass ever so slowly.

Weary, tired, thirsty, hungry and filled with hatred, he kept moving. Again, somehow, gathering strength, he staggered onto his feet.

Every millimeter was painful. Iron will propelled him a centimeter at a time. Every meter was traveled because he would never surrender and let them win. He would make it.

She watched from her perch. The large brown eyes followed his every step. A knot in her stomach tightened every time he fell. *Oh God, please don't make him walk another 24 hours. He might die.*

As the time wore down to the last hour, Gian gained strength. He was going to make it. They couldn't beat him. They wouldn't beat him. Then a funny thought crossed his mind. *What would happen if I stopped right now? They would have to make me walk another 24 hours. That is what Katsuro said. They would have to stay up and watch me. Then they would get tired, too.*

However, he did not stop. Instead he fell flat onto the grass as his right leg cramped. He rolled in pain, then crawled in pain, till finally he heard the words he had been waiting to hear: "It is time to stop, *Juko*. Now you know what tired means. Whenever you think of tired, think of this 24-hour walk." Gian got up.

With every ounce of resolve, Gian did not stop walking until he came to his house. He crawled upstairs and fell onto his bed, utterly exhausted.

Dog licked his face. Gian slept.

* * *

While Aaron slept his nightmares away, Anna talked to Ted. "Doesn't Aaron have a new girlfriend? I think he asked for her the last time he woke up. Maybe she should come over and see him like this. If she can handle this, she can handle anything."

"Good idea. Her name is Ali. She belongs to the gym where Aaron and I work. I'll call the place and get her number. Aaron really likes her."

Ali sat transfixed while Anna told her stories about Aaron she had never heard before. Gasping in disbelief, Ali listened and cried. There was nothing else she could do.

CHAPTER TWO

MARCH 1976

To tell the story of Gian, it is important to begin before he was conceived.

Red tiles covered the roof of the old wooden structure, hiding the demonic life of its inhabitants. The house, with all its windows clamped shut, with its heavy, old-fashioned curtains always drawn, and with the ceiling fans whirling in each room, provided little ventilation and no fresh air. Most of the swingers who inhabited the many couches and beds didn't notice and certainly didn't care. The rhythmic music bounced from the living room to every nook and cranny of the old Spanish-style house. Nobody heard it.

Mostly they smoked pot. Inhaling the smoke satisfied many of the participants. Many were simply excited to be invited to swing. Many had only envisioned being active participants of this lifestyle, and now they truly were part of it. None of them minded paying the fifty dollars at the front door to gain entrance to the old house. The money was for the food and drink. The pot was extra, or one could bring his own and share. Sharing it might mean your prey was easier to catch and seduce.

Jeff Hughes was not interested in swinging, although he had been a swinger for many years. His interest was in selling. He brought every known drug to these events and waited for someone to ask what he had. He was the unofficial supplier. For those who didn't know about his business, they soon found out. The drug of choice for this crowd was pot. Jeff rolled each cigarette in its own light-brown paper. That way he could control the amount he supplied. He mixed the marijuana with regular tobacco to make a milder drag. It also made for a greater profit.

He set up shop in a hall closet. Not a normal closet, it was larger than usual, with collapsible doors. Jeff was out of the way of the heavy human traffic. He sat next to a small table and sold his packs of smokes.

Isabella, or Ibell, as she was known to her friends, who was a very tall, trim woman with the body of an athlete and the thighs to prove it, remarked to her husband, "Jeff, you look ridiculous in that closet. It looks like you're hiding from the kids in a game of hide and seek. Can't you work in the den?"

"Are you kiddin'? There are three couples in there now. This space keeps me in the flow of traffic without being in the way. And sales are good. Here, take a pack. Send everybody to see me."

Ibell drew a smoke from the pack and lit it. She inhaled the smoke and blew it out her nose slowly. "You made some good stuff here, Mr. Drug Dealer. I'll have to come back and screw your brains out later for free smokes."

"The hell you will. You haven't done me in nearly three months. Go screw somebody else."

Ibell laughed. "Shit, man. You just don't turn me on no more. Besides, what the hell are you complaining about? You get non-stop action all the time. You probably can't even get it up for me no more. So go t' hell."

Ibell's long stride carried her down the hall quickly and into the living room. There she saw Carlos. "What's the matter, Carlos? Your wife not here with you again? She said she didn't want you to swing no more. And I guess she meant it."

"Stop it, Ibell. She's a pain in the ass. Come on. Give me a smoke. God knows I need one."

He limped toward her. "Your knees still botherin' you? Maybe you should get your knee replaced. I hear it works."

"Yeah, right—and a year of rehab. Great! That's all I need."

They smoked together and fell into a cozy embrace. Ibell always felt like a drifting cloud after a few drags; her mind went numb. Her body relaxed and Carlos began to explore her. She enjoyed every touch, every kiss, every finger penetration. Carlos lifted her skirt and caressed her crotch. Their tongues met. She gripped his manhood and stroked it. She laid her head in his lap and engulfed his member in her mouth.

He pushed her back on the couch and penetrated her. Both forgot the condoms that were in ample supply.

Jeff opened the door to their house. Ibell staggered in behind, still feeling the effects of too much pot. Neither heard the soft beeping of the answering machine. They wouldn't get its message until the next morning.

"Ibell," screamed Jeff, "that son of yours died. The Collinses called to tell you." It didn't matter to Jeff that it was his son, too. It only mattered that it wasn't his son anymore.

Ibell staggered into the kitchen. "What the hell you screamin' at me for? I ain't deaf. What you want?"

"Your son, Matt. He's dead."

"Matt, dead? Dead?" But she couldn't bring herself to cry. All she kept saying was, "Matt's dead. They said he wasn't going to live very long. Retarded and all."

"Yeah, givin' that kid away was the best decision. Raisin' that kid with all those problems and him not gonna live a life worth livin'. Besides, boys are hard to raise. My mother used to tell everyone I was no good compared to my sisters. She hated me. Bitch! I hated her back. Did you know I didn't shed a tear when she passed? Not a tear. Bitch!"

Ibell didn't say anything. They had talked through this before. When she got pregnant with their first child, Jeff told her, "I'm tellin' you, Ibell, if this is a boy, we're not keepin' 'im. I don't want no boys. Hard to raise and expensive. What if they would turn out like me, a drug dealer? I'd kill 'im. Uh-uh! Not on your life. If it's a boy, we put 'im up for adoption. Just remember that."

Ibell patted her swelling belly. She hoped for a boy since she really didn't want any children. *Hell, they would ruin my lifestyle. I wouldn't be able to go to any parties. Shit! Uh-uh, not for me. Little bastards. Good. A boy it will be.* And a boy it was. Given up through adoption.

But Matt's death did raise a question in Ibell's mind. Matt was her second born. Jeff had gotten her pregnant when she was in her freshman year at San Diego State. She never forgot the day she found out.

"Ibell, I don't understand. Your time in the mile has gotten slower even though you've been training well. The season is almost half over and you're getting slower. You feeling okay?" Coach Dragone asked, half a smile masking her concern for her best miler.

"Coach, I don't know. I think something is wrong. Besides, I've even put on some weight. Damn, what is the matter with me?"

Coach Dragone had seen it before, pregnant and not knowing. "Come on, let's visit the school dispensary. They have a nurse over there. Maybe she'll have an answer."

The nurse's answer was to go to the university hospital and to see an obstetrician. Yes, she was pregnant. When Ibell found out she was pregnant for the third time, she might have considered keeping the child, except it wasn't Jeff's and he wouldn't consider it. Ever.

They never named the boy. They just put him up for adoption. Ibell never held him, never saw him. He was a mirage, a passing event in her life. One she would forget, except for occasional brief moments that were a little painful, but quickly forgotten.

*   *   *

He stood erect and then slowly bent forward. Carlos Molina' back ached, but he knew stretching those aching muscles would help. His outstretched arms reached toward his toes. When he was growing up, touching his toes was easy. Stretching out in any direction was like doing a Chinese puzzle. All the pieces, all the joints fit together perfectly. His high-school coach had said he had more potential in the decathlon than any student he had ever had. "Carlos, you are tall, agile, powerful, and fast. I can teach you to master each event in the decathlon. You might become great if you work hard."

Now he had a hard time touching his toes. "Damn back! Damn knees! Damn!"

"What's the matter, Dad?"

"One day you'll be my age and your body will stop being so . . . so . . ."

"Flexible?"

"Right, flexible."

Carlos laughed at his eldest son. "Are your hands still sore from your pole vaulting? I remember how it bothered me."

"Naw, they're okay. I've got calluses now."

Sitting nearby, Papa Gian, Carlos's father, entered the conversation, He loved to reminisce. "Sore hands? Calluses? You should have seen my hands when I was in the Spanish Army. Those rifles they made you carry were heavy—over ten pounds. Doesn't sound like much, but when you carry that weight all day and then have to clean those rifles, treating them like babies, they get very heavy. And when you tried to load them, you could get your fingers caught in the clip latch on those M1s. Damn, almost took my thumb off a few times. There were guys who walked around with smashed fingers, broken bones, crushed thumbs and blisters. Big ones, too. But I don't complain. Why should I? I got to ride a horse. I love horses." Papa Gian barely took a breath when he talked about his army experiences.

Carlos let his father finish. "I'm mad those damn Germans didn't invade northern Spain on the French border. We would have drilled the bastards. We were battle hardened and ready for a war. That range of mountains, the Picos de Europa, would have stalled the bastards at every turn. We woulda stopped them. I wanted to kill those Nazis! Those bastards!"

Papa Gian loved to ride horses and talk about his war days.

CHAPTER THREE

PAPA GIAN RAUL MOLINA

Spain's government, fearful that Germany would break its pledge not to invade Spain once World War II started, sent many of its forces to the French border. Gian Raul Molina, the son of a Jewish merchant, was a hardened horseman, a duelist, and a sharpshooter, and he was one of those men sent to the border in the Cantabrian Mountains

He left his mother with her words ringing in his ear. "Stay neutral, Gian. We lose no matter who wins. Just remember the pogroms and the Spanish Inquisition. Jews never win a war. We just survive. Our family goes all the way back to the Conquistadors. We are patriotic Spaniards." Raul Molina smiled at his mother's concern.

"Raul, you must take care of yourself. What would I do without you? You are my youngest. Pedro is in America already. He writes and says what a wonderful country it is. Maybe you should go there after the war so I know you are safe."

Momma could read Raul's mind. He wondered where she got that ability. "Yes, Momma, I will think about it. So, wish me well. Maybe I will improve my French living on the border."

"You just stay safe and watch out for those French women."

"Come on, Momma. I am a Spanish Jew."

Momma smiled. "Stay that way."

For six months, Raul stayed true to his mother's words. But his manly needs supplanted his word. French women beckoned. The small city of Pamplona was a haven for Spain's fighting men: it filled their physical needs with both Spanish and French women.

The Barin Inn was known for its Spanish ale, friendly women, and roughhouse men. Raul had promised himself if he ever went to Pamplona, Barin's would be among his first stops. The bar's front bore a caricature of a man dressed in shorts and holding a beer with its foam cascading over the side. "Pretty provincial, I would say," thought Raul.

Raul stepped inside the smoke-filled room, walked directly to the bar and ordered up a "Alhambra Mezquitas." Raul shouted to be heard over the din.

"No use shouting," the bartender replied. "I ain't deaf."

Raul, finding no empty table, sat next to a man dressed in what looked like an old Cossack coat. Next to them sat a trio of Spanish soldiers high on too much beer. One soldier tried to stand, wobbling; he hovered over Raul and his drinking tablemate. "You," he said pointing to Raul's fellow companion. "You're dressed like a Cossack. I hate Cossacks. You Russian?" His voice was slurred but filled with anger.

Speaking in perfect Spanish, the other man, standing tall, assured him he wasn't. "No, my friend. It is cold and I wear these warm clothes."

"I don't like your clothes. Take'em off. Dress like a real Spaniard."

Raul bolted up from the table. "My friend may wear whatever he likes. These are his clothes. Leave him alone."

The soldier whipped out a knife from under his shirt, and before anyone could react, cut through the man's black belt holding up his pants. They fell to the floor. Raul leapt at the knife-wielding soldier. His fist caught the soldier under his ear and sent him reeling across the room. Two other soldiers stood and pounced on Raul while the stranger picked up his pants.

Fighting with one hand while the other held up his pants, the stranger decked one inebriated soldier, while Raul kicked the third man in the groin, taking him out of the fight. Before another blow could be struck, several hands wrestled the two back to their seats. "Easy, soldiers. They are on our side," said a hulking patron.

"Okay, soldiers," said the bartender. "Any more of that stuff, and both of you are out of here."

"Damn," swore the stranger. "They cut my belt. I'll need a new belt. Where will I get that kind of money?"

Raul noticed a large piece of cloth under the man's ripped shirt wrapped tightly around his middle. The cloth, a crazy maze of patches, fascinated him. He thought he saw pockets sewn into the cloth. Curious, he didn't say anything

After tying his pants with a rope, the stranger introduced himself to Raul. "Thanks, my friend, for your help. I owe you a drink. The name's Juan."

They drank until after midnight. In the early morning, they staggered out of the Barin Inn. Raul put his arm around Juan and held him close. "Come on old friend, let's get some sleep. There's a hotel right here. At least I think it says hotel." The two staggered in.

After paying the hotel clerk for the room, they walked past the hotel bar and climbed the creaky steps of the ancient hostelry. "Second floor, my friend. Room 202, says that right here on the key." Raul muttered.

Juan walked into the room as Raul flicked the light switch on. Juan turned to thank his new friend when a large metal object smacked him in the forehead and he tumbled unconscious to the floor. Holding a metal baton, Raul bent over Juan, "Let's see my new friend, Juan, what do you have in your cloth belt."

Raul cut the sash, removed the cloth band from Juan's middle and stretched the cloth belt on the bed. Raul opened each small compartment on the belt with his open knife blade. Inside each packet was a small bag filled with diamonds. "Just as I thought. Maybe you are a thief, Juan, or a diamond merchant." Raul also thought he might be a Russian deserter, based on his clothes.

Using his own belt and the rope, Raul tied Juan's feet, bound them with the empty sash, and put a gag in his mouth. Raul carefully folded the cloth belt and placed it in his bag.

Raul went downstairs to the hotel's bar and whispered in the bartender's ear. "He happens to be right over there. Where else would he spend a good night like this one?"

Raul walked over and sat next to a short, slender man with a smooth-shaven face and a waist jacket pulled tightly around his middle. "You are the Commissioner of Police?"

The policeman looked up from his nightly chore of guzzling a stein of beer. He licked his lips, removing a wisp of foam. "What can I do for you on my night off?"

"Sorry to bother you during your time off. I, too, treasure my time off. I wonder, is there a reward for a Russian officer who has gone AWOL? And if there is, how much is it, and would you like to arrest him tonight, on your night off?"

The Commissioner of Police put his stein down. Officers didn't drink beer from a bottle. "You know there is a standing reward for any Russian who is captured. And you know it is £25,000."

"Do you want to arrest him tonight? It could ruin your evening off."

The Police Commissioner said, "No, you made my evening. I get £10,000 for arresting him. Take me to this Russian."

The Commissioner stared down at the figure tied securely on the bed. "I got a feeling he is a deserter just from his clothes. There are many still around here," remarked Juan.

Raul knew Juan would never mention the diamonds, because if he had stolen them, he would end up in the gulag. If not, he still took them out of the country without registering them. He would have been tried for taking precious metals off Russian land for profit, which is illegal under Russian law.

Three police officers took Juan out of the hotel. "Goodbye, Juan. It was nice sharing a drink with you."

The Commissioner handed Raul a slip of paper to write his address. The Commissioner took the completed paper and left the room saying, "Come down to the station before ten tomorrow morning so we can do some paperwork. You'll get your money sooner that way."

The Commissioner looked at the address Raul had written. It was Raul's mother's house.

Raul spent the night sewing small packets of cloth into various sections of his clothes using a needle and thread he had borrowed from the bartender's wife. Each packet was filled with the uncut diamonds.

Raul kept his secret and his diamonds from all eyes until after the war. Intent on going to America, he found an old diamond cutter to appraise a few diamonds from his cache. The old man, Russian by birth, cut several diamonds into smaller gems so they could be sold easily. He cashed in those smaller stones for Raul.

"You said you wanted to go to America. I can suggest a manager in America. He will open up many markets for you."

"Who is this person?"

"Who else? A Russian. The market for diamonds is unlimited. He knows the international market. He will get you the best price and his cut will only be fifty percent."

"Fifty percent? Isn't that too much?"

"No. He will offer you a good price and he will protect you from *goniffs*, thieves who might want your diamonds."

"Who is this person?"

"My cousin. Arkady Petrovich. In America, he is Art."

"Where is this Art?"

"San Diego."

He shook his head from side to side. Raul had never heard of this city, San Diego.

CHAPTER FOUR

AMERICA

On the final leg of his journey to San Diego after leaving New York City, Raul met Maria Rose on the train. He invited her to lunch as the train wended its way south from Los Angeles to the border city. Maria Rose promised to help Raul in San Diego.

True to her word, Maria Rose showed Raul her city. She was very familiar with San Diego and took time off from her job at the naval base. Maria Rose found in this stranger from Spain to be a man of adventure and mystery.

Raul was in no hurry to make contact with his diamond dealer, Arkady. He had enough money to last for many months. Maria helped him find an apartment just off the coast in a place called Coronado. Raul had to outbid several others for his new living quarters.

The owner of the building, a grizzled old sea captain, was a bulldog to deal with. With rent control lifted after the war, rents were sky-high due to the influx of naval personnel returning to the area. The captain, whose name was Oliver Tompkins, intended to make plenty of money—now.

The old captain stood in the middle of Raul's rental apartment. "Glad to have you aboard, Raul. Nice to have someone who fought against those German bastards. Damn bastards trying to take over the world. Bastards! Besides, you were the highest bidder. I like a man who pays in cash for the first three months. Just look at that view. Hard to believe those waters were infested with German subs at one time."

"Really? This far in? Did they do any damage?"

"One got a shell off the coast near Santa Barbara. That's north of here. Nope, the Navy got 'em."

"You had this apartment building before the war?"

"Yeah, bought it from my former commander. He wanted to go back to Texas. Rent control clobbered me during the war. But things are different now. Demand is the name of the game."

"It sure has a great view. That's worth every penny to me."

That evening, Raul and Maria went to the Seville nightclub. It was owned by Señor Alphonse Maimon, a Spaniard.

"Tapas! I haven't had tapas in many years, Raul. How did you find this place?"

"You, my dear Maria, are my contact here in San Diego. Yet my contact goes all the way back to Spain. Being a Jew, I made a promise to my mother to remain a Jew and honor my name, Molina. Maimon is also a Jew, who honors his family name."

Maria was impressed.

Two days earlier, Raul had approached Señor Alphonse regarding his diamond contact. They had agreed to meet at the Seville. Maria did not need to know what Raul was about to do. Yet she was indispensable to him. He did need her as a cover for his business. Besides he missed her when they were apart.

Raul looked around the restaurant nervously. He was suddenly anxious to meet his contact, Art. Maria noticed a sudden change in him. "You are looking around like you are expecting your worst enemy, Raul. What is it?"

Raul took her hand. "I cannot hide anything from you, Maria. You are always on my mind."

Maria liked his words. She had been lonely in San Diego since her parents left. Now this man had entered her life, and she felt drawn to him.

She gripped his hand more firmly. Raul relaxed, until a man of incredible girth stood above him. Alphonse Maimon leaned over and whispered into Raul's ear. "You will find your contact at the bar in the back. He is wearing a blue ruffled shirt with a large bowtie loosely drawn. I will stay with your lady friend."

Raul beckoned Alphonse to be seated and introduced Maria to him. "Please excuse me, my dear Maria. Alphonse will be your companion for a few minutes. I will be right back."

Art sipped his drink while nervously tapping his fingers on the bar. He wondered if his potential client would accept his terms. He had little cash and needed to leverage his investment. Only with Alphonse's backing had he been able to bargain prior purchases.

Raul greeted Art, and they spoke very briefly. They would meet back at the Seville the following day, along with Alphonse, to discuss possible terms for the sale of the diamonds.

That night, Raul and Maria made love for the first time. She lost her virginity to this man she was drawn to for a reason she did not understand and did not care. Love had seeped into her heart, and she found it with this man from Spain.

She never told her parents about Raul; they wouldn't approve.

The two Spaniards and Arkady, the Russian, sat in Alphonse's office. "Raul, the first thing we need to do is get the stones evaluated and set a price."

It was simple—the first thing. But to Raul it was never simple. "How do I know your appraiser can be trusted? Who is he? What experience does he have?"

Arcady, called Art, laughed, "All good questions. But, you see it isn't an appraiser like you think. It is a fence that needs to see how much he can sell your diamonds for on the open market. These diamonds are not clean even though my cousin cut them into precious stones. What they are worth depends on what he can get for them. Diamond dealers like to know their sources. You are a source they would question. They won't buy hot stones. We need to contact those who will."

"There are an awful lot of people involved in this deal. What is each of their cuts? What is your cut?"

Alphonse spoke, "Your cut is fifty percent. We pay the expenses of the others involved. We take our cut from what remains."

"Fifty percent. I did all the work in getting the stones and I get only fifty percent?"

"Correct. You gambled on getting them and keeping them during the war. Our gamble is getting them through to a fence. Ours is a big gamble as well."

Raul took one packet from his shirt pocket and splayed the contents on a black velvet cloth. The diamonds glistened even in the weak office light.

The three gentlemen met again three days later in Alphonse's office. Art held a green folder. Inside was a carefully typed proposal. "According to my cousin these diamonds are not perfect stones. A diamond's quality is based on clarity, color, cut and carat weight. Your diamonds fit into a category, shall we say, of 'medium quality'. So, not being high end is actually good, to your advantage. They can be sold more easily."

Raul really didn't give a damn about what Art was telling him. He wanted the deal.

Art went on. "Considering all this. Here is our deal."

Raul was puzzled. He thought he would be offered cash and that would end his diamond deal. Not so. He read through the offer, placed it on the table and said, "I don't know what to make of this offer. There is no cash involved. You are offering me properties: some apartments, some vacant lots, a couple of houses. Where do these properties come from? How did you get a hold of them?"

"Fair questions. The vacant land is land held in homestead status. We acquired it from people who homesteaded them long ago and needed cash. So we bought it from them on spec that maybe the properties would be valuable in the near future. Most of the properties are in Costa Mesa. The truth is, one day this area will be very valuable. The apartments are units we purchased from the United States Government. They are former Navy barracks that were on Federal land and are now being rented as income property. There is an extreme shortage of rental units in this area. They are worth your collection of diamonds. The three houses are on plots of land zoned for agricultural use. When they are rezoned, they will be very valuable."

"And how am I to get the money to get this property rezoned?"

"That is something you will have to decide. This property will have to be transferred to your name and the principals need to know your decision in twenty-four hours."

Raul was confused and angry. He left the bar without saying a word. He called the one person he felt he could trust, Maria Rose. They met for lunch. Raul felt better after conferring with Maria. She was smart. In fact, she would make a great partner. That night in Raul's apartment, the two met with Captain Oliver Tompkins. A partnership was formed that would lead to a real-estate dynasty.

The diamonds were traded for land and property.

Oliver Tompkins, Maria Rose, and Raul Molina met with real-estate attorney Samuel Abel in his office. A fourth partner was about to be added to the group, forming an investment firm that would eventually own a variety of properties throughout the San Diego area.

In 1965, on a warm February day, Raul sat tabulating rent checks. He marked the total checks for each apartment house they owned. His days were filled with operating the finances for the partnership. He also ran *RAFT* Real Estate, the partnership's joint venture. Oliver Tompkins had died the year before, and the partnership, through life insurance, had bought out his share. So only the three partners remained. Samuel Abel handled all the legal matters associated with their business; Maria Rose helped run *RAFT* RE and was in the front office when destiny walked through the front door in the shape of Katsuro Tachigi.

Dressed in traditional western garb, a pin-striped gray suit, a light-blue dress shirt and solid deep-blue tie. He sat perfectly straight in his chair, waiting for Maria to finish her telephone call. Maria extended her hand. Katsuro stood and bowed, not taking it. "I would like to speak to the owner of the company. I have an inquiry about one the properties you have for sale."

"I am the owner, Mr. Tachigi. What property are you interested in?"

Katsuro hesitated. Once again he asked for the owner.

"I assure you, Mr. Tachigi, I am one of the owners."

"I see. In Japan, women are not allowed to own property. Their husbands are fully in charge. I beg your pardon for being so rude. I hope I have not offended you."

"I do not take offense easily. I understand perfectly what you are saying. Would you feel more at ease talking to my husband? He is also a partner."

Katsuro was most appreciative of this woman's understanding. "Thank you. I would feel more comfortable."

RAFT Real Estate evolved over the years. Eventually it became the exclusive property of Gian Raul Molina and Maria Rose, who married shortly after the partnership was established.

They had three sons. In 1975, Carlos Molina, Raul and Maria's eldest son, married Jennifer Sanchez. Carlos and Jennifer embarked on a lifestyle of drugs, free love, and swinging.

CHAPTER FIVE

KATSURO
AFTER THE WAR

Katsuro Tachigi was philosophical about the Japanese surrender and even more circumspect about the atomic bombs dropped on Nagasaki and Hiroshima. He was a physician, but as a black belt he understood the need for the victor to completely dominate his adversary. "Don't give your opponent any hope. If you give him hope, he may think he can beat you. Never let him have hope." He could hear his father's words echoed so often through the wooden halls of the dojo where he trained. His father, a Samurai, and the son of a Samurai, never blanched from an enemy, nor subsequent combat. Katsuro's father saw himself as a modern-day warrior. He wanted Japan to spread its dominance around the world and let the world know Japan was the master.

Out of respect for his father, Katsuro never argued with him. He bent to his will until the time came for him to assert his own philosophy on the world he lived in. It certainly was not world dominance. It was dominance of the human spirit: Willing one to be the best he could through a strict and disciplined life. Katsuro lived that life.

Studying to be a physician was his way of being precise and dominant. He knew what most people didn't: how to preserve life and how to take life, how to take care of one's physical self and how to take care of one's spiritual self. But, he was also a pragmatist. He needed money to live in the style he wanted.

He started his career working as an emergency-room physician in a small Tokyo hospital. His all-night shift allowed him to get a few hours sleep each day with time left to hunt for another job. "A job I can be proud of and help the most people," he told his friends. It was early Sunday morning, the streets outside his hospital were quiet. The three-story brick hospital built in the late 1800s stood in stark contrast to the new auto plant with its gleaming glass exterior in the Azabu-Hiroo District in Tokyo. Being Sunday, he did not expect any activity at the plant. However, walking back and forth in front of the auto plant were workers carrying placards. HEALTH CARE . . . WE NEED A HEALTH PLAN . . . WE HAVE FAMILIES . . . Katsuro knew some of these employees from his duty in the ER. He walked over to a large Japanese man he once had as a patient, "Friend, what is your health-care issue?"

Listening to the workers gave Katsuro an idea he knew would succeed. His desire to find a job of substance to help the workers was formulated. Over the next several months, Katsuro drew up a proposal for the car manufacturer. His entrée into the corporate world was easier because of his contacts in the hospital.

The name on the office door read *Yutaka Katayama, Vice President.* Katsuro was guided into Katayama's small office, simply furnished with a cherry wood desk and chairs to match. The Vice President was as diminutive as his guest. Each bowed, and Katayama nodded for Katsuro to be seated. "I have read your proposal. You are very creative, Mr. Tachigi."

Katsuro nodded without revealing any emotion. He felt it a great honor to be accepted by one of the leaders. "Tell me what you want for yourself."

Katsuro was taken aback by these words. He bowed his head and said nothing.

Katayama sat and waited for his guest to reply. Finally, Katsuro spoke. "I want the honor of helping my fellow employees. I want to make their lives better. I want them to realize the company they work for is helping them."

The Vice President nodded. He gathered his thoughts. "What do you need to make our health center a success?"

Katsuro lifted his head and glanced out the window at the cloudless blue sky and beautiful mountains surrounding Tokyo. "Your full support allowing me free reign to operate the health center as I see fit. No cost boundaries, only my word that all expenses will be necessary. In other words, trust me."

Katayama rose quickly, like the martial arts expert he was, and bowed. Katsuro had his job. A new career in the private health world had its beginning with this company.

Several years later, after the auto plant continued to receive accolades for providing its employees with cost-effective health services, other companies beckoned. Katsuro opened another clinic in a second manufacturing plant.

With a diverse number of companies using his medical services, he opened offices to provide medical insurance. Eventually, he headed an umbrella organization, *Kuretzu*, under which all his businesses operated. He was his own holding company.

Now a successful businessman, Katsuro knew he must keep the competition from stealing his contracted companies. Katsuro's companies were so successful that others tried to provide the same services. Katsuro didn't mind as long as they never touched his clients. That he would not tolerate.

Sitting in his new office, he addressed his cousin about the company that was threatening his new business, "Those bastards are stealing our business. Make sure they never touch our clients again. Do you hear me? Never again!"

Yon, who was a powerfully built man in his late twenties, a master in *Akin Jitsu*, nodded and bowed. He turned and left the office and headed for the lunchroom where his fellow martial-arts experts and friends waited.

He addressed them in whispered tones. "You," he pointed at a heavy mustached man, "You know where the president lives?"

The man nodded.

"Good. Break his car window and leave this typewritten note in his vehicle. You," he pointed at a second aide, "slash the tires of his wife's car. You," he pointed to the last accomplice, "slice up his children's stuffed animals and leave this note."

The man read the note: *"The next time it could be your child."*

"I will stop by his office and talk to him before all this is done. Start your work in three hours."

Yon looked at his watch. That gave him two hours to make contact and set the man up for his warning. Yon gunned his new sedan down the wide streets and parked in the lower level of the modern, opulent edifice erected just the year prior. *Tokyo is being rebuilt one building at a time. But what happened to the Japanese architecture? America's influence stinks,* he mused.

Yon took the staircase. He never drew a deep breath even though he ran to the eighth floor. He entered the appropriate door and spoke softly to a secretary. He stared at her well-shaped legs, no longer hidden by a long skirt. *American short skirts are better designed than their architecture.*

"You may go in, sir." The secretary smiled prettily.

The man behind the desk rose and bowed. Yon bowed while observing the office. "My secretary said you are from Mr. Tachigi's office and you said it was important."

"Yes, yes it is. We are asking you not to do any business with our clients. Any time you talk to our clients, an accident could happen. You may do business, but never touch *our* clients."

The man behind the desk sat down heavily. "You are threatening me?"

"No," Yon shook his head. "Threatening is too mild a word. I am promising you that something will happen if you ever step even in the direction of our clients." Yon wagged a finger at the man now sitting white-faced and slumped back in his chair. "We provide all the services our clients will ever need." Yon smiled. It was a smile of death.

On Yon's return to Katsuro's office, Katsuro listened attentively to what Yon had done. Katsuro thought to himself, *It is my fault. I should have taught him better. We must deal with our opponents in an honorable manner, just like my ancestors did.*

Katsuro rose and faced Yon. He slapped him forcefully across the face and sent him to his knees. "You have dishonored our name. When you deal with our opponents, their family should never be brought in as a potential target. We shall deal only with that individual. Punish that person. Bring that person to his knees. Never the children! Never the wife! Never! Always keep our Japanese honor in your heart and in your mind. Get up and get out."

Yon rose shakily. He knew the next time he might never rise again.

To expand his business empire, Katsuro started his own protection company. He signed up businesses on the premise they needed protection against supposed gangs of marauders who might vandalize them. Katsuro kept meticulous records of his clients and when their payments were due. He sent only family members to collect payments.

Many months into this new venture, Katsuro noted a client who had balked at paying. "Yon, our favorite market hasn't paid us in two months. You need to see Mr. Ayaka. No check, just cash. And bring back some summer squash and some beef for my barbeque."

Yon rounded up his other business partners, a.k.a. thugs, and headed for downtown Tokyo. Ayaka's Market was a series of booths that Mr. Ayaka leased out to local vendors. Yon's driver parked his van along the crowded streets filled with bargain hunters, street vendors, and old people out for a stroll to fill in their lonely days. Pushing past the crowd, the four men scrambled into the market seeking the owner. With a singular focus Yon learned from his martial-arts training, he led his men to the back office. Mr. Ayaka was at his desk when his door burst open and the four men crowded into his cubicle. Ayaka reached under his desk and pressed a buzzer. He stood and pointed his finger wagging it at Yon, "Get out. I am not paying you thieving bastards anymore. Out!"

Yon signaled for the other three to grab Ayaka. "Some of his workers will be right in here. You hold him. I'll take care of whoever comes through that door."

Just then the door burst open and several men pushed through the opening. Without a word Yon grabbed the first one and clutched his head in his arms and snapped his neck. The crunching bones of the death-blow could be heard. Yon's stiffened hand dug deep into the second man's stomach and blew the wind out of him. A right upper cut struck the man's throat. He slumped to the floor unconscious.

One of Yon's men grabbed the third and struck him to the floor.

"Stop," a paralyzed Ayaka said in a screaming whisper as his throat was being squeezed. "Take your money in my top drawer. Just leave me alone."

"Can't do that, Mr. Akaya. You need our services. You can see how vital they are." Yon reached across the desk, pulled out the top drawer and took the cash that was due while he instructed one of his men, "Get Mr. Tachigi his meat and vegetables. This should take care of our order, Mr. Akaya. Have our money on time next month." Yon waved his crew out.

Yon was pleased with himself. He was good at what he did and felt pride in his loyalty to his boss.

CHAPTER SIX

TAKAYAMA, JAPAN, 1977

Katsuro looked down at the tiny creature. He held out an extended finger and the baby grabbed it. "One day, little baby, when I have finished teaching you, you will be the greatest fighter of all time or die trying. You are not my blood, so I can train you like no other. You shall be my greatest protégé."

Rita, Katsuro's oldest child, watched from the half-open door and heard the words. She wondered about many things. Why had her father, at age seventy-two, adopted a child? What did he mean by saying *"You will be the greatest fighter of all time or die trying?"* Her brow furrowed even more when the tone of his voice changed and she heard him say *"You are not my blood."* His laughing voice sounded evil. Fortunately, she only heard it a few times. She knew when her father wanted something he would get it by any means possible.

Yes, Rita wondered, yet she would never understand until years later, when the words would haunt her very being.

* * *

THE NANNY

She was a large woman. Her hands were cradle-sized and her heart was in tune with the person who wrote her paycheck. She was only seven when her mother took a job away from their home. She was raised by her father. Lonely and afraid, many nights she climbed in bed with him. It was on one of those nights that he, also lonely and angry, because his woman was not in bed with him, began touching his child.

It was a drunken touching at first, but through the years it became wanton and lustful. As she lay next to her father, then under him, she began to hate her parents—her mother who left her and her father who cared nothing about her. By the age of ten, she swore never to marry and never to have children. She kept that promise. She ran away from home at the age of twelve.

Wandering the streets of Tokyo, sleeping in doorways of grand homes or crowded onto a large grate that covered an opening to the subway, she was molested and prodded too often to ever soften and love. Instead, she understood the need for survival and self-preservation.

It was under these circumstances she was taken into the house of Kobayashi. Found shivering by a servant on the Kobayashi apartment doorstep, the servant took her in and fed her. In a quiet manner, this kindly old woman fed and nourished the lonely child she named Tamika—*child of the people*. She dressed her in a maid's garb and taught her how to clean and take care of the owners without being intrusive.

"Remember, Tamika, you are living your life at the behest of another. Be courteous at all times, and above all never steal. They will take care of you, but first they must trust you." So the Kobayashis took in this child. It was only after several years that Tamika learned that her trusted tutor had betrothed her as a surrogate companion for the son of the Master Kobayashi. Her life was now that of both a servant and an on-demand lover and sex object for the Master's son. Uneducated and living on her instincts, she learned to survive.

As she matured and grew older, Tamika learned her place and how to care for herself. She was told often by her mentor, *Take care of yourself, for nobody else will*. When she was no longer needed by the Kobayashi family and feared being returned to the street, she took the job as nanny to the white child that had come into the household of Tachigi.

Master Kobayahi, a business friend of Katsuro, worked with Katsuro in one of the clinics, "You will like her. She works hard but is cold and strict when she needs to be. Just the person you need as a nanny to this white child."

Up to age six, Gian lived in the Tachigi house. Shortly after that birthday, which was never mentioned or celebrated, Gian was moved to a small house on the property several hundred feet away from the family house. Here he lived with his nanny and Dog. Dog was the only thing Gian owned, the only thing Gian was allowed to love. Dog was a large Akita. With its soft, bushy white fur, Dog showed Gian unconditional love. His nanny was cold and detached: *The perfect person to be with Gian,* Katsuro would tell his wife Rita as they lay together each night. Many times, especially when Katsuro had finished having sex with Rita, he would tell her about his plans for Gian. She would just listen, glad his sexual demands had somewhat diminished over the years.

Dog was Gian's only companion when he was in his two-story house. Gian ate his meals alone and played alone. No one was allowed to visit him.

It was at this time that living alone was never even a thought in the child's mind. His martial arts teachings began and Gian learned the meaning of pain.

Katsuro, the Master martial arts expert, began training Gian in his way of thinking, his way of fighting pain, his way of enduring brutality. Katsuro was his only teacher.

Training took place in the family dojo. In one corner of the large barn-like structure was a collection of mats to simulate actual martial arts encounters. Floor-to-ceiling wooden poles were spaced in several sections of the room. Each pole had a cord of rope tied around it at various heights. The trainee would use the ropes as others would use a punching bag. Using very lightweight gloves, similar to those used in actual matches, the trainee would punch the rope *"to toughen the hands and mind against pain."* Katsuro would repeat this over and over. The room lacked weight lifting equipment. "Weights are not good. Nature is better," Katsuro would say when asked about the set-up of his dojo.

As he had done since the age of three, Gian sparred with two of Katsuro's grandchildren. They tumbled to the mat, practicing some of the basic moves Katsuro had taught them. Katsuro, the grand master, also trained his grandchildren and children.

Tiny for his age and very thin, Gian was a runt compared to Katsuro's grandchildren. He was a year younger than any of them. Katsuro recalled Gian's tall and athletic birth parents. He was disappointed in the child's size.

"We are going to do a new exercise today, little one. Always do as I say. Never ask why, just do." Katsuro stretched Gian's arms wide and ordered him to hold them out straight. Katsuro spread Gian's legs slightly apart. "Legs apart to keep your balance."

Katsuro placed a book on top of each outstretched hand. "You understand?" Without waiting for Gian to respond, Katsuro continued, "Don't drop either book or you will have to pick it up and start over again."

Gian did as he was told. But under the sustained weight of the books and for what seemed like an eternity, Gian winced as his outstretched arms quivered. Then it happened; a book slid off.

"Pick up that book!" screamed an enraged Katsuro.

Gian bent over to pick up the book and felt a searing pain melt the flesh on his back.

"Pick them up quickly, for the longer it takes you to pick them up, the longer I will beat you."

Gian fell to the wooden floor of the dojo and started to crawl away from the bamboo stick lashing at his flesh. Katsuro held the *Shinai*, a bamboo stick used in Kendo Martial Arts sword fighting. This was Katsuro's way of inflicting pain so the trainee would understand what pain was really like. Gian did not understand. He was only six and the agony drove him to cower and cry out in terror.

Katsuro rained the bamboo sword across Gian's back and legs. The lashing continued until Katsuro's arms grew tired. He bent over the hysterical child and inspected his wounds.

None of the grandchildren in the dojo said a word. They glanced, turned away, and went about their training. Gian was alone with his pain.

Katsuro shouted to his son, "Ryuu, bring me the bucket of mud medicine, now."

Ryuu stopped his training and took a small bucket hanging from a hook on the wall and brought it to Katsuro. The old man dipped his hand into the bucket and pulled out a handful of sticky goo. Gian whimpered. "Mud is the best for a cut. It sticks on and stops the bleeding." Gian inhaled the awful odor of the concoction as Katsuro rubbed it onto his torn flesh.

Gian cried out.

"Do not whimper. Pain is only in your mind. You must learn to understand pain and deal with it. Put it out of your mind. Do it now!" It was an order Katsuro would repeat at almost all training sessions. "Put away your pain!"

"Get up, *Juko*, you still have your book exercise to do. This time you will not drop the books; and if you do, you will feel the bamboo against your flesh again and again."

Six-year-old Gian got to his feet. Katsuro's threatening words pierced his brain. But he could not help thinking, *What is this man doing to me? Why is he beating me? Don't drop the books, Gian! Don't drop them!*

Again Katsuro readied Gian for the book exercise. With his legs slightly apart and his arms fully extended, Katsuro placed the books on Gian's outstretched hands. Katsuro walked away. With his back in pain and his arms weary, Gian did not move.

Time stood still for Gian. When Katsuro finally returned, he said to Gian. "When your stomach growls, it says you are hungry; but you do not have to eat. When your arms are weary, it is like a growling stomach. Your arms are weary but not tired. You can hold on longer."

Katsuro walked away and Gian could feel his arms begin to quiver and quake. He shut his eyes and forced his arms to stop shaking. *Please don't drop the books. He'll beat me again, only worse. Don't drop the books.*

After what seemed like an eternity, Katsuro returned again, "We will do this again and again until you have the strength of a lion." Katsuro took the books from Gian's quivering arms, "Now go to the punching bag and work out. That will relieve the tension in your arms."

As Gian walked to get his gloves for the punching exercise, he heard a weak call of distress from Frank, one of Katsuro's grandchildren. Katsuro went quickly to the boy, put his arm around him, stroked his head, and kissed him gently on the arm where he had bruised himself. "That kiss will make it better. Now go finish your workout. Just be careful."

Gian watched and wondered why Katsuro had never held him, kissed him, patted him, or hugged him. He really wanted that. It drove him to work harder. Maybe one day Katsuro would put his arm around him and say he loved him.

With his house separated from the family house and not having a bathing room, Gian was allowed to use the Japanese ritual bath as needed. It was the only time Gian was permitted in the Tachigi family house. That night, Gian allowed Nanny to undress him and bathe him before he entered the larger bathing area as dictated by Japanese lore. *Clean your body first before entering the bathhouse, Juko. With a clean body you can then clean your thoughts and spirit.* Katsuro's words came to mind often whenever he entered the ritual bath. As Nanny tended to his scarred back, Gian winced. "Quiet my child. Do not make a sound. The pain will go away. But your Master will inflict more pain on you if he hears you make a sound. Bear the pain, my child. Think of peaceful things. School begins next week. You will like school. You will learn all about Japan, about our history. You will learn to read. Yes, think of school. It will take the pain away."

Gian did not understand what Nanny was talking about. *What does "bear the pain" mean? Everything hurts, especially my back. But maybe thinking of school will help. At least it will be time away from this house.*

Later that afternoon, Gian dressed for his daily workout. Nanny had packed that smelly, awful mud on his back. Even though he didn't like it, he had to admit, it did ease the pain, a little.

In the dojo Katsuro's grandchildren, ranging in age from one year older than Gian to the teenage years, were working out with their parents. Even Katsuro's daughters were working out on the other side of the dojo. With his robes tied neatly for his lesson in *Akin Jitsu*, Gian faced Katsuro.

"Today, *Juko*, we will learn additional stretching exercises that must be done in the correct order. So, listen to me carefully. Do exactly as I do. Repeat what I say. Do you understand?"

"Yes, sir," and Gian bowed.

Katsuro began the exercise routine he wanted Gian to follow. Gian, age six and with the attention span of any other six-year-old, tried to follow Katsuro. Gian worked through the exercise but forgot the exact sequence, and then the beatings began. "Gian, you are not paying attention."

"But I tried, sir."

"No, you did not pay attention."

"Yes, sir. I did my best."

Katsuro's hand struck so quickly Gian never saw it coming. Katsuro's hand whacked across Gian's face hard and intense. Gian fell to the floor. He cried out in pain grasping his left cheek. Tears flooded his face.

"Don't ever talk to me like that again. If I say you weren't paying attention to me, you weren't. Now get up and do it right this time."

Gian lay on the floor crying.

"Get up and stop crying, *Juko*. Do exactly what I say and never talk back to me."

Tears flowing, but fearing he would be hit again, Gian got up slowly. Finally, he stood as he had been trained to do from age three. "I will show you what to do. Watch me again, and don't fail this time."

Through his tear-filled eyes, Gian watched. He counted the moves in his head and began the exercise routine. When he finished, he smiled at Katsuro. "That was better, but wipe that smile off your face." Katsuro's left hand smashed across Gian's face, wiping the smile away and sending the six-year-old to the mat crying.

Katsuro stood above him. "Stop sniffling. You are not hurt. If I wanted to hurt you, you would know it. Get up and do it again. Now!"

Terror filled Gian's body and soul, his heart and mind; every inch of him was riddled with terror. His faced ached. He crawled backwards away from this monster. "Yes, sir."

Gian wobbled to his feet. Would the monster hit him again? He must do what he is told. He cowered before his tormentor.

"Do not pull away from me. Stand up straight. No fighter who is a true champion ever shows fear of his opponent. Fear me, nobody but me. Now get ready to defend yourself."

Katsuro held Gian's hands. "Block my punches with your hands."

Gian held his hands up near his face as Katsuro's hand crushed Gian's tiny arms down. The small child's arms were unable to block Katsuro's powerful and well-aimed punches that sliced through Gian's defense and smashed into his face.

Gian stumbled backwards. Katsuro kept throwing punches. Gian was overwhelmed and fell to the mat, his face bleeding, his flesh torn. The child, thoroughly beaten, didn't rise. He crawled off into a corner, cowering, screaming in pain and fear. "Go back to your room and have Nanny bandage your face. Then come back, and we will train on the punching bag."

Katsuro walked off. "He is not my flesh. I will train him like no other. Just like you would do, father." Katsuro looked toward the ceiling of the dojo and the sky beyond.

The lessons and the beatings continued relentlessly, every day, without rest.

Gian was alone every night except for Dog, who snuggled close and licked his hand as he rubbed Dog behind his ears. "You're the only one that loves me, Dog, and I love you, too." Gian squeezed Dog until he whimpered.

CHAPTER SEVEN

SCHOOL

"Stand up, Gian, while I fix your tie. You look very handsome in your uniform."

"Why do I have to wear a uniform? Will the other children wear one, too?"

"Of course, they will. Why do you think I dress you like this? I have already told you they do. All the children dress in uniforms. That way nobody gets special attention. You will like school. You will learn to read and write."

Gian was happy he would learn to read and write Japanese, but, sadly for him, he was the only Caucasian child in the school. All the other children were Japanese, and many of them made fun of him.

Nanny took Gian's hand and led him to his first class. The children stared at Gian. One boy called out, "You white. You different." He pointed and laughed at Gian. The children took their seats on the rug in front of their teacher. All the children wiggled as six-year-olds do, all except Gian, who, because of his training, sat rigid and listened.

At lunch Gian ate alone. Every other child ate with a friend. Katsuro's wife, Rita, packed Gian's lunch. The box had two layers of plates. The top plate had meat and vegetables and the second had rice. Not only did Gian eat by himself at school, he ate all his meals alone at home.

Tokyo and other larger cities each had several American schools. This small, rural area where the Tachigi family lived was far from any American presence and American children. Close to Takayama, all of Gian's fellow students were Japanese.

Each day Katsuro waited for him to return from school to continue the training. The beatings continued! The pain continued! Katsuro's hands smashed against his body, the *Shinai* pummeled his flesh. Gian had to learn to protect himself or the beatings would have been worse. He learned not to cower but to fight back, to use his small arms and legs as protection.

Sometimes Katsuro wasn't his opponent. One of Katsuro's grandchildren would take his place and be the antagonist. It really didn't make any difference to Gian. All the blows stung. The pain was intense. But at least the grandchildren were more his size, so he felt he had a chance.

On a bitterly cold day in January, Haro, a grandchild, was in uniform to train with Gian. After a short workout on the punching bag, Katsuro showed each a new move. Three times Haro mercilessly downed Gian and pummeled him as he fell to the mat.

The child of many beatings gritted his teeth and slid under a blow aimed for his face and drew his foot under Haro's, hooking the knee, sending him to the mat. With his tiny fists flying, Gian pummeled Haro. Katsuro pulled Gian off and held him while Haro kicked the child in the stomach, sending him to the mat holding his middle.

Katsuro lifted Gian with one hand and struck him in the shoulder with the elbow of the other while screaming at him. "Punish him. Use your elbows. You want your opponent to feel pain like you feel now. Never let your opponent off without punishing him. Make him afraid of you. As you get older and stronger, this must be your law. Be feared. Now, never hurt my grandchildren."

Gian sank to the mat and held his shoulder. He glared at Haro and said nothing. Katsuro's advice came to mind: *"Let fighting be your words."*

I will never forget today. I will get even with him. To Gian, Haro symbolized the different way Katsuro treated him and his own grandchildren. For now, Gian fought back tears. He had learned that crying brought only more pain. So the tears stopped.

"Come, *Juko.* It is time to balance the books on your hands. Today, we will balance the books longer than yesterday. Just remember the rules. We are building your endurance. You will not understand this until you are older. But you will understand—someday."

Gian did not like the name *Juko.* It was a bad name—an insulting name—a name he would one day fight to overcome.

Gian stood feet apart, arms extended, palms up, arms rigid, holding the books on his small hands. His mind went back to yesterday. He could still feel the bamboo ripping his tender, pulpy flesh, and he feared it would happen again. His arms remained rigid. His mind flushed all thoughts from his brain. He placed himself in a trance. The fatigue in his arms that had led to such exhaustion and brutality the day before was barely felt. *The real pain is in your mind. You can handle all pain as long as you convert that pain to energy that leads to survival.*

Katsuro's words were beginning to have an effect. Fear strengthened his resolve even at the age of six. *Don't give up. Don't cry out. This feeling of exhaustion will end. Just make it now.* His arms quivered. Gian closed his eyes. The world of reality vanished. He was in a trance: his survival trance. It was the beginning of his new world.

*   *   *

Tomi Tachigi was a steely-eyed, taller version of his father. His closely cropped black hair had been well manicured by the cute beautician in the beauty parlor he frequented. He talked her into wearing pigtails and very short skirts when he came for his monthly haircut. But he could not talk her into sleeping with him. He liked the little-girl look. *Kinjo* was the subculture of hidden desires Japanese men felt toward young girls. Perhaps, due to growing up repressed in an uptight society, Tomi had these desires.

Tomi sat in his downtown Los Angeles office knowing his charade of being a businessman might be over. The meeting with his CFO had not gone well. "Your company in Japan has let you down. The last shipment of nuts and bolts was defective and not up to the standards here in California. Two of your contracting building companies pulled their orders. They also cancelled their checks. You don't have the money to pay your employees. This company is in trouble."

Tomi pushed on the floor with the tips of his toes and the chair rolled back from his desk, and he walked it over until he sat face-to-face with his CFO. "This company is not in trouble. We have just had a slight setback. Hold reporting this loss. Make a loan from our bank and plug in the figures as income."

"That is not honest. That is cheating."

"It is not. It is good financial practice. We must remain liquid. The loan will keep us liquid until I get another shipment from our manufacturer."

"You mean a new manufacturer, don't you?"

"No, I have a contract with Rowen Industries and we will keep that contract. Make the loan, put it on the books as income, pay the employees, including you and me. We deserve it."

After his CFO left, Tomi wheeled himself back behind his desk and picked up his private line. He paid no attention to the time difference between Los Angeles and Takayama, Japan.

Katsuro picked up the phone in the dojo. He did not like to mix his workouts with business, but he knew Tomi had had several business, setbacks so he needed to take the call.

* * *

Gian's eyes were shut tight. The world did not exist. His arms were like two paralyzed poles, rigid and firm. The telephone ring startled him. His arms began to shake.

"Tomi? Yes. I can talk. But wait a minute. I need to finish with Gian first."

"Gian, your arms are shaking. Your mind must be in full control. Go to your room. Meditate and read. Spend your time wisely."

Gian let each book down slowly. It was the best telephone ring he had ever heard. Gian raced outside, feeling the new-fallen snow on his feet. He stopped and looked up to the blue sky. He took a few steps toward his house and then fell backwards onto the snow. Icy cold engulfed his body. The white was so pure he could lick it and taste its refreshing chill.

The freezing snow felt very good on his torn back. He had been thinking what it would be like to die. Would pain be lifted by death?

Is this what heaven is like? I know I will go to heaven. I have been a good boy. Why does he beat me?

He lay in this icy heaven until he heard Nanny's voice. "It is cold out there, young man. Come in."

After a warm bath, Gian sought his loving companion. Dog licked his master's face while the two rolled on his bedroom floor. Gian enjoyed this short respite from the brutality of the dojo.

With the dojo empty, Katsuro listened to Tomi and said nothing. When his son had finished he said, "Okay, I will take care of it."

Katsuro hung up the phone and quickly dialed his son, Ryuu. "Rowen Industries is not using US quality control. Take a few of our boys over to the company and talk to the Production Manager. Tell him this is not acceptable. Get a check from them to cover our losses due to their failure to comply with California standards. Deposit it into our California account so Tomi can pay off his short-term loan. Do it within 24 hours. Then we will consider a trip to Los Angeles to talk to Tomi. I'm afraid he hasn't embraced the skills we have taught him." Katsuro handed Ryuu a neatly typed paper with the amount he was to collect from Rowen.

Ryuu never said a word. He just noted his father's words and felt fulfilled that his father had such faith in him.

* * *

Katsuro's goal was to develop Gian into the best fighter he could. This meant creating ways to improve his mental toughness and physical tenacity. "*Juko*, come here. To be physically strong you need to develop your upper body. Pushups. Pushups will make you stronger. You will do your pushups like this." Katsuro demonstrated exactly what he wanted. His sinewy body easily pushed up ten times. "Let me see you do your pushups just like I did."

Gian had done some pushups before but never as many as ten. He strained to do three. He collapsed on the floor in a heap and drew himself into a shell. He knew what was going to happen. Katsuro stood above him. "I said ten. Get up and do ten."

Gian slowly crawled into a corner and trembled. "I can't do any more, sir. I can't."

Katsuro took the *Shinai* from its place where it hung on the wall. Gian, in fetal position, cowered and shook while Katsuro lashed the small child once again. The leaves of the *Shinai* raked across his short legs. Gian prayed he would die right then and there. Maybe the pain would go away.

Gian cried as the bamboo leaves tore at his flesh. "Get over here and do ten pushups. Never tell me you can't do something. Force yourself, so you can survive the pain life will give you."

Katsuro bent down and grabbed Gian by his head and neck and pulled him back to the exercise mat. "Ten pushups!" The *Shinai* rained down on the small, quivering figure. And then it stopped. Gian, in perfect position, pushed himself up from the mat. One, two, three, four, and then his arms wanted to give out. "Keep going, *Juko*!" The *Shinai* whipped his legs again. "Keep going, *Juko*!"

Gian bit down on his lips hard until they bled. *Stop-pain-stop. Ten pushups.* The pain did not stop but the whipping did as the tiny, frail body pushed itself off the mat again and again. *Ten!*

"The last two push ups were not perfect. Always be perfect. Do two more." The *Shinai* pummeled his legs again and again. "Now, *Juko*! Now!"

Gian passed out. The beating stopped.

Gian awoke with his body covered in smelly mud. He lay on a rubber mat, Nanny tending to his wounds. Gian looked at her with haunted eyes, "Is it time for me to die?"

With his arms outstretched straight in front of him, Gian held the books while he stood on a round disc. Katsuro's words were ingrained in his head. *Don't move off this disc, little one. You must get stronger. Do not twitch. Keep your mind focused. Do not move and keep the books still.* After what seemed like an eternity, Gian's determination to stay rigid was broken by a wave of tiredness and weakness in his arms. His right hand quivered.

An open hand smashed against his face. "I said, don't move! Keep your mind focused!" The books flew to the mat under the round disc.

As Gian bent to pick up the books, he felt the *Shinai* on his back. Only the white uniform, often soiled by blood from his wounds, provided slight protection, keeping the pain down to a throbbing tremor.

Gian placed the books on his outstretched arms and prayed the *Shinai* would not flash again. "Hold them still. Don't move!" Gian shut his eyes from his life and dreamed of death.

CHAPTER EIGHT

ROCKS

Massive beds of white beauty turned to graying mush. Rivulets of water crept through the white mass until it disappeared into the exposed earth.

Katsuro, dressed in a distinguished-looking blue suit, white shirt and muted grey tie, sat perfectly erect in his office, growing increasingly angry at his son, Tomi. "Yes, Tomi. I understand the problem in dealing with California laws and US Customs. They can be baffling, I know. But that does not excuse a downturn in sales that could bankrupt our company." Katsuro listened, but the scowl never left his face. "You have displeased me, Tomi. I will bring the family to California and look into this mess myself." Katsuro listened. "Yes, I will call you when I have made all the arrangements."

Katsuro walked straight to the dojo. He always relaxed after a good workout. That also meant a good workout for Gian. The melted snow had left a rock-strewn barren yard that was part of the Tachigi property. Katsuro had waited patiently for spring to come. *It is time to move some rocks; time for Gian to develop muscle.*

As Katsuro entered the dojo, he saw Gian stretching and then doing floor exercises alone on a mat at the far end of the building. He changed into workout clothes quickly and addressed Gian, "*Juko,* come here. It is time to develop real muscle while doing yard work." Katsuro, who seldom showed any wit, smiled at his own words. "Come here, *Juko.* Run!"

The small lad dashed full bore toward his Master, stopping abruptly with a quick jerk to hear his orders. "Look at this yard, *Juko.* It is filled with rocks. Those rocks at the far end need to be moved to this near side. Today, you will move those rocks." Katsuro did not tell Gian that the next day he would move them all back. "Find the ones that are half your size first and move them. We have until dark."

Gian ran to the far end of the yard. He lifted a rock that was half his size but surely weighed more than he did. With grit and determination, he carried it slowly to the near side. "Keep yourself upright when you carry those rocks. Let your legs and then your arms do the lifting. We are going to develop strength." Katsuro watched as the small child, with almost Herculean strength, toted the rocks and boulders to their temporary place in the yard.

Katsuro was still exasperated by the child's size.

Many years before he had met with Gian Sr. and the child-bearing mother along with the sperm donor father. They were both large, well-proportioned people. Impressed with their size and athletic background, he agreed to take the white child and fulfill his dream of breeding a martial-arts world champion. But this child was small. Katsuro wondered what he could do to stimulate this child's growth. *When I get to California, I will check with the R.I.G.H.T Clinic. They have done research on human growth. Maybe this California trip won't be a waste of time after all.*

Gian was growing tired. The more he lifted, the heavier the rocks and boulders became. The trips from one end of the yard to the other were getting longer. His arms became weaker; still, he knew he was strong.

Gian let his mind go to other things rather than the task of lifting. Just the other day, Gian had a fight with a child who had been tormenting him since he had entered school.

He was large for a Japanese boy. He had broad shoulders like his bricklayer father. His hands were large with a grip that was surprisingly strong for a third-grader. Even some of the older students cut a wide swath around him. Mamoru had a short temper and an acid tongue just like his father. Slow in school, he made up for his lack of intellect by being a bully. Mamoru saw Gian as an easy target. As the only Anglo, Mamoru knew the other children would not come to Gian's defense. So Mamoru bullied Gian at lunch every day. "Yeah, you smell so bad nobody wants to eat with you, you white-skinned bastard. You were not even born to your mother and father. You are a bastard."

Gian had grown weary of Mamoru's tauntings. He thought of Katsuro's words. He lived by them. *Never give your enemies a chance. Beat them so they will never challenge you again.*

Gian usually ignored his tormentor, until Mamoru knocked his lunch pail off the table, spilling his rice and beef onto the floor. With a greater ferocity than Gian had ever shown at school before, he lashed out at his tormentor. Leaping to his feet, Gian drove a knee into Mamoru's groin. Lightning blows to the child's head and back crushed Mamoru. Gian was in a trance. The years of beatings had filled his head with hate. Now he hated this child. He never saw Mamoru, only the image of Katsuro. Mamoru's wailing could be heard throughout the school.

A teacher yanked Gian off the bloody child. "Look what you have done!" the teacher repeated on the way to the principal's office. "Look what you have done."

The principal was tall and had a fuzzy goatee, "This is the last of many fights you have gotten into, Gian. I will have to call your father and tell him you may not stay at this school any longer. Fighting is not acceptable."

"But, sir, he called me a bastard."

"What he said to you is not important. It is how you handle yourself and learn to ignore words that are meaningless. No, Gian, you fight too often. We cannot allow this any longer."

The principal called Katsuro and was surprised by what the old *Master* said, "Was this Mamoru able to get up and fight back?"

Puzzled, the principal said, "No, sir, he wasn't. Gian pummeled him badly."

"And what do you suggest we do about Gian?"

"I am suspending him from school."

"Absolutely not! I cannot permit that. I will arrange for a private tutor for Gian. He will be alone in school with his tutor and may not play or have lunchtime with the other students."

The principal winced. Did he dare say no to Katsuro? He had heard Katsuro was a strong, demanding person.

Katsuro anticipated the long pause. "You take care of Gian in school and you can be assured I will take care of your school."

Inwardly Katsuro smiled. *Gian, I would have given anything to have seen that fight. Maybe you will get tougher as time goes on.*

So it was arranged. For the balance of his third-grade year, Gian had a private tutor. It was the best of all worlds, because it took him away from his tormentors, and he was able to learn at a much faster rate than the others. At the end of third grade, he was far more advanced than anyone else in his class.

*   *   *

The winter passed; the training and beatings continued. Gian's flesh never healed.

One morning, before exercise, Katsuro announced to his family, including the grandchildren, they would be going to Los Angeles for the summer. He had rented a house. Gian never showed emotion, however, this time his heart was filled with joy. Still, he never said a word. He had heard about California. He knew, from talks with an older sister, Rita, that it was where he was born. He was excited.

Katsuro made a call to Ryuu late that night. "I need a passport for Gian. Tell the artist to make a birth certificate to show he was born in the United States, two years earlier than his actual date of birth. Get it for me by Friday."

*   *   *

The artist had perfected his craft over many years. During the War he had forged many documents for the royal family and friends. Now he catered to an ever-expanding rich clientele like Katsuro Tachigi, his family, and friends. The old artist went through his file of papers and found a copy of a birth certificate from another client in San Diego.

The many wrinkles on his fingers were covered with black ink he could no longer scrub off. *Too painful*, he told his wife. He squinted at the paper Ryuu had left him. He looked at the calendar on his desk: May 17, 1983. He brought the paper up to a sharper light: Gian Aaron Molina, born November 20, 1976.

The artist looked at the picture Ryuu had given him. *He doesn't look like a happy child. Sad eyes. But what a lucky boy he is, living with such a rich family.*

He changed the year of birth to 1974.

*   *   *

On the flight to Los Angeles, Katsuro sat with his family and Gian sat with his Nanny. The family occupied all the first-class seats. Gian didn't care where he sat. He was going to see *his* real family. During the flight, only Rita went to see him. She put her arms around him. "Gian, you are going to see your grandfather, the one you were named after. His name is Gian Molina. Maybe your mother and father will be there, too. I am not sure, so don't expect to see them. But, maybe they will surprise you. Would you like to meet them?"

Gian hadn't thought about seeing his mother and father. He swallowed his words, choking back tears. "Yes, I suppose I would like to meet them. Do they want to see me?"

Rita shrugged. "If they show up, I guess they want to see you."

CHAPTER NINE

CALIFORNIA

In a normal situation, Gian Molina would have led the idyllic life of a loved child. He would have had loving, caring parents and grandparents. He would have been part of a close-knit family that would have taught him how to become a warm human being. None of this happened. His was a life very few could have endured. Even those few never lived such an abusive, loveless existence and endured the excruciating beatings, the unbearable pain, and the devastating loneliness. How did he live through all those years of extreme cruelty? How did he survive?

*　*　*

Katsuro rented a limousine and a driver to take the family to their summer villa near San Diego. It was the only place he could find with a gym and a separate guesthouse for Gian, his nanny, and Dog. Without Gian asking, Dog was crated into a cage and shipped through in the plane's hole. To have Dog with him, gave Gian a faint bit of happiness. Gian wondered if he would ever meet his family. Would they hold him and love him? That answer would not be long in coming.

*　*　*

While Rita got the family settled, Katsuro headed for the offices of *RAFT* Real Estate. He wanted to check the current value of his holdings. He had purchased many land parcels from Raul years before. His main intent was to sell some off these investments or borrow on them to finance his latest venture: a bank. By owning a bank he figured he could lend himself as much money as he needed to finance the expansion of many more medical facilities and other businesses.

If he was right, and he always thought he was, his property holdings in California would give him the initial capital for the last brick in his financial empire.

Raul sat at his desk expecting his fellow investor. He had been overjoyed with the booming economy in California real estate. Raul had entertained many offers from developers for his land in Costa Mesa. After talking to Katsuro, they both agreed to sell some land and trade other land for a share of the profits the developers would make in their new housing and commercial projects. Raul was pleased beyond his wildest dreams.

Raul stood, as the well-manicured, handsomely dressed Katsuro strolled into his office. Raul bowed appropriately and then Katsuro extended his hand that Raul grasped warmly. "It is good of you to come. I hope you are not too tired from your long flight to see our latest project. Costa Mesa is becoming the hub of San Diego County."

Katsuro's two silent companions stood nearby.

Raul and Katsuro drove off in Raul's Mercedes. The companions sat in the back seat, silent, observant. Raul spoke, "The Germans still make the best cars. But I understand the Japanese have developed a new assembly line that fashions a tighter fit for their cars, making them more efficient and economical."

Katsuro smiled. "Not only more efficient, but they will last longer. We no longer build in graded-obsolescence like American manufactures have done for years. We want our cars to last many more years so the demand for them will become stronger. Then, Japanese cars will sell better."

"You know the President of a car company. What does he think of opening new plants in the United States?"

"He knows it will be cheaper to build his cars here due to the overseas transportation and import costs. His only concern is teaching American workers that built-in-obsolescence is not acceptable. Neither are unions."

"Those are big obstacles."

"Only if you think they are. This company will do it sooner than later."

"Where?"

"Probably down south where labor is cheaper and the land is less costly." Katsuro went on. "Yes, the company will come and prosper."

Raul had known none of this. He also had never heard Katsuro talk so much. Katsuro rarely made small talk. Perhaps he wanted to pass the time as they drove to Costa Mesa. Katsuro was curious to see the new shopping centers.

When he saw the areas growth, he was not disappointed. He had invested well and at the right time. His new bank project had found the money it needed. The property he owned and the shopping centers he had invested in would be the backbone of his new enterprise. The money from those properties and a host of American investors would make his bank a success.

The shadows sat mute in the back seat.

*   *   *

Gian Molina was very excited. His Japanese mother, Rita, was sitting next to him in the back of a rented Chrysler Imperial. Also sitting with them was Rita, her daughter. Gian could never understand why a mother would name her daughter by the same name. They were driven by a hired chauffeur and headed to the home of Raul Gian Molina. They would meet Katsuro later for a formal dinner.

Gian, who had learned many lessons from Katsuro, including *Never love anything you cannot stop loving easily*, felt his heart nearly pounding out of his chest. "Imagine, Gian, this is your real grandfather. He is the one you are named after."

Rita, who played a very small part in raising Gian, stroked his hair. She didn't dare do that when Katsuro was around. "Here, let me look at you. You look very handsome in your coat and tie. Your new suit fits you very well. Someday, however, you will grow out of it. You will be tall and strong just like your grandfather."

* * *

Rita recalled the night when she had confronted Katsuro after he had beaten Gian more severely than usual. She had watched and then turned her head when Gian was taped to the punching bag pulley and lifted off the ground to be beaten with the *Shinai* until he fell unconscious.

Rita watched until she felt faint, but forced herself to stay in case she had to intervene to save Gian's life. She shuddered to think what Katsuro would say and do. Rita turned her back on the small child when Katsuro finally took the *Shinai* from Ryuu after Gian had passed out.

Katsuro was agitated and sullen when he came to bed that night. Rita sat up in bed pretending to read a book. She watched her husband closely as he went through his nightly routine of combing his hair and rubbing oil across his hairless, tattooed body. His skin glistened. He patted himself dry, allowing his skin to glow. He drew a nightgown over his head and placed a long nightcap on his newly combed hair as he readied himself for bed.

"Rita, you have seen me go through my bedtime ritual all our lives. Why are you staring at me as if you have never seen me do this before?"

Rita bit her bottom lip. She purposely placed the closed book, with its bookmark protruding from between the pages, onto her nightstand and cleared her throat.

Katsuro knew what was coming. He was the Master of his house and Master at martial arts, but sometimes he wasn't the captain of his own bedroom. Rita, a small woman from an aristocratic family, was trained to be obedient to her husband, but also trained (by her mother) to speak her mind when necessary. "I could barely watch as you beat Gian today. You almost killed him."

Katsuro, with a dry sense of humor, said, "If you couldn't stand to watch my disciplining Gian, then you should have left."

"But why this child? Why must you torture him so? You never touched our children when you were training them. You never touched our grandchildren when you were training them. Why this child?"

Katsuro sat on the edge of the bed and looked intently at this woman he loved, and spoke softly. "Because he is *not* my flesh and blood. He is a project. He is an experiment. I am raising him by the principles according to the *Book of Five Rings*, as I interpret those tenets. I could never reach back and do those things that are necessary to make my own children Grand Masters. I can with him. If he has the will, the strength, and the determination, he can be a world champion."

"If he lives!"

"Yes, if he lives. Then, I will have created a Grand Master. That will be my legacy." He took Rita's hand in his. "I am a doctor. I will not let him die."

Katsuro got off the bed and looked down at his wife. "Never bring this subject up again. He is my child, not ours. My child. I will raise him *my way*."

* * *

Gian had learned never to ask questions. He had learned to live in silence. As a result, he withdrew into his own loveless world, a very lonely world filled with raging fury. Yet, here on the coastal plains of earthly beauty, on the drive along the Pacific Ocean, he found his body suddenly tensing, his stomach tightening. He was about to meet a complete stranger who was nonetheless, they said, his grandfather—his blood. Gian, not used to anything but his daily routine, almost relished that repressive regime rather than meet this new face.

How would this stranger react to him? Was he a loving relative or another in a line of adults who would mistreat him?

Gian was always cautious. He withdrew his love, because Katsuro's words were always in the back of his mind: *Never love anything that you cannot stop loving and leave behind. Never become attached to anything. That allows you to be weak. Weakness cannot be tolerated.* Yet he sought love as a sponge seeks liquid; but he did not have to have it in order to survive. Or at least that is what he had been taught. Would that change with this new person in his life? Despite all his fears, he held out hope. He was confused; his thoughts vacillated between what was real and what he had been taught.

The man was tall and strapping. He had a broad mustache that crept over his upper lip but with enough room for Gian to see his smile. The old man's eyes glistened as he stared at his grandchild. He held out his arms and beckoned for the child to come to him.

"Gian, your grandfather wants to hug you. Go to him," Rita urged as she gently pushed Gian toward his grandfather's waiting arms.

Instinctively Gian recoiled. But oh, how he wanted to jump into this man's arms. Katsuro taught him never to love and never to trust. So he stood still, nudging closer to Rita and holding her skirt.

"He is very shy," Rita said. "Give him time. He will come to you."

Gian Sr. looked at his namesake. "You are a sturdy looking lad. Why don't you come with me while your mother and your sister have a drink on the veranda? Come, take my hand."

Gian looked at Rita, clasped his hands tightly behind his back, then walked slowly following Gian Sr.

The old man smiled to himself, *What did you expect, you old fool? You allow this child to be sold to a family as an infant and then expect him to welcome you with open arms? Take him to see Juniper—maybe then he will feel more comfortable.*

The two relative strangers from different times strolled toward the back of the seaside property to a recently constructed barn. They caught a strong sea breeze blowing against the sturdy structure. "I had to replace the old barn. It almost got blown down by a really strong wind. That would have killed the horses. I wouldn't want anything to happen to Juniper. Come on, I'll introduce you."

Gian slid cautiously into the barn. Several horses neighed as the old man nuzzled each snout. He picked a carrot from a bin and fed an old gray mare. "This one is Hazel. She has one gray eye and one hazel eye. Take a look."

Gian looked at the horse's head and stared at its eyes. "Do you see, this left one is gray and the other hazel?"

Gian nodded. He saw the difference. "You want to feed her a carrot?" Gian shook his head *No*.

They walked past another few stalls. "This here stallion is Juniper. He looks just like the beast I rode during the war. Want to pet him?"

Gian shook his head again. The old man smiled and said, "Okay. This is my old saddle I rode during the war. My mother sent it to me after I settled here. Genuine leather. You know what leather is made from?"

Gian knew but said nothing.

The old man opened the gate to Juniper's stall. "I have to ride these critters a couple of times a week or they'll get lazy. I thought we could take a ride this morning."

Gian Sr. saddled the stallion without another word. He cinched the bottom tether and walked Juniper out of the barn. Juniper whinnied his approval. "See, he wants to be free and run. It's good to be free. No creature should ever be shackled."

Without a word, the old man grasped Gian under his arms and lifted him onto the saddle. Then he looped his leg around the horse and settled himself right behind Gian. "Ever been on a horse before?"

Gian shook his head and uttered, "No sir, I haven't. Juniper is a mighty big animal."

"Yes, yes he is."

Hi, ho, Juniper, away.

Exhilarated, Gian felt the strong left arm of his grandfather hold him firm with a warm touch. A touch he had longed for, dreamed about, and could only imagine. Now it was real. Juniper trotted freely across a grassy knoll and onto the beach. Sand then water slid under his hoofs. Gian shouted, "Hi, Ho Silver." He remembered seeing the Lone Ranger on television.

Juniper galloped up a final sandy knoll and grandfather pulled him to a gentle stop. "Off, my child. Time to get acquainted." The two dismounted and stood before the brackish-green algae-filled Pacific. Grandfather put his hand out, "My name is Gian Raul Molina and you are my grandchild, Aaron Gian Molina. How do you do?"

Gian stuck his hand out, "My name is Gian. I am glad to meet you." Gian then tugged on his grandfather's sleeve, "Is my other name really Aaron? I've never heard that name before. No one has ever called me Aaron."

"Would you like me to call you Aaron?"

"Sure, if you like. Who named me Aaron?"

"Your father named you after me. You are from a Jewish Sephardic family in Spain."

"I'm Jewish?"

"Yes, you are. Jewish people from Spain or Portugal or North Africa are Sephardic. Our family comes from Spain. I was born in Spain. Your surname is Molina."

"Wow, I didn't know that." It was hard for Gian to comprehend all this new information, but he wanted to know more. "You said Juniper reminded you of the horse you had during the war. What war?"

"The Second World War. I fought for Spain against the Germans and Russians. I was in the cavalry."

"That sounds exciting."

"It may sound exciting, but war is filled with death. No war is ever good unless it is in total self-defense of one's property."

Aaron watched his grandfather take a twig of grass from the knoll high above the murky sea and place it in his mouth. He pulled another long stem of green weed, twirled it in his fingers, and let it float back to the earth. "Why did you put that piece of grass in your mouth, Grandfather?"

"That piece of grass brings back memories of when I was a child with my father. We used to ride into the countryside, sit on a grassy knoll and suck on a tender shoot of grass. It is just a reminder of those times. Without memories, what do we have?"

Gian Aaron Molina wondered the same thing.

It was on that grassy knoll that Grandfather Molina told Aaron of his time in the cavalry. Aaron sat between his grandfather's legs and let him hold him. It was a peaceful moment in a life of turmoil.

*   *   *

Katsuro Tachigi sat in the back seat of a red eight-cylinder Cadillac convertible. He loved to be chauffeured in comfort and feel the power of a robust vehicle. Unlike Japanese cars, the Caddy exuded power that enabled it to hurtle down highways when the California roads weren't filled with traffic. The Cadillac engine purred like a mellow cat but could blast along the freeways whenever possible.

Katsuro knew to avoid the early-morning and early-evening hours. He watched the pavement slide by as his driver pushed his foot down full on the throttle. When the driver saw the blinking red and yellow lights of the Highway Patrol in his rearview mirror, he smiled. *Should I give them a run for their money and see what this car can really do?* Katsuro had given the driver careful instructions to drive swiftly but to obey traffic laws. In this case, Katsuro would talk to the officer.

The driver pulled off to the side of the freeway. Katsuro got out of the Caddy. He waited with a wad of money in his hand and his identification ready.

The CHIPS officer stood next to him. "You are not the driver. Get back in the vehicle!" Katsuro handed the license to the officer. "You were doing over ninety, Mr. Tachigi."

"Yes, sir, I was. Please take my card."

The officer looked at the document, handed it back to Katsuro, and said, "Please, sir, have your driver drive a little slower. It's a safety issue. You may go."

"Thank you, officer, for your trouble." Katsuro handed the officer a wad of money as was the custom when being released for diplomatic immunity.

Katsuro tucked the diplomat's card into his wallet and handed the leather folder back to his shadow. *That engraver is the best at making false documents. Very authentic!*

CHAPTER TEN

R.I.G.H.T

The Reed Institute for Growth and Hormone Technology, *RIGHT*, was founded by Phillip Zarkowski, PhD, in the late 1970s. He left his position as a professor at Stanford University following a paper he wrote which questioned the proper use of growth hormones and their effect.

In a letter he wrote to the University President he said, "Contrary to public policy and this University's stated goals, my research is being stifled by those who oppose these types of models. I am a researcher of great integrity. Therefore, for me to carry on with my much-needed studies to reach the highest goals without interference from those who lack vision, I have formed my own research institute and will conduct all further tests without said interference."

Dr. Zarkowski had a large following, especially from athletes interested in his experiments and research that might enhance their physical prowess. His money also came directly from pharmaceutical companies that wanted favorable publicity for their products. A few donors to his newly founded Institute were from foreign countries, and a few contributions came from athletes and their benefactors. Katsuro Tachigi was one of those interested benefactors who wanted the latest research on growth-hormone therapy and treatments.

Katsuro was on his way to the Institute, which was located just off the San Diego Freeway and Crestview Boulevard in Los Angeles. Not knowing Katsuro was coming, Dr. Zarkowski was busy with several of his, researchers reviewing recent data and planning further studies. Dr. Zarkowski found, as so many researchers do, that one study always leads to another in an effort to reach the bottom line and a conclusion.

More money is always needed for research. When test results warrant, those results are published and released to medical journals. Some questioned if pharmaceutical companies could have swayed Zarkowski's results. Yet, there was no doubt that these drugs did provide human growth and accelerated strength training.

Katsuro Tachigi had read with interest the latest data on steroids and their use in human growth. He saw the potential for his use of this product. Katsuro knew he needed these drugs.

The driver parked the red Caddy in a private spot just in front of the *R.I.G.H.T* sign. The slender, powerfully built Asian strode up the front walkway and ducked quickly into the glass structure, followed, as always, by his shadows. He gave his name to the receptionist and was ushered into Dr. Zarkowski's office.

The doctor left his meeting as soon as he heard about Katsuro's arrival. The renowned researcher extended his hand to Katsuro who bowed in return and took his seat. "Why didn't you tell me you were coming, sir? We would have prepared for your visit properly."

"No need, doctor. The purpose of my visit is to review with you the new formula you have developed for human growth."

"Certainly, sir. We have just completed a short video for the manufacturer. Come, I will show it to you."

"I would appreciate that very much."

Dr. Zarkowski wondered if Katsuro planned to inject himself.

Once the video was over, Katsuro turned to the doctor. "The video never mentioned an age limit for use of this drug. What are the limits?"

"All our research is done on adults. Therefore, it is understood, it should be used only on adults."

Dr. Zarkowski again imagined Katsuro using the formula on himself. His theory was premature. Innocence would be violated again.

*   *   *

Katsuro's next stop was to see his son, Tomi. It wasn't a pleasant stop for either father or son.

"Tomi, did you set the record straight and reorder the nuts and bolts?"

"Yes, I did."

"Did they give you credit for those defective pieces?"

"Yes, sir, they did."

Katsuro already knew this because he had asked Ryuu to take care of it.

He wanted to make sure it would be done correctly. "Did you contact the contractors about reordering and let them know we expect them to continue working with us exclusively?"

"Many of the contractors balked at this. They say we are unreliable."

"Unreliable? Crap! That will not happen. I will take care of it—myself." Katsuro leaned over his son's desk. "Get tougher, Tomi. Make sure this business is run right. You must call me if there is a problem." Katsuro slammed his fist against the desk. "Call me, did you hear me? Call me!" He glared at his son. *You were never strong enough to handle this business.* He thought his daughter Rita was stronger, but he would never make *her* a company head. After all, a woman's place is in the home as a servant. It was his father's way, and now it was Katsuro's way.

Katsuro would never admit it, but he had grown weary from the long days of travel, planning, and driving. He retrieved his briefcase from his shadow and looked for what Americans called *"the little black book."* He needed a massage and a little more. He found the number he was looking for and using the mobile phone he had rented made an appointment.

His driver and attendant escorted him.

He had one more appointment in Los Angeles later that evening. He registered at the Four Seasons Hotel and rested before his dinner date. Feeling good about his continued manhood, even at age 81, the diminutive warrior slept until he received a wake-up call at seven.

She was a tall woman, quite attractive. Her long legs showed through the full slit in her ankle-length flowered dress. "Mr. Tachigi, it was indeed a pleasure to hear from you. I am looking forward to doing business with you. Are you planning to move to Los Angeles?"

"Why else would I call you? You have the pictures of the homes that fit my needs?"

"Of course." She pulled a packet from her briefcase. She allowed her skirt to slip from her long legs, exposing them to appreciative eyes. Her hair was braided into pigtails, for she knew that Japanese men like Mr. Tachigi preferred *grown women dressed as little girls.*

Katsuro quickly went through the pictures of the houses. He looked at them all and then went back to the three he liked the best. "I would like to see these three tomorrow. Be here at nine."

She nodded her head.

Katsuro kept the three pictures and placed them on the chair next to him. "Allow me to order dinner, my dear."

* * *

Katsuro never made it back for the planned dinner with Gian's grandfather.

* * *

Promptly at 8:45 the next morning, she drove up the driveway of the luxurious hotel, again in pigtails, wearing a short skirt and flat shoes so she wouldn't appear taller than her client. Her long legs, veinless, met with great approval from Katsuro. He allowed her to drive his Cadillac so he could leer at her body. "Where are these homes?"

"In the Valley. It is the only area I could find that had enough space to allow for your project."

"Very good." Katsuro's words referred to her body rather than the location of the real estate. The shadows were silent.

The red Caddy roared North on the 121 freeway, past Woodland Falls, and exited at Las Nogales Road, which led into the quiet suburban community of Canyon Falls. This was horse country. Each home or lot was connected to horse trails that led to the far-off Falls.

"There are several properties for sale. The first one is on Tagert Road."

Katsuro got out of the roadster and followed her longs legs onto the property. Katsuro walked through the house to the yard, bowing courteously to the female owner and was handed a tape measure by his attendant. He instructed long legs to walk off thirty-five paces east. He watched her as she knelt down, exposing her long legs almost to her crotch. "Okay, now go fifty paces north."

Katsuro calculated the dimensions of the open space and shook his head. "Too small. Let's go."

The next house also met with his disapproval. The third house was a two-story colonial. Large white columns accentuated the front porch. Katsuro walked deliberately into the backyard, turned right and walked to the fence that separated two large properties. "You see that yard. That space is huge. That is the house I want. Buy that house for me."

"Mr. Tachigi, that piece of property is not for sale."

Katsuro stood on his tiptoes. "Young lady, this is going to be a big sale for you. You will make a lot of money, unless I have to find another agent who will follow my orders without questioning me. Buy that property! The people can even stay there for a year while my new dojo is being built. Do as I ask. Buy that house for me!"

The long-legged agent drove back to the hotel and shook at what was about to happen. The valet took the car, and she went with Katsuro back to his room. He beckoned for her to sit on the couch next to him. He unrolled a long piece of paper. "These are the preliminary plans for my new dojo I want built in the yard after you buy that property. Then find a reputable contractor with excellent references and have him build my dojo according to *my* plans. Now take off your clothes."

The old man's eyes watched her long legs slide from her short skirt; her blouse came off, and she dropped her underwear. He never worried that he wouldn't be able to perform. Two days in a row with a woman, but this was a new woman, and even more exciting than the one the day before. He was a warrior again.

The long-legged real-estate agent stared at Katsuro's body. It was covered with delicately drawn tattoos, each in a myriad of colors. All the tattoos from his shoulders down to his feet were a work of art. Large monsters were drawn across his back, down his sides, winding around onto his chest. They leered at her from all places on his body as he removed his clothes. They looked like they would leap out of his skin and engulf her. Ancient writings scrolled down his arms and onto his wrist. Carefully drawn figures covered his stomach. Each represented the creatures in his world of martial arts. Other drawings showed the five stages and positions for which he was a Grand Master. In all, they represented his status and his position in life.

To this long-legged woman, having sex with this octogenarian was repulsive—yet exciting.

Will I dare tell my children and grandchildren that I was laid by an old man and his menagerie?

The next day, the chauffeur-driven Caddy headed back to San Diego. He had missed his daily workouts and had missed training his protégé. He would have to make up for lost time.

* * *

Two days later, wearing a full skirt, a very conservative blouse, and high—heeled shoes, the real estate agent walked up the path to the house Katsuro had ordered her to buy. She clutched her purse holding the blank check with Katsuro's signature in place. *Fill out the amount needed to purchase the house, and do not try to cheat me. To do so would be a major mistake. Do you understand what I am saying?* She remembers nodding *Yes* and then remembers the pain as he penetrated her. Now she blocked out those thoughts. She thought only of her commission of nearly a quarter of a million dollars. She rang the doorbell and a heavyset housekeeper asked, "Yes, can I help you?"

Having researched the county records for the owner of the property, long legs said, "Yes, I would like to talk to Mrs. Lewis. She is the owner of this property, correct?"

"Yes, she is. What is this about?"

"Tell Mrs. Lewis, I have a four-million-dollar check for her." According to recent sales in the area, this was twice the value of the property.

The housekeeper gulped. "Did she win some sweepstakes or something?"

"You might say that."

"Come in and please wait right here." As she waddled toward another room, long legs could hear voices just above a whisper. "Mrs. Lewis, there is a real estate agent here to see you. She says she has a check for four million dollars for you."

Mrs. Lewis, who was even larger than her housekeeper, came bustling into the living room. "Four million dollars, you say! Hmmm!" Mrs. Lewis commented without even asking the name of the bearer of the check.

"Yes, I have a legitimate buyer for your house who is willing to pay four million dollars for your property and allow you to live here for one more year."

Mrs. Lewis dialed her husband and whispered into the receiver, "Four million dollars, Hugh. Four million dollars!"

Three months later, the Canyon Falls Planning Department received the plans for Katsuro's dojo. It was a place Gian would come to know well.

CHAPTER ELEVEN

CRIME AND PUNISHMENT

Back in Japan, Gian realized he needed to formulate a plan to survive, to lessen the pain of abuse without giving up his training. Even at eight, he knew that getting stronger and more powerful was the only way to insure he would have a chance to grow to be an adult.

Meanwhile, he had to learn to cope. This was a complex problem. He had to obtain a mindset where his standard of behavior would please his oppressors, his mentor, and his tormentors, and yet satisfy his own rage at being abused. An eight-year-old, even one as smart as Gian, can only do so much deep thinking based upon his experiences. Gian's experiences were built around beatings and abuse.

He needed to strengthen his resolve to survive this brutality—a tall order for a small figure. Part of that resolve involved following the discipline he was being taught by Katsuro yet inserting his own will and personality into his trials. He worked hard in the dojo, constantly resenting that Katsuro, Ryuu, and Yukio owned him. This resentment of ownership is what he rebelled against.

Gian always worked to his fullest capacity. This work ethic was ingrained in him, and it was part of his plan to make himself physically strong enough to eventually overcome his tormentors. He was determined to work diligently to reach his ever-increasing potential.

Gian's resolve would be severely tested. On this particular day, there was a sense that something was wrong. Something that a young Gian could not understand or know; still he sensed it. The scene in the dojo was the same as always. The family members were into their routines. Some worked together, some worked alone, sometimes in silence, sometimes in a bedlam of noise and yelling, but always in cadence, in rhythm according to the teachings of *Akin Jitsu.*

Gian tried his best to understand Katsuro's emotional outbursts. Now he had Yukio and Ryuu pressuring him as well. Tension filled the Japanese building. Distracted by his feeling that something was wrong, Gian was not training as intensely during his routine. He thought they would not notice. The day did pass peacefully, but with an undercurrent of tension that did not dissolve.

After the family left the building, Gian cleaned the dojo as he did every day. He put everything away where it belonged. Then he went to his house, ate the dinner Nanny had prepared, and returned to the dojo to finish his nightly chore of mopping.

From there he retreated to the bath and took a few minutes to relax. It was his respite from the tensions of the day.

When he returned to his house, Dog didn't greet him as was his nightly ritual. Instead, Yukio stood at the edge of the living room scowling. In a gruff voice, he ordered Gian to clean up the crumbs Dog had left on the living room floor from munching on his play bone.

Gian was baffled by Yukio's presence in his home, his sneering manner, and his demanding tone. Yukio screamed at him, "You need to listen!" Yukio repeated his words with an even greater fury. "You need to listen!" Gian stood with his head down.

Gian could only think he was being told he needed to know his place, know he was an object, a possession, a toy. Gian did not say a word. He just cleaned up the crumbs. Then he trudged up the stairs to his room, missing Dog's companionship. Gian closed the door and flopped on his bed. Suddenly and violently, the door flung open and the larger than life Yukio stood in the doorway. In three steps, Yukio was at Gian's bedside. He bent down and grabbed Gian's hair, dragging him to a small table, and pushed his head down on the wooden top.

Yukio grasped Gian's pants and pulled them down. Yukio smashed his hand across Gian's naked buttocks, screaming, "You son-of-a-bitch, you worthless piece of shit."

Gian did not cry. Gian did not say a word. Gian remained in a stoic trance he had developed when pain came to him. Gian tuned out the moment. Yukio continued to curse as he swatted Gian's flesh. Then Yukio in a soft, evil voice said, "We own you! We do as we choose!"

It was at that moment Yukio sodomized the eight-year-old child.

Gian let the pain and dehumanizing moment slip into oblivion. He felt the thrust and imagined a soft bed of fresh snow being sent from heaven to comfort him, engulf him and keep him safe.

Yukio never felt sexual pleasure from his act. He never came, never released his seed of contempt. Rather, he felt the pleasure of knowing he had taught this *worthless piece of garbage* his place. Yukio had dominated this lowly creature. Whenever Yukio needed to dominate Gian, he did so using blunt force, in the same manner he did that first time.

The act was short. It was violent. Yukio stood over his prey and scowled at the creature. Gian looked up at his violator. Was he that *worthless piece of shit* Yukio thought he was? Yukio stared down. "You need to know you are mine whenever I want you, you worthless piece of shit!"

Yukio stomped out of the room and slammed the door.

Over the next three years, Yukio, always in a premeditated, agitated state, with his need to dominate and torture, sodomized the *worthless one* many times. Each time it was violent. Each time it sent Gian into his own world, so he never felt the physical pain. Still, he knew what was happening and vowed revenge on the hated rapist.

THE LAST RAPE

Yukio never enjoyed the actual experience of sex with Gian. He only enjoyed owning something, possessing this creature and bending him to his will. That was his pleasure. This demented pleasure ended in the eleventh year from Gian's birth.

Once again, the act was the same as always, short, violent, terrifying, yet without Gian having physical pain. However, smart and learned in his own way, Gian showed a lack of fear. Over the years he had learned to challenge a person's psyche. Gian had thought of Yukio's attacks often. How could he stop them? What could he do to intimidate his violator? That is what Katsuro would have done. What could he do to extract revenge on his attacker, this brutal rapist? Based on the teachings of his mentor, Katsuro, he plotted a way to challenge his attacker.

Gian conjured a picture in his mind—a plan. He knew he could easily enter the Tachigi house. He knew where each family member slept. Gian knew Yukio didn't sleep in the same room with his wife. He knew that he could quietly enter Yukio's room and crush his head with a brick while he slept. Could he kill him? He thought so. He thought he had the right to kill him; a license to kill; a reason to kill.

What would they do to him if he ever did attack or kill Yukio? Kill him? Beat him? They already were doing that. No, they really couldn't do much to him that was not already being done.

Now this rapist stood above him. Yukio sneered, "You are always mine. My toy!"

Gian recoiled, and at the same time he gathered his strength. He rose slowly as he had planned. The defiant eleven-year-old stood with his hands on his hips. Gian stared unblinking at the loathsome creature. His eyes filled with a violent hatred of such ferocity it transcended even his violent world. He spoke slowly, deliberately, in a clipped voice. "Someday, you are going to be sleeping and I'm going to come. You can keep doing what you have been doing to me. You can do what you want, but at some point you are going to be asleep and I am going to come and get you."

Yukio stared back at the cold, calculating child. He wanted to smash his face, yet, he held back. Yukio knew Gian meant what he said. Gian would kill him.

That was the last time Yukio ever sodomized Gian. That part of Gian's nightmare finally came to an end. Gian realized he could stand up to his tormentors. It was the first time he had been forceful and aggressive. It worked. Shortly, he would learn that his power was a long way from being great enough to thwart another adversary.

Gian slept better that night knowing he had a plan. Would he ever follow through on his thoughts? Probably! Gian knew, deep in his heart that at some point, he would kill Yukio if the attacks continued.

Gian realized his threat might have frightened Yukio. After all, Katsuro was training him to kill. He was a non-entity who could endure all pain and then act on his own. The Tachigis were creating a frightening monster, a robot trained to act and react without thought. Did Yukio see that possibility and stop due to his fear? Gian could only guess after the attacks stopped.

*   *   *

"Enough is enough! You dominated this creature, but now he has sensed his own strength. You must stop! Never again!"

Katsuro walked away from Yukio. He did not like what Yukio had done to his protégé, but he had allowed Yukio to act on his own. Katsuro understood Yukio, maybe better than Yukio understood himself. Yukio thought all his acts through from beginning to end. Every act was premeditated. Yukio was calculating and clever, cunning and extremely violent. Katsuro knew that more than any of his other children Yukio wanted Katsuro's place of domination, his power, and his Grand Master status. Knowing that, Katsuro gave Yukio his space so he could see how he handled different situations.

On the other hand, Ryuu did not contemplate or premeditate his actions. He was not calculating and clever, but he was extremely violent. The old physics axiom that every action has an equal and opposite reaction was never truer than when Ryuu reacted, except for the equal part. Ryuu responded to any incident, large or small, without thinking. He reacted spontaneously with excessive violence, going far beyond what is reasonable or normal.

And Gian tried to fit in to this world.

*   *   *

Gian's eighth birthday slid by without being mentioned by any family member. Late one evening after a whipping, and after Gian had gone to bed, Katsuro went into Gian's house. Dog met Katsuro at the door with a never-ending growl. Katsuro hated that animal. It loved Gian and Gian loved it back.

It was evident that Dog hated Katsuro, too. He sensed evil in this man, an evil that meant his master would be tormented. Dog pulled back from the evil man who snapped at him with a cursing yell. "Move, you molten beast. Someday your hide will be toast."

Katsuro seldom came into Gian's house. Now he thrust his hand through the bedroom door, opening and closing it quickly as Dog followed him up the stairs. Katsuro barked his orders as he always did. "Gian, I want you to design a pen where Dog can stay during the day instead of being cooped up in this house. Tomorrow you will build it."

Gian did not like the idea but said nothing. He knew that Katsuro didn't like Dog. Dog usually growled with a low rumble in his throat. The idea of Dog trapped in a pen sent a shiver through Gian. "Build a shelter for Dog, and build it big enough for him to roam around in."

Walking down the stairs Katsuro called out, "Gian, come and get this beast and take him to your room so I can leave in peace."

Dog growled.

*   *   *

After school the next day, Gian found a shovel, logs, and wire lined up against the house. With his plan for Dog's outdoor pen in hand, Gian began his latest project. The note on the shovel said, *Cut the poles to the right length, measure the area you need, dig a hole for each pole, and secure the wire mesh. Finish by dinnertime.*

Katsuro, you must be kidding. Finish by dinner? It will be a late dinner for me. Gian knew Katsuro never joked. He was even-tempered with Gian, always angry and serious. Gian plotted out Dog's pen as Katsuro had drawn it, dug the holes, measured the poles, cut them to the proper length, and placed them in the ground. Several of the grandchildren walked by. None offered to help. Margaret smiled at him as she slid into the dojo for her after-school workout.

It was dark when Gian finished. His muscles ached. His small frame was soaked in sweat. He picked up the tools he used, placed them back in the shed and started to walk toward the baths. Katsuro's voice shattered his vision of soaking in the hot tub, relaxing his muscles and soothing his body. *"Juko,* you need to complete your afternoon exercises before dinner. Now!"

Gian breathed a deep sigh, trotted into the dojo dressed in his *gi* and set out on his routine. Gian looked around; he was alone. Katsuro wasn't there. He must have been having dinner with his family. He hesitated to start his routine, then remembered Katsuro's words: *Every day of practice means you are closer to being the best. Never miss a day; never flinch on any part of your workout. Always do your best.* Gian could feel the sting of the *Shinai* beating a tormenting rhythm on his flesh. *Always do your best.*

The thought of the *Shinai* and Katsuro's words drove Gian to a fierce workout as he punched the bag, smashed his fists against the ropes, and did more than 100 push-ups. His body, sleek and powerful, was energized.

Katsuro entered the dojo silently. At the far right side of the dojo stood a large wooden figure of a man. Gian stood before it. Gian had watched as Katsuro and his sons struck the figure with unerring accuracy on the various circles drawn on the figure. Katsuro came over to where Gian stood. "You have never asked why we have this wooden figure. Watch what I do."

Katsuro sent a sharp punch into the figure's sternum. An elbow to the neck. A chop to the other side of the neck. All points marked with a small circle. "Each of these marked points is the most vulnerable part on a human's body. A single, well-placed blow to any of these marks can send a person into unconsciousness. You will practice on this dummy soon. You will learn it is not how hard you hit the mark but how accurate you are. But for now, back to work."

It was by practicing on this wooden figure Gian would learn some of his deadliest moves.

Katsuro left Gian to his workout, only to return an hour later in a meditative, reflective mood. The old man sat in his chair without the *Shinai* and quietly watched his protégé finish his workout. He thought to himself how well this child had progressed. He was, indeed, the best of his fighting sons.

Gian toweled himself down and sat next to Katsuro when the old man patted the chair next to his. "Gian, we have talked about God many times before. We have talked about His will, what He gives, and what He wants from us. I want you to know there really is a God even though you can't see Him or feel Him or sit and talk to Him at His side. He really exists."

"Why should I care?"

"Because you must have faith. True faith places everything in harmony—keep the faith. Find yourself with faith."

This small child looked at his mentor. "But if I can't see Him, why should I believe in Him?"

"Maybe you're not old enough to understand what I'm going to say, but with you I never know, since you are very smart. Believing in something you can't prove strengthens your faith muscle. It is the muscles in your mind that need to be challenged. Believing in God, this unseen God, will give your faith muscle added strength."

"But why should I do that? Does God really care about me?"

Katsuro bent closer to his protégé, "He really does. He cares about all His creatures, even you, the lowest of them. Your mind must expand and take in the world."

"Have you done that? Taken in the world?"

Katsuro rose from his chair. "My father, the great Samurai warrior, taught me to take in the whole world. The world we can see and feel as well as the world in our mind. He was a true physical warrior and a man of the world. He wrote poetry, and he dabbled in art to create pictures of his thoughts. That's what a true Samurai warrior does. That is what you must do."

"Write poetry?"

"No, my son, you are too young and inexperienced. But later in life you will write poetry and paint to show your intellect and your beliefs. Just like I have done on my body. All the paintings on my body are the art of the mind and of my life here on earth and in all the other realms I have visited."

Gian had often wondered about what the pictures on Katsuro's body represented. *His life on earth and in other realms.* Gian sat with his mentor in the dojo. The old man's arm around his adoptive son was a moment he would cherish for a long time. Katsuro leaned even closer to Gian. "Remember, Gian, *God* only gives you what you can handle—only what you can handle."

* * *

Margaret was excused from the dinner table and went straight to her room. She walked to her window and stared out into the yard. The dojo lights were still on. *Could Gian still be there?*

Even though he was three years younger than she, Margaret admired the body of the Anglo. She moved silently into the dojo. He was alone. She watched him finish his routine, stash the equipment away, and saunter to the baths. She followed him. She paused a minute and then opened the door. He never turned. He never saw her. He was stark naked; he showered, washed his body carefully, and then floated into the bath.

She moved in, closed the door behind her and watched him bathe. She slid out of her kimono, Gian was startled. "What are you doing here?" He covered himself up with his hands and started to get out.

"Stay. Let me wash your back. It will feel good."

"No, no, you're a girl." Gian's voice rose to a high pitch.

"That's a clever observation."

"No, no, you must not be here. Leave me alone. Damn girls!"

"But I helped you before. I *am* your friend."

Gian fumbled for words. He was embarrassed. "Yes, yes . . . friend. Not now. I just needed a bath and now I'm done."

She pulled him back toward her and rubbed his back with a soap filled loofa. "Now you're done. Get out if you wish."

Gian, more scared than anything, stumbled out of the bath, dressed while he was still wet, and left while putting his clothes on. "You could have at least dried yourself, Gian," Margaret called as he rushed from the wood-boarded room. *Boy, he sure is shy.*

*   *   *

Four six-foot-long, large dowelings lay along the fence. The yard was filled with rocks and holes where Gian had previously dug. Pockets of dirt were piled high with fresh soil, all evidence of Gian's exercising, building his strength and developing his muscles so he could be the best and strongest fighter. But why the six-inch-diameter poles?

Using two of his children, Yukio measured off a three-foot square in the dirt. They wound string onto small pegs already in the ground. Yukio explained to his children, "We are going to pound these poles into the ground right where these pegs are. We are making a perfect square."

"Why?" asked a razor-thin son.

"Your grandfather wants to make a square of balancing poles for your training."

"How?" came the voice of the same son.

"Enough questions. Just do as I ask and shut up!"

The children, under Yukio's supervision, sharpened one end of each pole and then pounded it into the ground so it protruded exactly thirty inches above the earth. When they finished this task, Katsuro gathered his clan around him. Barefooted, Katsuro climbed onto a stepstool, stepped onto the top of the six-inch poles, and assumed a squat position, one foot on each of two poles. Gian would soon understand why the poles were in the ground, but he would also learn to hate them.

"Now watch what I do." Katsuro shifted his left foot back. Then he moved his right foot back. Now he stood on the back two poles. "Watch!" He shifted again pivoting his left foot back, then his right. Now he faced the inside of the square. There he stood without moving, in perfect balance. At eighty years old, he was the Master.

Each of the children tried standing on the poles. Most fell off the first time. Each time Katsuro helped them up and held their hands while they balanced themselves. He was gentle and kind to each one. His demeanor was soft. Finally, Gian took his turn. Katsuro's voice changed as he addressed his protégé. Gone were the soft caring tones. His voice was harsh and critical of every move Gian made.

As the others did, Gian stepped up onto the poles using the stepstool and squatted. His bare feet gripped the round, flat pole tops. Hirohsu spoke firmly. "There is no reason you should not be able to do all my commands. You have practiced balancing on paint cans for the past few years. This is exactly the same thing except you are higher up and the platform is narrower. Get used to these poles."

Katsuro stood in front of Gian and illustrated the move he wanted Gian to do. He did a reverse pivot, all the time remaining in the squat position. Gian did the same on the poles. Gian smiled as he found his balance.

Katsuro moved and pivoted as Gian imitated him. It was the dance of mentor and protégé, to be repeated many times. When Katsuro felt they had done enough he turned to his protégé. "Tomorrow, faster. Balance is the key to being the best fighter."

The following day, Gian once again danced on the poles. This time the Master barked out his commands from a chair next to the square of poles. Across his lap lay the *Shinai*.

And then it happened: his legs weary, Gian fell. The old man got up. "Never fall! Not allowed!" Gian rolled on the ground. He knew what was going to happen. He scrambled toward the stool. Yukio grabbed the stool and cast it across the yard.

Katsuro laughed, "Get up, *Juko*! Now!" He waved the *Shinai* over his head. It cracked as the old man whipped it toward Gian. The tormented child grabbed the tops of two poles and in a single motion vaulted onto them, balanced himself, and squatted.

The *Shinai* waved in the air and Katsuro laughed. "Power move, *Juko*. You have learned. Now back to work." He wasn't laughing as he barked out his commands with ever-increasing speed.

Agile and alert, Gian played the game to its fullest.

At the end of the balance exercise, Katsuro ordered Gian to squat on the two front poles and extend his arms. "It is time to build your strength." Gian knew what was coming. Yukio, having watched the exercises silently, placed three large books onto Gian's extended arms. Katsuro growled, "Hold them still until I say to let them go."

Gian held his position. When his arms grew weary, he didn't move. He never wavered. Instead, he set sail into a beautiful sunset. He remembered his grandfather and the soft beaches near San Diego. He felt the steady breeze filling his face with the warmth of love and comfort. Gian was not alone; he was with family.

Each time Gian worked in the yard digging holes, filling them back with the same dirt, moving rocks from one area to another, pulling buckets of rocks, or pounding truck tires with a sledge hammer, he stared at the poles. They had become another symbol of abuse. Katsuro would have him mount the poles without the stepstool, do his balance routine and then hold books or rocks on his weary extended arms. Gian's back ached from this forced stance. His arms throbbed. His muscles became sore. The soles of his feet became callused and hard. The poles were another source of torture. Lashes from the *Shinai*, words of derision, hours in a hot sun or freezing temperatures—all would have dealt a lesser soul a deathblow. But Gian withstood it all and moved on.

*   *   *

It had never happened before. Katsuro left a note for Gian. The note listed Gian's workout routine. Katsuro would know what Gian did but he wouldn't be there to watch him. The note simply said, *Move all the rocks at the far end of the yard to the space next to the fence. Do this after you follow your normal workout routine.* Gian wondered where Katsuro was. He seldom missed a workout.

*   *   *

Katsuro was busy on the phone forming his new bank's board of directors. He needed a distinguished group to convince large corporations to use his new bank for their business accounts. He needed this money to help finance his businesses and make loans at a very favorable rate. Katsuro believed he had the power and business acumen to get what he wanted. So far, he had been right.

Katsuro took the call from the real-estate agent. Her voice was filled with excitement. "They have agreed to your terms. They are selling the house furnished as you asked. I had to pay another quarter of a million. I hope that is okay."

Katsuro bit down on his lip thinking of the night at the Four Seasons Hotel with this woman. His manhood grew. He was angry at that. Man's greatest weakness is his sex drive. Even now he found it hard to control. That and the failure of his children to develop their martial arts skills were Katsuro's greatest failures. But he whisked those thoughts from his mind and nodded his approval of her purchase, as if she were standing right in front of him.

"Yes, that is fine. I will send you my request for building the dojo. Hire an architect and send me his drawing and concepts. A Japanese architect would be best. I will send him pictures of my Japanese dojo."

He hung up the phone. He smiled. He got what he wanted. He had the money. Money equals power. He had both.

The next afternoon was a beautiful fall day. Occasional small puffy white clouds disturbed the nearly perfect azure sky. Katsuro was waiting for Gian in the backyard to come home from school. "Today you dig. Build your muscles. I have placed four shovels in various locations in the yard. Pick up each shovel and dig a hole as deep as you are tall. Then fill in that hole."

It was then Gian saw Dog in the pen he had built. Dog yapped happily to see his Master. Gian went over to pet him. Katsuro rushed after Gian and smacked him across the face. "Too much love for anything is wrong. It causes you to be weak. Go dig your holes." Gian held the side of his face. The slap had stung rather than hurt. He didn't cry anymore. He would just pull himself up to the task at hand and do as he was told. He knew that frustrated Katsuro. He wanted Gian to cry, to ask him to stop hitting him, but he never did.

Katsuro began to run around the yard. He usually did five miles a day. His only concession to a modern device was the pedometer he had attached to his waistband. *This way I know how far I have run. Wonderful device.*

Katsuro finished well before Gian had completed refilling his last hole with the dirt. "Gian, stop. Bring that shovel over here to the pen. They stood together at the pen looking at Dog sitting and wagging his tail. Katsuro's words were simple and said quietly: "Take your shovel and kill Dog."

Gian, now nine years old, was stunned. "What did you say?"

Katsuro shot his fist into Gian's jaw. The child barely felt it. "I said, take your shovel and kill Dog."

"Why? Why would I do that? I love Dog."

"That is why you must kill Dog. Never love something so much you can't kill it. If you love, you show a weakness that will prevent you from becoming a great champion. Therefore, you must kill Dog to prove you understand love is not important. One day you will get in a fight and you may need to kill. Will you be able to do it? Killing Dog will prove you can. Understanding you are capable of killing is important. Can you kill the thing you love the most? You must!"

Gian had learned to obey Katsuro without questioning him. But this scared him. "I won't kill my best friend, so you can see if I can kill. Never."

Katsuro's voice went up as he screamed. **"Do as I tell you. Kill Dog! Do not disobey me! Never question me. Never!"**

Gian threw the shovel to the ground. Katsuro shot a straight jab to Gian's face. The child clutched his cheek as he fell to the ground crying. Huge sobs burst from his body. "I won't kill my dog, I won't." The sobs weren't from the blow but from the realization of what he was being told to do.

Katsuro drove his right foot into Gian's middle. He picked up Gian by his hair as he handed him the shovel. "Take this shovel and smash in Dog's head. Do it now!" The back of Katsuro's hand sent Gian to the ground again.

For the first time Gian wanted to strike back at Katsuro as he bunched his fist. Seeing the small fist, Katsuro sent a right hand to the child's temple while he was still on the ground. "I said, take the shovel and smash in Dog's head."

"I can't. I can't do it. I love Dog." Hearing his name Dog barked at his Master. Dog, agitated, barked incessantly at seeing his Master being beaten. Dog pawed at the fence trying to reach his Master's tormentor. Gian called out, "I can't do it."

Once again Katsuro lifted Gian by his hair until he stood next to him. "I have taught you to do as I say. Now I am telling you to kill. Do it now!"

Katsuro's hand smashed back and forth across the child's face, ripping the skin as he held him by his hair. Droplets of blood surfaced and formed rivulets. "Kill now!"

Suddenly, Gian faded into his world. This was his way of relieving pain, his way of seeking a better place—in another time, his way of facing life as it was now being dealt, his world where there was no Katsuro, no Dog, nothing. His world was void of people, void of emotion, void of thought, void of love. It was his void, his hiding place. He was a tormented soul striving to survive.

Gian blinded by his tears picked up the shovel and moved closer to the pen. Somewhere in his void he found his place, his place to follow the orders—*Kill! Dog, I love you. Because I love, you I must kill you. Katsuro said I must kill the one I love.* Gian was in his self-induced trance, his escape trance. His mind snapped. He was no longer human. He was the robot Katsuro trained him to be. *Kill, I must kill. Sit still, Dog! Sit still'*

"Kill him, Gian. Kill him!" Katsuro's voice came from a surreal place. Lost between his training and his only love, Gian had lost his sense of restraint. His training took over. He would kill. That was what he had been bred to do. Kill!

Dog sat at the middle of his pen. Gian entered the gate and raised the shovel above his head. "Dog, I love you. I love you!" The shovel came down with a powerful thud that shattered Dog's skull. The animal gave one final groan and fell over, his brains bashed in.

Gian felt nothing. He had done his job. He had killed. Ryuu, a witness to this event, came forward at Katsuro's call. "Bury this dog in the last hole that Gian dug, then fill it."

Through a fog of unreality, Gian barked his objection. "No!" he screamed. "He is my Dog. I will bury him!" He pushed his way through the two men, lifted Dog into his arms, carried him the few feet to the hole he had dug, and carefully placed the beast in the ground.

He picked up the shovel and threw dirt on the only thing that loved him.

* * *

Her brown eyes filled with tears. Her body trembled uncontrollably. She turned from death and ran from the dojo into her grandmother's arms. "What is it, my child?"

Margaret said nothing. She had witnessed the making of a monster. At that moment, she hated her grandfather. She loathed him, and she felt helpless.

*   *   *

Katsuro put his arm around the Gian's shoulder. "Come, boy, I will take you to your house. You shall rest and then it will be time for you to finish your afternoon workout."

Gian went to his house and asked Nanny for a bath. She walked with him to the family house and the bathhouse. He entered, undressed slowly, and showered his shame away. His mind flashed to the events of the day. *I killed you, Dog. I'm sorry, Dog. But that will never happen again. I was weak; now I must be strong. I didn't protect the one I loved. Isn't that part of what being strong means? I have to be stronger. I will be stronger.*

He cried out in anguish and frustration at his own weakness. *I will never kill anything I love again. I swear.*

He stepped into the bath and used the loofa on his tormented body. He stopped his tears. Suddenly, in that moment he felt stronger and more in charge than he had ever before. *I will never kill because someone tells me to kill. I will never kill someone I love, but I will kill if I have to. I can do that.* At least he thought he could. The future would test that resolve many times.

*   *   *

Dressed in his *gi*, Gian walked into the dojo and began pounding the ropes with his fists. His hands were like leather, tough and calloused. His skin was thick. They used to bleed when he hit the ropes, but no more. His body, still small, was wiry, and his strength showed through every rippling muscle. His mind was free of thought.

*   *   *

The grandchildren looked away when Katsuro glanced at them. He left Rita's side and she continued to direct them in their daily routine. Katsuro carried a box with him. That box became part of Gian's present and future.

The Parcel Post package had arrived from the United States, just as *RIGHT* promised. Katsuro tore open the package and tersely read through the instructions provided. He knew what to do. He was a doctor. He remembered Dr. Zarkowski's words: *"This is a new formula. It is experimental. It is formulated to be used as shots and in pill form, not every day, but in a series of shots and pills to be taken over a period of time. This is not what you are used to using."*

"Yes, I understand, doctor. Could the patient experience negative side effects?"

"Swelling in the legs and pain in the joints around the skeletal-muscular areas could happen. A rash might also appear. That means lower the dosage, then see how long those side effects last. Remember, do not use this on a child. That could be very dangerous."

Katsuro reddened. *"That last remark was uncalled for. I will do as I see fit for my patients. You understand that, doctor?"*

Dr. Zarkowski froze in terror as Katsuro's demonic face thrust his worst fears out into the open. He put his hand to his face in horror. He knew at that moment he had made a deal with the devil.

Katsuro had bought his way into *RIGHT* and Dr. Zarkowski had sold his soul.

*   *   *

"Sit down here, Gian. It is time for you to grow bigger. Sit still while I give you this shot in your arm. You will be getting these shots every day for the next two weeks. You will also begin taking one pill a day at dinnertime. As I said, it is time for you to grow taller."

Katsuro plunged the needle into Gian's arm and Gian went back to work.

CHAPTER TWELVE

THE AKITA

An hour later, Katsuro placed a pair of 2x4s near the mat where Gian was stretching. "*Juko*, do a split so I can measure the distance from one heel to the other." Gian stretched his legs laying them out to each side, flat on the mat—doing a stretch split. Katsuro then placed one 2x4 under each heel. Gian's body was now resting only on his heels and completely off the mat. "Okay, Gian, in your split position, set your crotch down on the mat so you are really stretching your quads. Bounce a little—stretch."

Gian could feel the muscles stretching. He felt vulnerable. He had no control over his body in this position; but, as instructed, he included it in his daily routine after that day.

* * *

A month went by. The injections and pills continued. The use of the *Shinai* was seldom abated for any reason. Gian liked his private tutor at school. But he knew if he got too close to her, she would be dismissed; so he stayed detached from her and just listened and learned.

Gian was advancing well beyond his former classmates. This was a happy time for him.

* * *

Rita's driver drove slowly over a back road outside of Takayama. Rita had tried driving when she was younger, but Katsuro didn't want her to continue. She remembered the night she first talked to him about it.

"I am tired of being driven everywhere. I have to wait for you or one of the children. I want to learn to drive, Katsuro."

"Women don't drive. They stay home and tend to the children. That is what I want you to do. Tend to the children."

"First, I am not *women*, I am your wife and mother of our children. Our children drive, poorly sometimes, but they drive. If they can drive, so can I, your wife."

"You are a woman of the home. Driving by yourself can lead to no good. There is no reason for you to drive. As you said, our children can drive, and they will drive you wherever you want to go, or I will get you a chauffeur."

"Katsuro, you go off every day with a driver; you choose to be driven. I stay home. I am tired of the four walls. I want to learn to drive here in San Diego. I called a driving service to teach me, so you won't have to."

Katsuro was in no mood to argue with his wife. He was going to Los Angeles for a few days and wanted to go with a clear mind. He sighed. "That is very thoughtful to call someone to teach you so I don't have to. So be it. Take your driving lessons. But don't smash any of our cars."

Rita wasn't a bad driver, just inexperienced. She took the California driver's test and passed. "You're a little nervous, lady," the oversized driving instructor said. "But better than most. Good luck. Be sure to practice your parking skills." He laughed. *Damn Japanese, they are the worst drivers.*

Despite the driver's license in hand, she hired a driver when necessary or would have the children drive her. She won her battle with Katsuro but lost the war.

Now determined to right a wrong, she was being driven to a country estate on the outskirts of the Takayama. She had visited there many years before. She remembered exactly where it was, as she told the owner over the phone. "Yes, yes, I do recall. It is that lovely house on the hill. Do you have any other breeds of dogs now? Or, is the Akita your breed of choice?"

"Yes, Mrs. Tachigi. We only breed Akitas, just like always."

She never asked Katsuro; she didn't want to. She had mentioned it indirectly to him the week before. "You made your point with

Gian. You have trained him to obey even when he knows what he is doing is wrong or hurtful. You took away his only possession. That was not a good thing to do. Even you have possessions. Even you have things you care about."

"What are you talking about?"

"Now Gian has no possession he can call his own." She knew better than to say something he could love. "It is time for him to reclaim a possession. That is what I am saying."

Katsuro, for all his tenets and beliefs, saw some wisdom in what his wife was saying. Besides, she would keep after him until there was some resolution in her mind. Behind bedroom doors, this Japanese woman had secret powers.

Katsuro threw up his arms as he was prone to do when he was losing an argument with this woman he had been married to for almost fifty years. "Do what you want, just don't tell me. Do what you see fit to do."

The puppy farm was really an estate. The car stopped. "Okay, Gian, get out. You can pick your new puppy."

She had picked him up at school. Gian could not have been more surprised. He always ran home as part of his daily workout. Riding in a car was more fun.

He scoured the pens. He felt sorry for pups cooped up in those pens. He flashed back to Dog and immediately threw the picture from his mind. He had that ability. It scared him sometimes that he was able to do that; but it was his best defense against pain.

He looked at all the puppy faces, yapping dogs, and sleeping puppies. He knew that when he saw it, it would be the one. Then he saw it. The pup was sleeping on its back. Its tail hung through the bars of the cage, and its tongue hung out of its mouth. "That's the one, Mrs. Tachigi. That one." He pointed at the sleeping creature.

"Are you sure, Gian?"

"Yes, Ma'am. Looks like he can sleep through lots of noise. In our place I need a calm puppy." The child smiled.

Rita smiled back. It was the first time she had ever seen him smile with such hope.

Gian hugged Dog lovingly as they drove back to the Tachigi house. *I willl give you the same name as my other dog, and I will protect you. Don't you worry!* Would Gian be able to keep his promise? He hoped so.

That night Dog lay at the foot of Gian's bed and cried. "It's hard to be away from your family, isn't it, Dog? But don't you worry; I will love you as your family would. I will be your new family." Gian turned on the television. "That will keep you company while I get some sleep. Sleep well, Dog."

*   *   *

Whenever Gian went into the dojo he would look up on the wall to see if the *Shinai* was on its hook. He would shudder if it wasn't. He went through his normal workout routine, including the 2x4s used for splits. Katsuro was with him when he mounted the boards. He would adjust them to fit his reach and do the splits. Once in position, Katsuro barked at him, "Down! Stretch! Get down." Then Katsuro brandished the *Shinai*. "Down!" The leaves of the *Shinai* raked across his back. "Push down, harder." The *Shinai* stung his back again. "Push down!"

Katsuro reached over and pushed down on Gian's shoulders. At first Gian thought it was just a strain until he heard it pop. The pain seared through his groin. He knew right away he had torn a muscle.

Katsuro grabbed the boy as he plunged to the mat in agony. "Ryuu! Rita! Carry Gian to the table. He popped a groin muscle." Katsuro, the doctor, felt the muscles of Gian's groin area. He grabbed some massage warming oil and began rubbing the now swollen area. Gian could feel the muscle relaxing.

Katsuro wrapped the pulled groin in a surgical bandage and barked at his pupil once again. "Okay, time to get back to work. You have had half an hour to relax. Too much time."

For the rest of his career, Gian Molina always felt the twinge from that pull.

The next day Gian was back on the split boards. Never again did Katsuro push Gian down. He knew the danger of a groin muscle rupturing.

For the better part of a year after Gian had started his splits on the 2x4s, his life remained about the same. He returned to a regular classroom after more than a year of private tutoring. He had promised the principal he would behave and not beat up any students. His fellow students had grown to fear him, so no one befriended him.

Periodically, according to Katsuro's schedule, Gian was inoculated with the growth hormones and took the special pills designed, or at least Katsuro believed they were designed, to enhance his growth. Gian grew. His body filled out. Katsuro believed Gian's growth and strength were due to the shots and pills in addition to his strength training.

Gian continued to move rocks and boulders to one side of the yard one day and then move them back the next. He dug holes and reset the dirt from where it came. He moved like a cat in the gym: quickly and aggressively. He danced like a ballerina on the four poles set in a square.

No one ever came to visit him in his house—no one. It was at this time his Nanny left. No one told Gian. He came home from school on a Thursday and found the house empty. No food was on the table. The house wasn't cleaned. He checked the refrigerator. It was filled with food. Nanny was gone. Only Dog was there. "I guess it is just you and me, Dog. Just you and me."

When he asked Katsuro where Nanny went, he said, "She left and will not be coming back. You are ten years old and you no longer need a Nanny. Now you will grow up faster."

*   *   *

Katsuro found himself spending more time with his fledgling bank. Even a man of his immense wealth and power had some reluctant investors and questioning board members. Some questioned his loaning policies. At a board meeting, one member said, "You can't just loan your company money without some collateral. Our investors will question your motivation and your integrity. A bank is built on integrity and honesty. They will question our actions."

Katsuro kept his eye on the complaining board member and watched the man's body movements. Was he afraid of Katsuro? Was he speaking for himself or a group of investors? What were his weaknesses and how should he be handled? Katsuro decided to confront the board member straight on. He was about to make a mistake that would affect Gian indirectly.

"Sir, you question my integrity when you question my loan decisions. I have directed our loan officers to do business with only the most reliable and most prestigious companies, including mine. Yes, our bank has loaned my company money. That is as it should be. Never question my integrity again." Katsuro stared at the board member; and he suddenly realized he had made a mistake.

The board member stood up and pointed his finger at Katsuro. "You asked me to be on this board and I was honored. I have always thought of you as a fine businessman. I followed your career as a doctor, a manager of clinics, a banker, and a businessman, so I joined you. However, now I see a man who would disrupt his own bank. Your bank is filled with impressive and prestigious names of honorable men from our community. They trust you. The question is, should they? You sir, have shattered my image of you. I strongly disagree with your policies. Let me go on record to say I am resigning from this board and I will withdraw all my company's money from your bank today. Good day, sir."

Before calling the board meeting to an end, Katsuro, told the stunned board members, "I would never want a yes man to be part of this board. You can see that gentleman is definitely not a yes man." Feeling the tension in the room, the remaining board members laughed at Katsuro's comment. "Yes, I have authorized our bank to make the loans mentioned, but I have also authorized your companies to have a separate loan policy from non-board members. I will handle this matter. I call for an end to this meeting until this matter is settled. Agreed?" The other board members, deeply in debt to the bank, shook their heads nervously.

Back in his office, Katsuro summoned Ryuu. "Go see our board member with a couple of our associates. I am sure, after you talk to him, he will come around and he will reverse his decision. Let me know as quickly as possible. Go." Katsuro sounded a little less sure of himself than Ryuu could remember. Katsuro was worried.

His bank had attracted many major companies. He, personally, had talked to CEOs he knew and to some he had met for the first time. The pitch was almost always the same:

"We are a bank for the future of Japan. We pay the best possible rates, charge no fees for checking and make you a board member of the bank. You will be paid, personally, for attending each board meeting, and you will receive a substantial number of shares of bank stock. Also, we will have several junkets to various countries to promote the bank; you will be part of those junkets."

The number of stock shares would change depending upon how badly Katsuro wanted that individual and his corporation's money in the bank.

Background checks and extensive research on these executives frequently showed a proclivity toward young girls or boys. Those men would be part of the junkets to Thailand, where young children were sold as sex slaves. Once those executives had committed to that type of behavior, Katsuro had them, as he often said to Ryuu, "by the balls!"

So it was with this board member who had spoken up. Ryuu would present him with pictures of himself with Thai children in various sex acts. "I think you should recant your statement to the board at the special meeting Katsuro will be calling next week. Don't you agree?"

The board member now knew his instincts regarding Katsuro were correct, but he could do nothing about it. He swallowed hard, took the pictures, and burned them. "I'll be there and do as you ask."

Nevertheless, that board member's threats had upset Katsuro. As timing goes, it was very bad for Gian, yet that day would change Gian's outlook on life forever even at the age of ten.

* * *

Gian had been feeling good about his workout progress. His fight training with several of Katsuro's grandchildren had been successful. Katsuro watched Gian flip Sam on his back and pin him quickly with great power. Even Margaret watched with amazement. Nevertheless, Katsuro never complimented Gian. Everything Gian did was criticized. '*You should have done it faster. You weren't quick enough. You missed a punch. Your upward thrust was too meek.*' There was never any praise. No words of encouragement. No '*nice workout.*' Gian lived for those moments, but they never came.

Katsuro watched Gian go through his punching-bag routine. It was a routine Gian knew without thinking. It was engrained in his brain by words, beatings, demonstrations, beatings, and more beatings, frequently with the *Shinai*.

As Gian completed his workout on the punching bag, Katsuro came over and scowled at the ten-year-old. "You've been doing this for years, and you still can't get it right. The sequence of punches is critically important, and you screw it up every time."

The *Shinai* Katsuro was holding lashed across Gian's neck with a sting that Gian barely felt. He wiped the blood away from his neck. He was almost inured to the pain by now. Gian stood tall and pointed his finger at Katsuro, "You know, old man, if you were a better teacher, I might do better."

Katsuro stood stunned. "You insolent little bastard. How dare you disrespect me! Old man? Bad teacher? How dare you you!" With every ounce of strength in his 83-year-old body, Katsuro shot a straight jab into Gian's face.

Gian dropped to the mat. More surprised than hurt. Katsuro propelled his foot into Gian's ribs. That kick lifted Gian up a few inches and knocked the wind out of him. Another kick followed. Katsuro waved at Ryuu and Yukio. The two men ran over to their father and took turns kicking and stomping on Gian, driving brutally hard kicks into his middle. The boy rolled over, gasping. Ryuu, Yukio and Katsuro continued to kick the writhing child indiscriminately. Katsuro repeated over and over, "Never talk to me like that. I should kill you for your insolence." With his face in a twisted rage, Katsuro drew back and with great force viciously sent a kick to Gian's forehead that opened a huge gash.

Yukio picked up the writhing child by his hair and sadistically drove a straight right into Gian's face, breaking his nose. The bloody forehead and the broken nose sent a stream of blood to the mat and all over the three savages.

Gian lay on the mat, shrieking in pain. "Did that hurt, *Juko?* Maybe this will hurt, too. Katsuro's right foot stabbed into Gian's groin, sending a bullet of pain to his brain. Katsuro waved at his children and grandchildren. "You heard what he said to me. Show him what it means to speak to me that way. Show him!" Katsuro's voice quivered in rage.

Katsuro's children, men in their forties and fifties, took turns kicking the still figure on the mat, trying not to slip on the blood as it seeped from the tiny frame. Gian was losing consciousness. He could barely feel the blows as they punished him in every part of his body. He barely heard the grandchildren laughing and giggling, kicking the tormented figure into his final respite: unconsciousness.

She stood apart from the others in disbelief. Her brown eyes filled with tears as she watched her brothers and sisters drive the now silent child into another world. She gasped as they took turns pummeling him with their hands, feet, and even the *Shinai*.

Ryuu took the unconscious figure and placed him on another mat. "Margaret, get some water. Now!"

She brought a glass and watched Ryuu throw the water in Gian's face. Gian shook his head slightly and moaned at he clutched his stomach. Ryuu held him up. He pointed to the children. "Now, hit him again, straight shots into his face. Enjoy yourself." Fists bound tight by bandages and unsheathed from their fighting gloves rained blows onto Gian's face and nose, splitting the nose apart and worsening the gash on his forehead. Katsuro grabbed another glass of water from another grandchild and poured it on Gian's face. Gian stayed in his other world. "Bring me the smelling salts, Sam."

Katsuro waved the shaker under Gian's broken nose. Gian moved his head slightly and moaned. "Hear me well, *Juko*. I told you not to fear anybody but me. Never disrespect me like that again. Next time I may not let you live. **You understand me, *Juko*?**"

Somehow Gian knew if he didn't respond, he would be killed. He nodded and fell back into his other world.

"Ryuu, carry this piece of garbage to the table." Gian lay still breathing shallow breaths. Katsuro checked the nose. The pulpy flesh moved too freely. Katsuro snapped it back in place. "The nose is straight now." Gian never felt anything. Katsuro washed the blood from the child's skin, put the Green Vomit on every area of the body that needed it, and wrapped it all with gauze. He kept checking to make sure the bleeding had stopped. He felt the rib cage. "Broken! Let's see, two or three?" His skilled fingers pressed into the lonely figure. Even in his own world, Gian winced. "Three!" Katsuro taped the ribs together.

The battered and bruised body did not move. The others had left. Only Katsuro remained. "If you live through this, you will follow my orders every time I tell you to do something. You can be sure the next beating will be worse."

Katsuro left Gian without another word. He turned off the lights to the dojo. Gian lay still. Night came and he still did not move. It was sometime during the night when he regained consciousness. For a few minutes he did not know where he was. He only knew that he hurt but was still alive. He wished he wasn't.

Gian tried to lift his head; he couldn't. The pain echoed through his shattered body. He moved his hands slowly to check out what damage had been done. He felt the bandages. He felt his broken ribs. He felt his nose no longer out of place, but in excruciating pain. He moved his hands over his belly and cried out in agony.

He finally realized he was on a table. He moved very slowly to get off. He cried out in pain as he toppled to the mat. He reached his arms up to the table to pull himself erect. The pain shot through to his brain. He slumped to the mat and rested. *Okay, Gian, start crawling,* he thought. *Pain or no pain, you can't stay here. Katsuro will get you.*

One knee in front of the other, crawling was slow. The pain was intense. He felt nauseated. He stopped every few feet to muster strength. And then he thought of Dog. *What if they did something to Dog? No, not Dog.* Gian slid a little faster until he reached the door of the dojo, when he began to feel dizzy. *What is the matter with me? Why do I feel dizzy?* Overwhelming nausea came in a constant wave. He wretched.

He shuffled through the vomit, momentarily feeling better, but still in constant pain. The trip to his house felt like an eternity. Straining to reach the handle, he pushed the door ajar, and collapsed at the doorstep. Dog greeted him. He lay there for a long time, Dog licking his face. Crawling continued in inches. The stairs to his bedroom loomed, as Everest did to Tenzing. Dog flew up to the top of the stairs and waited It would be a long wait. But just as Tenzing made it, so did Gian.

Gian felt dirty and violated. He crawled to the bath and turned it on. A rib popped free of the bandages. Pain shot through to his spine. Dog kept licking incessantly.

"Go away, Dog. I have to wash."

The water felt cool to his skin. The gauze, wet and sticky, made him feel alive as it clung to his nakedness. Gian crawled toward his bed. He smelled something. He looked up and saw a lone figure sitting at his desk. "I was told I could not help you, but I could bring you dinner. Are you okay?"

Gian coughed. He stared at the big brown eyes. "You hit me, too?"

Her eyes became wider and tears welled up. "You think I could do something like that?"

The next cough sent a message of pain to every part of his body. He shook his head. "What did you bring me?"

"Food! Does it make any difference? I just wanted to see you and make sure you were okay. It must really hurt, what they did to you."

"Yes." He pulled himself up onto his bed. He needed to show Margaret he could do it. He was glad she was there. "Margaret, would you feed Dog, please?"

"Sure!" Margaret got up from her seat. "Do you want me to change your bandages?"

He shook his head. "That's not allowed in this game. Katsuro has to do it himself."

"Is this a game to you, Gian? Almost getting murdered? This slow torture? These sadistic beatings?"

"No, they are part of my education: learning not to love, not to care, to have no feelings." He coughed again. The pain wracked his soul. He felt like passing out. He turned white. Margaret bolted toward him.

"No, you must stop. You must go. If they ask you why you were here so long, tell them I passed out. I don't want you getting into trouble because of me. Maybe I will die and save them all the trouble of beating me to death."

Margaret grew pale. She began to cry. "I really want to help you."

"I *really* want you to help me." He shook his head slowly. "But you can't. I have to win or lose this war on my own. Go, Margaret. Feed Dog. He is not part of this. Go." Gian knew he was slipping away. The pain now came in waves. It was overwhelming him. He felt like he was about to faint but didn't want Margaret with him when he did.

Margaret left. He passed out. The pain went away temporarily.

When he awoke during the night, he found himself talking to God. *If you are real, God, why do you let them beat me? Why don't you protect me? I'm not a bad boy. I'm a good boy. But I'm in so much pain, God, I just want to die. Please take me to a better place. I can't do this anymore. I don't want to live like this. I can't take this pain. Please, please, God, let me die!*

CHAPTER THIRTEEN

THE KOREAN WOMAN

No one heard Gian. His unspoken words forced him to think through and relive the day. Suddenly a mysterious calm enveloped him. It was like a shroud. It blotted out all his previous thoughts, and he began to think in another direction. It wasn't that he doubted the existence of God and what good God could do, but he began to rethink his existence and his relationship with Katsuro and the Tachigi family.

Yesterday they could have easily killed him. Although pleasant in its possibilities, death would have meant he had lost the battle. Katsuro and the Tachigi family would have won. If he had given in to death, they would have beaten his resolve, his never-give-in attitude. He had to survive. He did not want death to cheat him of his ultimate victory: to never give in to Katsuro. Never show weakness. Never pray for death. Pray for ultimate victory and be stronger than all the Tachigi family put together.

Death could not be an option. He would live and he would win. How did he arrive at that decision on the day following the worst beating of his life? There could be no other alternative. The will to win was too strong. Gian Aaron Molina had decided winning meant surviving and surviving meant winning.

He forced himself to sit up. Dog licked his face. He rose from his bed gingerly and with great determination limped over to the table where Margaret had placed the plate of food. He drank thirstily and ate the slab of beef slowly. His jaw tortured him. He stared at the empty glass plate and noticed his reflection. It wasn't a pretty sight.

Somehow he managed to get back to his bed and slump onto the mattress. It was extremely difficult. It took all his resolve. He had made up his mind. He would no longer cry or whimper or show any weakness. He would be the Master of his own fate.

Katsuro's words came back to him. *God only gives you what you can handle.* Those words gave him strength. *If I can handle this, then I can survive and grow.*

Gian was allowed to rest in his room. Margaret brought him food and fed Dog. When Margaret was in school, mother Rita made his meals.

When Katsuro came to visit him, he treated his wounds. The Master never said a word about the beating. He just allowed Gian to rest. On his final visit, Katsuro said, "I will see you tomorrow morning in the dojo." Gian got his two days off.

* * *

Katsuro listened to Tomi and shook his head. He knew he needed to move to Los Angeles to oversee Tomi's business, a business run by an incompetent son. He bristled but could do nothing until he went there.

He called Rita, his daughter, who had moved to Los Angeles after marrying her *no-good* Chinese husband. However, even Katsuro had to concede the *no-good* had been very successful. He had invested in a chain of fast food restaurants called Burrito and Taco. Katsuro would never admit the moniker of *no-good* was only because he was Chinese. The Tachigi family had never intermarried successfully. Those marriages never lasted very long.

Katsuro remembered when his son Yukio had married a Korean woman, a marriage of convenience to cement one of Katsuro's business partnerships. The Korean wife died—unexpectedly. Katsuro remembered that day clearly.

"Gian, go upstairs and tell your Aunt Igi she needs to get ready for our company party."

The five-year-old hustled up the stairs to his aunt's bedroom. He knocked—no answer. He opened the bedroom door slowly and peeked in She wasn't there. He looked again and called her name. *Aunt Igi. Where are you?* He walked slowly into the bathroom and saw her shock of black hair in the tub. There, staring back at him, with her eyes wide open and her fingers wrapped around a radio, she lay in the tub, not moving. Gian had never seen anybody dead before. Then he smelled it. It was the odor of burnt flesh. Even at five, Gian knew she had been electrocuted by the radio, which was still plugged into a nearby outlet.

Gian raced down the stairs calling out, "Aunt Igi, she's dead. Aunt Igi is dead! Come quickly."

At the bottom of the stairs, Gian ran into Katsuro. "Calm down, Gian. What did you say?"

"Aunt Igi, she's dead in the bathtub."

"Yukio, come with me. Apparently your wife died while taking a bath."

Yukio joined Gian and Katsuro at the bottom of the stairs. They looked at each other and walked up together slowly.

"Hurry, hurry. She's dead."

"Why hurry, Gian? If she's dead, there is nothing we can do."

The police came, pulled her out of the tub, examined the body, and called the coroner. Thirty days later, Yukio had a new bride, one who was Japanese.

A few months after the death of his daughter, the father, the Korean businessman, died. Katsuro bought the business from the grieving family.

Many years later came Rita's marriage to a Chinese man. Katsuro was furious.

*   *   *

That evening, at dinner with his family, Katsuro made the announcement that sent his family reeling. "We are moving to Los Angeles. I have business there that needs my attention. Some of you will stay here to run our interests in Japan and the rest of you will come with your mother and me to Los Angeles."

And that was that!

Katsuro left for Los Angeles immediately, while Rita was left to organize the move for the rest of the family. Gian knew his life would be different for a while. He wouldn't have Katsuro for a few weeks.

Katsuro wondered if he would ever return to Japan. He would.

CHAPTER FOURTEEN

BACK TO AMERICA

Katsuro buckled his seatbelt and eyed the good-looking Japan Airlines stewardess. She poured him a drink and he sipped it slowly. The silent ones were seated near Katsuro.

His mind lapsed into memory, a memory so vivid it lived with him always. He was a young man when he first came to America with his father.

His father was short in stature but a giant to Katsuro. Tough-speaking and wily, the elder Katsuro barked at his family, "I have told you before, Japan is going to war, and we don't want to be in Japan when the war breaks out. This country is led by a group of warlords who will lead us into self-destruction. The world is not made for a single nation or two nations to rule it. Our leaders fail to remember our ventures in China. They are filled with days of short-term glory that will lead to defeat tomorrow. Obviously, this is way beyond their comprehension. We have a good business in Los Angeles. We will stay there during the war."

Katsuro wasn't convinced his father was right about the war, but he did know that Japan could never defeat the United States.

The elder Katsuro took his entire family to America. When the family landed at Los Angeles airport, the elder Katsuro's business associates met them. They rented a house in East Los Angeles near the old Jewish neighborhood called Boyle Heights. Some Japanese and other Asians had begun to move into the area as older Jews moved out. It was almost like a ghetto of Jews and Asians.

A young Katsuro sought admission to the University of Southern California to study medicine. Claude Andrews, Chief of Admissions, sat behind his oak desk twisting a Sheaffer fountain pen cap. "You have high marks from your University in Japan. We will see if we have enough room in our Medical school for you. We have many applicants."

Both father and son knew what that meant: a quota on Asians. The elder stared at the pen-twisting official, and asked, "I understand, Mr. Andrews, that this is a private institution and any donation to it is considered a tax deduction. Is that correct?"

"Yes, Mr. Tachigi. What do you have in mind?"

"I have in mind an amount that would get my son into your university, Mr. Andrews." The elder smiled a smile of contempt for the man in the dark-blue serge suit.

"I am sure your generosity will be looked upon with favor by this institution. Would, say, twenty-five-thousand dollars be within your means?"

The elder was simmering inside but hid behind a well-controlled half smile. *How dare they try to get my favor by such a paltry amount? Don't they know I could buy this place if I wanted to?*

Actually, the elder was expecting a sum three times that amount. So he continued smiling and accepted the insult to his wealth. He wrote the check. Katsuro watched with great interest. Lesson one: power is gained through money.

Unfortunately, that wealth would be eaten up by war, confinement, and a wicked series of events.

* * *

A stewardess who asked him if he wanted a drink interrupted Katsuro's vision of the past. He shook his head and saw the elder Katsuro again in the misty past.

* * *

The Tachigi family settled into their new home and swiftly established themselves as leaders in the Japanese community. The elder Katsuro was busily engaged in his produce-shipping business. Many of the farmers from San Bernardino through Ventura County were Japanese. They planted, harvested and packed their produce to sell to Los Angeles markets. The elder Katsuro even trucked his produce as far north as San Francisco.

The elder Katsuro helped the farmers set up local farmers' markets to sell their produce. He supplied the trucks and workers. Katsuro was impressed at how well his father did in attracting growers and retail food markets together, until one late Sunday afternoon. Katsuro was home studying. A neighbor, Mr. Nekkei, was talking excitedly to the elder Katsuro.

"I had a run-in with Mr. Larsen today. He and a bunch of his goons emptied my truck into the gutter and warned me about delivering goods to the Cuban market. What should I do?" Mr. Nekkei twisted a copy of the *Daily News* in his taut fist.

Slowly the elder stood erect and lifted a dragon-carved cane into the air. "Where do I find this Mr. Larsen? I want to talk to him."

"They tell me he hangs out at the Bimini Baths. He likes the waters there. Katsuro, we can't afford to lose the Cuban market group as a client." A worried Mr. Nekkei wiped his brow even though it wasn't hot.

"We won't lose them. Mr. Larsen will pay for his transgression. I will see to that."

After Mr. Nekkei left, Katsuro listened while his father made a few telephone calls. The rotary dial phone clicked slowly. The elder Katsuro spoke to an operator and was connected to Lieutenant Amos Cooper of the Los Angeles Police Department. Katsuro knew his father had several friends on the police force. "Amos, Katsuro here. I need a favor. I need to know what day and at what time a Mr. Larsen goes to the Bimini Baths. Would you get back to me on Monday at six?"

Katsuro, the elder nodded. "Yes, same terms as always. Cash. Only cash." He replaced the receiver and grinned. *Absolute power corrupts, and money makes it happen.*

Katsuro had no classes Monday, so he made it a point to be home for dinner when his father would receive his call. The phone rang right on time. When the conversation ended, the elder Katsuro excused himself. He called Mr. Nekkei, who sometimes acted as his chauffeur. Later that evening, the two of them met and drove off together. It was not until two days later that Katsuro read in the *Los*

Angeles Examiner about the severe beating of a Mr. Samuel Larsen and two of his men near the Bimini Baths on Western Avenue. From this gangland savagery, Katsuro learned how his father handled interlopers.

Never again did he hear about his father being bothered by anyone in the same business.

*   *   *

It was December 7, 1941, when the United States was attacked at Pearl Harbor. The next day's headlines screamed the President's words, *"A day of infamy."* It was then that Katsuro realized how brilliant his father really was. It was there in black and white, **WAR**. The Tachigi family was about to be thrust right into the middle if it.

Shortly after the United States declared war on Japan, President Roosevelt gave Executive Order 9066. Its intent was to identify all persons of Japanese descent living on the West Coast of the United States. Considered security risks, they were to be incarcerated for the duration of the war. The elder Katsuro sat with his family and outlined his plan. "I have read this edict from the President. I am deeply disappointed in President Roosevelt for his thinking. We should be treated as individuals and not lumped with the masses as possible persons of interest."

Katsuro listened to his father and said, "We aren't citizens of the United States. We have visas. Could we be deported?"

The elder scratched a faux itch and thought, "I doubt it. America is afraid of us—our people and our intentions. I don't think they would send us back. But, I do think they will send us to some internment camp."

"Where?" a startled Katsuro asked.

"I don't know. Even they haven't decided yet."

"I read many Japanese are being attacked by Americans. There is much discrimination here. Maybe we would be better off returning to Japan," Katsuro's mother offered, her hands wringing a napkin tightly.

The elder went on. "Order 9066 is a voluntary order. There are no sanctions for failure to obey. No penalty if we don't turn ourselves into the authorities. But, I am sure that will change. The government will make it a mandatory order soon enough."

"So what will we do?"

"Several things. I have arranged for some of our American employees to take over the business. I had documents drawn up to indicate they are owners. Then I made some contacts in Chinatown to have documents forged to show we are Chinese citizens, not Japanese."

Katsuro sat up straight, impressed but puzzled, "Father. I have several questions."

"Ask."

"We have Japanese visas. How can we be Chinese?"

"Good question with a simple answer. We will have all new documents including a passport that says we are Chinese citizens who lived in Japan for a few years. The State Department didn't check our visa request and our passports very thoroughly. The only bad part is that this process will take some time before it can be completed for all of us. Does that answer your question?"

"Yes, it does. But what about our business? What will happen to it? Are we selling it to our employees?"

"You have little faith in your father. Did I not get you into the university without a problem? You can be sure I will get our business back when we are free."

"How?"

"I had another set of papers drawn up that I left with an attorney who will represent us when we are out of the camp. Then, we will go to court to defend the legality of our documents and argue the illegality of the United States government imprisoning us without a fair hearing and a trial. I set aside money for this defense in a bank account with an old friend."

Katsuro shook his head and was proud of his father's plans and his insight. "Who is this friend, father?"

Hirohsu nodded to his son. "His name is Manfred Siegman."

Robert Burns wrote, "The best laid plans of mice and men sometimes go astray" ("The best laid scheme's a'mice an 'men Gang aft agley"). The elder Katsuro's plan did in part go astray.

After Order 9066 was signed on February 19, 1942, fate would have its way. Four days later a Japanese submarine attacked an oil field off the coast of Santa Barbara, California. That attack sparked an outcry about filling the loopholes in 9066 in order to make the internment of persons of Japanese extraction mandatory. War Relocation Authority (WRA) Executive Order 9102 stated "to provide for the removal from designated areas of any persons whose removal is necessary in the interest of national security." As a result, thousands of Japanese and Japanese Americans were imprisoned.

Those persons interned lost all of their property and nearly all of their belongings. They were permitted to take some clothes and bedding and a few personal items. The Tachigi family was interned in Manzanar, located in the upper reaches of the Mojave Desert in the Eastern Sierra Nevada Mountains of California.

* * *

J.W. Hood was a graduate of Stanford University, a scholar in international affairs, and a strong believer in the WRA. He regarded the surprise attack on Pearl Harbor to be the most evil act ever perpetrated against the United States.

When Manfred Siegman walked into his office in September of 1942 and handed him a packet of papers proving that the Tachigi family were really Chinese and were being treated unfairly, he flinched.

After waving Mr. Siegman to be seated he stroked his beardless face with the tips of his thumb and index finger. Flabbergasted, he said, "President Roosevelt swore to this country he would only assign those persons of actual Japanese origin to be interned and only after careful scrutiny to their being a danger to this country. I am ashamed this mistake has taken place."

He liked his speech but truthfully didn't give a damn who the President incarcerated, as long as he could make money. He saw the war as a great opportunity to ply his trade and get rich. "Mr. Siegman, where are your friends?"

"Manzanar."

"A very unpleasant place. I have visited there. It is like being in a cage. Shameful!"

Manfred sensed a little bit of sarcasm in lawyer Hood's voice. "Yes. My friends wrote to me. It is infested with rats and rattlesnakes."

"So they feed the rats to the rattlesnakes to keep them well-fed?" J.W. liked his joke.

"Hardly. They are not laughing. So, Mr. Hood, let's get down to business. How long will it take to get them out of prison?"

JW pushed his chair back and stood gripping the lapels of his dark blue suit with the same digits he had used to stroke his face, and said, "How much money are you willng to pay to expedite their release?"

"No bullshit from you, Mr. Hood. I expected that. How much to get them out by October?"

"October? Nothing! They can't even process the paperwork by then. December at the earliest, and that might be pushing it."

Manfred nodded. "How much by December?"

*   *   *

Manfred greeted the entire Tachigi clan as they left the Manzanar compound. Their faces were drawn, their skin pasty. They trooped out to freedom without a word, only a nod from the elder Katsuro.

Katsuro never got his business back from his former employees. The courts ruled that all prisoners could have no financial interest in any properties in America. Therefore, the elder Katsuro had to dig deep into his hidden reserves to survive.

Katsuro went back to the University of Southern California. Katsuro Sr. went into the trucking business hauling liquor: moonshine, to be exact, produced using homemade stills in the Imperial Valley by illegal Mexican laborers. His investment paid off handsomely. Katsuro avoided military service, because he was studying medicine and doctors were in short supply. He would have been drafted if the war had lasted longer.

Meanwhile, the two Katsuros continued to develop their martial-arts skills in a specially designed dojo Katsuro had converted from an old barn.

* * *

The elder Katsuro faded from his mind as Katsuro's plane descended onto the tarmac in Los Angeles.

CHAPTER FIFTEEN

LOS ANGELES

The long-legged real-estate agent met Katsuro at the airport to drive him to his new home in Canyon Falls. "Did you do everything I asked?"

Still a bit nervous about being stared at by the steely eyes of the old man, she shifted in her seat, tried to pull her short skirt down, failed, and drove onto the 121. Her voice cracked slightly as she thought about his requests. "Yes, Mr. Tachigi, I did. I have a wonderful group of servants ready to take care of you. A housekeeper, a chef, and a chauffeur, all now expecting you."

Katsuro wanted to slide his hand over and touch the slender legs of this woman whom he couldn't help admiring for her good looks and gorgeous body. "Fine. Are you planning on staying for dinner tonight?"

Her face flushed. Her stomach churned, She wanted to tell him she was a real-estate agent, not a prostitute. But she squelched her disgust and nodded, "If you would like."

"I would like that."

The shadows sat quietly.

All three servants met Katsuro at the front door. Introductions were made and the servants went about their business. The long-legged agent showed Katsuro around the property, including the newly constructed dojo. "I will see the inside after you leave. It is better I spend my time with you, while you can stay."

She nodded, swallowed hard, and thought of her bulging bank account just from the sale of this property and the money Katsuro had sent her for overseeing the construction of the dojo. She had done as he suggested and hired a Japanese architect to design the building and its interior. As Katsuro had instructed, the architect left a large space in another section of the dojo building for housing Katsuro's automobile collection.

They dined together. She then excused herself and changed into an outfit that a teenage girl might wear. She put her hair into pigtails and waited for Katsuro to come upstairs. She was watching TV as he entered. He held his head and walked slowly into the bedroom. "Mr. Tachigi, are you ill? You don't look very well."

"Tired. I suddenly got very tired. I want to rest. Will you come back some other time and look like you do now?"

Relieved, she said, "If you like." She hurried to change back into her regular work clothes and scampered out of the house.

Katsuro undressed slowly and realized it was sixteen hours later in Japan than in California. He fell into bed and was asleep in an instant.

The next morning he awoke early, dressed in a full suit, and toured the property. For a man who was always surrounded by his extended family, he felt intensely alone at that moment. He wandered across the landscape and entered the dojo. He knew what to expect, for he had designed it. The first glimpse of his new dojo engulfed him with memories.

It was his father's dojo. He envisioned his father standing on the mats jumping rope, punching the poles and practicing the rituals of *Akin Jitsu*. He stood in a corner and watched his father. *"Watch me, little one. Watch my moves."* When he had finished the routine he called his son over. *"Come now and imitate me. Do as I do."*

"Little one, move your feet faster. Get your full body into rhythm."

The elder grew weary of his son's failure to follow him. *"You are not listening. You are not taking this training seriously. Let me show you what serious means."*

The elder went to the wall and took down a *Shinai. "When you see this Shinai, you will know I mean business."* The elder whipped the coarse cords of the weapon across Katsuro's legs. *"Now move them."*

Katsuro cried out in pain. The elder hit him again. *"Never show pain. Never call out in pain. Pain should never enter your brain. Devour pain, or it will eat your flesh."*

The old Samurai leered at his son. *"You shall be all your twin brother could never be."*

Katsuro nodded. He would meet his father's expectations and more. But the old Samurai never adjusted to the new world that entered his life. It was too complex for him. That world wasn't his world—a world filled with Samurai warriors and their code of conduct, morals and customs. That era was dead and the elder never understood.

Katsuro recoiled. The *Shinai* hung just where he had drawn it to hang. He walked over to the weapon and stared at it. "I learned to tolerate the pain, father, and so shall Gian." He took down the *Shinai* and placed it next to the chair he would use when instructing his children and Gian.

He continued his slow walk through the dojo. His strongest memory of his father hung with an X on the wall: two Samurai swords, crossed dramatically, handles worn, blades nicked, their glistening steel dimmed by time, holding a history never tarnished.

He thought of his father and his profound teachings. Katsuro had never beaten his own children the way his father had beaten him. The *Shinai* that the elder always carried when he gave instructions to his sons would be used as a severe reminder that it was time to work harder. The elder would take this ancient sword used in the teachings of *Kendo*, loosen the binding cords holding the bamboo flaps in place, and then use the instrument as a whip. *"To whip you into shape, my son. To remind you that life is full of pain and you can only endure that pain by feeling it and understanding it. So this Shinai, this sword of my father and his father before him, gives you pain and pleasure: pain in how it feels against the flesh and pleasure in knowing you have mastered the pain."*

Katsuro remembered those beatings. His twin brother could never endure the pain and crawled from it. He was castigated and shunned by his own father. Katsuro, as he grew older, understood the teachings of his Master father, one of the last true Samurai.

Katsuro unwrapped the cord from this *Shinai* and flicked his wrist, hearing the crackling sound caused by the lashing bamboo. Katsuro never used the *Shinai* against his own flesh and blood. He would flick the sword at them when they needed reminding of their duties and their warrior needs, but not until Gian began his training did he use the full effect of this powerful tool.

Gian was a true warrior. He had tolerated and withstood the pain, even revered it. Now he would need more training and fiercer tests to prove his mettle. Gian would need more of life's teachings. He would be taught to understand the Ring of Fire. Yes, Gian, it is time to teach you about life.

CHAPTER SIXTEEN

HIGH SCHOOL
IN AMERICA

Just twelve, Gian stood in the principal's office at Carrington High School. His fake birth certificate said he was of high-school age. Although not tall, he was solid. His chest was massive. His legs were pure muscle. Still, he wasn't sure if he really looked sixteen. But he knew he was ready for high school academically. His advanced education in Japan had left him far better educated than the average American student. However, his English writing and spelling skills were not up to grade level.

Katsuro hired a tutor to develop Gian's skills commensurate with high school. Even though he lived in Canyon Falls, Gian attended school in the Los Angeles Unified School District.

The principal had no choice but to let Gian enroll in the fall.

During that summer, Gian and family visited Raul near San Diego. Katsuro had rented a house with the same configuration as in Canyon Falls: a main house, a gym and a casitas for Gian.

Gian had become very aware of his fighting skills, but his abilities sometimes scared him. He didn't mean to hurt anybody. When he fought his brothers and sisters, he always held back. He didn't hit them as hard as he could. He didn't follow through with his punches and certainly never kicked them when they were down. This pleased Katsuro and bothered him at the same time.

He would never want his grandchildren hurt. Yet, he wanted more from Gian, more of a killer instinct. It was under those circumstances James Garston came into Gian's life.

* * *

Riding his bicycle through his San Diego neighborhood, Gian saw a group of boys playing in a nearby lot. He parked his bike at the edge of the vacant lot and walked over to them. They were playing war games. Of the five boys, one was the most vocal and seemed to be the leader. He was a big kid, tall and heavy set. Before Gian could even say a word, the boy, James Garston, said, "What do you want, kid? We're playing a game and you're not invited." James sidled up to Gian and poked him in the chest. "How'd you get here? Walk?"

Gian said, "No, I rode my bike."

"Come on, guys. Let's look at this kid's bike."

James strode ahead of the others and picked up the bike. "New, eh? I like it. I'll give you a quarter for it."

"No, I'll just leave."

James then did something he would regret, not at that moment but very soon: he smacked Gian across the face, knocking him to the ground. It wasn't that Gian was hurt, but rather surprised at James' savagery. Gian rose and stood his ground. James shot a tight fist into Gian's nose— it split. Another right crashed into Gian's cheek. Gian finally ran from the group of boys who were laughing. "What a jerky kid he is. Now I get his bike for nothin'."

Standing on a hilltop, Yukio witnessed the one-sided fight. He ran to tell Katsuro. He delighted in bringing his father all the failures of his protégé. Katsuro waited for Gian to walk back home. He strolled out to meet him. He put his arm around Gian's shoulder and gently touched his face. "You have a pretty bad gash. Let me clean it up." They went into the backyard. Katsuro took out the garden house and showered Gian. Water dripped from his clothes, but he shook it off. "Come, I will take care of your cuts." Katsuro cleaned the wounds and helped wash the blood from Gian's face. He gave him some water to drink and stood over him, now scowling, all pretense of caring gone.

"Did that boy hurt you when you let him hit you?"

"No, sir. I didn't really feel anything."

"Did he cause you any pain?"

"No sir, he didn't."

Then, with a swiftness and hardness Katsuro had used before, he sent a powerful jab right into Gian's face. The boy fell to the ground like a sack of potatoes. He saw nothing but darkness. He reeled almost to unconsciousness.

Katsuro threw a glass of water at Gian's face. The boy moved, stunned. He saw the rage in his mentor's face and heard it in his voice. Katsuro screamed, "Did that hurt?"

Of all the blows Gian had ever felt, this was the most painful and the most unexpected of his young life. That single blow shook Gian to his core. In shock at Katsuro's sudden fierceness, Gian broke down and cried out silently. He shook his head, trying to clear the blackness only to see the light of fury.

Katsuro, nearly eighty-four-years-old, grabbed the boy by his hair and pulled him up. Again, his fist drove straight into the youngster's face. His cheek split. As the boy lay on the ground, the Master drove a powerful kick into his midsection. Gian gasped for air, his face turning purple. Katsuro's right foot stomped onto his face. "Get up, boy!"

Gian struggled to his feet, holding his stomach, his mouth open, still gasping for a breath. "Did I hurt you?"

The boy could only nod. "If I ever hear you backed down from a fight again, I will beat you worse than this. And for every day you do not go and beat that boy for hitting you, I will give you another beating ten times worse than this. You understand me?"

Once again, the boy could only nod.

"Now, get into the dojo so I can stop your bleeding and then you can work out. Go! Now!"

At ten the next morning, Gian walked back to James' house where he saw his bike parked in the driveway. James was standing there with three friends making plans for the day. Gian was about to spoil those plans.

He walked up to James. As James was about to speak, Gian hooked a punch to James' ear, splattering him with blood, causing a shriek of pain. As James grabbed his ear, Gian sent a jarring uppercut to his jaw, straightening him up before he collapsed to the concrete. Gian fell on James and drove a flurry of punches into his head. James fell unconscious in a pool of blood.

Katsuro, who had followed well behind Gian, unseen, now pulled his protégé off the stricken boy and walked off with him. "You beat him badly. That was well done."

Gian's bike never left James' driveway.

* * *

Harold Swartzman, a detective in the San Diego Police Department, had earned his promotion the old-fashioned way, by being the best. He had studied the ancient Israeli art of self-defense called *krav maga*. He worked out daily in a gym. He knew he was in the best shape of any San Diego detective, so when he stepped into the dojo where Gian and Katsuro's family were working out, he was in awe.

He introduced himself, gave Katsuro his business card, and asked, "Is this the way a dojo is normally set up?"

Katsuro, with a bit of pride, responded, "It is set up in the tradition of the Samurai warrior like my father. This is his dojo design. Not like the ones you have in the United States."

"And these twisted ropes? What are they for?"

"Rather than just punching a punching bag, these ropes toughen up your hands so they become calloused. When you are fighting, your hands feel no pain."

Gian stepped forward with his gloves on. He demonstrated how to use the ropes. Then he took the gloves off and continued his punching routine.

"Officer Swartzman, you are not here to see our dojo. How can I help you, Sir?"

The officer shuffled through his notebook. "Sir, I am afraid your son has badly injured a boy named James Garston. He had to be treated at the hospital. They tell me your boy beat him mercilessly. Is that true, young man?"

Katsuro intervened, "Did they tell you that James Garston severely beat Gian the day before?"

"That true, young man?"

Katsuro said, "That is true. I just told you it was true."

"Please let the young man answer for himself, sir."

Gian nodded and softly said it was true.

"Is it also true you beat this James boy the next day in his driveway?"

"Yes, sir. I did. But he started it, and I finished it."

Officer Swartzman took his notes and left.

At eight that night, Yukio and Katsuro drove over to the Garston residence.

The next day, the Garstons dropped all charges against Gian.

*   *   *

Yukio sat in his father's office. "I have lined up most of the businesses in Chinatown, Koreatown, and Little Tokyo in Los Angeles as customers. I have a few stragglers. But the boys are meeting with them this week."

"Good work, son. Did you also take care of the hospital bills for that Garston kid?"

"Yes, sir. I did. Goddamn, father. Couldn't he have been a little more civil. I hated to threaten to cut his fingers off if he pressed charges against Gian. I like it better when they just cooperate the first time."

"He may not have had his fingers cut off, but he sure gobbled up that ten grand we paid him for dropping the charges. Piss-ass bastard. I would have rather cut off his fingers. Cheaper!" They both laughed.

CHAPTER SEVENTEEN

THE BATH

Life in Los Angeles wasn't any better for Gian than Japan had been, except in school, where he wasn't teased by the other students for looking different. He still lived by himself in his small house in back of the main house. He was still trained by Katsuro and he was still beaten regularly with the *Shinai*. He still sparred with Katsuro's grandchildren and still showed restraint. Ryuu and Yukio continued to torment him whenever they could. All this while he attended high school at the age of twelve.

In addition to his normal exercise routine, Gian was introduced to pliametrics, a series of exercises designed to make him more explosive, able to jump higher and farther. These exercises entailed repeatedly jumping atop a series of progressively higher boxes. Gian did this better than any of his brothers.

On his visits to San Diego, Gian worked for the man who lived next door to Raul. Earl Kaplan was a retired war veteran. Unable to do much physical labor any more, he hired various people to do whatever work he needed. He had seen Gian lifting boulders on his grandfather's lot and admired his strength. He offered to pay Gian to move some of his orange trees to a planting area far up on the hills surrounding his property.

Earl provided a wheelbarrow for Gian to move the large trees. As Gian proceeded up the hill with his first load, Katsuro watched. The old man waved his omnipresent *Shinai* at Gian, "Gian, strength training takes all forms. One is to carry things great distances. Take all those trees and make sure you carry them where Mr. Kaplan wants them planted. That would be a good exercise." Katsuro tapped his bamboo sword on the wheelbarrow. "You will not need this any more."

Gian grabbed the first tree around its base and lifted it with awesome strength. Earl Kaplan was impressed. The young boy strode up the hill and deposited the plant in the hole he had dug earlier. He replaced the dirt in the hole and prepared for the next tree. It took Gian a week to plant the grove of trees.

His grandfather, Raul, had him shovel horse dung and carry it to fertilize his garden.

For Katsuro, Gian still toted boulders from one end of the yard to the other. He lugged large baskets of rocks from one pile to another and back. He pounded large tires with a sledgehammer over and over. He still received injections in his buttocks, legs and stomach on a routine basis. As part of his normal workout routine, Gian continued to hang from the punching bag pulleys by his wrists. "That will help you grow taller," Katsuro assured him.

He still used the communal bath; this was the only time he was allowed in the main house. His devoted roommate, Dog, faithfully barked at Katsuro, the abuser. On the rare occasions Katsuro visited Gian's house, Gian had to lock up Dog. Margaret remained one of Gian's few friends.

Gian's responsibilities included painting the dojo twice a year. Katsuro never allowed him to use a roller. "It is better to use a paint brush and stroke back and forth. That will build your endurance." From age ten, Gian also did his own laundry and cooked his own meals. "No need to have dinner made by a cook. You are old enough to cook for yourself," Katsuro said.

What did not remain the same was Gian's strength, his endurance, and his agility, similar to a young ballet dancer's, and all gained from his lifetime of workouts, lifting, human-growth-hormone shots, and formal martial-arts training. Taut and sinewy, his stomach muscles were like an iron grate. His body had no fat. His muscles extended and rippled.

Although Margaret was three years older than Gian, they were in the same grade. However, she attended a private school. She had her own car at sixteen and was parking it in the garage when she saw Gian moving rocks in the field in back of their house. She could not help looking at his muscular body. Her own body was changing, and her desire became full blown when she saw this man-child's muscles gleaming in the sunlight, naked to the waist. She wondered what his manhood was like.

She went to her room on the second floor of the house and watched Gian drag a full basket of rocks from one side of the yard to the other side. Katsuro egged him on, "Get your ass moving, you worthless piece of shit. I don't think you put enough rocks in that basket. Put some more in when you drag it to the garden. Then drag it back." Like a slave-owner from the Deep South a century before, Katsuro took his ever-present *Shinai* and raked it across Gian's back. The man-child flicked the pain from his mind, packed more rocks into the basket, and hauled the rocks even faster across the yard.

Katsuro applauded him sarcastically. "You think you can fool me? You must have taken some rocks out when I wasn't looking on that last trip. This time I'll pile some more rocks in that basket. Then let's see you move it so fast."

Gian smirked. *Let the games begin, old man. You know damn well that load was full of rocks, and you watched me like a hawk. So let's play the game.*

Like a plow horse, Gian gathered his strength and dragged the rock—filled basket even faster across the yard, smirking all the way. "Satisfied, old man?" He whispered so the Master couldn't hear him. *Old men don't hear so well either.*

As Gian dumped the load of rocks from the basket, Katsuro came over and lashed the *Shinai* across his back. "You insolent bastard. Don't ever whisper under your breath at me."

Gian tossed the pain from his back aside and strode off. "I'm washing up and making my dinner."

Margaret bolted from her perch overlooking the yard and raced downstairs into the communal bath area. She undressed and hid in a small alcove outside the shower area. Gian came marching in, full of himself. It had been the first time he had told Katsuro what he was going to do and Katsuro did not whip him for being rude or insolent. *Maybe the old man is getting tired of whipping me.*

Gian slipped out of his work clothes and flexed his muscles in front of the mirror. He liked what he saw: thirteen and still growing. Margaret could see the reflection, too. She giggled to herself. But something stirred in her. Something strange. A chill went through her body, and it did not diminish when she saw Gian leave the shower and enter the bath.

He lay in the soothing waters of the tub as it warmed his body. As he reached for a loofa, he felt a hand touch his back. Startled, he turned and saw Margaret's smiling face. "Stay still. Last time, you left me alone in the bath. That was not nice. I'm here to make you feel better."

Gian was suddenly very afraid, not afraid of Katsuro, but afraid of the feeling he was having. It was a strange feeling. His body ached and he tried to control his emotions as he had been taught. Margaret slid around in front of him. He stared at her nakedness. She saw his body respond. She wanted to giggle but controlled the urge. She took the loofa and began washing his chest. Her emotions were now totally out of control which was what she wanted.

As she continued bathing him, Gian pulled himself up in the tub and attempted to scramble out. He had no control over his body's emotions. He was scared of how he felt. Nothing before had ever caused feelings like he was experiencing. Margaret grabbed him by the legs and pulled him back. She bounded on him.

He became lost in his own emotions.

Gian reached the point of terror. What was she doing? Her motions suddenly stopped. She gasped. As she pulled free of the terror filled man-child and stood up in the tub she asked, "Did you like that, Gian?"

The expression on his face told her 'No'. She smiled down at him. "You'll like it better next time."

Gian tried to get up. "Not yet! Be polite! Ladies first."

That night Gian did not sleep well. He could not understand what had happened.

AIR-WATER-EARTH-FIRE=METAL

Gian had heard the muttering before. It was almost like a Gregorian chant but with no melody, except it was the same five words over and over. Gian had been taught never to ask questions about his routine, his workouts, his physical development. But these mutterings provoked his curiosity.

The late-afternoon workout was over. There had been no use of the *Shinai*. No derisive words. No praise. It was just a laid-back, melancholy afternoon. Katsuro was pensive, which was very unusual for him. It appeared that his mind wasn't totally involved. Katsuro was in deep thought. It was the anniversary of his father's passing. It brought great sorrow to him. *The least I can do is revere his memory.*

So when Gian asked him what he was saying as he muttered those words, Katsuro was startled, yet reflective.

"Sit, Gian." The uttering of his name was a surprise. He was usually called *Juko* or just pointed at. Most of the time, he was never formally addressed. It was like he didn't exist, but he was there. So Gian took special interest.

In this instant of candor, Katsuro talked about his memories. "Today is the day of my father's death. He was the Grand Master who taught me to become a Grand Master. He taught me the elements of *Akin Jitsu* that make up the forms used in marital arts training. What you heard were the words that make up the elements of this art: Water, Earth, Fire, Air, and the ultimate form, Metal."

Gian shook his head. "I don't understand."

"There is no reason you should. Let me explain the elements to you."

"The system of *Akin Jitsu* is meant to be everywhere. The forms are meant to move continuously, circling around an opponent, striking in ways that are often open-handed but meant to be devastating with every position and every blow. So, it is not just a hand slap, but also a soft, supple, continuous attack from every direction.

"You start with Air by learning to breathe. Air is the force around everything. Air is supple and it moves. It has no form. It is soft. It surrounds you. It comes at you from all directions; yet, without it, you cannot survive. It is vital.

"Water is also supple because it can take any shape yet can be devastating. Water is giving and it is soft, yet it can erode a rock. Water is a substance you can put into a container. Many techniques are pushing and pulling at the same time, like the ocean. Undercurrents go in the opposite direction of a wave.

"That is why you have practiced in a large vat of water, moving and strengthening your body. That water has no distinctive shape. It surrounds you, engulfs you. It is gentle yet so powerful it can transform a mountain."

Katsuro went on. "Earth is solid. You are born of the Earth. You are tempered by heat and then heated into a shape. You are cooled by Water. Earth doesn't move. It stands and delivers. It isn't fast. Still, it isn't meant to be slow or to be taken off its roots. It is meant to be powerful. It is meant to deliver force. Earth makes you strong enough to survive the mastery of all four elements."

Gian listened intently. When Katsuro was in this type of mood and shared his experiences with Gian, he reveled. He hung on every word. These moments were sacred and their impact lasted a lifetime. It was the teachings of Katsuro that Gian loved. He didn't love the man. Never! But he always loved Katsuro's wisdom. Gian found his words fascinating and these times precious.

"Fire is the hardest of the disciplines. It ravages. It is always straight ahead. Yet it can move from side to side as well as straight. But it never backs up. Fire never retreats. Fire is not love. Fire is not passion. It is hate in its purest form. It is meant to consume. It is meant to be focused and yet unfocused at the same time. Fire can be direct. It can burn straight up a hill, in a line. Yet, with a little whisk of Air, Fire can carry across an entire hillside. It is finite at one point, attacking at another. If you have one thing you want to accomplish, then Fire is how you do it.

"Without discipline, Fire destroys everything. If you have an out-of—control burn, you must destroy it.

"So this is the system. Part of the form is that way. It is always attacking. It never stops. It goes until it consumes." Katsuro's words were drawn out and enunciated with great clarity to make his point.

Katsuro continued, "All four of these elements create Metal. It comes from the Earth. It is heated by Fire, cooled by Water, and finally completely quenched by Water. You are Metal.

"Strong, ferocious like a sword, yet gentle like the back of a blade. All create the foundation of *Akin Jitsu*. Its roots are those four elements. Every Grand Master has to learn these. Kicks and punches go into the elements but they are only for the Master.

"*Qichon* is the Chinese equivalent of Japanese martial arts. The sophisticated intensity of Earth, Water, Air and Fire are for the Masters. Each of these pieces gives a foundation for the Masters. The Grand Master chooses a description to characterize and describe himself. I am Wisdom."

Gian had a question, but he allowed Katsuro to continue.

"To watch this form of martial arts is to watch art. To experience it, is to lock everything into place: your mind, your soul, your body—it is art. You are involved in this experience. You are positioning the pieces. Your training will help you perfect these forms that will give you inner peace and total harmony. They are the very core, the strength of what you do. You are learning the foundation. You are learning to fight, to be devastating. You are involved in all these disciplines."

Gian now understood what Katsuro had been muttering—*Earth, Air, Fire, Water*—the forms that make up *Akin Jitsu*. During Gian's training, punching, kicking, attacking, Katsuro repeated the form Gian was using.

"You had another question, little one."

"Yes, sir. You mentioned that the word *Qichon* refers to the Chinese form of martial arts. Why?'

"Because our ancestors were Chinese. My great-great-grandfather was a monk in China and developed this new form of martial arts. But that is a story for another time. Remind me someday and I will tell you that story. Not now, I am too tired."

Katsuro walked out of the dojo and into his house.

CHAPTER EIGHTEEN

AARON'S ANSWER

When Gian entered his junior year in high school, he couldn't help but admire the old man. At 86, he was agile, tough, and in peak condition. But so was Gian. Slender and well-muscled, with broad shoulders, stomach muscles that rippled like a washboard, and powerful legs that looked like tree stumps; all this defined his fourteen-year old body.

Now, major changes were part of a life still evolving.

The first one occurred on a visit to his grandfather's ranch near San Diego. Raul was waiting for his grandson on the veranda of his home, moving slowly back and forth in a rocker, his head nodding in the early afternoon sun, when he heard the car door slam and saw Gian. The old man eyed his grandson and marveled at his growth spurt from the last time he had seen him nearly six months prior. Gian's driver stayed in the car.

Raul got up and gave his grandson a powerful hug. "It is good to see you again, Aaron. You have grown quite a bit." He put his hands on the young man's shoulders and felt the power. He hugged Aaron close again and they walked inside. The two shared a pitcher of lemonade, then walked out to the stable. "Do you remember when we first met, when you were six, Aaron?"

"Yes, sir. We rode down to the ocean and chewed on grass."

"And you were reluctant to talk to me. Bashful, I guess." Raul drew his grandson close as his arm encircled his shoulder, "But, now, look at you; growing tall and strong. I understand you will be trying out for the United States Martial Arts Team. Katsuro says you will have no problem making it."

Gian stood straight. "Whatever Katsuro says is usually right. Katsuro says that American fighters are not tough. They train like sissies. I train like a man."

"Aaron, I have a feeling you are about ready to become a man. I am sure you will do well in the qualifying tournament this weekend."

Gian smiled for one of the few times in his life. "In your honor, Grandfather. I will fight under the name Aaron for the tournament."

"I will be looking forward to your fights . . . Aaron."

THE TRUTH

The man-child and his grandfather walked to the barn where they first became acquainted. Aaron bent over, plucked a reed of grass from the field, and twirled it in his fingers. "We chewed on this weed the first time we met and you told me about your time in Spain's cavalry. But you never told me about my parents. My birth parents and how I wound up in Japan to be raised by the Tachigi family. Why? How did that happen?"

Grandfather Molina stopped and placed his hands on Aaron's shoulders, "Are you sure you want to know the truth?" Aaron nodded. "I'm not sure you will understand. The truth will hurt, Aaron."

Aaron drew a deep breath. "Pain is part of what I experience every day of my life. Maybe this pain will be worth hearing. Maybe it will answer some questions. Maybe it will relieve some painful doubts."

"You are fourteen years old. I know because I remember when you were born. I knew your mother wasn't going to keep you. She didn't want you. You would have interfered with her life of pleasure."

"Life of pleasure? She gave me up for her pleasure?"

Raul looked at his grandson and a tear trickled down Raul's cheek. "I could not convince her to keep you."

They both sat in the middle of the field overlooking the Pacific Ocean. The waves slipped in and out over the sandy beach below. The soft sound belied the torrent of confusion Aaron was feeling at that moment.

"Your mother was never sure she ever wanted children. Your mother's husband was a drug dealer and he didn't want a boy to grow up like him. I think they really didn't want any children. They had given your brother up for adoption many years before. He was autistic and died when he was three. So when your mother became pregnant, not by her husband, but by my son at a swinger's party, she knew she wouldn't keep you."

Aaron almost laughed. "It seems nobody wanted me, except . . .."

"Yes, except Katsuro. My son's wife, Jennifer, didn't want another woman's child, so you were in never-never land. I knew Katsuro very well through our real-estate dealings. He was in town one day when we began to talk about what to do with our new baby coming soon. He had met both your mother and my son. They were both large people, both fine athletes, both smart even if they were narcissistic and selfish."

Aaron now laughed out loud. "Katsuro saw my parents as big, athletic people and decided I would grow up to be big and athletic. What a son-of-a-bitch! So that was why he chose me. I was going to be his world champion because I was going to be bigger, stronger, and more athletic than his own children. Damn it!"

Raul shook his head. "Right you are! So Katsuro suggested that he might want the baby. He would take the baby to Japan and raise it. Your mother liked that idea. You would be far away and out of sight." Raul paused.

Aaron looked at Raul, waiting for him to continue. Raul shook his head. "I'm am going to tell you the next part—but it's painful."

Aaron smiled. "I can handle pain."

"I hate to tell you this, but your mother can be a conniving woman."

"How so?"

"When Katsuro offered to adopt you, she just stared at him until he said, 'What do you want?' Your mother continued to stare at him and finally asked, 'How much is he worth to you?'

Aaron asked, "What did Katsuro say?"

"Well, Katsuro, the Grand Master of con men, put the ball right back in her court. He said, 'You set the price.' So your mother wrote down what she wanted and handed the paper to Katsuro. She said she wanted her demands in writing so there would be no misunderstanding of what she wanted. Katsuro looked at the paper and simply said, 'Done'."

"What was on the paper?"

"Katsuro was to buy her a $75,000 house and give her thirty-thousand dollars in cash. He told me later he would have paid more."

"So I was sold on the open market. Just like slaves of old. Sold!"

"You okay with that?"

"You know, Grandfather, I really don't care. I've been given this life, and I'm living it the best I can. These are the cards I've been dealt and I'll play with this hand. Thirty-thousand dollars and a $75,000 house. Son-of-a-bitch!"

*　　*　　*

Aaron stood in the corner, dancing to a slow ballad he had been listening to in the dressing room. He found that the slow, melodic music calmed him and gave him time to search his soul for the confidence he needed to battle successfully.

In the ring at the United States Martial Arts tournament, he eyed his first opponent. He was tall, well-muscled, and had a small tick that caused his head to bob. *Maybe he's nervous.* Aaron's mind flashed back to his first fight as a twelve-year-old. Aaron lacked size. All his opponents were taller and larger than he was, but he had unusual muscle development for his age. He pranced in his corner. Katsuro rubbed his shoulders to calm him down. "Just remember all I have taught you. Use your hands to protect and attack. Use your legs as a whip, to drive him to the mat. Use your instincts to fight as a fighter should."

The referee called the two to the center of the mat. "Keep the fight honest and clean." Aaron shrugged with an arrogant swagger to hide his nervousness.

His opponent was a head taller. They touched gloves. Aaron strolled back and assumed the fighter's position. The tall kid sent a sharp right jab to Aaron's face. He barely felt it. A leg tackle failed to drop Aaron as he stood squat to the mat. Another right bounced off Aaron's forehead. He felt none of them. *Katsuro said I wouldn't feel any pain. Now it is my turn to attack.*

Aaron sent a powerful kick to the tall kid's middle. He buckled, his head bent forward. Aaron hooked a left to his face and sent the kid to the mat. He pounced on him and drove lefts and rights to his face. "Stop it! I said, stop it."

The referee pulled Aaron up and raised Aaron's hand.

Katsuro rushed to the ring and sent a jarring jab to Aaron's chest that hurt more than all the punches in the ring. "You let him hit you on purpose. Why?"

"To feel somebody else's pain besides yours."

"Did you?"

"No, not really. You hurt worse."

The next day the *Shinai* raised welts on Gian's back. "This, *Juko*, is real pain." Gian barely felt the *Shinai* as it whipped him. *This is a game, Katsuro, and I will win it. Keep the Shinai with its pain, I can handle it.*

The banners filled the arena proclaimed this tournament would determine the United States Martial Arts Team. The announcer strode to the middle of the ring and turned slowly, gazing at the audience. "Ladies and gentlemen, welcome to this wonderful event to select our country's representatives to the World Martial Arts competition. All of our contestants have met the qualifications of entry. They have all won local tournaments and have been selected as worthy contenders. Good luck to them all."

Aaron had been told that Americans trained their fighters using pads, thick mats and thicker gloves. All were trained in American-style dojos with typical American-style training techniques. They were tough but not tough enough.

In this first fight, Aaron fought a tall, well-muscled kid with a football player's neck. When they met in the middle of the ring, Aaron just stared at his opponent to intimidate him. Aaron made the traditional bow and backed away, but his eyes never left the tall kid.

The kid looked back over his shoulder and felt Aaron's gaze. "*Juko*, hit him hard. He looks like he will simply fall over." Aaron's eyes never left his opponent even as Katsuro gave him advice.

Aaron strolled to the center and continued his stare. They touched gloves and Aaron shot a left hand, striking the kid high on the forehead, and at the same time he moved his left foot under the kid's right ankle and pulled him forward and down. A sharp right hand to the chest found the kid sprawling to the mat. He didn't get up. He just cried.

"Americans are sissies," Aaron muttered under his breath.

The referee awarded Aaron his first point in the competition. A few moments later, the referee raised Aaron's hand. "The winner, Aaron Michaels."

The tournament lasted two days. Gian gained strength and confidence as the fights continued. He fought eight times. Each bout lasted just a few minutes, if that. Katsuro smiled inside. *He is better than these other fighters. He is tougher and better trained. He will qualify.*

* * *

A couple of weeks prior to these trials . . .

Katsuro waited impatiently in the outer office. He twisted in his seat and squirmed. The shadows sat motionless. Katsuro wasn't used to being kept waiting. He looked at the name on the door, Harry Sigrowski, Director; World Martial Arts. President; United States Martial Arts. Katsuro wondered how you could do both. Finally, the hawk-nosed secretary ushered him into the Director's office.

Harry Sigrowski was outfitted in full martial-arts dress. His *gi* was extra white. The black belt that tied the gi was covered with travel badges—sewn in. His hair was cut very short, topping a square face marked with years of battle. "Mr. Tachigi, I am honored to have a protégé of yours trying out for our United States team. This World Federation guarantees your protégé will meet only the finest competition."

Katsuro said, "He is my son and he is the finest fighter your Federation will ever see. But you already know that since you have seen him fight."

"Yes, yes, I have. He is very good, a little ruthless though."

Katsuro shrugged off the negative observation. "Would you rather have a fighter who hasn't got that killer instinct?"

"No, I would rather have a fighter who displays respect for his opponents, something your son does not always display."

"My son understands how good he is. Being a confident fighter does not mean he lacks respect for his opponents."

Harry tightened his cloth belt. It felt snug on his flat stomach. Harry knew this was Japanese swagger. The Japanese felt they were the best fighters and resented others who thought otherwise. "I will have his coach teach him more respect for his teammates, if he makes the team."

Katsuro straightened in his chair. "I am sorry, sir. I am his only coach. No other person has ever coached him. No other person ever will. *That* must be understood."

"It certainly is not understood. We train our own fighters with the finest teachers in the business."

Katsuro rose slowly. "Let me say this, Mr. Sigrowski, Gian is well beyond what your teachers can teach him. He is superior to any member of your staff already—even at the age of 18."

"Which means, Mr. Tachigi that you know more than any of my teachers. Correct, Mr. Tachigi?"

Katsuro smirked. "Correct."

Harry studied this old man. How old was he? In his seventies? Harry pressed the communication key on his desk, "Miss Finkel, send in Mr. Morrow, now."

Momentarily, a stocky, broad-shouldered, crew-cut young man in his twenties bounded into the room. "Yes, Mr. Sigrowski, you need me?"

"Yes, Mr. Morrow, I need you to demonstrate your routine to Mr. Tachigi. He has some doubt about our training ability."

Mr. Morrow took his stance and went through a series of very impressive, but standard martial-arts moves. The routine amused Katsuro. He removed his jacket and hung it neatly on the back of his chair. He removed his shirt displaying his tattoos and kicked off his shoes. He stepped in front of Mr. Morrow and in his shadow imitated his routine. He then looked at Mr. Morrow. "A quick self-defense lesson, please, Mr. Morrow." Katsuro took his stance.

Mr. Morrow stared down at the old man who was challenging him. "You kidding me, old man?"

"Katsuro never kids about a challenge."

Without another word, Katsuro sent a powerful kick to Mr. Morrow's knee, lurched forward, and drove a sharp elbow into Morrow's shoulder. Katsuro's knee met Mr. Morrow's face and he fell off balance. Mr. Morrow tumbled to the floor, his shoulder dislocated. Katsuro stepped next to the prone figure and with medical hands adjusted Mr. Morrow's shoulder with a loud snap.

Harry had left his seat and rushed to his fallen teacher. "You okay, Mr. Morrow?"

Mr. Morrow wasn't sure. He had pain in his shoulder and a painful bruise on his left knee. His face was already swollen from the blow. He arose slowly.

Katsuro dressed. "As I said, nobody teaches my son except me. As long as we have that agreement, we can continue."

Sigrowski was torn. He had just seen his best teacher reduced to a bruised warrior; yet he admired the old man for his technique. At the same time, he hated his arrogance. "Mr. Morrow, go get an X-ray."

Without saying a word, Mr. Morrow left. Harry stood behind his desk. "You attacked him unfairly. He did not deserve that."

"A good soldier is always ready for battle, always ready."

"What do you want, Mr. Tachigi, now that I know what I'm dealing with? What do you want?" Harry's voice quivered in anger.

Katsuro leaned forward in his chair. "I want to invest in your athletic group. I want to donate money to the United States Martial Arts Team."

Harry was taken aback. "Are you talking about buying your son a place on this team, Mr. Tachigi?"

"No, Mr. Sigrowski. I am talking about guaranteeing that this United States Team has enough money to compete all over the world. And you, sir, know you need money to continue in this competition.

My son will make this team because he is the best fighter and he deserves to make this team."

"How much are we talking about, Mr. Tachigi?"

"Enough to make sure this team competes in all the world tournaments in a competitive manner."

"And what else do you want, sir?"

Katsuro knew he had struck a financial nerve and could get whatever he wanted. "I will be the only instructor for my son. I will travel with the team, but my son and I will travel first class. I will be an official of the team and be allowed to attend all bouts freely."

Harry didn't know what "freely" meant, and he didn't care at that moment. He had the finances he desperately needed. "Mr. Tachigi, I will provide you with a report stating our financial needs for the year through our accounting firm. I will put you in their capable hands. Thank you, sir, for your generous offer. On behalf of the Board of Directors, we accept."

"A financial report is not necessary." Given his checkbook by a shadow, Katsuro scribbled his signature on a check and handed it to Mr. Sigrowski. One hundred thousand dollars was cheap to pay for guaranteed acceptance. *This is what money is all about: power.*

Later that day, Katsuro gave the World Martial Arts contract and written pledge to Gian to read. "Read this carefully, especially Section A, Paragraph 3, so you understand how important it is. You need to be clean of drugs and stimulants. Since you know I have injected you with a growth hormone for several years, you need to cleanse your body of any impurities, any residue. It is two days before the trials. Drink this."

Katsuro handed Gian a gallon of light-orange fluid. Drink this. Drink every drop. Half today, then finish it tomorrow morning. Start now."

Gian poured out a glass of the concoction, took a mouthful, and swallowed. He gagged.

"I said drink, not gag. Drink!"

"I have the right to know what I'm drinking."

"Vinegar and apple cider diluted with water. That will clean you good."

Forced with drinking that quantity of foul liquid, Gian thought this was the worst of all the abuse he had suffered. *Your mind will allow you to do anything. Just do it.* With the first smell, the first taste, the first swallow, Gian went into his survival mode. He learned very quickly to hate this concoction.

Almost always, well before a fight, Gian had to drink that drink. Whenever he was tested, he always peed clean. When he didn't drink the drink, he knew Katsuro had paid somebody else to give a sample for him. Tests were random, but Katsuro always seemed to know when they would need that random sample.

Gian was always clean, officially.

Gian thought he had made the team but there was a lingering doubt nestled in his head. Katsuro had tried to relieve his worry but to no avail. Gian needed the letter of confirmation from the committee. It came a month after the trials. Katsuro saw the heading on the envelope and gave it to Gian. He had made the team.

Gian's swagger grew. His arrogance and self-confidence swelled. In this respect, he was just like Katsuro. Now his summer was set. He and his team would travel all over the world.

Different from the local tournaments he had participated in beginning at age 12, the USMA Team traveled and contested against the best martial-arts experts in the world, men from age 18 through 26. Up to this point in his career, Gian had never lost a bout. He usually defeated his opponent very quickly, as Katsuro always ordered him to do.

This day was another one of those milestones in Gian's life. The letter changed how Gian saw himself and how the Tachigi family saw him forever.

Gian was a member of the USMA at the age of 15. Since a fighter couldn't be on the team until they were 18, Gian's forged birth certificate was his entrée into another phase of his life at a very young age.

* * *

Seven members of the Tachigi family were doing their daily routine in the dojo when Gian entered. His small frame, 155 pounds at five-feet-nine inches, as measured by the USMA, was well muscled. He carried himself with that haughtiness he had learned by decisively defeating everyone he fought. Being raised Japanese by a man like Katsuro, he had assumed their sense of superiority in martial arts. His self-esteem grew even more when he received the letter of acceptance. *I can beat anybody.*

On this warm Southern California spring day when he entered the dojo, the family stopped their workout as soon as they saw him. As if by a signal, they stood. Only Ryuu approached him with his usual sneer. "You think you're some sort of fucking god just because you made this team? You're still a piece of shit to me."

Gian had heard those words and much worse throughout his young life, but they stung strongly at that moment. His sense of pride in making the team overwhelmed him. Usually, he kept himself under control, but not this time. Fifteen years of anger burst forth in a torrent of rage at a level he had never experienced before.

Gritting his teeth and spitting out his words rapidly, Gian hissed, "Step on the mat with me, Ryuu, and I'll show you what I got." Dressed in his *gi*, barefooted as always, Gian motioned with his fingers for Ryuu to come at him.

Ryuu's insolent smirk turned to a fierce grin he had shown many times, but now, with even more intensity. Ryuu waved to his brothers and children to gather around the mat to watch.

Katsuro took a seat near the corner of the mat, placed the *Shinai* across his lap. This was an encounter he had expected for some time and that time had arrived. Gian felt the rush of hatred. His heart raced.

With his brothers and several of Katsuro's grown grandchildren watching, Gian lashed out at his Japanese tormentor. With fists cocked and limbs flexed, he attacked with astounding ferocity.

Gian drilled a right hand into Ryuu's chest, taking his breath away. Ryuu blocked a left-footed kick to his head only to have Gian twirl through the air and with his right foot blast a deadly kick to Ryuu's temple. With every blow, years of anger were unleashed.

Ryuu tumbled to the mat half-conscious. Teddy, ten years older than Gian, attacked Gian from his blind side. He pinned Gian's arms with his arms and drew back to crack his back. Instinctively, Gian dropped to his knees as he delivered a sharp elbow to Teddy's stomach, knocking out his breath. Gian stood, whirled, and grabbed Teddy's head, bringing a devastating knee to his face, spraying blood all over the mat.

Gian sneered in contempt for the fallen. Every blow felt more rewarding than anything he had ever done. As Yukio sent a sledgehammer blow to Gian's middle, Gian took Yukio's arm, flipped him to the mat, and stomped on his face while pulling his shoulder from its socket.

Still game and filled with revenge for his pummeling, Ryuu smashed a strong right hand to Gian's jaw. The man-child never felt it. He only saw the man he hated before him. Gian drove his right foot into Ryuu's knee, sent a devastating left hook to his neck, and then dropped his other knee into Ryuu's throat as he crumbled to the mat. It was just like he had practiced on the wooden figure with the circled marks on the spots that, when struck, could render a person useless. He punished Ryuu, almost killing him.

The grandchildren, four of them, dove at Gian as one. With his bare feet planted firmly on the mat, Gian felt none of their blows. Yet Gian's arms and feet were a blur. He fended each blow while in a world of ecstasy. His fists connected on faces unseen. His ears heard the moans and the crunching bones.

Each grandchild fell to the mat moaning. Each held a broken part of his body. Haro, an old antagonist, was writhing in pain. Only the man-child stood. Gian towered over the fallen gloating, "Come on, you sons-of-bitches, get up and fight some more."

Katsuro looked on with despair at his fallen children and grandchildren and remained in his chair, stunned. Even he could never have imagined this devastating carnage. His eyes swelled with fear for his family and pride for what his protégé had done.

"That is enough. Stop the fighting. I have seen enough. Gian, go to your room. That is enough work for today." Katsuro said firmly

Finally Michael spoke. He had watched the fight but had not participated. "Katsuro, what did you expect? You made this child into a fighting machine. He is not a man! He is a robot! He is a machine scripted to fight, maim, and maybe kill. He feels no pain. He inflicts pain. You have made him what he has become. This is what you got."

Katsuro could only sit and nod.

Gian stood resolute staring at his family. His voice was strong and filled with conviction, "You, all of you, are very lucky I didn't try my hardest. I could have killed any one of you, all of you. But I let you live because I wanted you to know I am the best fighter in this family. Not one of you can defeat me. Not one. Not even Katsuro."

Gian gazed at the figures still down on the mat. Each suffered such severe damage they would not fight for many months. The marks on their bodies were signs of hatred fulfilled.

Gian returned to his room, found Dog sitting on the couch, and rubbed his head gently, saying, "I beat them all Dog—badly." He showered. The water never felt so good.

None of the family ever sparred with Gian again.

CHAPTER NINETEEN

UNITED STATES MARTIAL ARTS TEAM

There were two different fighting styles in the tournaments: Stand Up (kick and punch) and Olympic-style Kwando (kick, punch, hit, and fight on the mat.) Gian fought using all the maneuvers and competed in both fighting styles.

The tournaments ran three days. The first two days were devoted to team competition and the third to individual honors. The team with the most points was declared the winner. The United States team was not very good. But because Gian won all his fights, he competed on the third day.

Gian faced his toughest opponent in Germany. It was early July, the middle of the World Tour. Gian Aaron Molina lay in his bed at the GHOTEL near the Olympic Village district of Munich. The rest of the team stayed at the Mercure Hotel. Gian and Katsuro rarely stayed with the team. Since Katsuro financed these trips, he got what he wanted, and he wanted luxury. He wouldn't spend much money on food, but he insisted on staying in the best hotels. Katsuro and Gian partnered in everything during their travels. True to his request, Katsuro was the only one who trained Gian.

The USMA Team didn't like Katsuro, and most of them didn't like Gian either. "Too arrogant!" "Mean!" "Not a team player!" The team members whispered those words (and others) behind Gian's back. He was almost always alone.

The USMA team was being beaten by the German team, which was composed mostly of older, more experienced, and more technically adept fighters in their twenties. Gian had won his first two fights but would now face the oldest and most skilled member of the German team, Adolph Waechter, whose surname means "the warden." Adolph had watched the American team carefully. Now he leaned against a punching bag, tapping it lightly while talking to his teammate. "You see that skinny, muscular kid? The one with the shock of hair and meanness written on his face? They tell me he's the best on this American team. I want to fight him. I want to knock that smirk off his face."

"Yeah, I watched him, too. He's quick, Adolph. Very quick. He might out-point you."

"Quick, yes, but with just one blow I'll nail him. Did you know he's a Jew?"

"A Jew? He's with that old Japanese man all the time. I heard that guy raised him. A Jew? Are you sure?"

Adolph shrugged his shoulders. "I heard it from their team manager. He's a Jew all right. We didn't get them all when we should have. I'm going to get this Jew."

"The war ended a long time ago, let it go."

Adolph grabbed his teammate. "You let it go, asshole. It still lives with me."

Sipping their Cokes, Gian and John (his only friend on the team) sat in the bleachers just off the main fight area. "I thought the crowds in Korea were big. They have almost a full house here," John said.

"Ed says there are more than ten thousand people here."

"Really?" The crowd rose to its feet as the German fighter was declared the winner. "We are getting an ass-kicking today. These guys are older and tougher," John said. "Hey, isn't that Katsuro waving his hands on the far side of the mats."

"Yeah, I wonder what his problem is. I don't fight for two more fights."

"You better go down and see what he wants." John drew in his breath. "He can be rather demanding."

"Hey, you sound just like my English teacher. Okay, Katsuro, I'm coming." Gian waved back at him.

Gian jogged over to his *Master*. Katsuro was angry. Gian knew if they were alone, he would feel the wrath of the *Shinai*. "This German guy is tough. You need to stretch and get mentally prepared. Just because you are more skilled than he is doesn't mean you don't prepare properly. Get ready!"

Gian walked to the far side of the arena and down the corridor to the training area. The tunnel was only semi-lit. Gian did not see the shadowy figure standing in the tunnel's exit as it opened to the training area. Adolph stood blocking the entrance to the stretching room. "Where you going, dirty Jew boy? You thinking you're gonna beat me? Well forget it. I'm going to beat your ass until it's pulp," Adolph said in broken English.

Gian looked up at the giant standing before him, not recognizing him. "Move, big guy. Let a real fighter get by."

The German laughed. "You piss-ass, shithead. I should take you apart right here."

Gian stepped back a few feet to get a better look at the bearded face. Then he smiled, sneered, and spit at the giant. He stepped forward, driving his heel into the big man's ankle. The German shook his leg and winced. Gian darted by, but not before the German drilled a sharp elbow into Gian's shoulder. Gian sent a short leg kick to the back of Adolph's left leg. A short right hand crushed against Gian's face.

Ed Riso left the training room and was preparing to watch the next fight when out of the corner of his eye he saw the two combatants. "What are you doing, Aaron? This is no place to fight."

"Get him away from me, Ed, he's a dirtbag. He trapped me here to call me a dirty Jew. I have no idea what he's talking about."

"You, move away. I don't like my fighters being threatened, ever. Get out of here."

Ed watched as the bulky German walked off, turned quickly and shouted, "I'll see you in the ring. No mercy, Jew boy!"

Ed Riso, himself a large man and a former world champion, patted Gian on the back and stayed to watch him work out and stretch until Katsuro arrived. Ed explained to Katsuro what had happened. The old man shrugged. "That should make the fight more interesting."

The interesting fight was up next. Gian sat next to Katsuro. "Listen to me, boy. This guy is very big, but you can outpoint him. Stay away from him. Punch and run. Hit and retreat. Score points. Move quickly. Stay away from him. There is a time to fight and there is a time to fight and run. Winning takes many forms. This is one of those times."

Gian, a teenager and full of himself, listened half-heartedly, and mostly tuned Katsuro out.

Suddenly, Gian realized this German giant could kill him. He was back in the hallway where the German had attacked him. Gian felt like a dwarf, small and thin, a midget next to a monster. For the first time he felt vulnerable. He was scared. Why? He trembled.

Katsuro touched his protégé. "*Juko*, what's the matter?"

Gian would never let Katsuro in. "Nothing, I'm fine. Let me alone."

Katsuro sensed Gian was a bit awed by the size of the German. Katsuro stared at his son. "Let me tell you a story:

"*Juko*, there are three types of guys in this world. The first type says, 'I am going to climb the mountain.' And he does. He gets his ass kicked all the way up and he gets his ass kicked all the way down. He stands at the side of the mountain and screams at his friend, 'It was rough; it was brutal; but I made it. What a sense of accomplishment I have.'

"The second guy looks at the first guy, looks at his buddy, looks at the mountain, and sees a road. He takes the road. The road is clear and quick. When he gets back, he tells his friend, 'I took the road and it was much simpler. We're both in the same spot. We both succeeded. Take the road,' he tells the third guy.

The third guy looks at the mountain, puts his hands on the mountain and pushes it out of the way. 'I'll just push it aside.'"

Katsuro said, "Willpower can do anything. You have to choose to succeed."

The ring announcer bellowed out Aaron's name. "In the United States corner, wearing red, blue, and white trunks, Aaron Michaels. For our German team, the 'Monster Man,' in green trunks, Adolph Waechter."

Aaron turned to Katsuro. "He's going to kick my ass."

Katsuro turned in a sudden outburst of fury and smacked Aaron on the side of the head. "Don't ever say that. You are going out there, and you are going to do what you have been trained to do. Move that mountain!"

"Okay!" Aaron took a deep breath and came out when the bell rang. In his stand-up position, Aaron advanced to the center of the ring. The German, muscular, powerful, and eager for revenge, speared Aaron with a right. The punch stung, but nothing like the left cross that landed solidly on Aaron's temple and sent him sprawling to the mat. Gian stared up at the giant and saw the mule that had just kicked him. The blow was just that—a mule kick. Aaron shook the cobwebs clear. "Oh my God!" He rose slowly.

Katsuro yelled, "Get up, get up, get up!"

Aaron stood and backpedaled. The German, smiling through his mouthpiece, strutted forward. He swung but Aaron ducked under his blow. Aaron sent a right jab to the German's middle. Aaron danced backward. "You son of a bitch. Wait until I get you."

The referee took a point away from the German for unsportsmanlike conduct. The bell rang for the end of the first of three two-minute rounds.

Katsuro sponged his protégé with water and gave him a drink. "You are losing. You need to move faster. Jab, jab and run. Kick and run. Kick, pull him forward and collide with him. Push off and collide. Accumulate points. Technique wins. Use your speed. He's slow."

The bell rang and Katsuro pulled the chair from Aaron. "Kick and run." This time Aaron listened to survive. The German whipped a kick to Aaron's right leg. Aaron side-stepped the kick and whipped his right leg across the German's leg and the giant stumbled back. Aaron unleashed a hard kick to the right leg again and the German fell to the mat.

Aaron waited for the German to get up. When he did, he charged forward in fury, drove a sharp painful jab into Aaron's tender shoulder. Aaron grabbed his shoulder for a second, then drove a left hook to the bearded giant's midsection, followed by a knee into his right thigh. Adolph was wounded. He hobbled back. Gian knew he was even more dangerous now. Aaron continued to back step. As the German attacked, Aaron punched and ran.

The bell rang. Aaron turned to go to his corner. The German brushed by him and spit on his shoulder. "That shoulder is a wounded buffalo. I will hunt it down."

Katsuro washed Aaron down and pressed on the shoulder. "That was better, *Juko*. Hit and run. You have no pain. You feel no pain. Clear your head of pain. It doesn't exist." Katsuro massaged the shoulder and gave it a little jerk. "Remember, kick and get out. Don't stand and punch with him. Beat him, *Juko*."

They touched gloves and Aaron began his dance. Punch and run. Kick and run. The giant, frustrated and realizing he was losing the fight on points, nailed Aaron into a corner. He grabbed the smaller fighter and gave him a bear hug, driving his elbow into Aaron's shoulder. "Break it up, guys!," yelled the referee.

Slow to respond, the giant massaged his elbow into Aaron's shoulder and then broke. Wincing in pain, Aaron jabbed and ran. The giant ran at him and Aaron drove another knee into the German's thigh. The giant fell to the mat in agony. Aaron wanted to leap on the fallen fighter but was held back by the referee. His mind cleared in that instant. *This is not Kwando, Gian. Stand and fight. Kick and fight.* The fight ended as the bell rang.

The referee raised Aaron's hand. The German said, "See you tomorrow!"

Katsuro may have been a sadistic bastard, but he knew what to do to protect Gian. They walked back to the GHOTEL. "That guy doesn't like me, Katsuro. He fights dirty. My shoulder aches."

"I'll take care of the shoulder and you will fight that guy again, but I'll take care of everything."

"What does that mean?"

"It means, I will take care of everything."

Katsuro leaned toward Gian over dinner and said, "We need to have a special training session in our room tonight. I need to teach you a maneuver I have never shown you before. It is time for you to learn a Grand Master move."

Later, in their room, Katsuro showed Gian a move he would rely on many times to disarm an opponent and shut him down. Katsuro was his subject as Gian drew Katsuro near unconsciousness.

The next day the winners and best fighters from each team were in the arena. John sat next to Gian. "You going to fight that guy again?" Gian shook his head. "Why? He's bigger and older than you. He'll hurt you."

"Naw! Katsuro talked to the German coach and they agreed we would fight Kwando."

"Kwando? Why?"

Gian patted John on the leg. "Watch my friend. I am going to beat his ass."

The bearded giant stood at the far end of the ring and leered at Aaron. "That little shit. I'm going to beat him up good!"

Aaron smiled. "Katsuro, we have already lost the team championship to the German team, so this bout is just an exhibition, right?"

"Right!"

Gian pounded his lightweight gloves together. "Only an exhibition. Good!"

They settled into the center of the ring: the giant and the Jew. Aaron sent a jarring right to the middle of the German. His leg whipped the giant's right leg again and again with such quickness and ferocity that Adolph was unprepared for. Pain shocked the giant's leg. He limped backwards.

Aaron dropped to the mat and leg-tackled the bearded one. The giant dropped to the mat. Aaron sent a devastating right foot into his face, got up from the mat, and dropped a knee directly onto his right shoulder.

Again Aaron stood, and like a lightning bolt, dropped his knee into the giant's shoulder. The referee stepped next to Aaron. "Young man, that is an illegal move. I am taking two points away from you."

The referee went to the giant and talked to him. "You okay to continue?"

"Let me at that son-of-a-bitch!" The German struggled to his feet. The referee waved the fighters on.

Aaron sent a left leg into the thigh of the German. The sound could be heard throughout the arena. The giant grunted and limped backward. Aaron leapt after him. Once again Aaron dropped to the mat and leg whipped the German. Like a tree being cut down, Adolph fell. Gian fell on him and sent a powerful series of rights and lefts to the giant's face. Gian gripped the monster-man in a half-nelson and placed his other arm around his neck. Gian then flexed his massive biceps and pressed against the giant's carotid artery. The German fell limp. "Ring the bell. This man is disqualified!" shouted the referee.

The bellicose audience greeted Aaron as he left the ring.

Katsuro never, ever, said another word about that fight. He saw the Gian he wanted him to be, the Gian he had raised and trained.

John was horrified. He sat transfixed; yet he understood. Gian had been disqualified for breaking the rules of Kwando. Gian did what he had to do.

*   *   *

It was winter. A chill set over the usually warm climate of the San Fernando Valley, a suburb of Los Angeles. Hermansol, Katsuro's and Rita's fourth child, a noose around his neck, eyes bulging, face blue, swinging gently from the olive tree in front of the family house. A ladder lay on the ground. A note was attached to the third rung by a long string. The family stood speechless looking at the lifeless body suspended by the rope that extinguished his life. Katsuro was in the dojo working out. Rita called her father to come to the front of the house. Katsuro stood next to the fallen ladder. He looked up at his son, shook his head and said, "Cut him down."

Katsuro returned to the dojo. Rita picked up the ladder and set it against the tree. "Gian, get a knife so I can cut him down." Gian ran to the kitchen, pulled a butcher knife from a wooden block, ran back, and handed the steel blade to Rita. The rest of the family stood motionless. The blade sliced through the rope and the body plunged to the gravel below. Mother Rita cut the small string on the ladder and pocketed the note.

She called the police and the fire department, as her daughter told her to do. Teddy walked away. "Hermansol was gay. It was best he killed himself. He has already disgraced the family."

The two Ritas attended the funeral. They were the only ones. Rita Sr. took the handwritten note from her dress pocket and read it out loud, "You will no longer have me around to disgrace our family name. I am who I am, and I am sad you could never accept me for being me. I leave this world, knowing your life will go on as always. Forgive me. Goodbye."

There was no signature. She folded the note and placed it back in her pocket. *What a waste of life!*

* * *

It was a Sunday several weeks later, when the family, all fifteen of those who lived in the Los Angeles area, had gathered in the living room for a family meeting. For one of a few times in his life, Gian was allowed into the house for this gathering.

Not many people ever came to the family compound. So it was a surprise when they heard the doorbell ring incessantly.

A servant approached Katsuro. "There is a young lady at the front gate who insists on coming to see you, sir. Shall I let her in?"

Katsuro waved at the servant to let her enter.

A loud female voice echoed through the chambers of the mansion. Her words resonated off the tile floor. "I want to see that son-of-a-bitch. I'm pregnant! Where is he?"

A distraught servant came into the living room. "I'm sorry, sir, but she just . . ."

"It's all right. Bring her in."

The servant ushered a pretty Anglo woman into the large room. Her eyes quickly searched the room and found Yukio. "You miserable bastard. I'm pregnant. What are you gonna to do?"

Yukio didn't even look at her. He simply waved at the family. They all rose and left the room. Yukio's wife walked over to him, stopped, looked up, and said, "Do what you must!"

Gian turned to leave but Yukio called to him, "Gian, you stay. I might need you. Come over here."

"Listen carefully. This is how we deal with a problem."

The near empty room made the girl tremble. She was visibly shaking when Yukio walked up to her. He placed his hands on her shoulders and spoke softly. "You have invaded our house; nevertheless I'm going to tell you what I will do. You have two choices. The first is very simple. I will give you twenty-five-thousand dollars cash and put you in a hotel for a week. Then I'm going to give you another twenty thousand dollars after you have your abortion. You will never see me again, never speak to me again."

The girl, her face suddenly full of color and flushed with excitement said, "I don't want that. I love you."

"Okay, here's your other choice. My nephew will hold you while I kick you in the stomach so you will never have this child or any other ever again. So those are your choices." Yukio's voice was matter of fact. His words were clear and precise and calm.

The girl went pale. Her shoulders slouched and her head bowed. She began to tremble. She knew he would do it. She knew it.

"You have one minute to make your decision." Yukio peered at his watch.

Gian was shocked. Even in his ultra-violent world, to pick on an innocent girl like this made him feel sick. His breathing became uneven for the few seconds that the girl took to utter her words.

She muttered her decision so softly that she had to repeat them so both men could hear her clearly. "I'll take the money!"

Yukio stepped back. "My representative will call you after he arranges for your abortion. You will never contact me or any member of my family again. Is that clear?"

She nodded.

"Give all your information to my servant." Yukio called for the servant and gave him his instructions.

After she left, Gian stood next to Yukio and said, "I can't believe you said that to her."

Yuen looked at Gian, "You would have held her." And the fifteen-year-old Gian knew he would have had to. This was another reason to hate this man.

Gian knew what he had always known, Yukio was cold darkness. He had never shown any regret or remorse. He was deadly.

* * *

Gian was in San Diego representing the USMA Team. After he beat the German and fought in London against the street fighters, Gian had hardened. At 15, he had turned to open rebellion against Katsuro and the family. Beatings were no longer a threat to him. When Katsuro did beat him, Gian would laugh at the thrashing. "I am your robot, Katsuro. Beating me does no good. I am already programmed to do your work, the work your other sons couldn't do." Gian had already beaten many full-grown men. He was a proud bad-ass.

To show off his independence, he failed to follow the protocol of the matches. He didn't bow. He didn't have any respect for his opponents. "Why should I? I am better than they are. I can beat them all, and they know it."

"One day you will be a professional. You will be fighting the best in the world and you must follow protocol as a fighter. Otherwise, you will be a non-entity in the fight game."

"Is that all you care about, Katsuro? The game? I am better than they are, so my games go on. And, when and if I do become a pro, I will make so much money I won't have to listen to you, ever."

Katsuro slapped the *Shinai* across Gian's face. Gian wiped the blood away. "I will never hit you back and you know it, because that would mean stooping to your level. Hit me if you will, but I will feel no pain." Gian growled his words in defiance.

Gian walked away turning his back on his mentor. The old man's shoulders slumped. He said nothing. He just remembered Michael's words: *You made a robot of him. You turned him into something almost non-human. That is what you wanted and that is what you got.*

*   *   *

Madame Sung sat at the corner of the bleachers watching her fighters compete, but her eyes wandered to the muscular specimen sitting next to Katsuro. For years, she and her husband had taught the finer techniques of martial arts using several forms. When one of her fighters finished his bout, she walked over to Katsuro to say hello. He had barely acknowledged her in the past, but she wanted to talk to his fighter. "Mr. Tachigi, it has been a long time. You are looking well." Katsuro, who never made small talk, looked up at her, annoyed, and went on wrapping Gian's hands.

She sat there, silently. Gian got up when his name was called, and she watched the fight in silence while Katsuro acted as his second.

Gian did what he had gotten used to doing: not show any respect for his opponent. When they raised his hand as the winner, Gian returned to the bleachers to get his gear. Madame Sung grabbed his hand, "You have the tools to be a great fighter, but you will never be one, you will never be a great fighter as long as you listen to him."

Katsuro glared at her. "You old witch, you virgin mother, never speak to my son again."

"I don't know what you are teaching him to do, because he is not respectful, not honoring his art. This is as much about art as it is about fighting. We give a show for people who come to watch this. He needs to respect and show the beauty of this culture, its art, its visual forms in each style. All you give him is the art of a pit bull and the ability to hurt people."

"I won." Aaron grinned.

"But what did you win? You didn't win respect. You didn't win anything but people fearing you. Okay, so they fear you. So what? They know you are a bad-ass. You beat that man, my son. You knew you would win before you came to this tournament. This was a walk for you. But you really didn't win. You got a trophy that goes into a box. Good luck with that."

Madam Sung's words haunted Gian. *You didn't win respect.*

CHAPTER TWENTY

A LESSON

Katsuro placed the phone on its base. "Gian," he called from his office in the dojo. "On Friday, we are going to visit the software company I just bought called RedMark. I want you to see how I work with them."

Gian didn't miss a beat as he tattooed the punching bag, skipped rope, and did pushups. "Why am I going?"

"You will do as I tell you. You are going. You will listen and learn."

Periodically, Katsuro took Gian on business trips with him. Katsuro, always the teacher, took these opportunities to show Gian the superiority of Japanese culture and Japanese life. It was important to Katsuro that Gian, an Anglo, be taught more than just fighting skills: he needed a sense of pride in the culture within which he had been raised.

RedMark employees had been instructed to attend a business meeting to greet their new owner. It was Katsuro who sent a very strong memo to the CEO urging him to set up a meeting with all the employees. It was the president, however, who had founded the company, who was curious about the request, so it was he who arranged the compulsory meeting.

RedMark was a small company with about 150 employees. Gian sat with Katsuro on the dais and watched as every employee received an envelope as they entered the room. The instructions were clear, DO NOT OPEN.

The CEO introduced Katsuro, who spoke about himself and how he runs a company. "I believe that no member of our company team is any more valuable than any other member. That is why all members of this organization shall be treated with the same respect as every other member. Therefore, no one is better than the next person. You are all cogs in the same wheel. To be part of that wheel you must understand what part of the cog you drive. Who is the lowest person on the totem pole in this company?"

A janitor raised his hand. "How long have you been with this company?" Katsuro inquired.

"Six going on seven years."

"Then you are not the lowest person on the totem pole."

Another man raised his hand. "I have been here for two months."

"Stand up, sir, and open your envelope." The man took out a $50 bill. "Now, all of you open your envelopes." Katsuro waited until all the envelopes were open and the buzz had quieWil down. "Your CEO has $50, like everyone else in this room. Business is a pyramid. The strongest pyramids have the widest base. But every once in a while, the president has to invert that pyramid and be strong enough to stabilize the company on his shoulders. Everybody is important. The janitor is important because we all need a clean environment. Welcome to you all. It is good to be here."

Polite applause followed Katsuro off the dais and into the President's office. The CEO, the Vice President, and the Director of Human Resources followed. Gian was shocked at what went next. The company president was a mousy, bespectacled balding man in his fifties. Suddenly he began screaming at Katsuro. "I built this company from scratch, from the ground up, and you are telling the employees this bunch of crap. You slimy little turd, never speak like that again to anybody in my company." Gian was shocked at what he heard.

Katsuro rose from his red leather chair, stood quietly, walked a few steps toward the president and pointed his finger at him. "I am going to make you a deal. I will offer you one of two things. First," Katsuro pulled a folder from his briefcase, "I will buy any percentage of equity you have in this company and cash you out of your portion, whatever it is. Or, I will shut my briefcase, we shake hands, and you will trust me. This is all there is to it. I am going to lunch, and I will be back in one hour. You decide."

The two of them sat at the food stalls in a nearby mall. "Have what you want." Katsuro went on without a breath. "Maybe one day, I will buy this mall." Those were the last words Katsuro said during lunch. Gian sat on pins and needles. *What is this president going to do?*

They arrived at the door of the president's office. Katsuro turned to Gian, "What do you think he will do? Do you think he will shake my hand, or take the money and sign the agreement?"

Gian just wanted to burst and blurted out, "He will shake your hand and trust you."

Katsuro smiled, "I will give you 25% of whatever the check is if he doesn't take the money and run. He won't shake my hand. If I am wrong, I will give you the 25%."

"He's going to take your hand, I know it."

In the room, surrounding a large oak table, sat a squadron of lawyers with papers drawn up. "I will take your offer. The asking price is two and a half million dollars. Done?"

They signed the legal papers and Katsuro wrote the check.

"Just a minute, gentlemen. Before you go, let me show you something." Katsuro reached into his briefcase and took out another folder. He placed it on the table. "I will be right back, stay here."

Minutes later Katsuro entered the room with a woman. "This is Gail. Let me tell you what I am going to do. In my right hand is trust. In two years or less, a bigger company is going to buy this company and your interest would have been between five to ten million dollars. I would have made you even more money. All you had to do was listen to me. Instead, what I am going to do is give your job to Gail, because she remained under-budget on her project-manager's job, and she is generally a nice person. Gail, will you shake my hand and trust me?"

The slim, tight-lipped woman took Katsuro's hand. Katsuro turned to the president. "She trusts me, and you didn't. Get your shit together and get out. If I ever see your face around here again, you will regret it."

Gian sat in awe. After the president left, Katsuro took Gail's trembling hand, "I am going to send someone here tomorrow and he will mentor you so you cannot fail. You trusted me, and I am asking you to trust me a little longer."

As they rode off in Katsuro's chauffeur-driven limousine, Gian turned to Katsuro. "Why did you bring me along?"

"Because you have a leg up on Americans. They always think they have to have something in their hands, not in the bush. They are impatient. It is always about what they *have* rather than what they *could* have. You thought out the bigger picture. The CEO didn't. You thought what it would take to get to the next level, for the greater good. Japanese are for the greater whole. You thought about working for the whole. That guy thought about himself. He had no chance of shaking my hand. That American was of a certain generation and all he gave a shit about was himself. You have to understand, you and I are a team. I am giving you invaluable lessons that will make you great. So what do you do with these lessons? You have to trust me that everything I teach you is the gospel truth. It is what is best for you."

Gian looked at Katsuro, "Why are we having this moment? Why are you telling me this? Do you doubt my resolve?"

"There is an old American saying, that you can lead a horse to water but you cannot make it drink—but you can drown the son of a bitch. And, if I have to, I will drown you. I hope you will choose to do it my way. It will be easier for you."

Gian believed in the Japanese philosophy of concern for the greater whole. He also knew he was going to have to do what Katsuro wanted. After all, Gian was a product rather than a member of the family.

Katsuro never saw Gail again. A year later, he sold the company for over ten million dollars.

* * *

It wasn't the first time Katsuro had taught Gian a lesson. As he lay in his room that night after his workout, staring at the ceiling, he wondered if other kids had a teacher like Katsuro. In some respects, he hoped they did, except for the beatings. He respected the way Katsuro stood by his principles, his beliefs, and his philosophy. Gian actually took his mentor's advice and embraced it. In more ways than one he was the product he was supposed to be.

*   *   *

Gian never knew when to expect another lesson about life. They came in clusters, during a workout, during a beating, during a trip.

On the drive to his next tournament, Gian sat next to Katsuro. Margaret sat in the limousine, listening to her Sony Walkman. "Why is she here with us? I really need her for a second?"

"Yes, she was the only one available. You need her for a second." Katsuro paused, thought for a moment, "Gian, did you ever think about what is on the other side of life? What will happen when we leave this earth?"

Gian shook his head. "You must be kidding? I have enough trouble with this life."

Katsuro ignored his protégé's curt remark and went on. "Do you end where you begin or do you begin where you end? You have multiple lives in many existences. In each life, you are meant to understand certain principles before you can go on, or go to wherever you are sent. For instance, you were sent to me. To wherever you are ascending, to whatever you are becoming, you have to learn. I teach you so you can become the best. You are ascending to the upper echelon."

"I understand that, but how do I have multiple lives?"

"You live within the spirit of others and within yourself. Haven't you ever had an experience that you thought you had had once before?"

"You mean déjà vu?"

"Yes, déjà vu. You remembered! Very smart."

Gian smiled inwardly. It was one of the few times Katsuro had complimented him.

"You begin where you end. Each life experience is relearned but in a different form."

"How?"

"On one of your several journeys you might go through the same journey more than once, and you won't understand why. Through your journey you might meet people and know you know them, but you don't remember from where. That is because their paths have intersected with yours. You bring memories with you from every life: everything you have ever endured."

Margaret burst out in song. Katsuro reached across and said, "Young lady, not listening to your grandfather is okay if you wish, but I don't want to be interrupted by that stuff you call music."

"Sorry, Grandfather," her voice had a tinge of sarcasm that Gian would have been beaten for, but Katsuro ignored it.

"Try to remember what you have endured, Gian. But whether you can remember it or not, it still defines who you are. Use all your skills from this lifetime and from your previous ones to advance into the next lifetime. As an example, in America they say, 'He is an old soul.'"

At that moment Gian understood why he was where he was.

Suddenly, he realized he was in his last lifetime and that all his preceding lifetimes had intersected. *Because I have been through past lifetimes, I know I can and will endure this one. This is my final life, the last life I have on this earth.*

I know things "an old soul" would understand. That is the only thing that makes it okay for me. All the things I have dragged from my other lifetimes prepared me for this lifetime. I am meant to teach whatever I can teach and then go wherever I go when I am done. I don't know where I will go, but I will be prepared.

His sense of place was complete. *I believe you make the most you can of your free will. That is the only reason I can make any sense of what has happened to me and be okay with it: the beatings, the mental abuse, the physical abuse, the shit they fill me with, the compassion and love they took from me. It has to be. I hope I'm right. God put me to rest if I am wrong.*

So Gian recalled what he thought of as The Circle of Life Theory that Katsuro had preached to him on many occasions. He believed. He had no choice. It was cope or perish.

CHAPTER TWENTY-ONE

NEW FRIENDS

Gian still lived on the same property with the Tachigi family, but he didn't always train in their dojo. As he passed into his sixteenth year, Gian could sense a small separation from the 88-year-old Grand Master. He had become bored at Carrington High School, because it failed to offer a challenge for him. So he transferred to Century High. That move alone allowed him more freedom. The new high school was farther from the family home and gave Gian the opportunity to train elsewhere, to be away from the house during the day. Katsuro was displeased. He was slowly losing his grip on his protégé.

At his new training gym, Gian met Ted and Phillip. It was Ted he grew closest to: Gian's first real friend. They shared a love for martial arts, camaraderie of boys playing a man's game. Yet Gian could never open up and tell who he was and how he grew up.

Ted wiped the perspiration from his face with a small pink towel. "Come on, Phillip, stop washing all your clothes with the towels. Pink is a terrible color for a man's towel."

"What's the matter, Ted, pink too close to your delicate face turn you into a fairy? Besides, why don't you bring your own towel, like the other guys do? Think about it, Ted, two questions and not one answer from you."

"Two stupid questions. How about you, Aaron? You like pink towels?" Aaron stood at the side of the ring, a white towel draped across his broad shoulders. "Looks good on you, Ted."

"Get off it, you two. At least Aaron does his own laundry, not like you, our great little flower."

Ted perked up. "That right, Aaron? You do your own stuff?"

"Sure, man, and I can cook, too."

Phillip checked in another member to his gym and added, "He'll make a great wife for somebody some day. Not like you, Ted."

Ted walked over to Aaron and sat down beside him on a workout bench. "You know, man. I haven't seen you much around school lately. Where ya been?"

"You got a short memory, man. I enrolled at the JC. I only go to Century two days a week. It's boring for me. I'm taking some college courses for the UC."

"Good idea, man. What time you got for classes?"

Aaron checked his watch. "Holy shit, right now. I'm going to be late. Bad influence hanging around with you guys. So long, Phillip. See you tomorrow. Take care, Ted."

Aaron really wasn't late. He had signed up for two classes and it was the first day of class. It took a little while for the teacher to go over things. Still, he didn't want to be late.

The sixteen-year-old man-child walked into class at the JC. His school records said he was eighteen. He sat down at the front of the class. He had learned this was the best place to sit so he wouldn't get distracted. There he sat stretched out, legs askew, slumped in his seat like a typical teenager.

Catherine Tyler was black, with raven skin, the smile of the *Mona Lisa*, and the determination to succeed like a Jack Kennedy. She had listened to the junior-college school president give his usual canned speech on student needs and academic requirements too many times. She was going to school to become an art appraiser. Teaching gave her the money to pay for her own tuition.

Wearing a gray business suit hemmed just above her elegant knees, and with long ebony hair splashed across her back, she strode into her first class. There in the front row, sprawled across a chair like a blanket, sat Aaron Molina, until he saw her. He had never seen anything, anyone, so beautiful. He shot up, sat straight, and looked attentive.

"Good late afternoon, class. I am Miss Tyler and this is Art History, an overview from the Renaissance to modern art. Please respond when I call your name. It will be the only time I will call roll all semester. You are all adults and you know where you belong each Tuesday and Thursday afternoon at four.

If there was one thing Aaron knew nothing about, it was women. Being violated by Margaret and Yukio led to a fear of sex. Having lived a loveless existence, he was devoid of normal feelings about love. Yet at that moment he felt a peculiar set of yearnings. He only knew he couldn't keep his eyes off this tall, shapely black woman with the face of a goddess.

Catherine surveyed the room. She had used the word adult referring to her class. As she looked down at the hulking, good-looking kid in the first row, she thought she might be wrong in her original remarks. He wasn't well dressed. He had on a tee shirt that accentuated bulging muscles and a well-developed chest. He wore shorts displaying a pair of bulldozer legs, hairy but muscular. But he was handsome in a juvenile way. What was he, 16?

At the end of the class, Gian stayed. He had no idea why he was staying and what he would say, but he had to say something. He stood in front of his seat as the other students flocked out. She packed her lecture notes and tried not to see him, which was difficult, since he was well over six feet tall and broad. "Hi, I'm Aaron. I'm a fighter."

"Hi Aaron, I'm Catherine. I'm an artist. I thought your name was Gian?"

"It is. I fight under the name Aaron."

"Well, it is nice to meet you Aaron. I'll see you back Thursday."

Aaron stuttered, "Y . . . y . . . ou know Miss Tyler, I took your class because I love history. It is fascinating."

"Most kids your age—what is that, 15?—are not all that interested in history. What is the attraction for you?"

"That's two questions in one. "I'm 16 and a student over at Century High. And the reason I like history is I was born here in the US but raised in Japan."

"Well." She stuck out her hand. "I will see you later this week. Don't you have another class now?"

"Yes, yes, I do. See ya."

Aaron couldn't wait until Thursday. He even tolerated a beating by Katsuro with his *Shinai* for being lazy in his workout. "I don't know where your mind is today, but it's not here on what is important. Think! React! And then think no more, only react."

He went to bed thinking about her. "You know, Dog, she is really pretty, not as pretty as you, but really pretty. Catherine Tyler! Catherine Tyler! What a nice name."

Aaron left school at noon like he usually did and headed for Phillip's gym. "Time to train, Phillip. Got to stay in shape."

Phillip nodded to his right. Katsuro sat with his *Shinai* in his lap. "I came over to see what the problem is. Maybe you should be training more at the dojo? Better for your concentration."

"You don't trust me? You don't think I know how to train. I'll be ready for the next tournament. Santa Monica, right?"

"Right, *Juko*. Santa Monica." Katsuro just sat. "I think I will stay for your workout. I haven't seen you do your stuff lately."

Gian worked extra hard. He wanted to impress Katsuro and maybe win that long-desired praise. Sharp and focused, he pummeled the punching bag, bounced with vigor while jumping rope, and did a set of sit-ups with intensity. Gian's real problem was finding a willing sparring partner. They always complained he used too much power and had a killer instinct even in sparring. Phillip walked away one day saying, "You're punching too hard for me. This is supposed to be fun, a workout, not murder."

So this day with Katsuro watching, Gian said, "Ted, come and spar with me." Ted, being a good friend, nodded and got in the ring.

Gian, still intent on showing Katsuro he could be on his own, forgot about "fun" workouts, and sent a bullet to Ted's head and dropped him with a leg drag. "Hey, watcha doin'? This is a workout, not a real fight. Ease up!"

Katsuro appreciated the show and said so. "Good show, *Juko*. But it was only a show. Be ready for this weekend." He left.

Aaron went over to Ted. "Sorry, man. The old guy was upset with me, so I needed to put on a show. I certainly shouldn't have picked on you though."

"It's okay, man. Just give me a warning next time." Ted held an ice pack to his cheek.

*   *   *

Aaron was very early for class. Dressed in slacks, a button-down shirt open at the collar, and dress shoes, he read; or at least he pretended to read the text. He wanted her to be there so he could talk to her. He wondered how old she was. Maybe 21? Maybe? He fidgeted in his seat.

Several students entered the class and walked by the big kid sitting in the front row. Catherine still wasn't there when the clock read four. The guy next to Aaron whispered, "A rule of college is, if the teacher is late by ten minutes we can leave. Check your watch."

Aaron checked the second hand on the clock at the side of the class and prayed it moved slowly. At five after the hour, she strolled in. "Good afternoon, class. Sorry to be late—I had business."

"Let's continue from Tuesday." She rambled on, used a slide show to illustrate the various forms of art, and never made eye contact with Aaron. He was disappointed.

He waited for the classroom to clear. She eyed him. "How are you doing, little boy?"

"I'm okay, old woman. Good lecture today,"

"You would say that even if it wasn't any good."

"No, I'd be honest."

"How does it feel to be in college when you haven't even graduated high school, yet?"

"Better than you could ever imagine. I get to meet people like you."

Catherine blushed. *What is it about this sixteen-year-old kid that I like? He is good looking.* "You went to school in Japan?"

"I did. I lived there for eleven years. Japanese schools are far more advanced than US schools. I skipped junior high because I knew all that stuff."

"You're a smart kid."

Aaron gulped and blurted out, "Why don't you come and see me fight one day? I train over at the Kung Fu Gym, not far from here."

Catherine smiled, "I'll think about it." She started to leave but turned. "By the way, you look good today. I like it when you dress up like a big boy. See ya!"

Dressed as she liked, collared shirt and slacks, Gian would stay and talk to this beautiful black woman after each class. Every time they exchange a few words. Catherine wondered why she was drawn to this kid. She noticed a profound change in his dress, his demeanor, and her interest in him, but mostly she noticed his eyes. Despite all his bluster and youthful charm, she noticed his eyes. They were the saddest eyes she had ever seen, filled loneliness. Those eyes never changed. She knew about sadness and despair.

As the first semester wound down, Gian felt a surge of loneliness. Would he ever see her again? Would she be teaching another class? He checked for the Spring schedule every week. Finally, it arrived. He checked: Art History. Art History. There she was, Catherine Tyler, Art History, Van Gogh to Dégas (1865-1885). He would enroll.

After his final, he sat and waited as he always did for the class to end. "Thank you for a great class. I will see you next semester."

Catherine bit her lip, "No, Aaron, you won't. You are not ready to take this more advanced class. It is too complex for you."

"I'm getting an A in this class. Why is the next one so much different?"

"Because it just is. Take my word for it. It is too difficult!" She saw the sadness in his eyes even more. She had disappointed him. They had become friends over the semester, then she had shattered whatever dream he had. She needed to turn away from those eyes. They haunted her.

"I'm sorry you won't let me take your class. I really enjoyed this one. I'll miss you." The words blurted out. He had never spoken like that before. He felt a knot in his stomach. *Damn!*

She quickly gathered her books and ran from the room and those eyes. Aaron stood alone in the room, a tear trickling down his cheek. He wiped it away, sniffled, and became very angry. He ran from the room; she was not in the hall. He ran to his car, gunned the engine, and drove to the gym. He needed to kick some ass.

Catherine sat in the teacher's room sipping a too-hot cup of coffee, her head down, eyes misty. *What am I doing? I am ten years older than this kid. What am I thinking? I did the right thing. I shouldn't see him again. I won't.*

Catherine tried to work on her new art program, tried to forget the haunting eyes. The image didn't go away. "Okay, Catherine, grow up. What are you thinking about? That child is illegal. You touch him and you could go to jail. You have read about teachers who have had a relationship with one of their students and lived to regret it. Stop those thoughts now." Her voice echoed off the walls of her small apartment. Only the cat, sitting on the back ledge of her couch, listened. "You don't understand me either, do you, Cat?"

"Meow!"

'Good grief. What has happened to my life? I'm talking to Cat as if she's my best friend. Shit! Maybe she is!'

She found the number in the yellow pages. She dialed it, asked her one question, got her answer, and hung up. "This is the end of my sanity."

Cat reclined, stared, and purred, content with its life.

Gian sat alone in the corner of the dojo, daydreaming. "What's the matter, Gian? You look a little forlorn? You hurting?" Margaret asked sympathetically.

He shook his head not wanting to talk.

"Come on, Gian. We have been friends for a long time, you can talk to me."

Nodding, he got up and walked over to the punching bag. She followed. He drilled the bag with a stiff right. It felt good. He always got relief by fighting, by taking out his frustrations in a physical way. Margaret held the bag and felt the power of his punches.

Margaret, too, was feeling her own frustrations. Katsuro had discovered her affair with a Chinese lover. She needed to talk just as much as she knew Gian did.

"You know, Gian, Katsuro is very angry with me. He has forbidden me to see Lee. You remember him? You met him at your last fight."

Gian slammed a hook to the bag and said, "Yeah, I remember him. Nice guy. Katsuro wants to squash all of our affairs."

"What does that mean?"

"It means he wants full control over our lives. He has to be in charge." A right/left combination thundered into the bag. The pounding of the bag went on in silence except for the leather thuds.

"I have been sneaking out with Lee for over a month, but I'm afraid what will happen if Katsuro finds out."

"And you have reason to be afraid. You have seen what he is capable of doing." Gian danced around the bag and went on. "I'd really be afraid for Lee. Does he know about Katsuro?"

"Some." Margaret watched her brother dance and shadow-box. He is still so very young and hurting, but he has been hurt one way or another all his life. She admired his muscular frame. She saw the image of his young body and felt his fear of forced penetration in the communal bath. Every time she entered that bath she thought of him.

"Gian, what do I do?"

Thinking of Catherine, seeing her before him and wanting her, he looked more carefully at the now-grown woman who had raped him, and forgave her. "If this guy, Lee, is up to handling Katsuro, go for it. Getting away from your grandfather is worth it all."

Margaret sighed, ready to accept what she already knew would happen. She would be ostracized from the family if she didn't marry someone Japanese who was from their social class. "And you, Gian, what are you thinking?"

He shook his head. "If I told you, if Katsuro ever found out about this woman, he would do what he always does—stop my life."

"So, is this affair going on now? Did you meet her at school?"

Gian had to laugh to himself. Margaret asked the right questions; *Yes, I met her at school, but she is* **my teacher**. Margaret would be shocked if she knew. He shook his head again in silence. "Margaret, I really don't want to talk about this."

Gian knew even though he could trust Margaret, one slip of her tongue in anger at Katsuro would sink his ship. He saw the way Katsuro ignored Lee, making him feel inferior. He knew what Katsuro would think about Catherine. He wanted to maintain his dream. At sixteen, he needed that dream.

The spring semester had been ongoing for a month. She had seen Gian from afar on the campus. Each time, she remembered his eyes and felt a pang. Each time, she forced that longing out of her mind, but the urges were constant. Her need for love and a sense of belonging were taking hold.

At night she would awaken in a cold sweat from the nightmare that she experienced too often. He was on her. He was tearing her nightgown from her body as she fought him. He pinned her arms back above her head, then mounted her. The first time was the worst. Terrified and ashamed, she felt him push inside her tearing her virginal flesh. The pain was intense. *"Not a word to anyone. I saw you looking at me. You wanted me and now you've had me. Your mother would be ashamed of what you have done."*

"Oh God, father. Why? Why?"

She never said a word. The shame was too much. Her mother would be so upset. She would throw father out, and then where would they be? He had the job, brought in the money, and mother needed him. Catherine would be okay. She wanted her mother to be okay, too.

When, on a late Friday afternoon, father never came home, never called to say he was going to be late, just left without a word, Catherine wept for her mother and cried for her freedom from tyranny and fear. She never saw her father again. He had run away with another woman. A friend of the family told her mother this a month later. Mother and daughter carried on.

In search of love, of someone to care for, Catherine saw those lonely eyes, found her destiny, and fell in love. On a warm Saturday morning she entered Kung Fu. The smell of sweaty bodies filled the room. Martial arts, boxing, wrestling, karate, and any other form of fighting were going on at once.

Phillip saw the tall, slender figure out of the corner of his eye. *They come in all sizes and shapes, but never this nice.* "Can I help you, miss?"

Catherine looked around the gym. She didn't see Aaron. "I'm looking for Aaron Molina, the fighter. I believe his friends call him Gian."

"Yeah, yeah. He's working out in the back room. Practicing some of his take-down moves. Right through that door at the back of the gym."

She strode forward, eager to see Aaron again. Peering through the doorway, she saw his elegant figure wrestling on the mat. "Okay,

Aaron, great move. You really have nailed that drop maneuver. Quick and decisive," Ted praised his friend.

"Let's have a go again."

Aaron took his stance and prepared to attack. His eyes focused totally on his sparring partner. Ted called out directions, "Fake left, drop right, leg whip below the knee. Ready?"

The two men circled each other. Aaron, his mind clear and responsive, followed the move perfectly. The two figures lay on the mat and patted each other. "Thanks, buddy. Good workout."

"Okay, man. I like working out with you. You're really good. I learn a lot from you."

Buddy walked off the mat and turned to Aaron. "I hope she's waiting for me, but I doubt it. I wonder who she is."

Aaron saw Catherine just inside the small gym, watching. He had tried to drive her out of his mind but couldn't. She was still in his thoughts. Only when he worked out did he find relief from his yearnings. He threw a towel over his shoulders and ran toward her. "Hi. I've seen you around campus a few times. How are you?"

"I'm good. Better now that I'm here."

"Why are you here?"

"You know why. The same reason you ran over when you saw me. I missed you."

CHAPTER TWENTY-TWO

CATHERINE TYLER

Ted stood nearby. "You going to introduce me, Aaron?"

"Ted, this is Catherine, a friend of mine."

Catherine stuck out her hand. Ted grasped it. "I am very glad to meet you. I am a friend of Aaron's, too."

Aaron smiled broadly. He loved both these people. That felt very good.

Later, when they were alone, Catherine said, "I packed a picnic lunch for us. I hope you haven't got any plans today."

"I had, but I just changed them. That picnic lunch sounds really good."

Devonshire Park was smack against the San Gabriel Mountains. Gian thought, how beautiful these mountains were. They are like a beautiful woman. He told Catherine his thoughts. "That's what I like about you, Gian; you are so innocent."

"What does that mean?"

She smiled. "It was meant as a compliment. You need to learn so much about life. You're so young."

"Old enough for you to come and see me. Say, how did you find me?"

"Remember, we were talking one day and you said you work out at the Kung Fu Gym. So I looked it up in the telephone book, asked when you worked out, and came over. Aren't you glad to see me?"

"Oh my God, what kind of question is that? I think about you all the time. The best way to get rid of your image is to fight. Last week I thought of you all the way to San Diego, where I was fighting in a tournament. Katsuro—he's my father and trainer—knew I wasn't into the fight. So he promised me a few days off if I won in under a minute, and I did. I had to prove to him he was wrong. I was interested."

"I'm glad you got some time off. When is your next tournament?"

"Next week in Santa Monica."

They ate slowly while talking and relaxing. Gian could not remember when he felt so comfortable with anyone. He was so attracted to this beautiful black woman, he wanted to burst. But now he wanted to grab her and hold her forever. Time slid by, day to evening. "It's getting a little chilly," Catherine said as she crossed her arms and squeezed herself. Gian put his arm around her and drew her close.

"Better?"

"Yes. But I have to get home soon."

"Why not have dinner with me and we can talk some more."

"We've talked all day."

Aaron, socially inept, but too much in love for the first time, couldn't let go. "Come on, I know a great Mexican restaurant in Canoga Park. You'll love the food."

Catherine smiled, shivered, not from being cold but unwilling to let the day go, nodded. "Sure, let's go." She reached for and held his hand as they walked through the park toward his car. "I like Mexican food. I had a friend who used to take me to a very special place near the beach off Topanga."

Gian grasped her hand a little more firmly. He was jealous of this unknown guy. "So now you'll be able to compare places."

It was after eleven when Aaron parked his car in the family driveway, closed the car door quietly, and walked into his house. He flicked on the light and started to go upstairs. "Where have you been, *Juko*?"

Katsuro sat in the darkened room, *Shinai* in hand, fury on his face. Standing defiantly, Gian replied, "Having fun!"

"Having fun at the expense of not training, not working hard, not preparing, is a game that leads to failure."

"Every man needs some time off. Every man needs to have some fun in his life. God knows I've been short-changed."

Katsuro sprung to his feet. "You have a duty to be on time for your sessions to train and stay in shape." He pounded the *Shinai* against the chair. "Have you been out with a girl? Are you wasting your time on some girl who will take you from your destiny, your goal of becoming a world champion?"

"I have a right to be with a person I care about. I have that right. I need that person."

Katsuro walked toward the man-child very slowly. "You have no rights. I have given you everything you need. I trained you. I taught you. I educated you and I own you. You owe me everything."

Gian rolled his fingers together. He wanted to smash this horrible man, club him, and destroy him. *Easy, Gian. Don't be him. He isn't worth it.* "You have always told me to do something to the best of my ability, to be my own man, to react to things: not to think, but react. Well, I reacted to my feelings. I did as you taught me."

Katsuro walked closer to Gian as he stood on the bottom step. "I also told you never to love anything you couldn't give up easily. Love is hard to give up, if not impossible. You were taught to fight without feelings, because feelings limit your ability. If you become involved with somebody, you put that person first. That is what is wrong. You must have a single focus on being the best in the world, and you cannot be the best with distractions. Don't see this girl again. I am telling you, never again. You understand me?" The *Shinai* snapped across the banister and smacked onto Gian's shoulder.

Gian looked at the old man, noticing that his hair was graying slightly and askew for the first time. His twisted smile made him look even more sinister with the *Shinai* raised as if to strike Gian again. "Don't bother, old man. I don't feel any pain, only anger. Go back to your house. I need my rest."

Katsuro knew when a battle needed to be fought and when to withdraw. Now was the time to withdraw and fight another day. He was seething inside. Was he losing his son, his protégé, his world-champion fighter?

Gian slept well that night. He dreamed of a mystical black woman, dressed in a long gown, her black hair blowing in a mysterious wind, calling to him from a grassy knoll: *"Gian, I'm here. Come back to me."*

* * *

The Santa Monica Civic Auditorium was filled to capacity. Each club sat in their respective areas with brightly colored banners held aloft, floating and swaying with family members and friends. The Kung Fu Club sat quietly. Phillip made sure all gloves and equipment were fitted properly, all except those of Aaron Molina, who was being attended to by Katsuro. "You have fought several of these men before and beat them. Now it is time to beat them faster. Give them no hope. Crush this first guy. Take away any of his dreams that he can beat you. Destroy each fighter. You must do this so that when the pro scouts come to look at you they will see a destroyer, not just a battleship."

Gian smiled at Katsuro's metaphor. *Destroyer, indeed. I can be that destroyer.* Katsuro, seeing the smile, poked him hard in the chest. "You are laughing at my message, my words. You don't think they are sincere and needed? You will win quickly and savagely. Punish these men! Punish them!"

*   *   *

She fumbled through her purse, found money, and purchased her ticket. She was nervous and confused. Why was she here? It was her first martial arts tournament. She trembled. She didn't know what to expect. She found a seat in the first row of padded chairs, removed her short brown coat, and placed it on the back of her seat. Two large men, each holding a bottle of Coke, stared at her. "Jesus Christ, Henry, I've just been sent to heaven. I'm gonna have that sitting right in front of me."

"Stop it, George. We came to see our boys, not some tall, beautiful, snazzy black woman. Watch your kid!"

"Who ya kiddin'? That's a piece of meat worth eating."

"Well, just tuck your eyeballs in, or Marian will close them for ya. Here she comes."

Gian hummed softly to himself. Sinatra filled his ears with the smooth, soft melody of "Fly Me To The Moon." His feet moved slowly and rhythmically. Katsuro said nothing. *Every fighter prepares for battle in his own way.* He thought of his father in battle, the great Samurai warrior checking every facet of his gear, stretching,

176

praying to his God, and flexing his muscular frame to intimidate his opponent. Despite all the lectures, beatings, and coaxing, Katsuro could not get Gian to use this same reverent ritual. So Gian danced and sang to the quiet music of the *Great American Songbook*.

She twisted around in her seat looking for Aaron. Not seeing him, she thumbed through the program and finally found his name: Aaron Michaels. Fighting for the Kung Fu Club, Stand Up, Ring 2, at 11:15. She glanced at her watch, 10:50. She gasped as a fighter fell to the canvas after being hit by a straight right leg to the chin.

The fighter fell, his opponent dropped on him, sending wicked rights and lefts to the man's face. After a minute, the referee patted the victorious fighter. The fight was over. Blood streamed from the fallen man's face. She covered her own. She felt the tap on her shoulder. She turned to see a large man with a toothy grin handing her a tissue. "We carry these for those just-in-case-moments. Take it."

"Oh, thank you. It is my first tournament; I guess I have to get used to the blood."

"Well, our boy is fighting next in ring one. Who are you here to see?"

"Oh, Aaron Michaels. He's a friend."

The man drew back. "Yes, a friend." The man swallowed hard. "He's a hard fighter, undefeated!" The man sat back in his seat, the conversation over. The opening smile was now a scowl; his arms were crossed. Catherine didn't understand the man, so she turned around and watched his son win his match, then waited for Aaron.

The fighters came to the middle of the ring. The ring announcer's voice came across loud and clear: "In the green corner, fighting out of the Santa Monica Bay Club, Jess Montez." Heavy applause and whistles followed. "And fighting out of the red corner, representing the Kung Fu Fight Club, Aaron Michaels." A strong mixture of shouts, boos, and catcalls, along with minimal applause, filled the arena. Catherine did not understand why anybody would boo a young fighter like Aaron.

Katsuro rubbed Aaron's back and shoulders out of nervousness. He knew there were several pro scouts in attendance and wanted *Juko* to impress them for a pro contract. After the referee's instructions,

Katsuro whispered into Aaron's ear, "Get rid of him fast. Plenty of pro scouts here. Need to impress them. You can make a lot of money. Get rid of him!"

With his head down and his mind set on being that destroyer, Aaron raced to the center of the ring and waited for his opponent. When the kid met him, Aaron hooked a sharp, powerful left to Jess's middle, and a leg whip followed. Jess tried to block it, but Aaron was too strong. His physical presence dominated.

Jess withdrew in fear. That first blow hurt badly. It took his breath away, and now he felt the sharp, relentless torrent of punishment he had heard Aaron Michaels gave all his opponents. The fear he had tried to talk himself out of before the fight had become a reality.

Aaron sent a sharp jab to Jess's face. He bent down and drove another blistering blow to the downed Jess. A burst of boos shattered the arena. Jess was beaten before the fight was a minute old. The fear Aaron had spread throughout the amateur world of martial arts helped him win another fight.

The referee waved Aaron off. The bell rang and the ring announcer said, "The referee has disqualified Aaron Michaels for fighting after a warning. The winner is Jess Montez." The referee raised Jess's arm. Aaron Michaels waved his hand at the referee in disgust and left the ring. Katsuro smiled, patted Gian on the back. "That should impress the pro scouts. Hopefully, they won't think you should have beaten him even faster." Gian expected Katsuro's words, never a word of praise, but always some comment about what he could have done better.

The man in back of Catherine stood and booed lustily. "You're a dirty fighter, Michaels, a dirty fighter!" Catherine got up to leave shocked by the man's words. "What's a matter, lady? Your friend's a dirty fighter. That's the third time this year he's been disqualified. Find another friend!"

Catherine made her way to the back of the arena and waited outside the dressing room. Several fighters were crowded around, chatting. A heavyset bearded man was talking, "I hope I get a shot at that son-of-a-bitch Michaels. He's a bad ass, huh? Well, so am I. I'll treat him to an old-fashioned beating." The bearded man took out his false teeth and grinned. "He thinks he's tough. I got these knocked out by some bastard in the Houston tournament. Meanest bastard ever. Makes Michaels look like a pussycat."

"Yeah, yeah, sure. He's just a dirty fighter—he shoulda been disqualified."

The bearded man glanced over his shoulder, "See that little bastard? That's Katsuro, Michaels' trainer and father. He's a Grand Master, but power-hungry. He's taught Michaels to be dirty to impress the pro scouts, cuz Michaels will be turning pro soon. Hopefully not before I fight him. I'll beat him good and they'll look at me as a pro."

Catherine heard it all. *They are talking about a sixteen-year-old kid. What are they talking about? He's only sixteen and he's going to turn pro?* She wondered what she was getting herself into.

Then she saw Aaron, different than the shy child she couldn't get enough of. Here, he was a man, tall and strong with huge shoulders, rugged and handsome. She wanted him. It was lust, and she knew it, but she had no control. When she saw him, she was in another world, another life, another place than where she needed to be. He was her destiny.

Katsuro stood next to Gian and talked to two other men. Catherine stood in the corridor leading to the dressing rooms; it was hard to be in the background. There was no place to hide, but Gian's eyes found her. Their eyes met. He waved to her to move back. He mouthed the words, "Wait for me."

She mouthed, "Okay!"

Catherine slipped back down the corridor and disappeared from Gian's view. He became anxious. He tried to listen to what Katsuro was saying, but his mind wandered. He tapped Katsuro on the shoulder. "You don't need me anymore, right?"

Taken by surprise, Katsuro shook his head *No*, and Gian ran off with a broad smile. His heart pounded. Catherine was here and he needed her, desperately.

While Gian sought out Catherine, Katsuro continued his serious conversation with the two men in dark business suits. "Gentlemen, this is not a good place to talk. Let's adjourn to Rose's Café and have some lunch. Your treat, of course."

Aaron grasped Catherine's hands with his. "I am so surprised to see you. Why are you here?"

"To see you fight, of course." Her words were soft.

Aaron, like the awkward man-child he was, mumbled, "Wait for me. I need to shower. I want to look my best for you."

A few minutes later, the white sixteen-year-old high-school student (a potential martial-arts champion) and his black junior-college teacher walked from the auditorium touching hands. They didn't say a word, until they found her car. "We're close to the beach. We can walk and talk."

* * *

Katsuro ate slowly, swallowing his food after ten chews. He concentrated on his food. Eighty-seven and slowing down slightly, he loved to eat. "When you get to be my age, you chew every morsel and enjoy it to the fullest. This is my last time around. I want to make the most of it." He spoke to the two men, but more to hear himself talk.

The two men were puzzled by the old man's words but went on, "May we speak about business while you eat, Mr. Tachigi?"

Katsuro nodded.

"We are prepared to offer Aaron a contract to fight for our organization. We have access to every major arena in the world where martial-arts fighters are looked upon as gods. We are prepared to offer him a guaranteed income for the first two years and then incentives if he wins world championships."

"*If* is not the case, gentlemen. Rather, *when* he becomes a world champion, those incentives will come into play." Katsuro smiled back.

The taller fight rep leaned back in his chair, then shot forward and stuck his finger right in Katsuro's face, "Your fighter looks a lot younger than eighteen. You wouldn't be trying to scam us with your boy would you, Mr. Tachigi?"

Katsuro drew back in mock horror at the accusation. He ignored the finger-pointing as coming from an uncouth American slob and simply stated, "I will show you his birth certificate." Then he smiled and bowed while seated.

"That would be fine. But we still have two other hesitations about Aaron. His demeanor in the ring is not up to our standards or the standards we expect our fighters to follow. He does not bow when introduced. He is far too aggressive and clearly does not respect his opponents. All true?"

Katsuro stopped chewing. He swallowed, wiped his face with a napkin, returned it to his lap, and said, "Your lack of understanding of what it takes to be a great fighter is astonishing. Yes, he is aggressive. What do you want? A pussycat? He doesn't show respect? Nonsense! When you are fighting fighters who are so inferior to yourself, you not only show no respect for them, you show contempt. As for bowing, no, he does not do that well. I promise he will bow with great clarity before and after each fight. You said there were two things. What is the other?"

The taller rep spoke again, "I have been around the fight game for many years. I have seen fighters with astonishing bodies. Aaron has one of those astonishing bodies. Unfortunately, many of those bodies I have seen were a product of steroids. That is not our type of game. We check religiously since our fighters are licensed under the California Athletic Commission. Has Aaron ever taken steroids, Mr. Tachigi?"

"As you know, he has tested negative on every test he has ever taken, as required by the California Athletic Commission. He has tested negative in every country he has fought in. That alone should answer your question."

"Have you, Mr. Tachigi ever injected Aaron with any performance-enhancing drugs? Or given Aaron any pills for the same effect?"

"I believe I have answered that question before."

"No, you haven't, Mr. Tachigi. The prior question was has he ever taken any drugs. This question asks if you ever gave him any drugs. Have you?"

"Gentlemen, I have trained Aaron from the time he was three years old to become a world champion in martial arts. From the age of six, he has been lifting rocks, digging holes, pounding tires with a sledgehammer and using alternative weight-lifting equipment. He has incredible strength, none of which is gained through anything but real hard work."

In unison they asked, "You still haven't answered our question, sir. Did you ever give him any human growth drugs?"

"No, I haven't."

"We have attained documents from a drug lab in Los Angeles that states you bought these types of drugs from them. Did you?"

"Yes, of course I did. Why do you ask?"

"Because those types of drugs are illegal in our sport." The taller man raised his voice so others in the restaurant could hear him. "And you know that."

"Of course I know that. But only if the person taking those drugs is a participant in your sport. But when that person is pushing ninety-years-old and believes those drugs will enhance his life expectancy, that person can do as he wishes, right?"

"You mean to tell us you have been injecting yourself with human growth hormones to extend your life?"

Katsuro looked at the two men with doleful eyes. "Yes, I have."

CHAPTER TWENTY-THREE

PROFESSIONAL

As they walked on the beach, Catherine reached over and grasped Gian's hand. "You're my little boy. I really like my little boy. He's really cute."

Gian squeezed her hand and then held it by his fingertips. "I've never had a girlfriend before, let alone a grown woman girlfriend."

They swung their arms like little kids and giggled as they strolled the beach near Venice. Gian took off his shoes, walked into the ocean, and splashed in the salty brine. Catherine laughed as her man-child made a silly sound with his lips. "What was that?"

"A motorboat. I always wanted a motorboat. Hard to find one in Japan, especially Takayama."

"No need for a motorboat in the mountains?"

"None!" He splashed her. She reached down and splashed back.

"Hey, nigger, can't you see a guy is resting and enjoying the beach? Don't need a nigger gettin' me wet. That your boyfriend? A little young, ain't he?" The voice came from a dark-skinned man with a full beard and stained yellow teeth, reclining on a striped beach chair.

Aaron stepped forward. "You asshole. What kind of language is that to use on a lady. Your choice of words needs to be changed."

"What? She ain't a nigger?"

Aaron reached down at the reclining figure. The face covered with a shaggy beard and red eyes squealed as Aaron picked him up, "You need to apologize, sir. You are rude and need a mouth-cleaning."

The frightened half-drugged figure turned white. "Sure. Sorry mister. No harm. Just strange to see a black lady with such a young kid and holding hands. Sorry."

Gian let the man drop back into the sand. "Sleep it off, old-timer."

"I'm glad you didn't hit him, Aaron. Most people don't mean anything by what they say. He was just drunk and probably homeless. You did the right thing."

"I would do anything for you," Aaron blurted out. Then he got embarrassed and blushed.

Catherine gripped his hand and pulled him along the beach. "Come on, my man-child."

"Why did you call me that."

Catherine stopped. "Because you are. In some ways you are a man. In others you are a child."

"Give me an example." Aaron smiled.

"There, that was a man speaking. 'Give me an example.' A man would speak that way."

Aaron fumbled for words. "Thanks. And the child? When have I been a child?"

"Wanting to defend me from that bum. Playing in the ocean. Not being sure when to hold my hand. Being embarrassed and unsure of yourself."

"That's a long list of childlike behavior. So let's be more adult." Aaron put his arms around Catherine and pulled her toward himself and kissed her firmly. He had never tasted anything so wonderful in his whole life. She kissed him back with the same passion he gave her. "Was that a man's kiss?"

"Better than any man I've ever kissed before." She held on to him. Her inner kid wouldn't let him go. "You are my man-child. I like it that way."

Aaron stepped back. "You ever married?"

"Only to my work. Why, have you been married?"

"Only to Katsuro. He goes everywhere I go."

"He's not here now."

"Lucky for us."

* * *

"Well, gentlemen, do you have any other questions? If not, I must be on my way. I have an appointment I must keep."

They extended their hands. "No, sir, we have no more questions. But we are set to offer Aaron a contract. There will be a specific clause in that contract requiring a drug test before each fight. No random testing."

"I will discuss that with Aaron. Well, I am off to talk to PRIDE to see what they offer." The two men sat straight and gulped. They didn't want to lose their prize catch to the upstart organization known as PRIDE.

The taller man said, "Wait a moment! Maybe we should reconsider some of our restrictions on Aaron, like random drug tests."

Katsuro smiled and bowed as he got up. "No need to change anything, gentlemen. I just need to get information and decide which organization will best serve Aaron's interests."

"I would hate to see Aaron make the wrong decision, Mr. Tachigi."

"I don't make mistakes, gentlemen. I do my research quite well." Katsuro walked out the door and left the two to pay the bill. *That will make them think about their offer. More money will be expected.*

*   *   *

The afternoon turned into evening. The feeling inside Aaron was one he had never experienced before. He wondered if this was what love felt like. Katsuro had continuously warned him about the dangers of love. He had tried to prove his point by forcing Gian to kill Dog. And Katsuro had tried to prove he was the Master when he ordered Gian to kill the new Dog when they first came to Los Angeles. But Gian was adamant about never again killing anything he loved. A withering look from those sad, determined eyes told Katsuro Gian meant what he said. Katsuro relented but knew his time would come when he would have to teach Gian a lesson by killing something Gian loved: a lesson in dominance and control.

Catherine drove back to the Valley. "Would you like to see my place? It's not very much, but it's mine."

"Sure, why not? I'd love to see it." Aaron got excited. He could feel himself being aroused. He knew more about sex than when Margaret raped him, but not much. He was still self-conscious about relationships. He had never had a real girlfriend. He felt inadequate.

He had heard the other boys talk about their sexual conquests. He couldn't imagine himself in that position until now. With Catherine, he felt comfortable, but still unsure.

When Gian was growing up, Katsuro had never talked about sex, except to warn him to avoid girls. He said they were too controlling and would spoil his dreams of being a great fighter, so he left them alone, but now he had Catherine. He stared at her while she was driving. Her face was radiant. Her nose was perfect, not too small, but just right. In all the other girls, he saw imperfections. A nose too big, hips too large, ass too small, teeth stuck out, giggled too much, or something else, but not Catherine. She was perfect, or at least to a sixteen-year-old she was perfect.

Catherine's apartment was filled with artwork. "Is this your work?"

"Some of it. I do mostly modern painting, like Jackson Pollock—abstract expressionism."

Gian grinned. "Hey, remember you're talking to a man-child? What the hell are you talking about?"

"Now is not the time to explain my art work, but this is what I do."

"Do you sell many of your paintings?"

"If I sold a lot of them, I wouldn't have to work as a teacher and be studying to be an art evaluator and appraiser with a need to get a Master's degree in art."

"But you're good."

"Thanks. Want a cup of coffee?"

"No, thanks. I never have anything with caffeine."

"Would you mind if I have a cup?"

"Not at all. I'll have some water, though."

Sipping a steaming cup of coffee, she sat next to Gian on the couch. He reached across to her and placed his hand on her knee. She bent forward and kissed him gently on the cheek. He turned to her and kissed her mouth. "God, you taste so good."

"Maybe it's the taste of the coffee you like?"

"Very funny."

They snuggled, kissed and made small talk far into the night. For the first time in his life, Aaron was in love, and it simultaneously felt very strange and very wonderful. He was confused by how his body reacted. The strange impulse he felt in his body made him quiver, tingle, and shake. It threw him into unquenchable urges that made him lose control over his emotions more than once.

Love was a concept, a reality that Gian had been denied in every form from birth through childhood and into manhood. Nobody had ever loved him, held him, comforted him or cared for him. For this abandoned child set off alone, this was his first taste of somebody loving him. That taste would linger a lifetime.

* * *

After leaving the pro scouts, Katsuro instructed his chauffeur to drive him to the Hollywood Legion Stadium.

Katsuro knew that the famous old-time fight auditorium was no longer there, having been demolished several years prior, but he couldn't remember the name of the new building, so he just called it Hollywood Legion. His father used to take him to see the fights at the Stadium and at the old Olympic Auditorium in Downtown LA. His father knew the fight promoter, Eileen Eaton. *She knew how to promote a fight. She used minorities like Mexicans and blacks to headline her fights. Smart lady.* Now Katsuro would promote his white fighter in a world ruled by Asians.

PRIDE's headquarters was on the third floor of the Newman Building. He took the elevator up, turned left to Room 327, and entered. The room was in chaos. Boxes littered the floor. A small brunette was on her hands and knees collecting papers that had fallen from a container. Katsuro tapped loudly on the desk. She turned to face him. "Mr. Feinstein, please. Mr. Tachigi is on time for his appointment."

The brunette scrambled to her feet and scampered into another room. With the door slightly ajar, Katsuro listened as the woman called to her boss, "Mr. Feinstein, a Mr. Tachigi is here for his appointment."

"Damn! Well, bring him in and find a seat for him. Those movers will wait a long time to get paid for being so late."

The brunette waved Katsuro into the office and propped up a chair. Mr. Feinstein made his appearance and extended his hand. Katsuro bowed deeply and returned to his seat. He didn't like chaos and disorder and a lack of promptness. *This Mr. Feinstein had better offer Gian a great contract or he'll get no deal.*

* * *

The weeks passed very quickly. Aaron went to school only at Catherine's urging. He wanted to spend every moment with her. He shook with anticipation when they were apart. All these feelings were strange, wonderful, exciting, and joyful for Aaron, who had, for the first time, discovered love.

Due to a teachers' meeting, school adjourned early and the entire student body of Century High bolted from the buildings on their way to the beach or family pools or some other place to escape from an early-summer heat wave. Aaron headed for Catherine's place. Unannounced, but always welcome, Aaron rapped at her door. He heard the shout from behind the door and trembled. He was about to see her. He became excited and quickly became embarrassed. He was confused by his reaction to just thinking about her.

The door swept open and Catherine stood in the doorway in a see—through negligee, the outline of her body showing through the delicate fabric. Her skin was a silky brown, and her smile invited him in. "You said classes were cut short today, so I was expecting you."

Aaron slid through the door, closed it behind him, and grabbed her into his arms. Their mouths met fiercely and passionately. He could feel her body collapse into his. He pressed himself against her and rubbed. "Are you a little horny this afternoon?"

"God, who wouldn't be with that reception? I could eat you up."

"Then why don't you?"

Catherine led him to the couch and removed her flimsy cloth. She pulled his shirt from his firm young body and unbuckled his belt. She pulled his trousers down. "Easy, big guy. It goes better if it goes slower." She laid back on the couch and began what would be a day-long session of teaching lovemaking. "When I get through with you, sir, you will be a pro at more than just martial arts."

His body drenched in sweat, Aaron lay on the floor. Catherine lay next to him, her body equally wet, but sated many times over. He rolled over on top of her. "Was I good?"

Catherine laughed. "You were good; a good listener, a good student, and destined to be a great lover."

Aaron laughed that boyish laugh, "Oh, my God, I lost count."

"How many times you had pleasure is not important. It is what you do for your partner and how many times she has pleasure that should matter to you. That's when sex becomes even more fun, when you care more about your partner's fun than yours. You will learn that. It is what love is all about."

"I'll do better next time and all the times after that. I'll become that pro." Then he turned serious. "Do you love me?"

"Yes, I do. Why would you ask that question when we just made love almost all day?"

"Why? I'm ten-years younger than you. That's why!"

"The first time I saw you I saw sadness in your eyes—that deep, disturbing sadness—and I wanted to know why it was there. I wanted those eyes not to be sad anymore." She leaned over and kissed each eye. "Sadness, go away forever."

"I'm never sad when I'm with you. I feel so fantastic, so alive."

"Yes, you are alive."

He rolled over on top of her and they made love again.

Her breath came in short bursts as she collapsed onto him. "A woman can have fun many more times than a man with an appetite that is insatiable. Those feelings are what I live for at times like this." Aaron's education was coming full circle.

CHAPTER TWENTY-FOUR

DESPERATION

Katsuro had finished his negotiations, read the documents from each professional company, and waited patiently for Gian to come home. Catherine dropped Aaron off at his house in Canyon Falls. "You know you can't come in. Katsuro will be very angry. I missed my afternoon workout."

"What will he do to you?"

"I don't know and I don't care. I am happy when I'm with you." Whatever he does will be worth it." Aaron leaned over and kissed her. "I'll see you tomorrow."

Catherine nodded. Her face grew pensive. "I worry about you. Does he beat you?"

Gian laughed. "Beat me? It is more like torture. Do you know you are the first person who has ever told me she loved me? Do you know how that makes me feel?"

Catherine drew her lover toward her. She held him and caressed him slowly, lovingly. "Now I know where you get those sad eyes. Everyone needs someone to love. You can love me. Okay?"

Aaron smiled at the thought. "Okay, I would like that. Meanwhile, my love, I have to go. It is my time to perform."

He left the car not knowing what to expect, not caring. He had found love.

The old Master saw the lights of the car in the driveway and knew it was Gian. He heard the gate to the driveway open and close quietly. He left his chair and walked outside to talk to Gian. His protégé looked taller than the last time he saw him. He looked broader. He looked different. Gian walked with a lively step as he approached his house.

"You missed your afternoon workout, *Juko*. That is not acceptable for a fighter who is about to become a professional."

"You negotiated with those two men after I left?"

"Yes, and with another company to see which one made the best offer. Come, I will tell you about it while you work out now. Get your gear!"

Gian dressed, half expecting this to happen even if the hour was well past midnight. The dojo was dark, except for a small set of lights near the mats. Katsuro flicked on the remaining lights and the dojo glowed. Gian automatically started his stretching routine. "Tell me about her, *Juko*. Who is she?"

Gian had already decided to tell Katsuro if he asked. "I met her at school. She is a good friend."

"Are you having sex with her?"

"Yes!"

"Are you wearing protection? You can't afford to get any sexually transmitted diseases."

"She makes sure I'm wearing protection."

"Good. When will you be done with her? When will you not want her anymore?"

"Never."

"Use her as you wish; then get rid of her. Screw her brains out and then dump her. You need to concentrate on your career."

"I love her."

Katsuro walked close to Gian. "I have told you before, you must get rid of all things you love. Get rid of them. Love will consume you. Never love unless you can walk away from that love at a moment's notice. Love diverts your mind to things that are not important. Your career is what is important."

Gian pounded the bag with thunder fists. *Never tell me what I must do or whom I can love. You want me to perform as a professional? Then respect my loves.* His fists were like lightning. The bag swayed and bounced from each blow. "I am going to be the best fighter this pro club ever had. I will become their world champion. I will devote my life to being the best anybody has ever been. But I will never let this love go. It is what drives me now." The words hissed through his tightened lips. The blows to the bag became ever more intense. "I can do both. I will do both."

Katsuro stepped forward, his *Shinai* grasped firmly in his hand. "You think you can have two loves: your career and your woman. Never! That woman will drive you, direct you and eventually conquer you. You cannot win with a love you cannot cast aside instantly. I know that for a fact."

"You know that for a fact? But you don't really know me. I am not you. I can do both and I will do both. So, I have had my say. Now let's get on with my workout so we can discuss my pro contracts."

Katsuro drove Gian well past three in the morning. Gian, the teenager filled with excitement, loved challenging Katsuro. He felt more powerful than ever. Suddenly, Katsuro needed him, needed him to be *his* world champion. Gian wanted to be that world champion but knew he held the upper hand. Gian, arrogant and brash, had his best workout in a month.

He bathed in the family bath, dressed, and met Katsuro in his house. "Okay, tell me about my offers."

Katsuro gave the contracts to Gian. The pages were filled with small print and long, complicated paragraphs. "Read them over and let me know what you think. Or do you want me to give these contracts to my lawyers and have them break them down? You may be smart, but you are not that smart. You are just an arrogant son-of-a-bitch who now thinks he knows more than I do, someone who can do more for himself than I can. Just remember you still need me, *Juko*, so don't be so arrogant and so smart."

Katsuro left. Gian shrugged Katsuro's words off and went to bed. Two hours later he was readying himself for school.

His phone rang as he was leaving. Catherine spoke quickly. "Aaron, I have to leave for a few days. It is important. I will call you when I get back. Please be careful. Just remember, I love you." The phone buzzed.

Aaron began to tremble. His face grew pale. His body shook, and he couldn't control it. *Where is she going? Is she going to come back? Maybe she's leaving me? But she says she loves me. God, what will I do without her? I'll never find anybody else to love. Why didn't she take me with her? She knows I love her. Maybe I'm too young for her and she knows it.*

He sat next to the phone. His trembling hands cradled his head. His nerves jumped. He felt sick to his stomach. *Is this what the loss of a love feels like?* Suddenly he felt calm. *Wait! She said she loved me and she would be back in a few days. She's not leaving me. I'll be okay.*

Just as suddenly the trembling began again. An unjust fear crept into Aaron's head. *will I ever see her again?*

And so the same words bounced around his head over and over. He had conquered the beatings, the abuse, the mental torment by accepting them and by placing himself elsewhere. But this was different. He had found love. *Am I being abandoned? Again? Will I be alone again? Will I face a loveless world forever? Will I . . .?* The phone rang again.

"Aaron, this is Ted. Why are you answering your phone? Why aren't you picking me up so we can get to school on time?"

Aaron looked at his watch. *God! Look at the time.* "I'm sorry, Ted. I just can't make it today." His voice cracked.

Ted could feel the torture in his friend's voice. "Aaron, don't move. Stay home. I'm coming over. I'll be there in twenty minutes."

Knowing Aaron would say no, Ted hung up and left his house, shouting as he went, "Mom, I'm going to see Aaron. He's not feeling well." Before his mom could answer, Ted was out the door and into his car.

When the doorbell rang Aaron snapped from his lethargy and ran to the door. He was sure it was Catherine. Ted's face brought him back to reality. "Ted!"

Ted stood at the doorstep. "What's with the look of surprise? Shit, I told you I was coming over. What's the matter with you?"

"Nothing, Ted. Nothing!"

"Sure there is. You going to let me in or what?"

Aaron smiled without feeling like smiling. He had never had a visitor before. Ted was the first guest to ever enter his house. "Sure, Ted, come in."

With two large steps, like a child stepping over hot coals, Ted entered the house of Gian. "Not a lot of furniture. Somebody live here with you?"

Dog had been sleeping on his couch and wagged his tail at the visitor. "Only Dog, and he isn't a very good watch dog. Just me and him," Aaron said absentmindedly.

They sat on the couch, and Aaron began to tremble and shake uncontrollably again. Ted thought Aaron was having a spasm of some sort. Aaron wiped his eyes. He collapsed in fear. His head rolled back on the couch and he stared at the ceiling, not seeing it. Ted patted his hand. "Aaron, what's the matter?"

Ted ran to the kitchen, grabbed a glass of water, plucked a handful of ice from the freezer, and raced back to his friend. He rubbed the cubes over Gian's neck, face, and hands. Revived and alert, Aaron sat up. "Okay, Aaron, what gives?," Ted inquired. "What happened?"

Aaron took several large gulps, swallowed hard and said, "I got a call from Catherine. She said she was leaving town for a few days on an emergency and she would get back to me."

"And for that you passed out?"

"I didn't pass out. I got . . . I got . . . I got scared."

"Scared about what?"

"That . . . that . . . that she won't come back. I know it! I just know it! She won't come back."

"God damn, you had a panic attack."

"How do you know?"

"Because I've seen fighters who've had panic attacks about fighting or being nervous in the ring. Never about a woman though."

"You think that's funny?"

Ted shook his head, "No, I don't. But I take it seriously. Let's go out and talk. Maybe you'll come to my place for dinner. Mom would like that."

Aaron grabbed his jacket. "I don't want to, but I will. Let's go. I need to get the hell outta here."

* * *

Harry Simeron had been an attorney for nearly forty years. He had started in contract law and migrated into sports law by a fluke.

Simeron was called in to evaluate the contract between the Los Angeles Coliseum Commission and the Los Angeles Rams, back when that football team was still based in the city. He concluded the Commission had no case, since he deemed the contract flawed, and he was right. It was then he began receiving calls to draw up contracts between athletes and various teams. This is how it came to be that Katsuro Tachigi called him.

Harry Simeron sat in front of a very large picture window on the seventeenth floor of the Century Plaza Building in West Los Angeles. His view encompassed the western section of the city, its beaches, and coastal towns. It also prevented Harry from suffering his greatest fear, claustrophobia. In his first office building, his daily trips in an inside elevator caused him to break out in red, prickly dots across his chest and back. "Nerves," his dermatologist would say. So Harry found a building with a glass exterior elevator. He relocated.

Katsuro walked into the lawyer's office, bowed, and handed the large man sitting across from him two envelopes. "These are the contracts. Please read them and give me your suggestions" Katsuro sat cross-legged, arms folded across his chest, looking straight at the attorney.

"Mr. Tachigi, it will take me several days to review these contracts and write you my opinion. I cannot do it right now."

"Mr. Simeron, your fee is $330 per hour. How many hours will it take to complete your work?"

"Maybe ten hours."

"So, I could come back tomorrow and your suggestions would be ready?"

"If you were my only client, yes, but you are not my only client. Next week at the earliest."

"You don't understand, Mr. Simeron, I will pay you $660 an hour to get these done by tomorrow. Therefore, I will be here tomorrow afternoon, and we will talk, right?"

"Wrong! Next week! No matter what you pay me, I cannot be bought. I have loyalty to all my clients and I need time to evaluate their contracts, too. I will treat you equally and fairly—and your contracts will be ready next week."

Katsuro bowed, smiled, stood erect, and said, "Tomorrow at three." He left.

Harry took the envelopes and opened them. He read the contracts carefully. "Damn! This new wave of extreme fighting companies and their contracts are filled with inconsistencies and ambiguities. By tomorrow?"

Harry read each contract and decided that the best for this client was to write him brand-new contracts. The International Fight Federation (IFF) and Extreme Sport Karate (ESK) would have to agree to these new contracts.

* * *

Ted's mother's house was homey. It was filled with pictures and mementos of a life well lived. Cabinets were filled with trophies. Aaron had no pictures, no memories. He had no mementos, just a few trophies that Katsuro kept in boxes, never to be taken out. Ted's mom was a striking blonde with gentle eyes and a smile that lit up the room. She extended her hand. "Ted has spoken of you often, Aaron. Welcome to our home."

Home! Aaron never had a real home. A shiver went through him. He suddenly realized he had lived alone from age ten. No real mother or father, just Katsuro's loveless, cold teachings. His fear of intimacy and loneliness filled every crack of his emotions. He felt overwhelmed by being in a place called "home."

Ted's mom, Anna, talked on and on, well aware of Aaron's silence. He remained quiet. Anna didn't know what to do about it. Therefore, she did what she did best: talk. As she talked, she also looked at the sixteen-year-old more carefully. He was big and broad, with a thick neck, powerful well-defined hands with long fingers and the saddest eyes she had ever seen. She thought they looked like willows ready to weep uncontrollably. Yet at the same time they were staring out into space, not seeing anything. She could tell he wasn't listening to anything she was saying, nor did he seem to care. He was adrift in space and nobody was getting into that space, not now, and maybe never.

They ate in silence except when Aaron gave a one-word response to Anna's questions or just nodded. Anna served cannelloni for dessert. Aaron perked up a little at the delicious flavor of the cream-filled Italian dessert topped with whipped cream and asked shyly for a second helping.

After dessert, Aaron and Ted retired to Ted's room. Trophies lined the walls. Aaron's trophies were never seen by anybody, including Aaron. This was a home. Aaron lived in a shelter, cut off from the real world of wonderful people and love. Sitting on Ted's bed, Aaron's space became very small. His very existence was being squeezed. He suddenly withdrew and became depressed. *Why did she leave me? Where did she go? Will I ever see her again?*

Aaron saw Catherine's flickering face fading in and out and then disappearing. "No!" he shouted. "No! Please come back."

Ted was startled at the verbal outburst. "Mom, Aaron is out of it. Come quick"

Anna burst into her son's room and saw his friend's blank stare. She sat down next to Aaron and put her arm around his large shoulders. She drew him near and he slid under her arm. She stroked his hair and whispered, "Whatever is the matter, we can talk about it and you will be fine. Just talking makes things better. You won't be alone then. You will have me." She repeated those words over and over and never let go of this boy with the blank eyes.

Aaron sat silently. Hurt so often in so many ways, he drew inward as he had taught himself to do. *What is this woman doing? Stroking my head feels really good. What is she saying? What does she want? That dessert was really good. Talk about what? Talk, and I'll feel better?*

Then he heard Ted's voice, but he couldn't make out his words. "Mom, he doesn't hear you. I have been with him many times when he is like this. He told me he can detach from anything."

Anna put her forefinger to her mouth. Ted stopped talking and Anna continued to cradle this sad teenager. He did not know how long Anna held him. Time meant nothing to him. It only held the secrets of abuse and abandonment. After this extended period of unmeasured time, Aaron sat up slowly. "Thank you, ma'am. Thanks."

"Did you hear anything I said?"

"Yes!" Alienated and fearful of talking to anyone, Aaron sat quietly.

Ted rejoined the conversation. "I do know, Mom, that Aaron's girlfriend called him today to say she wouldn't see him for a few days."

"Is that the problem, Aaron?" Anna asked.

Taking a deep breath, Aaron nodded.

"She's never coming back?" the pretty blonde woman asked.

Aaron shook his head. "No, she'll be back, one day. Soon, I hope."

"Where did she go?"

"I don't know."

As if adrift alone on the sea, Aaron followed Ted and Anna to the living room. The painstaking talk continued. Anna sat stunned at the remoteness of her son's friend. *He is so distant. Why? So painfully far off!*

It was when Anna asked about Aaron's family that his sullen nature came to the forefront. He spoke in clipped terms about the Tachigi family. And then Aaron asked, "Do you know what a *Shinai* is?"

Anna shook her head. Ted shrugged, not answering the question. "It is a bamboo sword that the ancient Samurai warriors used in the feudal days. The bamboo is wound tight with a slight, wiry-like cord that holds the leaves in place. If the cord is removed, the leaves hang loose. My father beats me with those leaves almost every day." Aaron's words fell like a sledgehammer on Anna's ears.

"Every day?"

"Yes. He says it is necessary to train me to withstand pain so I will become a better fighter." The words were slow in coming. Anna could barely hear them with her heart pounding so hard.

Aaron had never uttered those words before to anyone, not even Catherine. He was afraid she would report Katsuro for child abuse. He also feared Katsuro would seek her out and hurt her if he knew she was aware of his torturing ways. Anna was different. She was a stranger Katsuro would never know.

Anna could not speak. But Ted said, "Oh, my God! So that's why, when you fight, you never cry out from pain. You've withstood real pain already. Wow!"

"It isn't a wow, Ted. It's a horror. Does anyone know about these beatings?"

"No, and they never will. You must promise you will tell no one, not a soul, or I will never be able to trust you again." Aaron was now fully alert, no longer detached.

Anna put her arm around Aaron and held him close again. He did not protest. "I will never break your trust. You can talk to me anytime about anything whenever you like. I will never judge you."

CHAPTER TWENTY-FIVE

CATHERINE'S NEW JOB

Harry Simeron never left his office that night. He brewed a fresh cup of coffee, sprinkled in some non-dairy creamer, and sipped the liquid as he drafted a new contract for Aaron Michaels, the IFF, and the ESK. Daybreak came. The sun rose across the San Gabriel Mountains and sent electric rays of yellow light dancing through his office windows. He made several copies of his new contracts, used the john, and began reading the two documents.

At six-thirty, he called his partner and faxed the contracts to him. "Read them carefully. I have my client coming in at three to pick them up. If I made a mistake, correct it, and be ready to give them to Betty by ten."

The building coffee shop opened at six so he ordered breakfast. "Please deliver it to my office ASAP." *At least I don't have to take that elevator down.*

* * *

Katsuro accepted Gian's call at ten the night before. "I am working out with Ted and I will sleep at his place. Not the girl's. She's out of town." Aaron hung up the phone and grinned. "Damn! Free for the night!"

* * *

While Anna was comforting Aaron, Catherine sat in Simon Zarwicki's studio. He was the President of Evaluator's Insurance Group. "Miss Tyler, we like your resume. You have come highly recommended.

You are young enough to attract clients and experienced enough to hold on to some of our older clients."

"Where would I work? I don't want to leave the LA area. I call it home."

"So do we, Miss Tyler. We have reps in every West Coast area. You would be our Southern California rep."

"And you will supply all the names for me?"

"Yes, but we do expect you will bring in new names. We always need to expand our base."

The office Catherine sat in was hung with paintings. Each had an envelope taped to its frame. In each envelope was the estimator's evaluation of that piece of art. Some works were being donated to charities and the donor needed a fair market price for tax purposes. Others were being sold or exchanged and needed an evaluation for comparison. Still others were art pieces being loaned to museums and needed an estimate of value for insurance purposes.

This wasn't what Catherine really wanted to do, but she loved the money. "How often will I need to come to San Francisco to meet with you?"

"Not often. But all expenses will be paid by the company, and you will stay at the best hotels."

"You are offering me a sign-on cash bonus of $10,000? Correct?"

"Correct. I took the liberty of drawing up a contract for you. Please read it over and we will meet again tomorrow to answer any other questions you may have."

"Fair enough, sir. Tomorrow at two?"

Simon Zarwicki stood, extended his hand, and admired the beautiful black woman he had just hired for his company. Her dress reached just above her knees. When she sat, the dress slid up, exposing a slender pair of legs that Simon could only dream of touching.

Catherine took a cab back to her hotel. It was late in the afternoon. She showered, dressed in a miniskirt with her blouse open at the top and no bra. She walked out of the lobby and took the cable car at Powell that was destined for Fisherman's Wharf. At the final stop, the Embarcadero, she leapt from the cable car and walked quickly to her favorite restaurant on the Wharf, Cioppino's. She sat in the back room and knifed a slab of butter onto sourdough bread, waved off the server, and waited.

A handsome young couple entered, looked around, and walked steadily toward her. The beautiful raven-haired woman bent down and kissed Catherine full on the mouth. "Hello, my dear. Nice to see you again."

A short, stocky man, his hair pulled straight back and tied in a pony-tail, shook her hand firmly. "It is always good to hear from you."

"Order what you like, both of you. I will have the Cioppino. It is the best."

The conversation was light. "It has been several years since we have seen you. I hope everything is going well for you."

"Yes," Catherine spoke easily. "Everything is good."

"We have set up the room as you requested. Everything is ready for you."

"That sounds great! When you have finished eating, we will be on our way. I am looking forward to the evening."

The threesome walked up the hill toward Coit Tower, made a sharp left, and strode up Stockard. The girl produced a key, opened a latched door, and entered the two-story townhouse. "The bedroom is upstairs." The three took the stairs. The man rubbed the girl's rear sensually. She responded by playfully shaking her ass.

As the last one up Catherine watched. The man stood at the edge of the bed and began removing his clothes. The girl helped him undress, caressing his manhood. She took him in her mouth and he stiffened. Catherine watched, sliding her hand under her skirt to pleasure herself. The man unsnapped the other woman's bra and caressed her breasts. The woman moved closer to Catherine and bent forward, kissing her full on the mouth.

Catherine's hands sought the woman's genitals.

Catherine devoted the following morning to reading the contract. She was prompt for the 2:00 p.m. meeting with her new boss, Simon Zarwicki.

*   *   *

Before school, Aaron spent the early morning at the gym. Feeling guilty about not having worked out for a few days, he slashed through a complex set of exercises while thinking about Catherine and when he would see her next. Ted patted Aaron on his broad back. "Come on big guy, a few rounds in the ring will be good for you and for me. Just remember this is a workout, not a real fight. Okay?"

"Sure, Ted, okay. I wouldn't want Anna not to speak to me. I'm looking forward to having another terrific meal."

"That's great. I get treated well in the ring so you can have a good meal." Ted laughed. "If that's all it takes to satisfy you, the next guy should cater your dinner."

"Very funny, but not a bad idea."

*   *   *

Katsuro did not bother to knock at Harry Simeron's office door. He entered, bowed as he always did as he slid into a chair, folded his arms, and waited. Harry was reading through the last suggestion his partner had made, routinely crossed a T, and looked up at his demanding client. Harry's eyes were heavy from lack of sleep, but he knew he had done a terrific job rewriting the contracts. "Mr. Tachigi, I rewrote the contracts you gave me for both companies, IFF and ESK. I believe they are fairer for the fighters and equally fair to the companies. Now it is your turn to review them."

Katsuro leaned forward. "I hired you for your opinion, not mine. You work for me and Aaron Michaels; you speak my opinion."

"Very well, sir. My opinion is you should have more control over your son's fights. By this I mean selection of opponents and how often he must fight and under what conditions. They had Aaron fighting no matter what physical condition he is in. This is very insensitive to his well being."

"And what would you have me do with these contracts, Mr. Simeron?"

"Submit them to the companies as the only contracts you will have your son fight under and convince them they are a good standard contract for all fighters. You might even mention that I drafted them and that they have my permission to use them."

"Make a copy of them for me, sir, and I will take them with me to read over." Katsuro was handed an envelope by his shadow who had been carrying it in his jacket pocket; Katsuro passed it to Harry. "I trust this will cover your expenses."

The following week, Katsuro kept his appointment with the International Fight Federation. He handed the directions to his driver and reflected on what he should do about his fighter. *He is better than any fighter I have ever trained. He is bigger, faster, tougher, and oblivious to pain. He is able to detach himself from what is happening to him and, through dedicated training and constant repetition of actions, he never needs to think, only react. Michael said it best—he is a robot. He has got to give up this woman who is poisoning his mind with nonsense about how love can fight his fights. I don't like the fact that she even showed up to his last fight. God damn black woman! She may be beautiful, but that beauty is dangerous.*

* * *

The greatest misconception about a fighter is he has to be large and muscular and have a face realigned by having been in the ring too many times. Micah Sandervol was a short, slender man, but he had been trained to be a fighter by his father so he could survive the gang-filled streets of Detroit. He might have been small in stature, but he was tough to the core. He was a highly decorated ex-Marine fighter pilot who had been a POW in Korea.

A relentless fighter, Micah was known as The Stalker. He was quick enough physically and mentally to outsmart the gangs of his neighborhood. Knowing his father would kill him rather then let him join a gang, he learned the gangs' colors and wore only neutral clothing. He learned gang signs and when to use them. He befriended all the kids and was mainly left alone until, of all days, his sixteenth birthday.

He found himself in the middle of a gang fight in an alley he used for a shortcut home. "Which side you on, Micah?"

Without hesitation, he called out, "I'm the lookout. Two whistles if the cops are coming, three if another gang shows up."

Micah went up a short fire escape where he could see the main drag. He rarely looked back at the knife fights happening below. Only when he saw his father walking the main drag did he realize he couldn't be caught as a fight participant. If another gang should come, they could enter the fray or just watch and enjoy the fun. If the police came, they would arrest the gang members they could catch.

So Micah slid his fingers in his mouth and blew out two blasts. "Cops!"

"Cops!" he repeated. The knife fighting and scuffling ended, and the sound of retreating feet could be heard through the alleyway. Micah's father barely saw his son coming down from the fire escape. "What are you doing up there, Micah?"

Micah hopped down from the metal ladder. "Visiting a friend."

"Well, don't get caught by the girl's father. That would be worse than being a lookout for the gangs."

Micah was taken aback. "How did you know?'

"No big secret. After you yelled "Cops!," a gang member running by me stopped and said you were not part of the gang, just a lookout. Nice kid."

Micah asked, "Who was that guy, Dad?"

"I think he said 'Harlan' when I asked him."

Micah Sandervol had been expecting a call from Mr. Tachigi in response to his offer. Surprisingly, the call never came. Meanwhile, Micah went over his fight club's proposed schedule and penciled "Aaron Michaels" in each venue. He also scheduled time to take publicity pictures of his new fighter. Of all the mugs Micah had in his stable, Aaron was the best looking. He was even considering changing his fight name to 'Aaron Tachigi' to give him that authentic Japanese name. But his plans changed when Katsuro never returned the signed contract.

His phone rang. "Micah, Harlan here. I'm over at the printers to help him design the new posters. What gives with this guy, Tachigi?"

"Your guess is as good as mine. I'll have to call him, but I hear he is difficult to deal with. They say he is used to getting his way. They even say he bought his way into our National Martial Arts Team. Maybe he's a control freak."

The phone buzzed, so Micah begged Harlan off and said, "Micah here."

"Mr. Sandervol, this is Katsuro Tachigi. I am coming over to see you now. I will be there in about fifteen minutes. Please be ready for me." The phone clicked.

Micah sighed, cursed, and drummed his fingers on his desk. "I hate people, especially fighters and their managers."

Katsuro walked through the office door, dropped an envelope on Micah's desk, bowed, as was his custom, and sat down. "Our new contract."

Extremely intelligent is how his law professor described Micah. "Young man, you have a good mind; just make sure you use it properly and wisely." Micah practiced law for a few years, but although he loved the money, he grew bored quickly, so he set out to create a new world for himself. An enthusiast of martial arts and all its mysterious underpinnings and Oriental intrigue, he found himself fighting behind closed doors and in clubs to attain the excitement he craved.

However, it wasn't until he formed the first legitimate martial-arts extreme-fight club, the International Fight Federation, that he found his dream, and it wasn't until he saw Aaron Michaels fight that he found his first charismatic pugilist. A good-looking, strapping young man with a killer's sense in his eyes and lightning in his every move, Aaron Michaels fit Micah's image of the commercial champion he needed to make his club a success.

So when Katsuro exploded Micah's world with his own version of a fight contract, Micah realized he wasn't in full control of his own destiny. He needed the fighters and managers. He hated the reality that he required their help to make his ambitions come true.

Without showing anger at his potential meal ticket, Micah picked up the envelope and scanned the contents with his lawyer-trained eyes. *This son-of-a-bitch wants full control of Aaron's training: when he will fight, how often, where he will train. And, after being undefeated for ten fights, he wants a shot at the world title.*

Micah squirmed in his chair, coughed into his hand and continued reading. Katsuro sat and stared, wordless.

He wants a percentage of the gate receipts. As the gate expands, following Aaron's fights, he wants a ten percent increase in revenue. Any commercial use of his Aaron's name will be subject to a fifty-percent share of potential revenue. Aaron Michaels will be paid for appearances outside the arena to promote any activities of the IFF; and, when he becomes world champion, he will be given a twenty-five percent increase in all revenue. Micah drew a very deep breath, puckered his cheeks as he blew the air out slowly and made a loud, piercing low whistle.

"Why don't I just give you my business? Wouldn't that be easier?" Micah smiled at Katsuro and then stared at him, menacingly. "What do you really want, Mr. Tachigi? Full control over every aspect of your fighter's life and my business?"

Katsuro's face never broke. His face was placid and blank. He didn't respond.

"Answer me, old man. You have something in mind more than I am reading here?"

Katsuro unfolded his arms, leaned forward, and spoke. "I want all the assurances I can have for my son to become the world champion. You have never had such a wonderful fighter. He is young, he is saleable, he is your next champion, and you know it."

Micah pounded his desk. "I know only one thing: you want too much control. I am the fight promoter. I own this business and I have the contacts around the world to make it work. So you need me. You got that, old man. *You need me.*" Micah hissed his words

The phone rang. "Harlan, what is it?"

"I need to know what's going on, that's all."

"What is going on is highway robbery. I'll get back to you. Don't call me. I'll call you. Understand?"

"Sure!"

Micah spoke slowly, "Now, Mr. Tachigi, let's talk turkey."

In the end, Katsuro's contract held. Micah knew Aaron was a find. He called Harlan to print the posters.

CHAPTER TWENTY-SIX

THE OTHER
FIGHT CLUB

A week after signing a contract with IFF, Katsuro and Gian made an appointment with Extreme Sport Karate, a competitor. "Gian, in our contract with IFF there is no mention that we can sign with only one group, one promoter. And since I have full control over who you fight and how often, we can play both ends against the middle and also sign with ESK if their offer is the same or better than IFF's."

Gian, who had taken to questioning Katsuro more often and with barely any consequence, asked, "Is that a smart thing to do? How often can I fight? And are other fighters doing the same thing?"

"You are full of questions, *Juko*. I have told you many times and I repeat it now. I have your best interests at heart. I will make sure you are the best fighter you can be no matter whom you fight. So it is okay to sign with more than one fight club, and we will, unless it is not in your best interest. Besides, you can and will be the world champion in two clubs."

The last words excited Gian: world champion two times over. "By the way, Katsuro, when is my first fight with IFF? Is it next Tuesday in Santa Monica, right?"

"Right. And we will be training seriously this afternoon—*all afternoon*."

The receptionist at ESK was used to seeing men of all sizes traipsing through the office. When she looked up, she saw the ruggedly handsome face of the developing teenager, his massively broad shoulders, his square jaw, and eyes that could penetrate a brick wall. Those eyes sent a chill through her soul. "Mr. Manley is expecting you," she said, pointing to both men and their shadow.

Phillip Manley was the definition of living to excess. His portly body struggled to rise from the cushy chair behind his desk. His girth almost matched his height. But that look of excess belied strength and toughness Gian did not expect. Manley shook hands with both men. His thick fingers grasped Gian's with a grip of steel. "Don't let the rubber tire fool you. I tried out as a sumo wrestler many years ago and never lost the weight. I still do plenty of weight lifting, though."

Gian clasped the man's hand longer than usual in a test of strength, the type of game Katsuro would appreciate. "I have read your contract offer, Mr. Tachigi. I know this Harry Simeron well. We have had dealings before. He has been trying to become our legal counsel for a few years. And now this—a circuitous route to our office, indeed, but, nevertheless, a beginning."

"And what is it about the contract you don't like?" Katsuro asked.

"Most of it. It is written with your son's best interests at heart, I understand. But, and this is a big but, I am willing to work with you and offer you more money than you have indicated in the contract based on your client's draw, how much money he brings to the table, or more precisely, into the arena."

"And . . ."

"Let me finish, Mr. Tachigi. I am offering a share of the TV revenue if that should become an issue, or more correctly, a reality."

Katsuro was angry. Harry had overlooked television revenue or any broadcasting rights for Gian as the contract was now written. Gian sat transfixed. This business was all new to him. He looked at it as another training experience by Katsuro and his lessons on life.

As Katsuro calmed down and thought about the situation, he began to realize what Harry had had in mind. *"We can cover many aspects of the contract in detail, or hold off until we are sure what some of those details might be. All media rights are negotiable. The contract states that those shall be discussed at the appropriate time, and any disagreement could force the contract to be null and void,"* Harry had said to Katsuro when he gave him the contract. *'If we lock in terms to any media without knowing how high the stakes are, we may be cheating ourselves. If your son is as good as you say he is, they need him more than you need them. So, bite the bullet now, and the big payday will come."*

Katsuro could see Harry's face and now understood what he had meant.

"That's okay. Leave that alone."

"Besides that, Mr. Tachigi, you have too much control."

"And Mr. Manley, how much control should I have?"

Phillip Manley shook his head and said, "I don't understand your question."

Katsuro leaned forward in his chair, hands together locked in his own fingers. Gian had seen this stance before. He knew that Katsuro was about to do something unexpected. "Mr. Manley, I want to buy into your management company. I want to be in control of my own fighter and own a percentage of your firm."

Phillip Manley was taken aback. "You want to take over this company?"

"No, I want a small percentage of your business, not full control, but I don't want you to interfere with my fighter. So, I want you to accept this contract and let my son fight his fights. You see, Mr. Manley, a very simple concept."

"What about my other fighters?"

"What about them? They can fight under your company with a different contract that has nothing to do with us. As long as the championships are settled fairly and honestly, they shouldn't care, and neither do I."

Gian took all this in as best he could. He didn't understand all the ramifications of what Katsuro was doing or saying, but he did know he wanted to become a world champion.

It took two weeks for Katsuro to invest in ESK and become a silent partner with his own contract in tow.

* * *

Aaron spent every spare moment he could with Catherine after her return from the Bay area. He worked out with Katsuro during early morning hours, attended school until noon each day, and spent several hours with Catherine in the afternoon. His body always ached when he approached the townhouse Catherine bought after her new job emerged. There were a few days each month she had to go out of town for work. "I know you don't like when I leave you for business, Aaron, but it can't be helped. Look, I love you. I care for you. And I want you. I love having sex with you and teaching you everything I can, but, still, I have to earn a living."

"I know, but I still miss you when you leave." Aaron sounded like a lost soul when he said goodbye to Catherine.

"Come over here, Aaron. Let me show you what I will teach you today." Catherine stripped off her housedress and stood naked in front of him. Gian's emotions exploded. "Just relax. You will enjoy this and more."

Aaron thought of the angels he made in the snow in Japan, his heavenly spot of peace. His heaven was still ahead of him.

Catherine undressed Aaron, one button at a time. Gian's lessons in life continued. They made love the entire afternoon.

Spent, Aaron lay next to her. His body seemingly limp and weak while soaked in sweat. In the middle of this mind-blowing experience, inexplicably and eerily he heard Katsuro's voice. *A woman can sap you of your strength, just like Delilah did to Samson. Her cutting off his hair was a metaphor for a man losing his vitality and virility during sex. Never have sex before a fight. In fact, never have sex for the week before a fight. Your manhood may feel good, but your urge to follow through and kill your opponent will diminish, if not dissipate.*

Aaron rolled off the bed. He moved to a chair and sat. Catherine knew she had lost him. What happened? "Aaron, what are you thinking about? Talk to me!"

He stared straight ahead. "He follows me wherever I go. I can't ever leave him behind. I am his prisoner. Even in my greatest throes of passion, making love to the woman I love, he comes back to haunt me. I can't escape him." His voice started out strong and then grew weak and tentative. Talking about *him* made his life real, not the fairy tale it had become.

Catherine looked lovingly at her man with the sad eyes. He had told her about growing up in Japan. She knew about the abuse. She understood his tortured thirst for love and guidance, but she also knew she could never fully understand the torment his mind must be full of and the anguish he almost always felt. "What were you thinking about? What was Katsuro telling you?"

Aaron flopped back on the chair, his eyes gazing upward as he spoke. "Ever since he learned I was seeing you, he constantly warns me about having sex before a fight. It will sap my energy so I can't fight as well. It will diminish my drive, he would say."

"Is he right?"

Aaron laughed. "I don't know. I haven't had a real fight since I have been making love to you."

"So, why don't we test his theory? You have a fight this Saturday in Santa Monica, in two days. You will tell me after the fight how you felt before the fight and after. If you feel good and strong, then we can screw as often as you like whenever you like. If not, we will have to plan sex sessions around your fight schedule. That would mean no more screwing unless we check your calendar. Okay?"

"Okay, I guess." Aaron did not know what else to say.

They started their love making session again.

Aaron showered and dressed slowly. "That was great. But I need to go. I have to get in my evening session with you-know-who."

Catherine walked close to Aaron and cradled his head to her bosom. She stroked his head and gently massaged his back. Her long fingernails slowly caressed his muscular shoulders. She held him close, and he let her. He relaxed, even though he wasn't used to being held. It sometimes felt he was a prisoner, like when he had been tied to the pulley by his hands and beaten. At first he struggled with being caressed. Then, slowly, after Catherine had talked to him about loving and feeling like a prisoner, he accepted her fondling him.

Out of the blue, she startled him when she asked, "Gian, do you ever want to make love with another woman? Or just have sex with another woman? Do you ever look lustfully at a girl in your classes and secretly want her but wonder if I would object?" Gian was stunned by Catherine's questions. Not waiting for his response, Catherine continued. "Well, you wouldn't be my boyfriend if you didn't. Men are beasts of prey. They hunt and seek their mates. If you ever want to have sex with another girl or woman, go for it."

Gian pulled away. His body shook; it trembled involuntarily; his mind raced. "You don't want to see me anymore? You want me to have another girl?"

"Never, my love. I want you now and tomorrow and for all the tomorrows after that. But, sometimes a man's urges can't be controlled, and they shouldn't be controlled. One woman may not be able to satisfy you. And I love you so much, I would never want to stand in your way of having your physical needs met. If I can't totally satisfy you, then I do want you to have another woman to meet your needs along with *me* meeting your needs."

"You want me to fuck another woman?"

"If you like."

"Why?"

"I just explained it." She went over her words as Aaron nodded his head like he understood. "You understand what I'm saying now?"

"Sure. You want me to screw another girl and you, too."

"Well . . .. with one caveat."

"What's a caveat?"

"One condition."

"What condition?"

"You must screw this woman while I watch."

"You're kidding me, right?"

"No! I like to see my men happy, and I know you are happy when you're screwing someone."

Aaron sighed. Forgetting his "man," he went to his "child." "When do you want me to do this?"

"How about after you win your first pro fight? It will be like a treat."

Gian smashed his hands together. "Okay, I buy that. You have somebody in mind?"

Catherine laughed. "Hmm . . . not really. But there are a lot of groupies who follow the fighters wherever they go. I'll bet they would be willing to screw the winner of the fight."

"Yeah, I'll bet they would. Shake on that."

"Better yet, kiss me on that."

On his way back to Canyon Falls, Aaron stopped at a new restaurant, In-and-Out Burger, and ordered two burgers with a large side of French fries. Katsuro always said, *Get plenty of fat in your system, because you burn off huge quantities of calories and you need to replace them with fat. Keeps your body weight up while you work on your speed.* That wasn't what he learned in his health class, but he loved a good burger. Besides, Katsuro rarely ate anything but fast food and he was very trim at age eighty-eight.

Katsuro waited for his protégé in the dojo holding the *Shinai* in his hand. "Get dressed, *Juko*. It is time to train . . . hard.

"You still screwing that whore you screw every day?"

Gian stared down at his mentor. "She's not a whore. She's my girl friend, and I love her."

"Loving not good before a fight. You remember I told you that."

Gian nodded.

"Good, then keep your dick in your pants for now and come outside. Time to pound tires, lift tires, and dig some holes."

Gian loved it when Katsuro went back to his basic training techniques. He had learned long ago to like the game of "tire rummy," as he called it. Beat a tire—Move a tire—Dig a hole. Pound a tire—Lift a tire—Drag a tire. Throw a tire! The game never ended, but now it was a game Gian would always win.

They were out in the yard for more than three hours. Margaret watched from her window. *Doesn't he ever get tired of doing those workouts? I know I get tired of watching.* She showered, then dressed in a miniskirt and a low-slung top that revealed her well-tanned breasts. She was going on a second date with Lee, a Chinese man of great wealth who had a wonderful family. Margaret had told her mother about Lee after her first date. "Your grandfather will not like it that you are going with another type of man, as he calls them. After our daughter Rita married a Chinese man, he disowned her. It is very sad."

Margaret, who was ready to move out on her own just as soon as she finished college, shrugged, "You know, Mother, I don't care what Grandfather says. I'll be free of him pretty soon. He tries to control all our lives."

"That's not fair, Margaret. He is only trying to teach you about being Japanese and its wonderful history and tradition."

"Yeah, sure, a great example of that is Gian, his slave. Is that what we Japanese are all about?"

"No, sadly, you are right. But Gian is not Japanese, not really family. He is an experiment. Can you teach another human being to be so detached from his own reality that he feels no pain and suffering while in battle? It was the way of the Samurai, like his father. So it says in *The Book of Five Rings*. And, it seems his experiment is working."

"Working for Grandfather, but how about poor Gian? To maim and torture until one breaks, or master the pain, that is a horrible legacy to leave anyone."

Mother threw her arms in the air. "Go out, my child, and have a good time. You are right. It is time for you to leave the nest and spread your wings."

CHAPTER TWENTY-SEVEN

FIRST PRO FIGHT

Charles Umber was of German descent. He was a powerfully built man in his early thirties. He had been fighting professionally for three years. His greatest strength was his quickness. He usually ran around his opponents, tiring them, and then leg-whipped them into submission. It was no secret how he fought. It was just a secret from Aaron.

"It doesn't matter who you fight. You are so well-trained and prepared, you will beat anybody. Only worry about how well you are prepared. Don't worry about your opponent." Katsuro said

"Where did you get that stuff from, John Wooden?" Gian asked sarcastically.

"Who?"

"The UCLA basketball coach."

"I don't know who he is." Katsuro looked puzzled.

"It doesn't matter. His philosophy is to get his team so well-prepared that he never worried about the other team and how they played."

"Well, whoever he is, he is right."

A grizzled old man wearing horn-rimmed glasses and a fedora came into the dressing room. "Okay, young fella, need a urine sample before ya fight. Pee in the bottle." He handed Katsuro a glass receptacle and left.

Aaron drank that "vinegar crap" off and on during the day. He took the bottle into the bathroom and peed. *Damn.* He rubbed the needle prick Katsuro had sent into his leg the day before. *He's been putting that stuff in me from the age of nine. I got more holes than Swiss cheese.*

The old man came back, put some drops in the bottle. "Clear." He went on to the next dressing room. Micah came in. "Good luck, kid. This guy Umber likes to hit and run, then leg whip. Fast, too."

"Why are you telling me this? He's your fighter, too."

"Just a courtesy. I told him about you in case he hasn't seen you fight before, and he hadn't."

Katsuro said nothing until Micah left. "Pay no attention to him. You just go after this guy and finish him off quickly. We want to scare the shit out of all the fighters in this club."

She settled in the third row of seats. She knew better than to sit too close. *Blood flies everywhere.* She crossed her long legs, and her short skirt slid high above her shapely knees. *No dimples in those knees,* her first lover had told her. Her black outfit accentuated her slim figure, a sight every person in the audience, men and women alike, took into account. She wore a push-up Wonderbra to cap off the Venus effect.

But more than anything, she dressed for Katsuro. She wanted him to know she was a full woman, not one of those pigtailed, short-skirted teenagers Japanese men had fantasies about. She was Aaron's woman.

Micah answered his walkie-talkie without thinking it might be a disaster in the making. "Yes?"

"Boss, we got a problem. Umber went crazy in the locker room and smashed his hand into the wall. Something about his wife leaving him. The doc is sewing him up now. What do we do?"

"Shit!" Mentally, Micah went through his roster of fighters to find one that might test his new fighter. "Benny, is Rich Gold available now? I know he fights later on in the undercard. But tell him we'll pay him double to fight on short notice. He likes money."

"Yeah, boss. I just saw him. I'll ask. Hang on."

Micah could hear the voices in the background, then a new voice came in, "Micah, Rich. Give me a shot at the title if I beat your new guy, and I'll do it."

Micah didn't hesitate. "You got it, Rich—a title shot if you win. Be ready in fifteen minutes, okay?"

"I'll be ready. Just get your new guy ready. He ain't fought anybody like me before." Rich laughed. "I'll pulverize him."

Micah made a beeline for the locker area and entered Gian's room. Katsuro was just lacing up Gian's gloves and rubbing his shoulders. "We got a change in your opponent. Umber is sick, so Rich Gold is taking his place. Make any difference to you guys?"

They both shook their heads. Micah left as Ted came bursting into the room. "Sorry I'm late, Aaron. Got hooked up in traffic."

Katsuro looked over at Ted. "Why is he here?"

"He's my second. I chose him. I want him with me."

Katsuro really didn't care. This fight would only take a matter of minutes. Aaron reached for his headset and turned to his music. Ted readied his equipment. Katsuro sat and wrote a short note. He gave it to Aaron. *Two minutes and six seconds, no more. Destroy him.*

And the countdown began. Aaron settled into his own world, a world without pain, without thought, without caring, a world of destruction so thorough that victory was inevitable. There was no opponent, only an object to be defeated without mercy.

Catherine was getting nervous. The announcer announced the change in opponent for Aaron. She drummed her fingers and felt the tightness in her stomach. *What if he lost? What if he got hurt? What if . . .*

The fighters came down the aisle, Gian in the red-and-black trunks he always wore and Rich Gold in a robe with a Jewish star embroidered on his sleeve. *I wonder if he knows he's fighting another Jew?* Catherine stood and applauded. A shrill whistle blasted her eardrum as her lover entered. The whistler shouted, "Kill the Jew bastard! Kill Aaron!"

Catherine wanted to punch the guy for his remarks and for trying to break her eardrum.

The announcer took the microphone as it came down from the ceiling. "Ladies and gentlemen! Welcome to this mixed-martial arts-match, an open-weight-class fight. Introducing your two combatants. In the red corner, weighing 180 pounds, a title contender, *The Fighting Jew*, Rich Gold. And his opponent, in the black corner, fighting in his first professional fight, weighing in at 185, Aaron Michaels."

Aaron walked to the middle of the ring and stared at his opponent. His eyes never left Rich during the instructions. As they walked back to the corner, Katsuro whispered, "Show him no mercy. Make him fear you. Let him be the example for the rest. You can't be beat!"

Aaron, the fighter, the killer, heard the bell, bowed, and rushed to the middle of the ring. Without any time to feel out his opponent, without caring about being hit or hurt, he swarmed over Rich landing heavy blows to his head and midsection. Rich tried to fight back, but when he swept his leg to send Aaron off balance, Aaron blocked the leg sweep and kneed Rich in the stomach as he brought both hands crashing onto his neck. Rich crumbled to the mat and Aaron dropped a knee into his kidney. Aaron gripped Rich's right arm into an arm bar and yanked back with the strength garnered from years of torturous training.

The snap could even be heard over the din of the crowd crying for blood, but just as suddenly, silence. Rich screamed in pain, his right shoulder dislocated. Aaron pulled away from his victim and raised both his arms, remaining in his zone far away from reality, totally focused on his triumph.

Rich, writhing in pain, bellowed. After attending to Aaron and cooling him down with a sponge, Katsuro bent over Rich, gripped his shoulder, yanked it back into place and disappeared backstage with Aaron.

The ring announcer grasped the mike. "Time: one minute, seventeen seconds, the winner of his first professional fight, Aaron Michaels."

Ted patted his friend on the back yelling words of enthusiasm. "You got him, man! You really nailed him!"

Katsuro smiled to himself, never letting Gian see him pleased. Katsuro always demanded improvement from every fight. He wanted Gian to complete the task quicker and with more destruction while showing his contempt for his opponent. That, Katsuro believed, would create fear in the next opponent, and the next, and the next. That fear gave Aaron an edge for each fight and built his reputation as a bad ass.

Gasping for air, Catherine raised one hand to her mouth, the other clutching her chest. She heard the crack, the scream of pain, and the man next to her shouting, "Next time, kill the Jew!"

She left her seat to go to the dressing area. "Sorry, Miss, can't let you in there. No women allowed." Catherine stepped back.

Aaron dressed quickly and found Katsuro talking to Micah in the tunnel leading to the arena. "Great fight! Aaron looks really good in there. I'll build him up for the next fight and bill him as a contender for the World Championship."

Rich Gold's second passed the twosome in the hallway and tapped Micah on the shoulder. "Great fight? Great fighter? Bullshit! Practically tore my fighter's arm off. Shit! Dirty fighter, that's what I'd call him." The second pushed his way past them, muttering obscenities.

Micah said, "This is a tough game. The bastard shouldn't complain about nothing. Besides, he didn't even thank you for resetting his shoulder."

"And what media are you going to use to announce Aaron as a title contender?"

"Why do you asking?"

"I want an ad in the *LA Times*."

"Well, we don't have that kind of money." Micah resented being told how to handle his business.

"Yes you do. I know your finances. Do it!" Micah felt an unexpected chill run through his body. *Damn, I hate this son-of-a-bitch. I'd ditch him here and now if his fighter wasn't so good.*

Aaron saw Catherine at the end of the hallway and brought her over to Micah and Katsuro. He introduced her to Micah, who said, "Hi," and to Katsuro, who didn't even look at her.

Later, in bed with Aaron, Catherine cuddled with her lover. "Don't fret about Katsuro. He's just jealous that I have you now and he doesn't."

Catherine would soon find out how wrong she was.

* * *

It was the Sunday following the fight, and Catherine was busy making breakfast while Aaron read the *LA Times* sport section. "Hear this, the article about my professional debut says: "Aaron Michaels finished off Rich Gold faster than anybody ever did in ESK history. Aaron Michaels won his first pro fight with a bone-cracking arm bar. An ESK official says Michaels is now a contender for a championship fight."

"And I say, it's time to eat breakfast. Come on, honey, let's eat."

"And then we can have sex?"

"How about the three of us having sex?"

Aaron, was flabbergasted. "What are you saying?"

"You know what I'm saying. Remember our deal? You need to have sex with another woman, to experience what another woman tastes like, and I'm going to watch to make sure you enjoy every moment of this woman."

Gian poked a fork of French toast dripping with maple syrup into his mouth. "Who is this woman?"

"You just wait, lover boy. You will be delightfully surprised."

Gian was aroused just thinking of this unknown woman.

She rang the doorbell. A well-manicured index finger pressed on the black button three times. She shifted her legs and thought back to when she first met Catherine Tyler. Catherine was a fellow student. She couldn't help notice the tall, beautiful black woman, always well-dressed, hair attractively coiffed, with a face of stunning beauty. She knew she was also pretty, but she needed constant validation, so she slept with many of her lovers on the first date.

However, she wondered why she didn't have many orgasms. She enjoyed her vibrator in the solace of her bedroom many times more than the company of men. She began to recognize the truth about herself: she liked men but she loved women.

Feeling melancholy one Saturday night, she stopped in at a bar, ordered a drink, and sat alone enjoying her solitude. The bartender broke her self-imposed isolation. "The person down at the end of the bar would like to know if you want a drink."

She looked to her left. A well-developed blonde with too much makeup saluted her with her own drink. She wanted to say no but the blonde waved her over. She moved over and sat next to her. The blonde said, "I'm Olivia. No last names are necessary."

"Jeanne." They clanked glasses.

They left together about an hour later and settled into Olivia's spacious apartment. "My roommate won't be home tonight. Is that okay with you?"

"It's okay with me, as long as you know this will be my first time."

"It will be the first of a lifetime of pleasure like you have never known."

It was that way when Jeanne met Catherine. They had dinner together and settled into a strong sexual affair. On their first evening together Catherine said, "I have to be honest with you, Jeanne. I like my men just as well as my women. I even like watching other men and women together. Is that okay with you?"

Jeanne had heard the question before and always answered it the same way: "I like that idea, too."

Now she waited to be buzzed in. Catherine stood at the top of the stairs and beckoned her up. Then Jeanne saw what Catherine had said would be a great experience. Jeanne thought, *He is indeed a gorgeous man-child.* Her body began to ache.

"Jeanne, this is Aaron. Aaron, my friend Jeanne."

Aaron could not help but get excited. It wasn't the figure of Jeanne that he lusted after, but the thought of making love to her in front of Catherine that excited him more than he could have ever imagined. Catherine, dressed in a long bathrobe asked Jeanne, "Would you be more comfortable wearing this?"

Jeanne smiled. "No, I'd be more comfortable hugging naked with Aaron. Come on, big guy, show me what you got and how long you can last."

Jeanne practically tackled Aaron. He let himself be pulled onto the open bed playfully falling onto the sheets. Catherine lounged in a chair, enjoying the scene in front of her, a vibrator in hand and driven by lust.

Aaron let Jeanne undress him; as he helped her out of her clothes, she said, playfully, "I didn't wear a bra or panties just for you, big guy."

Aaron lay spent. "You were really great, little guy."

Catherine shut the vibrator off gasping a deep sigh. *This will not be the last time, Aaron. It is only the beginning of your experiences. You still have a lot to learn.*

CHAPTER TWENTY-EIGHT

THE PROM

Chester "Chet" Procter was a defensive tackle on the football team. He had met Aaron in his first year at Century High. It was after a game that a group of football teammates were exalting Chet for sacking the quarterback on the game's final play.

Aaron was watching with friends when Chet came over and stood above him. "Yeah, chickenshit, how come you never came out for football? Afraid of getting beat up?"

Aaron really didn't know how to respond. New to the school and not knowing very many people, he finally said, "I'm not into football, shithead."

"Naw, you're just afraid, a coward. Chickenshit!"

Knowing his fighting abilities, a friend grabbed Aaron before Aaron could get into trouble and said, "He's full of himself. Just let him talk. He thinks he's a BMOC. Actually, he's full of hot air."

Aaron turned and walked away. Chet thought walking away meant Aaron was a coward. He never stopped riding Aaron the next two years.

"Come on Catherine, you'll have a great time at my prom. You'll be the prettiest girl there."

"And the oldest."

"Not true. I have teachers who are older."

Catherine smacked him with a wicked right on his shoulder, hurting her hand. "Damn, you are just too hard-skinned."

"Hard-skinned?"

"You heard me, hard-skinned and hard-headed. If it means that much to you for me to go, I'll go, but I better not be bored."

Irene Marcusi's mother thought Chet Procter was an arrogant S.O.B. "You're going to the prom with him? I don't like you going out with him. Can't you find someone else?"

Irene at eighteen knew everything. Thus, Irene and her mother often got into arguments about various subjects. They were a grating team. Each rubbed the other the wrong way. Irene's mother did not understand the new generation and its mores. Irene did not understand much of anything because she was a teenager. She hated school, she hated her mother, and she hated her body because it was her body.

So Irene found Chet to be charming, fun, and arrogant even though she did not know what the word meant and really didn't care. After all, if her mother thought he was arrogant, he was definitely not arrogant. Having sex with Chet was like loving a freight train. He would charge through her body without one thought of her needs, settling back after he expired, forgetting about her. At these times, Irene wondered if her mother was right and if this is what arrogant means. Thoughtless! He was full of himself.

Just before the prom, Irene and Chet had an argument in the backseat of his car. "Jesus, Chet! How about waiting 'til I get my panties down before you stick me. What am I, a package of dirt to be bored into?"

"Come on, Irene. You want me because you like being seen with me. It makes you the big girl on campus."

It was at that moment Irene decided she was through with Chet Procter, but not until after the prom.

It was around this time Irene took notice of Aaron. She began to flirt with him. Aaron and Irene shared the same homeroom and a desk. "How's my friend Chet doing? I see he got a scholarship to Idaho. Not exactly the most elite football program but it is an NCAA Division I school."

"Oh, he's okay. I haven't seen him in a few days. Too busy with football, doing spring training with the Varsity."

"You going to the prom with him?"

"Why, you need a date? Good-looking guy like you shouldn't have a problem getting a date."

"No, I have a date. I just want to know if he'll be there and try to spoil my good time."

Irene sighed. There was something about this guy she liked. She guessed he wasn't arrogant. He was rather shy around girls.

Somebody had told Irene he was into martial arts. She giggled as teenage girls often did. "This date of yours, is she cute? Does she go here?"

Aaron shook his head. He thought Catherine would really resent being called cute. "No, she is a real woman and quite beautiful. She doesn't go here."

"Well, I'll be looking forward to meeting her." Irene grinned, showing a mouth full of braces.

Irene would soon find out just how happy she could be.

The next day at school, Chet saw Aaron on the quad. "I understand you got a real beautiful woman for the prom. I'll be looking forward to seeing this beauty. I know she's not nearly as pretty as Irene. Shit, man, you couldn't even get somebody that close to Irene's looks."

As Katsuro taught him to do, Aaron channeled his anger to other things when provoked. *Don't waste your energy on those who are not worthy of you. Select your battles and conquer those who deserve conquering.* Aaron wasn't sure he always understood what Katsuro meant at the time he espoused his words of wisdom, but he knew those words were meant for times like this. There would come a time to let Chet know what he thought of him. It wasn't now. Chet wasn't worth the consequence of a battle at school. Aaron was too close to graduating with almost all 'As', and he was heading for the University of North Carolina.

When Gian approached Katsuro with his acceptance letter, Katsuro read the letter and simply said, "You can't fulfill your contractual obligations with the IFF and ESK if you attend North Carolina. A University of California school is better. Go there." Gian shrugged, disappointed, but said nothing.

Aaron had the Century High office send his transcripts to the UC. His SAT scores were very high and his grades were very good. He received tentative acceptance because the UC needed to see how many applications they received from incoming freshman. Along with the classes Aaron took at Placer Junior College, he had also enrolled in several classes at Cal State while at Century.

The cycle never seemed to end for Aaron. If he had gone to North Carolina, he would have been separated from Catherine. But he was also ambivalent about the UC. It meant he would still live close to Katsuro, a place he really didn't want to be.

But at the moment, he played a cat and mouse game with Irene and Chet. Aaron liked that game.

*   *   *

The prom was festive. The gym turned into a dance hall with a local school band playing 80's music: Bon Jovi, *Livin' On A Prayer*; Madonna, *La Isla Bonita*; U2, *With or Without You*; REM, *The One I Love*; Genesis, *In Too Deep*. The room rocked with sweaty bodies and hormones ready to explode. And nobody was closer to exploding than Chet.

He watched and waited for Aaron to make his entrance. Arriving early on purpose, the Idaho-destined Chet dragged Irene to the gym as the dance started. "I don't want us to be the first ones there, Chet. I want to make an entrance so I can be seen with you." Her friend Emily had given her that line when Irene told Emily Chet was picking her up so early.

"Guys like to think they're such big cheeses. Chet is more like Limburger. That big jerk doesn't deserve you, Irene. You ditching him after the prom?"

"If he isn't nice to me, before the prom is over. I just wanted to make sure I had a date for the prom. I can always come over and hang with you, right, Emily?"

"Sure, Irene, sure," Emily knew her date would be upset to hear that. He was counting on getting laid that night.

Aaron made his grand entrance with Catherine on his arm. It would be unfair to say everybody—every student, every staff member, every band member—was staring at Catherine: unfair because some were outside enjoying a nip from a bottle or sneaking a smoke. Almost all the others wound up gazing at her. "Aaron, I

227

feel like a piece of furniture. Too many people are asking how old I am."

"Nonsense. They are just looking at you because you are so beautiful, and licking their lips wanting to be in my place."

"Don't you let them get near me. I will only dance with you."

"You bet, honey. Dance only with me." Suddenly Aaron became detached. He was lost in a zone. Catherine knew the drill. He had seen something. He was focusing and couldn't release that focus. Aaron spotted Chet. He was dressed in a tuxedo with a red cummerbund, a black bowtie, and a flat flask of bourbon tucked neatly in a jacket pocket. Chet raised his hand to Aaron, signifying he liked his date.

"Who is that big kid with the raised hand in the middle of the dance floor, Aaron? A friend of yours?"

"No, not exactly. More of a jerk I have yet to slap down."

"Well, you're not slapping him down here. Not with me, you're not."

"I promise to be a good boy, Catherine, as long as we are at the dance."

"Come on, lover boy. Show a girl a good time." Catherine ground her hips into Aaron's groin, making him dance better than ever.

A number of guys tried to cut in to dance with Catherine, but Aaron said no and so did Catherine. Even Chet walked over to get a closer look at the statuesque woman. He maneuvered Irene close to his target and said, "Hi. Nice date, shithead."

Catherine could feel Aaron tightening up and moved him away. "Not here, big boy. You promised."

After the dance ended, Chet and Irene were looking for his car in the school parking lot just as Gian was swinging by with Catherine. "You know, Catherine, Irene would be a great woman for you to have. Maybe we should take her home and show her what real pleasure is like."

Filled with bravado fostered by too much bourbon, Chet stopped abruptly in his tracks. "What the hell you talkin' about, shithead? My girl is too good for you or your black-cat friend."

"I'll tell you what, Chet. You and I will settle the score once and for all. The winner takes all. You take me out, and you can have

Catherine. If I take you out, we take Irene home with us and show her a good time. Okay, Irene? You are going to leave this schmuck after you graduate anyway. So ditch him now."

Before Irene could answer, Chet blurted out, "You know, man, I'll really enjoy fucking your little girlfriend here all night. I'll show her what a big dick can do."

Catherine burst out laughing. "You are a big dick, buster."

Chet blustered, "I'll kick your ass, Aaron. I'll smash you to bits. To the winner goes the spoils."

Catherine repeated the deal; "If you kick Aaron's ass, Chet, I'll go home with you and show you what a woman can do for you. But if you lose, Irene goes with us. All agreed?"

Irene, feeling a little light-headed from a few sips of booze but very interested in Aaron, nodded her head. She helped Chet take off his coat. "Give it to him, big guy," she said meekly.

"Hold my jacket, honey. It's gonna be you and me and blackie tonight." These were Chet's last words for the night.

With their hands raised in a fighter's position, Aaron leaned forward and smashed Chet in the mouth, hard. His head snapped back and Aaron hit him again on the side of his head. Chet faded to the left and Aaron unloaded a crisp right that knocked Chet down and out cold: a three-punch fight.

Irene looked down at her date and said nothing. She stepped over him, grabbed Aaron's arm and walked with him to his car. Catherine drove home as Aaron and Irene got acquainted—intimately. "If you're doing her now, you'll have to do her again so I can watch," Catherine said from the front seat.

"Your wish is my command," Aaron said as he came up for air. Irene called her mother and said she would be home around noon the next day.

*   *   *

It was an unusually cool summer in Los Angeles. Gian, with a towel wrapped around his well-developed body, stood in the bathhouse talking to Katsuro. The old man's splendid physique, still chiseled despite the supposed ravages of old age, was a body any forty-year—old man would have been proud to display. His various tattoos seemed alive.

"That reporter from *Martial Arts Magazine* was certainly impressed by our dojo. He said he had never seen anything like it in the United States."

"I was with you, Gian, when he did the interview. I know what he said. Just contain your excitement."

Gian started to dance around the old man, stabbing the air with lightning blows. "He said he had never interviewed a fighter with only two fights under his belt. I guess I must be pretty good. Besides, I'm fighting for the world championship after only two fights. That's never been done." Gian smiled as he continued his talking and dancing.

Katsuro muttered to himself, ducked under a right jab, and walked out of the bathhouse. He slammed the door behind him so Gian would know he left. Moments later a slim shadowy figure entered the bathhouse dressed in a flowered kimono and rubber clogs. "Gian, it's me, Margaret. I need to talk to you."

Gian remembered the last time Margaret had seen him in the bathhouse. This time he made sure his towel was secure around his waist, forcing him to stop his dancing and jabbing. "Come on, Gian, ease up. I just want to talk."

"Right here? Right now?"

"Yes, my grandfather will not come back now and I want to talk to you alone."

Gian slid onto a wooden stool. "Talk to me."

"I am leaving the house and getting my own townhouse. I want to lead my own life. Katsuro won't direct me anymore. I must have my freedom."

Gian sat motionless. "So why are you telling me this?"

"Because you need to be free of him, too. You need to get away."

Gian rose from the stool, cinched his towel, placed his hands on his hips, and looked right at Margaret, "You are his flesh and blood, Margaret. You are part of his family. I am not. You have his love, no matter what you do. He loves you. I bet he has told you that a hundred times."

"Yes, but so what? He loves you, too. I know he does."

"He has never told me that. He has never held me, never said a kind word to me. Never! I am his beast of burden that will carry him to the promised land of championships and renown that nobody in his family could ever achieve. So he calls me his son, calls me his champion, but never calls me his beloved child."

"I don't understand, Gian. I see what he has done to you. I see how he trains you. I see the time he takes to make you the best you can be. Does that not show his love?"

Gian put his arms around Margaret. He held her close. "He has done this to you. He has cradled you when you are hurt, loved you when you needed love, told you he loves you. He has done none of those things to me. I am his surrogate champion. When I win the world championship, I take him with me because he has been my trainer. He might love me then, but not for who I am, but for what I have become. The thing that he made me."

"Oh God, Gian. I am so sorry. He has stolen your childhood, your soul, and made you a robot. But, if it will make you feel any better, I love you. You are my brother and I will never forget you." A tear trickled down Margaret's cheek.

"Hey, come on, Margaret, I didn't mean to make you cry." Gian picked up his older sister and placed her on the stool. "Now you are the queen of my attention. Where are you going?"

"I am going to live with my Chinese boyfriend. Grandfather doesn't approve, but I don't care. I am out of here as of this Saturday."

"I am glad for you, but it is not my time to leave yet. I owe that man something. I owe him the world championship."

"When are you going to fight for that prize?"

"In three weeks in Cologne, Germany. There will be a hundred thousand fans there. I owe him that, if nothing else."

"I'm excited for you. When did you find this out?"

"That reporter who just left about thirty minutes ago said he was writing an article about the fight for his magazine. I will be on the cover."

Margaret jumped into Gian's arms. His towel dropped to the floor. He held her. She looked over his shoulder. "You dropped something."

"I don't care as long as I don't drop you."

Aaron and Catherine drove to the beach that night. They stopped at the Fish Shanty, picked through the crab and talked about the fight. "Cologne, Germany? Why so far away? Why not in the United States?"

"Those are a lot of questions." Aaron thought for a moment. "I think I know why. Katsuro met with Micah, the owner of the IFF. Micah says the best offer he got was from the promoter in Germany. They're really into martial arts. They are having many international bouts and several world championship fights in various weight divisions, including my light-heavyweight bout."

"Who will you fight?"

"Charles Umber."

Catherine flashed back to Gian's first professional fight. "Wait a minute. Isn't he the guy you were scheduled to fight for your first fight?"

"Yup! He's the guy. Apparently being from Germany, he has great appeal as a fighter."

Catherine frowned. "If I remember correctly, he's had many years experience and he's older than I am."

"Yes, you are right. Still, I can beat him, but I'm not sure about you."

She punched him in the arm. "That is probably harder than Charles will ever punch me." He held her close. "Maybe the next time I go overseas, we will go together and vacation. I would like that."

Catherine smiled. "So would I."

Sometimes what one wishes for is better left unfulfilled.

* * *

Margaret told Katsuro she was moving out that Saturday morning. She kissed him gently on the cheek. "Thank you, Grandfather, for all your caring and love. I am like a butterfly that needs to leave her cocoon. Every creature needs to find a life of her own, so I go."

"To your Chinese boyfriend?"

Margaret smiled. "You knew all along, didn't you?"

"I have my ways. You know I don't approve. But what can I do? I will miss you, child."

Margaret got up and hurried out of the house. A tear trickled down her cheek. She fumbled for her keys and spun out of the insulated world that was the Tachigi compound.

Katsuro needed to work out to remove the sadness from his system. Margaret was his favorite. She had more guts than any of his other grandchildren. She also had a conscience. He remembered she was the only one who had helped Gian. She had helped him dig out of his Earth home, cared for him when he was beaten, fed him when he was unable to feed himself, took care of Dog when he couldn't. *Margaret was born female but had the gonads of a boy.*

Katsuro entered the family dojo. It was empty. The floors were clean, well scrubbed, just as Gian had always done. He stopped and . . . *Who cleaned the floors? Where was Gian?*

Meanwhile, Gian walked slowly through his old home. It hadn't changed. No one lived there now. The slight smell of Dog remained. He wondered how Dog was doing, living with Raul.

He left his house, passing the dojo. He heard the gloves pounding against the bag. He peered in. The old man was there alone. Something drew him into the building. He sat in the chair where Katsuro usually sat with the *Shinai* tucked next to it.

The old man stopped and turned. "Margaret left, but you already knew that, didn't you?"

"Yes."

"Why did she go?"

"She needed her freedom. But you already knew that, didn't you?"

"Yes. She went to be with her Chinese lover."

"So did your daughter, Rita. So what!"

Katsuro wiped his face with a towel. He pulled a chair next to Gian. "Did I ever tell you our family was originally from China?"

Qichon! Now Gian remembered. *The question that had never been answered so many years ago. Qichon. That was it.*

"My grandfather was Chinese. His ancestor was a monk. The monk took the basic tenets, the basic forms, of Shaolin Kung Fu and extrapolated them into animal movements. He took from the teachings of his Shaolin upbringing and mixed those movements with his own theories to create a simpler yet more effective system.

Those hybrid movements emulated the snake, monkey, crane, tiger, and dragon, in that order. The monk taught the people in the villages how to fight and how to defend themselves using his system and techniques.

"But his timing was bad. He left the temple and lost its protection. It was not a good time to be a monk at all, especially without the temple's protection. So he fled to Japan with his wife and daughter. There he became the servant of a Samurai warrior. His daughter and the warrior's son fell in love. The Samurai was furious and ordered death to the servant monk.

"But when the Samurai was under attack, the monk came to his rescue and earned the warrior's gratitude. The monk taught the warrior his form of jujitsu. The warrior secretly allowed the two lovers to marry. Their child was passed on as Japanese and was taught the three varieties of martial arts.

"The Monk created a system that became Earth, Water, Air, and Fire: equal parts Japanese and Chinese.

All the forms of martial arts are more than fighting and the techniques of fighting. It is to understand history, to understand warfare, and to understand why things were."

Gian rocked back in his chair. "So why are you so set against Margaret marrying this Chinese man?"

Katsuro slapped his hands on his lap and rose. "Through time, the Japanese religion and culture has prevailed in our family. It is called purity, my son, purity."

While driving back to Catherine, Gian laughed at the word "purity," Katsuro's one-word argument. However, Aaron dwelled on the other noun he'd heard: "son."

CHAPTER TWENTY-NINE

KATSURO'S DREAM

Katsuro was exploding with excitement. It was something he had worked for all his life, and now this child, his protégé, would reward all his hard work with a world championship. He thought of his father, long gone to his final resting place after he had fought his last battle. The Samurai warrior, the proud gladiator, was certainly looking down on his son with pride. He could hear his father's words: *Honor thy family's name in all battles. Let our family tradition of great warriors carry on forever.*

Into the ring climbed the family's tradition. Katsuro had often apologized to his father that his own flesh and blood could not be that great champion, but he would raise a warrior of superior skills to that level. So Aaron Michaels carried the Tachigi family flag with him whenever and wherever he fought.

Aaron Michaels looked out across the arena. He had watched as the German crowd rooted for their fighters in each bout. The huge crowd, roaring for blood, would have intimidated a lesser fighter. Aaron considered it another challenge and was rather bemused by the noise.

But Aaron was not what one might call a normal fighter. From an early age, he had had the fear of mere mortals knocked from his mind. The only person in the world he feared stood in his corner and cheered for him. Only Katsuro drew Aaron's fear, the fear of not being his best, the fear of failure, the fear of losing. Those fears were never allowed once Aaron entered the zone of readiness for each fight. He would not be beaten, for he banished all pain; the only pain he could possibly feel would be the pain of failure.

Charles Umber stood on the opposite side of the ring, waving at the crowd. He had fought many fights, always dreaming of this championship bout. Now it was here. He could hardly contain himself. His handler rubbed his shoulders gently. "Quiet down, Charles. Just concentrate on this kid. Your time has come."

Charles flexed his muscles and felt his powerful body ooze with energy. He knew it was his time. His place in history would be made tonight. He stared at the kid who was going to try and stop that history, and he grew angry. "Destroy him, Charles. Be quicker than he is. Be stronger than he is. Be more powerful than he is. Kill him, Charles." Charles stood in his corner. He was ready.

Aaron sat and hummed a slow ballad. He was now in his other self where he never felt pain, where he never heard anything but the thought of obliterating his opponent. He was ready to do battle. He ceased hearing the bloodthirsty crowd. "Kill the Japanese bastard. Kill the American bastard. Kill him, Umber."

Katsuro patted his son on the back and whispered to no one, *for my father.* Aaron never heard the referee's words. He only glared at his opponent with eyes so vicious they tore into Charles Umber's heart. Aaron's voice tore into Charles' psyche. "You will feel nothing but pain. I am about to destroy you. Get ready for pain, Charles!"

Aaron's words penetrated Charles' brain. No one had ever said anything to him before a fight. Charles lost his concentration just thinking of the words Aaron had uttered. *That son-of-a-bitch, I'll kill him.* Charles Umber had lost the battle of wills.

'Kill him, *Juko*, quickly. Give him no chance.' Katsuro's words echoed in Aaron's silent world. 'Kill him quickly!'

Charles Umber lumbered into the center of the ring. For that split second, he let his guard down. Touching of the gloves, a custom, was part of the opening routine. Custom is one thing, fighting for a world championship is another.

Aaron ran to the center of the ring, never touched gloves, never hesitated to deliver a roundhouse right hand that struck Charles Umber on his left temple and sent him sprawling across the ring. Aaron did not hear the boos, did not hear the chorus of verbiage that pelted the ring. He heard only flesh crushing as his knuckles met the flesh of Charles Umber and tore his skin. Charles stumbled backward and fell to the mat as his feet became tangled.

Charles's forehead ached and he felt blood dribbling down his face. But the pain in his head was nothing compared to the pain in his stomach when Aaron dropped a knee into his ribs, splintering several.

Aaron knew he had hurt Charles Umber when he fell on him, spun him around and wrapped his legs around his torso while squeezing those broken ribs. The crowd quieted to a hushed whisper as their hero lay in agony crying out in pain.

Charles raised his arm to the referee signaling he was done. He quit. The pain was like no other he had ever felt. His immediate hatred of Aaron Michaels was intense. Aaron had broken the martial-arts-fighters' code.

Micah hurried to Katsuro, who was grinning and bowing through the cries of derision from the pro German crowd. "Get your boy back to the dressing room, quickly, before this crowd mobs him. Now!"

Several German policemen pushed through the crowd shoving the howling mob out of the way before they could attack Aaron. Two more policemen gathered around Katsuro and Aaron and escorted them down the aisle and into the small tunnel at the back of the arena.

"Rather unfriendly crowd out there tonight," Aaron commented. "You'd think they would be saluting me as the world champion."

Micah fumed. "Not when you fail to follow tradition. You slugged Umber before you touched gloves. That was outrageous. My World Champion didn't follow our Federation's rules! That can't happen again!"

Katsuro bowed slowly while removing Gian's gloves. He cut the tape away and dipped his hands in hot oil to soften them. "A fight is on once the combatants come out of their corner. My fighters are always ready to fight. There is no time to relax in the ring. My son is the new champion of the world. You want to give this guy another fight? You're the promoter; do it! He will beat him again."

Micah stomped out of the dressing room, glaring at the two, but that glare turned to a smile as soon as his back was to them. *There is nothing like a little controversy to stir interest in a future fight.* Micah saw the green of money, as Charles Umber saw the red of revenge.

* * *

"Just sit still, Charles. You have a nasty cut on your forehead. I need to sew it up. Patching it won't keep it closed for long."

"That son-of-a-bitch, bastard! He cheap-shotted me. I'll kill him next time. You get a hold of Micah and tell him I want a rematch, quick!"

* * *

Micah was on the phone to a promoter in Brussels talking up his fighters when, "That son-of-a— . . ."

"Hey, quiet down. I'll talk to you in a few minutes."

Joseph Schultz was a large man with meaty hands and a round face flushed with beer. "I ain't quietin' down. I got a group of mad patrons out there who want the scalp of your boy. They want to see him get his ass kicked. I want to set another fight card for next week using your new world champion. I'll sell out the place."

Not being able to quiet Schultz, Micah hung up the phone without a word to his Belgian promoter. "You want Aaron back? Next week?"

"Yeah! And I want my boy to be fightin' him."

"Who's your boy?"

"The Son of Hitler!"

"Come on man, you're kidding me. The Son of Hitler?"

"That's the name he fights under. He draws big crowds and makes me all sorts of money."

"Tell me about him."

"Just come down and watch him train tomorrow at nine. Hell, he even looks like a blown-up Führer."

* * *

The next morning Gian awoke to rapping on his door. "Door's open. Come in."

Micah entered and sat on the edge of his bed. "Well, kid, you really caused a ruckus last night. Seems the Board of Directors is not going to allow you your championship due to unsportsmanlike conduct. They have ordered a rematch and the record of last night's fight has already been wiped off the map."

"You talked to Katsuro about this?"

"Can't find him. He went out someplace and hasn't returned yet. The Board is saying you have to give Umber a rematch. Umber wants you, and the Board wants you to fight him. But, this time, all the rules must be followed. Got it?"

"Yeah. Well, whatever you want. I'll take Umber just like I did last night."

The rematch would have to wait until Umber's cuts healed.

*　*　*

Katsuro sat at the back of the gym and watched the fighter work out. He smiled. *Juko will kill this guy. But we might want to have some fun with him. Some side bets should work well for us.*

He was a monster of a man. He was too heavy, though mighty powerful; too slow, yet extremely brutal.

He used this brutality to intimidate his opponents giving him great pleasure.

Katsuro watched for a weak spot. He found none. This would be a real test for Aaron Michaels. The Son of Hitler: Katsuro shook his head at the outlandish name. Katsuro remembered Hitler as being short and thin. This fighter had trimmed his mustache and that was the only feature that looked like Hitler's. This man was huge compared to Hitler.

The match was set. The city of Cologne became the meeting place for Aaron and the Nazi. Somehow the news got out that Aaron Michaels was born a Jew, and that news made the fight with an American/Japanese/ Jew even more interesting than Micah could have imagined.

The fight was booked as an open-class bout. There was no weight division. Even Micah had been caught up in the chaos.

Katsuro called Ryuu to catch a flight to Cologne. "I need you here. You are the only one I can trust with all this money that is being bet. They have this guy as a 5-2 favorite. I had one guy who bet twenty thousand and I put up ten. Another guy says the fight will go

239

three rounds. I bet him it would never make the second round. Just get here, fast."

Saturday arrived very quickly. The press, locals, and those curious to see an Anglo-Japanese-Jew fight attended Aaron's daily workouts. Katsuro had worked Gian very slowly. He wanted the Germans to think Aaron wasn't as good as he really was. Aaron put on a show. *Just like show business or monkey business,* Aaron thought.

Ryuu had contacted a German bookmaker who handled all the bets. The German was a small, wiry older man with a large mustache and steely eyes that Ryuu liked right away. This was quite unusual, since Ryuu didn't like very many people and trusted even fewer. "Old man, you have a fine reputation, but still I want you to know, do not cross me. That would be a very bad move."

The old man smiled. "My young friend and fellow bookmaker, I have dealt with Hitler and his men during the early years of my life. I survived that, and I will survive all your threats. We will both makes lots of money."

Ryuu met Katsuro later that evening in the hotel dining room. "This old German bookmaker is okay. He is honest and cagey at the same time. He makes the odds as he sees the take coming in. We have very good odds on Aaron."

"What is the over and under on the fight?" Katsuro asked. "That we have control of. If the odds say the fight will last two rounds, then I will have Gian end it in less time."

"Gian knows about overs and unders?"

Katsuro laughed. Gian only cares about winning and losing, and he never loses."

"I think we can makes lots of money on this fight."

The Stadium was in an uproar. Fans who had attended the last fight and those who had read about the man-child, as the German Press referred to Aaron, were fighting mad. Micah had pleaded with the German fight promoter to triple security, which he did but only when Micah upped his guarantee and promised a greater cut of the gate. Aaron was the only one who was calm during the entire week. He had called Catherine several times and talked dirty to her on the phone. "If that old man won't let us have sex before a fight, then let's talk dirty now. That should get you revved up real quick." Catherine sounded excited yet, her voice was very soothing to Aaron, who always worried about losing her.

Aaron kept grinning while he told Catherine what he wanted to do to her. She wiggled in her chair and stroked herself. "I can't wait for you to get back. Say, when are you coming back?"

"I don't know. Katsuro wants to travel a little bit in the United Kingdom and have me fight some Welsh fighters. He says they are a rough-and-tumble group."

"Well, just promise me you'll take care of yourself."

"I will. By the way, did I get any mail from the UC?"

"Yes! It's right here."

"Please open it for me. I enrolled in a couple of courses this summer and I want to make sure I got in."

Catherine tore the envelope and scoured the pages. "The letter says you were accepted to each of the two classes. Enjoy your trip without me, lover boy. Just be ready for me when you get back."

*   *   *

The noise of a European crowd is different from an American audience. Each ethnic group bans together in one section of the arena and carries its own colors, and its country's flag. They sing a wide range of songs throughout the match. Countries compete against each other as to who can sing the loudest, yell the loudest, waved its banners the longest, and make the most commotion. In this German arena, there were only Germans, waving German flags. Every single one of them was pulling for his hero and against the hated enemy, Aaron Michaels.

A raucous sound resonated across the arena and the old building shook. Gian was fighting last on the card. "I want to keep the audience in their seats through the evening. Quite a sight out there! Germans are great fight fans."

Gian, who had not yet psyched himself up for the fight, piped in, "Sure! Great! Especially when the press builds the fight as a Japanese-trained Jewish American fighting the embodiment of Hitler. Great publicity!" Gian stroked his chin. "Say, how did they find out about my being born a Jew and being raised and trained in Japan?"

Micah smiled. "That's why they call me a fight promoter. I promote fights, and I am damn good at it."

The Son of Hitler sat in his dressing room and had a swig of beer. His manager grabbed the bottle. "Stupid son-of-a-bitch! What are you doing drinking before a fight! This guy's tough."

Hitler grabbed the bottle back, threw the cap away, and guzzled the rest of the brew. He belched. "Fuckin' good stuff. Makes me fight better. Remember that last bastard I busted up, that Swiss guy. I drank a whole barrel of the stuff before I fought him. The only bad part was I had to piss so bad, I ran outta the ring before they announced my name as the winner."

"Listen to me, stupid. This guy is not a bum. He's hell on wheels. The crowd doesn't like him because he beat one of their boys and broke a code of ethics. Well, this game has no ethics. Tradition, maybe, but no ethics. Anything goes! Don't give him a chance!"

Hitler stood, fully erect. He was a monster of a man. He looked like a sumo wrestler of ancient times. Still, he could fight on the mat as well as stand up. He had quick hands and large, meaty fists. Slow and plodding at times, he was tough. He had a large scar across his right knee. His Hitler-like mustache was trim and neat compared to his slovenly appearance, only because his girlfriend insisted. "I didn't like Hitler and I don't like you being called the Son of Hitler," she told him often.

"I only get that Son of Hitler crap because of my mustache. Besides that little trick of being the Son of Hitler brings me lots of fans and good money."

The Son of Hitler's girlfriend cuddled up to him and said, "Promise me, if you ever get tired of fighting, you'll shave off that crappy mustache."

"I'll go one step further. If I ever lose, I'll shave it off just for you, sweetie." He stroked her chin. "Come on, let's have a little fun."

"Sex before a fight? Your manager says that's not a good idea. *Verboten!*"

"Screw my manager."

While the Son of Hitler cuddled with his girl, Katsuro met with Gian in their room. "This guy wants his revenge. There are no rules, so be on your guard."

"Come on, Katsuro, you know I can beat this guy. I'll cut him up."

"It would be better if you just rendered him unconscious." Katsuro laughed. "You remember that wooden figure in the dojo, the one with all the circles on it?"

"Of course."

"Then remember this spot." Katsuro touched a spot near Gian's middle. "A well-targeted elbow to this spot will knock the wind out of anyone, and an even harder blow will knock a victim out. This is what a Grand Master would do."

Katsuro went through another of his Grand Master moves, drawing Aaron closer to that illustrious position.

Gian would need all these techniques and all of his guile to defeat this German.

The crowd was in a mean mood when it came time for the last fight of the night. Too much beer, lack of air-conditioning, and a fervor against the American Jew combined to create a negative atmosphere in the arena, which was ready to explode.

Aaron was in his trance. Only Katsuro noticed the crowd and leaned over and whispered to Ryuu. "You go sit next to that little old bookmaker friend of yours and don't let him out of your sight. This place could explode, and I don't want him to explode with it."

Katsuro, always looking for an excuse for Aaron to end a fight as quickly as possible, had the best excuse of all tonight. "Juko, this place is not a friendly environment. End this fight as quickly as possible. Destroy this guy, so the crowd can see you are a much better fighter than he is. That way, they may not erupt if there isn't any doubt about who has really won. Get him quick!"

Even Micah was a bit nervous about the crowd. "Damn Germans! It's only a fight."

The old German bookie sat shriveled up in his chair accepting a parade of bettors as they walked up to him, whispered their bets, and moved on. He barely blinked but did nod his acceptance of each bet. On a rare occasion he would shake his head and the bettor would have to offer another bet. One large man with a fist full of marks stuffed the money in the bookie's pocket and moved on. The old man turned to Ryuu. "He likes your boy. Says he'll beat the crap out of Hitler. Some Germans bet with their hearts rather then their brain, but not him. Your boy in the first round at three to one."

Ryuu asked, "How do you remember all these bets? Do you know all these people?"

The old man was about to answer when another patron came over. "Hitler, second round, three thousand. Number 635," the patron said in German.

The old man spoke into his lapel. "See this thin piece of metal? A microphone goes to my son, who records all the bets. I have it all on tape and in my son's computer. Modern stuff is great for accuracy."

"How are the bets going?"

"Never worry about what somebody else bets. For the bookie, it all levels out. You make your personal bets, pick on the differences in the odds, and all will be well."

Ryuu reflected on the old man's words and said nothing. He had made his bet on Aaron at 5 to 2 for $50,000. That would make the fight worthwhile.

Ryuu watched the parade of fighters in the preliminary fights. Then he saw the big German walk down the aisle. Ryuu sized up the monster until he came to his vulnerability. Ryuu, the savage, always looked for an advantage, and he found it in the right knee of the Son of Hitler.

He scrambled to the ring and leaned over Katsuro. He said a few words and returned to sit next to the old bookie.

Katsuro seldom pointed out Aaron's opponent to him, not wanting to break Aaron's concentration. But he thought he must in this case. He leaned over to Aaron and told him to look at the German giant's surgically repaired knee.

The referee called the two fighters to the center of the ring, each bowed, touched gloves after the instructions, and took their fighting poses. The crowd roared. Aaron heard the crowd for the first time. "Kill the American Jew. Kill him!"

Aaron moved slowly around the German waiting for the right moment. Finally, he stopped moving and motioned with his hands for the German to come after him. Hitler stopped, puzzled. Usually fighters ran from him and relied on quickness. None had stood still beckoning him in. So for that fatal moment, Hitler stood still. It was in that instant Aaron Michaels, bending deeply, sprung up and forward, left his feet and sent a powerful left foot into the German's right knee. The German winced and cried out. He felt a shock of pain and collapsed to the mat grabbing his knee. Aaron stomped the right knee again and again and finally dropped his full weight onto the German's knee. He dropped to the mat and grabbed the German's right leg and bent it back, using his left leg as a bar.

Aaron heard the knee crack. Silence! Weird silence! The crowd sat, stunned. As if in slow motion, Aaron got up. The referee raised his hand. The announcer yelled, "The winner and still undefeated Light-Heavyweight Champion of the World, Aaron Michaels." The fight announcer ignored Micah's statement about Aaron being disqualified in his previous fight. The slow motion ended as Aaron left the ring.

From the crowd that had been screaming kill Aaron Michaels, only silence and a few catcalls could be heard. Only the shuffling of the stunned crowd leaving the arena could be heard above the air of expectation that had been drained from the stadium.

Ryuu stayed close to the old man as soon as he left his seat then quickly left the arena, and walked into Micah's temporary office. There sat Micah, the German promoter, and Katsuro.

Cash was distributed: over and under money, some of the betting money, and then the winner's purse. The German promoter said, "The other money will be transferred to your bank accounts as you wish. Thank you, gentlemen, nice doing business with you." A private security company with several armed guards walked with Katsuro to Aaron's dressing room. He found Gian lying on a training table being vigorously rubbed by his second.

The security guards left the threesome at their hotel after being paid in cash. Katsuro called his bank in the United States and had the hotel wire their cash winnings to the bank. Katsuro took fifty percent of his gambling profits and placed them into a trust account held in Aaron's name. He looked at Ryuu and nodded. "A well-earned bonus for my son, the world champion. Maybe he might want to buy his own house one day."

Later, in the car as they were being driven back to their hotel, Gian said, "I told you I didn't need any special move to beat this guy, Katsuro."

"But you will one day. Practice it and use it when needed." That would be at a special time.

Gian thought about that move. Katsuro showed him how to kick the inside ankles of both feet, then grab the upper portion of the *gi* with both hands, pull the opponent forward, drop one arm, and drive an elbow into the ribs. Air is knocked out of the opponent as he falls to the mat, then one drives another elbow to the stomach area as the opponent is knocked unconscious. Swiftness, power, and accuracy all lead to defeating any victim.

CHAPTER THIRTY

THE STREET FIGHTERS

The Pen and Wig Tavern in Cardiff, Wales was a narrow building with a huge oak-covered ceiling, a variety of beers displayed on shelves, and a bustling clientele from near and far. Frequented by college students, it served good food, good ale, and an assortment of characters who interested Katsuro. He and Ryuu and the ever-present silent attendants made their way to the far end of the bar and ordered pints of bitter. "Nothing better than some bitters from our friends in Wales."

And they waited.

A former prizefighter and natural-born bad boy, Trevor Wiliams was born in Wales. He still had a serious acne problem at the age 42. A swatch of red hair had been severely removed by a bottle of acid from a jealous husband, and there was a wide red scar from a knife attack on his left cheek. He zoomed down Cardiff's main drag, racing in and out of cars, knowing he was late for an appointment he shouldn't be late for, and hustled into the Pen and Wig. He saw the two Japanese at the far end of the bar and moved toward them.

The bartender, a husky-voiced mountain of a man, saw Trevor enter and pressed the buzzer under his counter. The bar's owner, alerted by the buzzing sound, looked down from his office and saw the shock of red hair and the disfigured face, and buzzed three times. His security guards looked up at the window of the boss's office, followed his eyes to the red hair, and closed in on Trevor Wiliams.

They caught him as he neared Katsuro and Ryuu's table. "Steady there, lad. You were told never to enter this place again. Out you go."

Trevor was surrounded by four security men. Now alert and in a crouching stance, "Come and get me gentlemen. I don't go easy."

The former professional fighter was overmatched. The security guards quickly surrounded him. One punch and Trevor was reeling around in a vicious circle as he bounced from one fist to another. The tortured face was bleeding profusely.

Katsuro and Ryuu nodded to each other. They took off their jackets. "Don't want to mess our nice suits," and stepped into the skirmish.

Ryuu delivered a quick kick to one guard's ribs and sent him tumbling into the bar. A chop to a second guard's throat dropped him gasping for air.

Several students, always looking for some excitement, entered the fray. Katsuro sent a hard chop to a student's neck and floored him. Trevor, no longer the center of attention, scrambled from the fight. A melee ensued. Trevor signaled to Ryuu and Katsuro. They grabbed their coats as the trio exited the club's back door.

"I owe you gentlemen. Trevor Wiliams at your service."

A little winded, Katsuro walked briskly toward their car. "Why are you not welcome in the club?"

"The owner and I have a mutual dislike for each other. I was accused of forcing my attention on and screwing his brother's wife. A lie, of course. I screwed her at her request."

Ryuu puzzled asked. "So why did you have us meet you there?"

"I don't like to be told where I can go. I want what I want. Besides, I don't like the man. If I can cross him, I will."

They reached Katsuro's rented car and scrambled in. "Just drive around the corner and we'll go to the Blackweir Tavern about three blocks down on the right." Trevor said addressing the chauffeur.

Seated in a private booth at the Blackweir, Trevor went on, "The owner wasn't supposed to be at his tavern. He was supposed to be out of town. But, obviously he wasn't. So I got hammered. If you guys hadn't been there, he would have probably had me beaten to death. I'm not the most well-liked guy in town."

"But you do handle street brawlers, right?" Ryuu asked.

"You got the right guy. You got a fighter who needs a lesson in all-out war fighting—anything goes—anything?"

"Yes, my son can handle all that. Besides, he needs a couple of real tough characters to know what a true battle is like."

"Your son? He ever street fight before? It's dirty stuff, guys!"

"Yeah, he's a bad dude. That's what he calls himself."

"You got a hundred grand to put up? I'll need that to guarantee the toughest fighters show up, to rent a place, and to get publicity. We will need a CFO, though."

"CFO? What's that?"

"A fancy name for a bookie."

"You have a bookie; how do I know that bookie is working for both of us?"

"I've checked into you guys. You hire your own security who work for you, not me. So I'm sure you'll cover your ass."

Ryuu hired security, Katsuro met with Trevor to see the site and Gian took his daily workout with his weekly injections. "No tests for this fight," Katsuro noted. "But you will have to wear this iron jock. This is a no holds fight. Everything goes, including groin kicks. Be prepared, *Juko!*"

On the last trip to check out the site, Gian went with Katsuro. They walked with Trevor to an abandoned warehouse. The ring was set up and two fighters were working out.

One fighter, a shaved-bald black man with no teeth, was shadow-boxing as he waited for the other man to get ready. "Yeah, Sid, get this piece of shit up here so I can crush some bones. Where did you get this guy, off the trash heap?"

Sid, finished rubbing down the sparring partner with linseed oil and yelled back at the toothless black man, "Shut your pie hole, man. Just let me get my fighter ready. You want a war, he'll give you one."

The toothless black man burst out laughing. "Shit man, I'll eat him for supper."

Without a referee, the two entered the ring and went to war. Toothless shot a rocket jab to the middle of the linseed oil-guy. The black man, showing no fear or any reaction to pain, attacked linseed. He drove him to the mat with a body slam and elbowed him in the face. Blood spurted from the man's torn flesh. The blood soaked the mat. Toothless ground the man's face into his own blood. He drove a series of knees into the man's kidney.

The man rolled over and held his side while the black man smashed elbow after elbow into his face. The linseed man collapsed in pain all the while his body continued to be abused. Without thought, Aaron leapt into the ring. He pulled the black man off the now unconscious man. "He's out, man. Off!"

The toothless giant, much taller than Aaron, shoved him across the ring with tremendous power. Aaron bounced off the ropes and elbowed the incoming black man. Toothless took the blow without feeling it and stood his ground. "You going to be my next meal, kid?"

Despite his advanced years Katsuro bolted into the ring. "My son is not a kid. He will fight you here next Saturday."

"Trevor! This the tough kid that wants a street fight? Can't you get me a real man. I don't like to fight children."

Katsuro knew when he was in tough and withdrew. "We will see you next Saturday. Just be ready for a whipping."

Toothless smiled toothlessly. "I'll be ready for legalized murder."

Trevor walked the two out, "Will he be tough enough?"

Katsuro shrugged. Gian smiled at the idea of fighting the toothless guy. "If he's so tough, what happened to his teeth?"

Trevor laughed, "That son-of-a-bitch just pulled them out so he wouldn't get them all knocked out fighting. He's a tough guy, real tough!"

Katsuro was a little worried for the first time. This guy was mean and tough. *I will need to teach Gian a few new tricks.*

*   *   *

Katsuro spent the next afternoon with Gian, reviewing with him the parts of the body circled on the wooden figure in the dojo. Katsuro's instructions were always the same, "It is not how hard you hit someone, it is where you hit them. A sharp blow on any of these spots will render a man unconscious."

Gian closed his eyes and marked the spots in his mind. "Be accurate!"

* * *

Saturday night a storm stood off the Isle. The rain pounding against the old building caused several leaks. Fortunately, the mat was left dry. Yellow rain slickers decorated the leaking structure. Gian had his music on his portable Sony and drank in the soothing sounds of Ella.

Katsuro met with the CFO and placed $100,000 on his underdog son at 3 to 2.

With his security entourage in tow, Ryuu watched the CFO for the balance of the week. The news about Aaron and Toothless caused an uproar among the fans. They knew it would be a war. Wagering was heavy and Ryuu's job was to make sure they got their percentage of the action.

Trevor sat with Katsuro and went over the fight card. "We can't just have the main event. We will have two events before Aaron fights."

Katsuro balked. "No, Trevor, wrong. I want Aaron to have a preliminary fight before he fights Toothless. That guy got a real name?"

"Yeah, but everybody knows him as Toothless. Makes him more fierce, don't you think?" Trevor paused, "You really want a preliminary fight before Toothless? That's a lot!"

"I said another fight before Toothless. That's what I want. Do it!"

Trevor shook his head at the unusual request and changed the calendar of fights.

When they were alone, Ryuu asked, "Why do you want this preliminary fight?"

"Two reasons. First, Gian needs the challenge. And I want to increase the wagering, so I want the patrons to see what Gian can do. They will bet a lot and we will make a lot of gravy."

Ryuu shook his head. Even though he didn't like Gian, he questioned Katsuro's judgment. "It's a lot."

"Yes, a lot. But he needs to be toughened up a lot. Grow up and know his potential. Get hit and know how to take a hit. He can't be beaten. I have trained him to survive and win."

* * *

If Aaron thought the German crowd was raucous, this one was worse. Maybe it was the combination of rain pelting the water-soaked barn, or the bloodthirsty crowd that followed street fighting to see someone killed, or the drunken wagers that were being made over the din of the crowd. Aaron needed his headphones to dull the noise. He shut his mind and went slowly into his own world. But for the first time, that world was tainted by the thought of Toothless and the helpless man on the mat he would have killed. *Come on, Aaron Michaels, cleanse your mind, go into your own world, deflect the present and become the warrior of old. You are a Samurai warrior.*

The announcer yelled at the top of his lungs from the wooden box he stood on. He announced the first fight that few in the audience heard. When the crowd saw the two contestants they yelled and booed. "Get those two bums outta the ring. We want Toothless and the Kid."

The fight lasted three boring rounds and the crowd was restless. The announcer read the winner's name and the two fighters left the ring. This time using a Rudy Vallee megaphone, the announcer read Aaron's name as he bounced into the ring. When he read another fighter's name, the crowd booed, "Toothless! Toothless! Toothless!" They chorus chanted.

Aaron Michaels walked to center of the ring with the announced fighter. There was no referee. Aaron looked squarely into the guy's eyes. "You got a wife and kids?"

The fighter not knowing what to do, answered the question by nodding. "Then know you will never see them again. I'm going to kill you."

"Shit man, what are you talkin' about?"

Aaron shook his head back and forth, "Your funeral!"

The crowd screamed, "Fight! Fight!"

"Fight, man, and try to stay alive!" Aaron hit him with a leg kick to his middle. The man backed off and threw several rights and lefts; only one landed. With the man's last punch, Aaron gripped his arm and threw him across the ring. Aaron did not follow him to the mat. "Get up! Fight for your life."

The fighter suddenly became scared. He got up and began to run around the ring. Aaron stalked him slowly, carefully following his every step. When the man finally stopped running and took his normal fighting stance, Aaron made his planned move. He dropped to the mat, brought both legs up into the inner thighs of the fighter, and tattooed his groin area. The first blows were right into the leg muscles, and the next succession of blows sent the groin into paralysis.

The man toppled to the mat, grabbing the pain in his inner thighs. Moving like a cat, Aaron sprang to his feet and dropped a knee right into the guy's groin and inner thighs over and over. Once Aaron's blow hit the man's iron cup and he felt the shock in his knee, but that was only once.

Aaron spread the man's legs, forged a figure-four leg lock, and jabbed the groin with his fists. "No, not again," he pleaded. "I have a wife and kids. Not again!"

Aaron drove his fists into the man's inner thighs, and only stopped when the man lay motionless, gripping his crotch.

From the box, the announcer raised Aaron's hand as the winner and announced to the crowd, "In five minutes we will have the feature bout, Toothless and Aaron Michaels."

Toothless stood at the entrance to the arena and watched the match. He smiled his toothless grin. "If he's tryin' scare me, he lost. I'm gonna beat his ass," he said to no one. "Yup, I'm gonna beat his ass. Maybe I'll even kill 'im!"

Katsuro rushed Aaron back to the makeshift dressing room and sponged down his fighter. "Toothless will be a lot tougher. But you must do the same thing to him. Soften him up before you beat him. That way he may quit. Other than that, you have to knock him out."

Aaron said nothing. He took a swig of water, allowed his face to be bathed and his body to be rubbed in linseed oil, then went into his own world.

The two men stood at opposing corners glaring at each other. The announcer made his introductions and the crowd went crazy. Toothless raced to the middle, "Come on, Bad Ass, fight."

Aaron circled Toothless and stared while jabbing him. Toothless just stood there and absorbed each blow. He waded in slowly until he could grab Aaron's arm and throw him to the mat. He dropped a knee onto Aaron's right arm and then used his leg to apply a cross bar. The hold, designed to dislocate the shoulder, forced Aaron to quickly roll up Toothless's torso and grab him in a headlock. Toothless, bald and slick with grease, slid out of the hold and grabbed Aaron's arm again. He sent his toes into Aaron's armpit, held onto the arm and dragged Aaron back to the mat. Toothless then yanked Aaron's arm viciously. He continued to yank the arm until finally Aaron was able to send a slew of hard kicks to his face with his bare feet. A toenail ripped the black man's ear.

The two grappled in the middle of the ring. Aaron tried to grab Toothless with his right arm. It had no strength. Toothless had dislocated his shoulder. He was fighting with one arm.

The bell rang ending the first round. Aaron staggered back to the corner. "He's torn my right shoulder."

Katsuro set his hands on his fighter, one hand on his right shoulder and the other on the elbow and yanked. Aaron felt the pop. The shoulder was back in place. "What do I do?"

"Practice what I have taught you. He is that wooden creature. Hit him accurately until he fades away. Knock him into another world."

Aaron looked at his mentor. "I'll take care of him."

"This is war. All is fair in war. I have prepared you for war. Learn it tonight."

The two stood in the middle of the ring. Toothless was not a trained fighter. He knew how to punish and take punishment but only because he was oblivious to pain. Aaron took his fighting stance and decided to box and prepare for the opening needed to dispatch the black man. Toothless was not used to straight stand-up fighting. Aaron punched viciously as Toothless chased him. Each blow had its effect. Toothless became slower and more unsure of himself. Aaron balanced on his toes, waited for his opening. Suddenly, like a ballerina he spun, swinging his right leg in a wide, powerful arc that caught Toothless on his left ear. The blow knocked Toothless to the mat.

Instead of following his opportunity, Aaron moved back and allowed Toothless to rise to his feet.

"You slimy toad. I'm gonna make you toothless, too."

Aaron grinned. He knew Toothless had lost his concentration. Revenge is never a good impulse in a fight.

Aaron took his stance. Again, balanced on his toes, he spun. His right leg hurtled down on Toothless. But the man was ready for the blow. He blocked it with his left arm. Like a cat on the attack, Aaron reversed his spin and brought his left leg over and clubbed the back of Toothless's head. The man tumbled to the mat.

Shaking his head more in surprise than pain, he rose slowly. Bewildered by Aaron's style of attack and speed, he glared at the man-child as he rose from the floor. His mind was an angry blank, confused by the attack he was under. Aaron, once again, backed off and waited.

Toothless rose even slower, shaking his head and trying to formulate a plan. The two stood again in the ring's center. Taking his normal fight pose, Aaron faked a looping kick, Toothless ducked. This was Aaron's opening. He saw the exposed neck and brought a steel-like open-handed chop to the wooden man's spot.

The jarring reaction stung like a sledge-hammer on a large tire. Aaron's brain was in Katsuro's backyard again.

Toothless sank to the mat unconscious.

Katsuro climbed into the ring. He wrapped his arm around Aaron. "Could you have killed him?'

Aaron looked down at his mentor and mumbled, "Maybe, for an instant! I thought I might have to."

The CFO met Ryuu at the door of the barn. "Your share young man. Nice to do business with you."

Katsuro depositedl Gian's 75% share into his trust account, and the trio left Europe for home and an old trouble that needed to be addressed. Aaron's call to arms.

CHAPTER THIRTY-ONE

A LOVER
TO CATHERINE

Aaron spent the next few months fighting, using mixed martial arts and stand up, defending his IFF world championship, and was declared the top contender by the NKF. The fight with Umber was still on hold.

He also spent time in Catherine's arms.

He even had the time to attend the UC for two summer-school classes. Everything was perfect until Catherine asked the question, "Aaron, why don't you move in with me?" Aaron liked the idea but was sure Katsuro wouldn't. "I can take care of you. I make enough money to support both of us, and you can get away from *him*."

Gian turned to Catherine as they lay in bed after a long love-making session. "I would like that. I know we belong together. Still, I worry about you and what Katsuro might do to you when he finds out. I am his possession. He doesn't want to let me go or share me."

She stroked his well-shaven cheek. "I'm not afraid of him. You know that. I despise the man for what he has done to you. You need to be apart from him, to be unleashed, to be set free." She squeezed his cheek tenderly. "You need to be with someone who loves you—unconditionally."

That afternoon he discussed the subject with Ted "What do I do, Ted? I certainly don't want to put Catherine into any danger. I'm torn between my freedom and Catherine's safety."

"Maybe you should talk to Katsuro. Maybe he wouldn't have objections to your moving. Maybe he . . . maybe he might think a little bit of freedom is needed."

"He won't. He's a possessive man. He needs to dominate within his domain."

"But to move in without him knowing? That would make the matter worse."

"How so?"

"Because, just like you said, he needs control. If you tell him and he says okay, he gives up that control, but at the same time he's still in control because you asked him and he gave permission. Does that make sense?"

Aaron winced at the thought of asking his tormentor anything, but he knew he must. He headed for the Canyon Falls house.

Gian arrived at home and packed his things. Then he looked for Katsuro.

Katsuro was in the dojo with Ryuu and Yukio. The old man patted his *Shinai* into the palm of his hand as he watched his two sons work out. Seeing Gian, he flicked his *Shinai* at him and said, "Get dressed for your daily workout, *Juko*. It is time to work hard."

Once dressed, Gian took his stance on the mat and went through the series of exercises he normally went through without saying a word. Katsuro walked around the mats, slamming the *Shinai* into the palm of his hand. He stopped and stood in one place. "You enroll in a class at the UC, *Juko*?"

"Yes, sir," shouted a sweating Gian.

"You still seeing that woman I told you to stop seeing?"

"Yes, sir. I am." Gian's voice was strong and resolute.

"You ready for your next championship fight, *Juko*?"

"Yes, sir, I am!" Gian's words came in breathless blasts.

"Why are you still seeing this woman, Gian?" Katsuro loved to repeat questions until he got the answer he wanted, another of his games Gian had grown weary of.

Gian stopped jumping rope after five hundred reps. "I told you before, I love her, and I'm gonna move in with her."

Ryuu and Yukio stopped their routines and watched their father. They could see the anger in his body as his defiant son told him he wanted to break the family bond Katsuro craved.

"So you love her. You want to live with her. You want to make this whore your own and leave the family. You will never leave our family until I give you permission to leave. And I don't!" Katsuro spit out his words, quivering in anger.

"Ryuu, take the pulley system off the punching bag. Yukio get me some tape. It is time to remind Gian that there is nothing as important as family, respect, and loyalty."

Gian knew what was coming. He remembered when he had beaten all his brothers and uncles. He knew then Katsuro would never stop the fight. Katsuro wanted to see what his adopted son could do and would do. Now, the timing was different. Gian could easily beat the trio that was about to punish him, but he wouldn't. If he did, he would have sunk to the low level of his mentor, using violence to solve all problems. Gian would not fight back. He would accept what he was about to receive and then be free of them, or so he thought.

Ryuu lowered the blocks and pulleys from the punching bag equipment. Teddy, the strapping 41-year-old son, now joining them, found a large circular package of plastic tape.

Margaret called out her mother's name as she walked through the house. *Damn, maybe they are in the dojo. They all work out too much,* she thought. She sauntered out toward the dojo and heard the sound of brutality coming from within its four walls. She looked through the slightly opened door and watched as Ryuu and Teddy elevated Gian up to the top of the punching bag pulley, dangling with his hands strapped high above his head.

Katsuro unwound the tethered straps of his *Shinai* and flicked it into the air. "You have defied me, Gian, for the last time. When I get through with you, you will be just a piece of flesh delivered to your whore." The *Shinai* stirred the rancid air and met Gian's flesh, cutting a patch of skin from his chest.

Margaret screamed! The foursome turned and saw the cowering girl sobbing at the entrance to the dojo. "Leave, girl! You have brought dishonor to this family; if you weren't my flesh and blood, I would have you up on this stake."

"What have I done? What has Gian done? And what are you doing to your son?" Katsuro walked close to his grandchild and flicked the *Shinai* at her.

"You witch! You have taken up with another not of our heritage. This thing, this no-son-of-mine has taken up with a whore. Both of you have disgraced the Tachigi name. Leave and let me take my pound of flesh, or you can stay and watch me torture this fool."

Margaret placed her hand over her mouth and gasped. Then she shouted, "I'm sorry, Gian. I truly am. I can't help you now. I can only curse my family for what they have done to you. I am so sorry." And she ran into the night. She never stepped into the dojo again.

Ryuu, reveling in having Gian in a helpless position, sent a powerful blow to Gian's stomach, knocking the wind out of him. Gian struggled to breathe. Teddy took a bamboo pole and pelted Gian across his chest and face. The blows tore the man-child's flesh again and again. His blood dotted the mat. Katsuro, angry at being betrayed and humiliated. allowed the beating to continue. Lost was the fact he was beating *his* world champion fighter senseless. Katsuro's anger swelled. He was in his own other world, slashing this no-son-of-mine into a bloody pulp. It mattered not to him that he had trained this man-child to be the finest fighting machine in the world. He wanted to teach this him to respect his mentor and obey his words. Katsuro only knew his son had committed treason against his family and himself. And, worst of all, he had become attached to another so that Katsuro was no longer in control.

When the flashing fists, the lightning punches, and the sharp, crisp lashes of the *Shinai* had finally stopped, Gian looked like a piece of beef hanging in a slaughterhouse. He was almost unrecognizable. "Lower him!"

Ryuu took a knife and cut the rope that bound the man-child's hands. Gian collapsed to the floor, barely conscious. Katsuro walked over to him. He delivered a surgical kick to his stomach. Gian refused to cry out. Ryuu stepped hard on his face. "His face was always too pretty." He stomped on it again. Teddy sent a toe into Gian's groin. Yukio followed.

"Katsuro, you may not have any grandchildren from this traitor."

"I have enough grandchildren, now." Teddy sent another toe into Gian's groin. Gian only saw the stars twinkling in an empty sky that didn't exist. His brain went from blue to gray and then into a swirling sea of darkness. He heard and felt nothing.

Katsuro pried open Gian's eyelids. "He's out. Ryuu, revive him!"

Ryuu found a pail and hooked it on to the sink faucet. The water splashed over the top of the aluminum bucket and spilled over into the sink. Ryuu turned the spigot off, lifted the bucket and doused Gian. He stirred.

"Can you see me, *Juko*?" Katsuro shouted.

Gian was still in a fog but he blinked involuntarily. "Teddy, he needs a face massage with your fists."

Teddy sat on the semi-conscious figure and rifled blow after blow to the Gian's face until his eyes turned black and the blood ran freely into his mouth and over his chin.

Katsuro dropped to his knees and took Gian's pulpy face in his hand. "You have just signed a pro contract. You have committed to a career in mixed martial arts, and now this. I warned you not to become attached and you didn't listen. And you want to leave me for what? A slut? A woman who will never understand what you could become? You want to leave me? Leave then! Just remember, you will always be part of me. You can't walk away from **that**." Katsuro spit into the pulpy mess.

"Ryuu, Yukio, pick him up and carry him to my car." Katsuro ordered.

"He's bleeding like a stuffed pig. He'll get your car all bloody!" said Yukio.

"Teddy, get some plastic and lay it in the trunk, then lay his body on the plastic," Katsuro said.

"I hope he doesn't bleed to death. Then we'd have to bury him. Where would we bury him, Katsuro?" Ryuu laughed.

"We're going to bury him at his precious girlfriend's house. We'll see if she wants him now, almost dead and useless."

Ryuu dropped the body into the trunk after Teddy had carefully laid a plastic sheet across the trunk floor. "Wouldn't want to ruin Katsuro's carpet, would we?"

Ryuu drove. "I know where she lives. I followed him there one day just to find out about this broad. She's some good looker. Must give *Juko* real good sex."

Yukio laughed. Teddy said, "He won't be able to perform for a long time. He won't be able to get it up for a long time. How's he gonna fight a week from Saturday?"

Katsuro smiled, "He will fight! There's no question about it. I know *Juko's* determination. He is going to will himself to fight, even if he is in constant pain, just to show me up. That is who he is."

Ryuu made several sharp turns on the now empty street in the San Fernando Valley. Ryuu checked his watch. "Three-fifteen, a nice time for witches and ghouls."

"Nice time to dump a nearly dead body on a girlfriend's lawn."

Ryuu stopped the car. "That's the house. Let's get out and get the body. Just like Dashiell Hammett, always dumping bodies." The three of them lifted Gian from the trunk and dumped him onto Catherine Tyler's front lawn. Gian's head bounced off the surface of the grass, and it jarred him awake.

"Well, look at that. Pretty boy is awake." Teddy sent a sharp toe into Gian's midsection, and he rolled over. Ryuu kicked him in the groin. Yukio stomped him on his head. "Just for good measure."

Katsuro picked up his cell phone and dialed Catherine's number. He heard the dull voice after the third ring. "Who is this? Why are you calling me at this hour?"

"Well, young lady, we have a present for you. It's not wrapped very well, and it isn't very pretty, but you'll find it on your front lawn. Happy days!"

"Who is this? Who is this?" She shouted not hearing the closing click on the other end of the line. "A present on my front lawn? What is he saying?"

She dressed and ran out the front door making sure it was unlocked. The present lay there, not moving. She screamed! Catherine dropped to her knees and cradled the face of her lover. Was he dead? She squatted in horror.

Aaron barely conscious found his thoughts wandering. *How could my best friend and someone who beat me so badly share the same name? Ted and Teddy!* He lost all consciousness without an answer to his question.

*   *   *

With the help of a neighbor, they carried Aaron gently into Catherine's townhouse and then upstairs to her bed. Aaron's bloody body, no longer dripping claret, lay motionless. The neighbor asked, "Do you want me to call for an ambulance?"

Catherine shook her head. "No, he wouldn't want that, and don't call the police. This is a family affair. Please, you have been very nice. Thank you. I know he will be okay."

As if on cue, Aaron moaned and put his hand to his head. "Don't move, honey, just lay still. Let me get something to clean you up." She turned to the neighbor, who was looking more than a little concerned. "Aaron is a professional fighter. He has been hit worse than this. Please don't tell anybody. I would appreciate that."

The neighbor shrugged and left after asking if Catherine needed anything.

It was then that Catherine dropped her façade of little concern. "Oh my God, Aaron. What am I going to do? I can't believe they did this to you. Why, my God? Why?"

Aaron, still in another world, stared blankly at the ceiling. His mind was a haze. *What happened to me? Where am I? Why is Catherine so hysterical?*

Slowly and methodical Catherine began cleansing Aaron's torn body. She winced at every cut, every bruise, every abrasion, every piece of torn flesh. Finally, she could no longer contain herself. She broke down and sobbed. Her body convulsed in despair and terror at the family who did this. *What kind of people could do this to their own son? And why? What provoked them?*

As the wee hours of the terrifying night passed into light, Aaron came out of his fog. Maybe it was the years of abuse that had trained him to go into his own world of no abuse, no pain, no feelings. There could be no other explanation for his survival. None!

Catherine lay next to him. He turned his head slowly. "How long have I been here?"

"About five hours. You're in pretty bad shape."

"I feel like I'm in pretty bad shape. Can you help me?"

"I wouldn't have it any other way, but shouldn't we call the police, get you to the hospital, something?"

His words were slow and measured. "Nothing! Just let me get some sleep. I will survive this with your help. Please do it my way. Say no more about it for now."

He closed his eyes and sank into oblivion.

Catherine removed all his clothes and dumped them. She finished bathing the rest of his wounds and put salve on them. She looked at the clock. Eight. She picked up the phone and called Ted.

Anna had finished preparing breakfast for her family when the phone rang.

"Hello, this is Anna."

"Anna, this is Catherine, Gian's friend. Is Ted in?"

"No, he went to work already. Can I help you?"

Catherine needed to talk to somebody. She decided to talk to Anna. Aaron had often told her how nice Ted and his mother are. "Anna, I have a real problem. Maybe you can help Aaron and me. Can you come over? It's urgent."

The word urgent made Anna's decision easy. "Yes, I will be right there."

She yelled upstairs to her family, "Breakfast is ready. Eat now and then clean up. I'm going out."

The two distraught women watched the sleeping body—ravaged by this merciless beating—as it took short, shallow breaths. Catherine told Anna all she knew. Anna shook her head slowly in disbelief. "They dumped the body on the lawn after they called you? My God!"

Anna went to the Thrifty Drug Store to get additional bandages, creams, and lotions. She knew they wouldn't solve the problem, but she wanted to cover the wounds. When she returned Anna sat with Aaron while Catherine made some business calls.

"I cancelled my calls for today. I have to stay with Aaron, but I'm so tired," Catherine cried bitterly.

Anna held her. "Emotions will make you tired. I will stay, too. You go rest now." Anna breathed heavily and bit her lip to hold back her tears. She took Catherine's arm and guided her upstairs to be with Aaron.

"What will we do, Anna? What will we do?"

"I don't know, except to pray. That is all we can do now."

Aaron slept deeply even though he was having a horrific reoccurring nightmare. He saw the image of a small child tied securely to a punching bag. The child's arms were tied with tape around the massive bag. His arms were stretched tightly. The child wore a tattered *gi*. Deep cuts were on the child's back and legs. Katsuro stood above the child plastering smelly salve on its back. The child never screamed or made a sound. Somehow the child untied his hands and crawled off the mat. Katsuro followed the child, still plastering the smelly goo on the child's back. The image was repeated through the blackness.

CHAPTER THIRTY-TWO

THE RECOVERY

On the fourth day after Aaron's brutal beating, he was resting downstairs when Catherine came back from an appointment. He was fully dressed. His small suitcase lay opened at the foot of the couch. "Aaron, you're dressed! Where are you going?" Her stomach suddenly ached. She sat next to him. "What's the matter?"

"I am going back home."

"No! This is your home!"

He shook his head. "No, this is *your* home. This can never be my home. I need to be with them. If I don't go back, they will destroy what I love the most, meaning you. You have seen what they can do. They will stop at nothing to keep me, to control me, and I can't stop them."

"No! Come and live here, with me. I'll protect you. I'll hire an attorney and get a restraining order against them." Her voice began to fade away as she saw the expression on Aaron's face saying, *No one can protect me from them.*

He reached across and held her hand. "I know you truly love me, just as I love you with all my heart. That is why I cannot stay here. They are very powerful. They are powerful beyond anything I have ever told you. They need to control everything and everyone around them. I can only protect us by not being with you."

Catherine spoke through her tears. "I . . . I . . . I feel so helpless. I want to protect you, but I can't. I want to hold you, but I can't. I want to be with you all the rest of my life, but I can't. What can I do?"

Gian wiped away his own tears, "Just love me. We will be together, just not living together. Nothing will change."

"How can you go back now? How can you fight again so soon after the beating? I worry about you."

"Thanks for worrying. Nobody ever did that before—worry about me. Let me explain." Aaron removed his shirt. "See this body. It has been taught to take abuse and pain and never feel any of it. It has been taught to take abuse and pain and to never let it interfere with fighting. I know what they did. I also know I can fight through anything. I can live through anything. A less-prepared person would have died under their last attack. But Katsuro knew I wouldn't die. He had toughened me up to take this punishment. I will not let him defeat me. I will fight this Saturday and I will win easily."

Catherine had to smile at Aaron's long speech. It was far more than he usually said. "I know you can endure the pain and the torture, for now, but for how long? Even the toughest of bodies can only endure so much. When does this body stop enduring the pain and give into it?"

"When I know you are safe. When I know I have protected you from them forever. Someday, maybe—not too far off, I hope." Aaron stood, picked up his bag, kissed Catherine gently on the cheek, and walked out the door without looking back. He couldn't. He didn't want to see Catherine in tears.

*   *   *

As if nothing had happened, Katsuro told Gian to dress for his training session. No "How are you?" No "Why don't we take a day off?" It was as if nothing had ever happened. It was over. The old routine started again.

Katsuro, who seldom spoke of an upcoming opponent, talked about Mathew Stamford as if he were the greatest challenge Gian had ever faced. "He is big, smart, and a very good fighter. He knows his martial arts well. Be prepared for him."

"Why are you telling me this? I don't care about who I fight. I'll whip his ass like I always do."

Katsuro didn't answer *Juko*. He knew that Gian might not be in the best shape. He wanted him mentally tougher. He wanted him ready.

At the weigh-in on Friday, Gian, carrying a bucket, stood next to this large, well-conditioned man. As the weigh-in wound down a sportswriter asked, "Hey Aaron, why you carrying a bucket? Got some water in there to revive the old guy after you beat him?"

Aaron, who had been waiting for the question, pulled a bottle of aspirin and a cold pack from the receptacle. "This is for you, Stamford. Free of charge. You'll need it when I whip your ass."

Stamford took a step toward Aaron, "You think you're so tough. You're a Bad Ass. But I'll kill ya."

The next night at the fight, Aaron talked to one of his seconds. "Stamford's wife and mother are coming to the fight. They don't know you. Tell them you work for management. Tell them they can't go into Stamford's dressing room because the commissioner is in there. Then, I'll take over." The second nodded that he understood and led the wife and mother down the hall to where Aaron was waiting, dressed in a suit and tie. Having never met Aaron, they listened to him. "Thank you, ladies, for your understanding. The promoter instructed me to take you to your seats. But first, how about a picture of the three of us?" The attendant Aaron had paid held a camera. Not knowing what to make of the situation, the wife and mother posed with Aaron for the Polaroid picture.

Aaron escorted the ladies to their seats and promptly left. The attendant gave the picture to Aaron, who headed for his dressing room. Katsuro didn't say a word as Gian arrived a few minutes late. They both remained silent while Katsuro bound Gian's hands and prepared him for the fight.

Just moments before, the attendant stopped Stamford as he was walking toward the ring. "Stamford, you know where your wife and mother are?"

Puzzled by the question, Stamford nodded, "Yeah, in their seats."

The second handed the Polaroid picture to Stamford, "They've been with Aaron for about an hour. He says they're nice and friendly." The second ran off quickly, not waiting for Stamford to answer with a punch.

"That son-of-a-bitch, I'll kill him. What the hell is going on?" Stamford was riled just as Aaron planned.

When the two entered the ring and met for instructions, Aaron whispered to Stamford, "Your wife is a really good fuck." Aaron winked. "She's damn good!"

Stamford, furious about the picture and now driven out of his mind by Aaron's comment, lunged at him. The referee pulled them apart. "Stop it, both of you. One more outburst outta you, Stamford, and you'll be disqualified."

Aaron pushed the enraged fighter away. "You're mother fucks well, too."

When the bell sounded, the enraged fighter had lost all control of his senses, and Aaron pummeled him for two rounds before the ref stopped the fight. In the corner, Katsuro grumbled, "You carried him."

"Just to make a point."

Ryuu cursed as he carried a large brown envelope with their winnings to Katsuro, "Would have won a lot more if he hadn't carried that bum for a second round. Damn, *Juko!*"

*　*　*

The phone rang. She looked at the incoming call and didn't recognize the caller's number. She put down her cup of coffee, slid her long legs from under her desk as they began to cramp, sat fully erect in her chair, and said, "Real-estate office."

"This is Katsuro Tachigi. Who am I speaking to?"

Oh my God, I haven't heard from Mr. Tachigi since I took care of his property in Canyon Falls. She flushed with embarrassment at the thought of what she did to earn the biggest commission of her life. She had been young and so clueless about real estate, and he had taken advantage of her innocence. Now he's back. "Yes, Mr. Tachigi. Nice to hear from you again. How are you?"

Not one for chitchat, Katsuro went on, "I want to buy a small townhouse in the Carrington area. Find one for me."

"In what price range, sir?"

"You know I have no price range. Just find me what I want."

She laughed to herself. Now that was the Mr. Tachigi she knew—abrupt. "When would you like it, sir?"

"By next week. Call me so I can see it. It is for my son."

Yukio sat with his father in his office. "Your son?"

"Yes, Gian. I am buying him a townhouse."

"You want him out of the house?"

"Yes. It's time to give him a little freedom, a place of his own. He is still going with that woman, and I am not happy about that. But sometimes I have to let my leash out. Now is that time."

Yukio sat forward. "He is almost ready to graduate from the UC. He is a world champion in martial arts. I hate to say it, but he has done well."

Katsuro stared at his son. "He has been the best of all my sons, even compared to you. He has done as he was trained to do. Now I am getting old. Ninety-one!"

Yukio, his mind always planning, flushed at his father's words, *The best of all my sons! Even you!* Yukio was enraged. His long-time hatred for Gian was rising to a boil. *That son-of-a-bitch, a world champion! What would happen if I beat the world champion? Or better yet, killed the world champion? It has been a long time since I dominated the bastard. Best of all his sons? That bastard!*

Nearing ninety-one, the old man still moved with a lively step of a gallant warrior filled with vigor. But even the old man had to clutch at the pain that sent shock waves through his big toe, ankle, and heel. He tolerated pain very well, but its swift incessant gnawing at his foot troubled him.

When the usual treatments, a hot bath, an oil massage and mind exercises, for pain didn't help, he scoured his own medical brain. "Gout! Damn, not me!"

After suffering intense pain for two days, he was able to absorb it and finally, tolerate it. Although he made the concession of walking with a slight limp, he no longer felt the full force of the painful attacks.

* * *

Sometimes nothing changes. It wasn't even Gian's birthday since that had passed many months earlier. Katsuro was buying this townhouse for Gian for a reason he never really revealed. On his last birthday, Gian had become eligible to vote. Like always, he didn't notice, nor did anybody else. Birthdays were never celebrated.

*   *   *

He barely remembered the tall, long-legged woman who stood before him. She extended her hand. "Nice to see you again, sir. It has been a while."

The old man took the soft fingers in his hand, something he would never have done when he first moved from Japan. It was an act he had embraced when he realized he could be that much closer to a beautiful woman. *Some things in America are better than in Japan.*

Gian drove his new Chevy to the townhouse complex. He arrived late, as was his custom, shook the hand of the real-estate agent, and greeted his father with a slight bow. "She will show you your new house."

Gian wasn't sure what he had heard, but he knew better than to start questioning. Katsuro stayed downstairs in the living room of the two-bedroom townhouse. Gian followed the long-legged woman upstairs and admired her short skirt as he walked behind her. He glimpsed at the inner thighs and suddenly didn't care too much what the townhouse looked like.

"The townhouse is under your name, not mine," the old man said. Katsuro signed the papers to purchase the house, handed the agent a check for the full amount, and left.

"How about having dinner with me tonight?" The eighteen-year-old asked the older woman. "I am sure you are dying to know how that man could be my father, aren't you?"

She looked up at the tall, powerful-looking stranger to whom she was suddenly attracted. "Yes, yes I am. I will cancel my other appointment."

Coming home that night, Aaron pulled up in front of his new place and parked. He leaned over and drew the long-legged woman to him and kissed her firmly on the mouth as he caressed her body. She wanted to withdraw from him but was turned on by his sheer brute force. She had never felt anyone so powerful in her life.

When his hand slid under her short skirt, she stopped his hand from probing her. "Not here. Let's go inside."

Inside, she pulled off his shirt and ran her hands over his massive, sinewy body. "I love your body." She kissed his chest and allowed herself to be drawn to the new carpet of the vacant townhouse. He removed her clothes. She lay prone in her panties and bra on the shag carpet.

When the rap came on the front door, Gian, like a cat, got off the floor. Catherine stood at the door, silhouetted against the night's light, and kissed Aaron. "I have a lovely house warming gift for you," he said as he let her in.

Long legs sat up on the floor and tried to cover up. "My name is Catherine and you don't have to cover up for me. The more I see of you the better I like it."

Startled, long-legs tried to stand but Aaron held her down. "It's okay. I still want to make love to you. Catherine just likes to watch. You'll like it. Besides, how many sons get to make love to a woman their father made love to?'

The trio initiated the new townhouse in a manner it would never see again.

Catherine moved some of her things into Aaron's townhouse.

During the summer before Aaron would become a UC graduate, the leash got tighter again. Katsuro, vacillating like a rocking chair tilting wildly, sensed that Gian had become distant and removed from his umbrella, an umbrella whose shadow fell across the lives of everybody within its reach. Aaron thought it was an obsessive reaction to his moving to his own place, training in a separate gym, and being under the influence of "that" woman.

Katsuro stood alone in the dojo. It was eerily empty. Usually filled with jabbering children and grandchildren for many years, Katsuro did what he knew was a dangerous thing to do: he thought. He imagined evil that might or might not exist. The old man trembled at the thoughts that occupied his mind. *I have lost my most valuable possession. He has been stolen from me, for what? Love? Never! It should not be.* He became angry and resentful, having been abandoned by his world champion—his. *That ungrateful child. I raised him to be somebody, and now he has turned to another to seek diversion from what is his fate; his earned right to be a world champion, the best of the best. A fighter like no other, masterfully trained by me, using my father's teachings and my father's legacy. I hate that woman for taking him from me, for taking my legacy. I have devoted nearly twenty-years of my life to making him an incomparable fighting machine. Now, you are not here; not training; not under my tutelage. Not under my command. I hate that woman for what she has done to you, for what she has done to me.*

He picked up his *Shinai* and slapped it into his ancient hand. The bamboo clapped against his bare palm, the sound echoed through the empty edifice. The bamboo stung, but the old man never felt it. His anger and his training against pain never allowed him that feeling, yet age had brought bitterness to him, a sense of urgency to accomplish what needed to be accomplished, for he knew this was his last time around. His life would end with this passage of time. His life had been evolving over many years. He had reached his final goal. He had developed his world champion. He had taken his father's teachings to the highest level, and his road had been paved with success. Now it would be time to join his father in the final life, but not until he had seen his son win another world championship: the heavyweight championship.

The boy had grown into a man. Well over six-foot-four, a rock-solid two hundred and forty pounds. He was the indestructible being Katsuro had trained . . . or was he? This woman, who had diverted his attention from this single goal, was an obstacle. Katsuro could not get her out of his mind. He was tortured by his obsession!

Ryuu stood at the entrance to the dojo. He saw his father standing, slightly stooped, in the middle of the mats, bouncing his *Shinai* off his hand and muttering. For the first time, he noticed his father had aged. His body wasn't as erect. His shoulders were slightly protruding forward. His spry gait lacked its bounce. His body was just as lean, but the once powerful frame lacked the forceful nature he had always exuded.

Although his hair was full, it was now salt and pepper. Age lines dug deep crevasses into his flesh. His facial skin sagged around his jaw and into his neck. Ryuu, mean and caring for nobody but himself, showed only a slight tinge of regret. Soon he would be the person in charge. *Soon, my time will come.* He was ready by decree. He was ready by his training. He knew. He sensed the time for him was close.

Without turning to Ryuu, Katsuro said, "You have arranged for the fight in Germany? Everything is taken care of?"

"Yes. We are ready! But where is *Juko*? Why isn't he here?"

* * *

The sweat poured from Aaron. The gym was hot. Too many fighters were crammed into a small place. The smell of sweat permeated the nostrils of all the fighters. It was a sweet smell to Aaron, the perfume of energy released. Bodies grunted and mouths swore: curses of frustration, voices of exhilaration, and muffled cries of a battered fighter being cuffed mercilessly. "Aaron, you son-of-a-bitch, this is a workout, not a war." The voice of the battered bleeped.

Aaron grinned. "Sorry, man. I was just imagining you were that German guy I'm gonna be fighting."

His sparring partner stepped out of the ring, cursing and holding his side torched by an aggressive knee.

Aaron had been working out for over two hours. He had noticed he was getting tired of working out. He questioned his own work ethic instilled in him from birth. He couldn't imagine getting tired of fighting, weary of the routine, frustrated by the repetition and mindless workouts. He had talked to Catherine about his feelings. She could tell his body had become worn out and he wasn't as anxious to fight and to work out. His dedication was waning. "Maybe you need a long vacation. We could take one in Europe after you fight in Germany; a nice long vacation."

Gian had never thought of a vacation. That thought excited him. Yes, he was tired, very tired. Tired of the beatings, tired of the fight routine, tired of life at the edge. It was too much pressure. A vacation. That idea dwelled in him as he fought. *I'm going on a vacation.* The man-child had returned. Like a kid in a candy store, he desperately wanted this vacation. A grin crossed his face.

After dinner that night, Aaron sat and talked to Catherine. She held his hand. "We need to plan this vacation. Something special.

274

Something we do together, not like we usually do when I plan everything. I want this to be *our* vacation."

"Our vacation! Okay, where?"

"Where do you want to go?"

"I know where I don't want to go: Japan. Maybe Barcelona. I understand it is the most beautiful city in the world." Aaron smiled. "If you're there with me, it will be the most beautiful city in the world for sure."

Catherine smiled the smile that made her even more glowingly beautiful than Aaron had ever seen. "Okay, I'll check with my friend. She's a travel agent. She'll do right by us."

"And I'll polish off this bum I'm fighting so quickly that we'll be in Spain before we know it."

Catherine cuddled with Aaron. That usually meant she wanted something and Aaron tensed up. She tousled his hair. "When we're in Europe, could we get married?"

Aaron tensed up even tighter. He hated when she talked like that. He sat back from her. "I told you before, I am only nineteen, and I don't want to get married. I'm too young. Come on Catherine, we've talked about this before. You are twenty-nine. I'm just a kid. Don't spoil the trip by bringing this up."

Catherine knew the question would anger Aaron, but she pursued the subject. She had a plan. She had been thinking about their relationship. She knew she wanted him. She knew it was right. "Aaron, if we get married, then Katsuro would no longer have control over you. I can then get a restraining order to keep him away from you. I will hire an agent for you to guide you through your fight career. You'll be free at last."

The pit in Aaron's stomach grew harder. "The only time I will be free of him is when he dies, and I'm not even sure about that."

"Why?" she asked in frustration.

"Because he has left me a portion of his estate in his will. The family has control over how much they pay me, if at all. And when I'm thirty, they are supposed to pay me the balance of what they owe me, but at their discretion."

Catherine coughed, "You need an attorney. He'll get your money."

"Not if it's in Japan. They will want me to come and get it. Reconcile with them if we split." He patted Catherine's hand. "You see, my dear, nothing is as simple as we would like it to be. I have a feeling this family will always try to control me. I wish you could make it better, but you can't. Someday, someday, I will settle this. Someday, but not today."

With a deep breath Catherine knew she had lost the battle—but not the war. She would fight again when the right time came. Would that time ever come?

CHAPTER THIRTY-THREE

RETRIBUTION

It had been a couple of weeks since Katsuro had seen Gian, so he was surprised when he got Gian's call. "I want to show you I have been working out and I am in good condition, so I will be over this afternoon."

Katsuro grunted, "Okay! Come!"

Wearing a form-fitting t-shirt, Gian walked through the door of the dojo. The old man stared at him. *He has grown since I saw him last. He looks good.* "You don't look in such great shape, *Juko*, you need me to make you tougher."

Gian knew exactly what the old man would say. He had never told him he looked good, he fought well, he loved him, he . . . Yes, Gian knew what he would say. Gian changed into his *gi*. "Give me your routine, *Juko*." Katsuro called out the key words in Gian's workout, and the man-child responded like the robot he was trained to be.

Katsuro never commented on what he saw. Secretly he saw the birth of a full man from the man-child. When the routine ended, Katsuro went to the mat. "Today I will teach you a new hold, a new technique you will only use when you are in trouble. It is a hold that will temporarily paralyze your opponent. You are the only one worthy in my family to know this technique. You are the best of my fighting sons. You are the strongest, the quickest, the most powerful. This technique was passed on from my father to me, and now only to you, the world champion."

Gian was stunned. It was the first time Katsuro had ever complimented him. Gian glowed and smiled.

The old man knelt next to Gian on the mat and said, "I will show you what to do. Listen and you will know exactly how to proceed."

Katsuro, at ninety-two, placed his thin arms around Aaron's neck and set his knuckles into Aaron's flesh. "The Samurai used this hold in close combat. It is a sleeper hold." Katsuro pressed his knuckles into Aaron's neck and slowly exerted pressure. Aaron suddenly felt dizzy. Katsuro released the hold.

"Now you try it on me."

"Are you sure?"

"Sure? Why not? You think you will hurt me?"

Gian shook his head yes.

"You will not hurt me."

Gian took his position. He placed his powerful arms around the frail old man. His knuckles pressed into his Master's neck. *They will always be part of me, even if the old man should die. I don't know if I will ever be rid of them. But, maybe when the old man is dead!*

"If you are thinking of killing me, don't. It isn't my time!"

The old man felt a swarming dizziness. The blackness crept slowly into his brain. Then there was a scream somewhere in the distance. "Don't kill him. Don't! You will always regret it if you do. Let him die in his time."

Aaron looked up and saw his mother, Rita, standing above him. He released the old man. Katsuro fell semi-conscious to the mat. She moved his head to the right and rubbed his wrists. "Getting his pulse back."

Gian knelt next to her. "I was only practicing this new hold he was showing me."

"I know. I have seen him use this hold on two others in a fight. He told me one day he would teach it to you when you were worthy. I guess you are worthy now." She patted his shoulder. It was the first time he could remember she had ever touched him except the time she had a workout with him and when he got a new Dog.

He was ten. Katsuro was away for the day. Rita was in the dojo working out with her children and grandchildren. During the session she went over to Gian and knelt next to him while he was stretching. "You want me to show you some new holds, Gian?"

Gian smiled. She had almost always ignored him. But here she was on the mat, with him, teaching him. She even cleaned a slight cut he had gotten on his arm while wrestling with Ryuu. She never beat him, never cursed at him. She simply tried to teach him—once. He had always wondered why she never taught him again. Rita quietly answered that question, now, so many years later, while Katsuro was reviving himself.

"He told me if I ever tried to train you again, he would beat you even worse. So you were always his to train and make in his image. It was as simple as that."

Rita's voice faded as Katsuro rose. He shook his head and said, "Remember, only use that hold when you must. Never show it to anyone who is not worthy."

The old man gathered himself. He looked over at his wife. "Rita, tell the chef to prepare an extra meal for Gian. I want him to stay for dinner and then we will show him several more holds he has never been exposed to yet."

At dinner, the first time Gian had ever been allowed in the family dining room since he was a little boy, Katsuro spoke slowly and carefully. "Gian, you are the only fighter in the world who is fighting using *Akin Jitsu*. It is a technique used by my father, me and now you. Yes, my children were taught this technique, but none mastered it like you. How you use this technique will be up to you. The only thing I ask of you is to use it honorably. Honor the name Tachigi," and he grew silent.

Gian felt uncomfortable. After nineteen years as a member of the Tachigi family, he was eating with his adoptive parents. It was eerie. *Why now? What did the old man want?*

After dinner, with the moon ascending in a fading amber sky, Gian and Katsuro met for another training session, each dressed in their *gi*. Katsuro began. His voice wasn't as strong as it once was, but it was still firm. "You have been taught about the universe: Earth, Air, Fire, and Water. Now it is time to learn about *Ki*, a spiritual awakening. It is a natural energy of the universe changed into *Akin Jitsu*. I shall teach you its dynamics in a form only you will know and use."

Rita saw the lights burning late in the dojo. She checked her diamond-encrusted watch, her only opulent possession, watching the hands as they crept past midnight. She smiled. *If he is really teaching Gian the family form of Ki, then he knows his time of life is wearing down faster than he would like.*

* * *

Yukio, who had been visiting the family compound, entered the dojo. He heard Katsuro say, "You are a world champion. You are the best. Soon you will become the heavyweight champion of the world."

Yukio had taken his father's words as an insult. *He is the best of all my sons.* The words had scorched his brain and tormented his soul. He had been rejected by his own father. He was a failure. In Yukio's world of devious thoughts, he dwelled on his hatred for this world-champion son. What would happen if he beat this world champion? What would his father say then? That son would no longer be the best. Yukio would be the best. Yukio's mind was demented; it was in anguish over his father's words. He knew he had to kill this world champion—kill him and be rid of him.

It was in this high state of angst that Yukio Tachigi entered the dojo. "Well, the boy wonder! The world champion! I should be honored to be in your company."

Gian stood and looked at this creature, the most despised of all his tormentors; the sodomizer. "Yes, you should be honored to be in my presence. Why don't you bow down to me, or, better yet, kiss my feet and worship me?"

Yukio raged at the words. "You piece of shit. I should have killed you when I had a chance. I should have taken you and killed you instead of only raping you. You have only been our toy, our possession, our . . . ."

Gian stepped toward Yukio and slapped him hard across the face. "I shouldn't soil my hands on you. You have always been a deviate, a child rapist, the lowest of the low."

Yukio held his face and lashed out at the man-child. Gian let the blows pepper his face. Yukio spit on Gian's face and hissed, "I am going to kill you now. It is what you deserve! It is time for you to die!"

Katsuro sat in his chair, as he always did, and said nothing. He knew this moment would come. Now that it was here, he would do as he knew he must: step aside. In the corner of the dojo stood Yukio's aide, his driver and companion ready to move . . ..

Katsuro pointed his index finger at him. "Stay where you are. This is none of your business. It is family business."

Yukio turned and slid out of his clothes. He dressed in his *gi*. His 48—year-old body, muscular, taut, and fit, gleamed in the shadows of the dojo. *I may not be the world champion, but I am going to kill him.*

Gian took a sip of water. He removed his gloves. He watched his tormentor, and his mind slid back in time to when he had first been raped. The huge figure hanging over the small child taking him from behind, the pain, the humiliation, the dehumanizing act, the rape, the continuous rapes for the next three years. *I could have bashed his face in with a brick as he slept. This is better. This will be my revenge.*

The two witnesses watched, the father feeling nothing. Why? Why wouldn't he? These were his sons. Katsuro knew this battle was inevitable. Now was the time.

The two men faced off in the middle of the mat. Gian slapped Yukio again. "Just to see if you are still alive."

Instinctively, Yukio reached across and slapped Gian hard. Gian rushed his tormentor and like a football player bowled him over. He knocked Yukio to the mat and pummeled him. He could have knocked him unconscious, but that would have been too easy. He wanted to punish him, make him feel pain.

Yuen squirmed from under Gian and rolled across the mat. His quickness surprised Gian. They both rose and sparred. Gian faked a right cross, dropped to the mat and attempted a leg whip. Yuen had seen Gian fight too many times not to know what to expect. He jumped away from the whip and dropped his knee onto Gian's knee. "Hurt? You piece of shit."

Gian had never fought someone who knew him so well, had studied under the same Grand Master, and was so devious and calculating. The robot had to think and quickly dig deep into his arsenal. He shot a straight hand grab into Yukio's chest and crushed his sternum. Yukio brushed off the pain. "I've been taught to disregard pain." Yukio's voice came in short pants. Gian heard the hint of blowing wind. Yukio mouth was open.

Conditioning! That was it. Gian went on his bicycle. He circled Yukio and jabbed him. Straight shots to his face, his throat, his shoulders, pressure points like on the wooden figure, all the time dancing to his left then reversing his movement to the right. With each move, Yukio followed, expending energy. Gian knew age would eventually catch up with Yukio.

He wanted Yukio to pay by feeling pain in as many areas of his body as possible. Then . . ..

Eventually, Yukio became winded; each breath was labored. Gian, young and spry, tortured him with slaps, punches, and blows that weren't always hard but were inevitably accurate. Gian concentrated on making every blow on target. He took his time slicing up Yukio. Time was Gian's ally. So he took that time and punished Yukio. *Only the Grand Masters know all the moves. Only the Grand Masters know all the techniques. Only the Grand Masters know all the vital spots on the human body. I am training you to know them all.* Katsuro's words had been prophetic.

The killing would be slow, but he had nothing but time—all the time in the world. This was his revenge for himself and all the other unknowns.

Slowing down, Yukio gasped. His body ached. Each blow felt like a ton of bricks, just like the brick that Gian wanted to use to crush his head. Yukio saw the punches coming, but no longer was quick enough to pull back. A fist paralyzed his neck. Then the huge creature leapt at him and drove an elbow into his neck on the other side. Yukio went black.

Gian allowed the figure to crumple to the mat. He dropped another sharp elbow into the throat of the unconscious figure.

"Enough, he is unconscious!" Katsuro shouted.

"Not yet. One blow for each time he raped me. And you have to watch, because you allowed him to molest me. *You gave him permission to sodomize me.*"

Gian stood and dropped another elbow into the chest of his attacker and heard the bones crush. Gian's knee shattered Yukio's rib cage. "That's three blows. How many times did he sodomize me? Eight? Yes, eight. I counted. I know."

Gian knelt over the reclining figure as Yukio was slowly reviving himself. Gian spat in his face and drove a ferocious blow to Yukio's mouth, knocking his front teeth out. Gian was splattered with Yukio's blood. He shot four more blows to Yukio's face, rendering him unconscious again.

Gian got up and walked away, passing Katsuro as he walked straight out of the dojo and into the bath. He cleansed his body and soothed his soul. He wondered if Yukio was still living.

Katsuro signaled Yukio's attendant to come over. Katsuro knelt next to his son. Yukio's pulse was barely discernible. He waved a packet of smelling salts under his son's nose. Yukio blinked in great pain. "Carry him upstairs. Put him to bed. I will be up shortly."

The attendant lifted Yukio and walked him up the back stairs of the Tachigi family compound.

Yukio's breathing was shallow. Katsuro sat next to his son on his bed. Katsuro bathed his face. He didn't say a word. He bandaged his son's wounds. During the night, Katsuro woke several times and checked on his son. His breathing was still shallow, but he was alive.

At nine the next morning, Yukio's wife went to see him after spending the night in another room. Her shrieking brought Katsuro from his office. "He's dead! He's dead! Come quickly."

Katsuro walked quickly. In tears Rita pointed to a note.

Katsuro read the note and pulled the dagger from his son's gut. The claret gurgled as it seeped from his body. Rita tore the note from her husband's hand: *I have failed you as a son. It is better this way.*

Rita wept. Then she turned and slowly whispered to her husband. "You killed him. You were never satisfied. You wanted this Anglo child to be what your sons could not be. You killed our son."

Katsuro drew back at his wife's words. Yet, Katsuro was proud of Yukio. His son had done the honorable thing. He had honored his family by killing himself in the tradition of the great Japanese warriors. Yukio knew he would never be the Grand Master he wanted to be so badly. The Grand Master—the reward he felt he deserved from his father. He had lost his battle with the other "son," the new

Grand Master. So he ended his life as his father would have wanted: by *Seppuku*, Japanese ritual suicide.

Katsuro had lost two sons who thought they were failures by suicide. Would there be another?

Two days later, Yukio's attendant brought a medium sized package to a Fed Ex office. The agent asked, "What is it you are shipping, sir?"

"A Ming vase. Priceless. So I bring it to Fed Ex knowing it will be shipped with great care."

The agent smiled and said, "Thank you, sir, for your confidence in Fed Ex. We will take every precaution in shipping your vase." He paused, lifted the vase, and a puzzled look appeared on his face. "It is very heavy, sir. What is in it?"

The attendant, doing as he was rehearsed said, "Ashes, sir, of the family dog, a shibu inu, a large dog."

The agent shrugged. "Any insurance, sir?"

"Two million. Even though it is priceless, the family wants to insure the dog gets back to Takayama, where it was raised as a pup."

"Very good, sir. I will wrap the package right now, so it is shatterproof. It will get to Takayama safely."

The attendant left with the receipt after using Katsuro's credit card. He was now working for Ryuu.

Katsuro did not blame Gian for Yukio's death. He, more than any other, understood the need for the battle between his two sons. Katsuro's way of coping with the loss was to never mention Yukio's name again. It was as if he had never existed. Katsuro moved on to the tasks at hand. The past was history, not to be visited or revisited and not to be discussed by any member of the family ever, no matter what the circumstance.

* * *

They sat on Aaron's townhouse patio. The valley lay before them, its lights burning magically like a series of candles held at a concert. Their hands touched, their fingers entwined. Catherine, her nightgown blowing gently in an early-evening breeze said, "My heart is pounding like a little girl's. We are really going away, tomorrow, to Munich and then Spain. Will you make love to me at the sea, Aaron? I know it's a child's dream, but it's my fantasy."

Aaron looked at the beauty holding his hand. "I promise to make your dream come true. I promise."

She looked at him and smiled.

"Your dream is my dream, but you know I have to train in Munich for two days after we arrive and I have to also do several press conferences. ESK is promoting this fight in Europe, plus five others in various European cities, in order to bring Extreme Karate to the continent."

"And then?"

"And then I keep my world championship belt, and we are on our way, alone."

"No Katsuro, no fight clubs, no nothing!" Catherine bit her tongue. She wanted to say more, *I wish you would stop fighting and I could take care of you. We could get married and start a family. I can support the both of us. You will have your degree from the UC, and you can always get a job. I want to marry you!* But she didn't speak, because she knew he didn't want to hear it—at least not now, maybe not ever, but especially not now.

They made love that night.

*   *   *

Catherine sat next to Aaron on the non-stop flight to Germany. Teddy sat next to Katsuro glowering as only he could. The few times Gian passed the glowering Teddy, he laughed to himself. *If I ever need a professional glowerer, Teddy would be my man. He is good.* But to Gian it was part of the game they played.

The game had grown very tiresome.

*   *   *

The cab rattled through the streets of Munich. The afternoon sun was warm. They crossed a bridge over the Isar River. The cab dropped them off at the Hotel Koenigshof Munich. Katsuro and Teddy stayed elsewhere. ESK would only pay for part of the expensive Koenigshof; they had told Katsuro, "We have only so much money to spend on accommodations. You have a daily stipend. Use it as you wish. The rest is up to you."

The two lovers, trying to adjust to the new time zone, walked the city before dinner. "I have to leave early tomorrow morning. It is my training time. I will be with Katsuro for most of the day, sorry."

"Can I come and watch? Would you mind?"

"Not me. It's a public workout. Even Carl Brennar will be there."

"Who?"

"The guy I'm fighting. You can watch him train also. He's a real brawler."

"You're not scared, are you?"

Aaron never took offense at her asking that question. She asked it before each fight. It was her way of taking care of him. It was her way of showing concern. It was her way of trying to tell him to stop fighting. Stop fighting! Yes, he had thought about it much more often lately. He found himself tired of it all. He had been fighting since the age of six. Fighting, surviving the beatings, the torture, the deprivation of his soul. All that made him tired at the age of nineteen. He was worn out physically and mentally. He never shared that with anyone. What would he do if he retired? *That* made him scared.

"Scared of him? No, not him. Only of losing you."

The late afternoon was warm as they stood on the side of the Isar River and watched the people walking along its bank. "My God, Aaron, look. Are those people laying nude on the river bank?"

Aaron squinted in the fading sun, "Sure looks like it. Men and women. Just what you like."

"You don't like it, too?"

"You bet I do. Maybe in Barcelona we'll find another woman to make love to. For you and me."

She squeezed his hand, and they moved on.

Katsuro was talking to Phillip Manley, his partner, who had come to Europe to visit each site and sell his products. Katsuro asked, "Why are we using a smaller venue? We could fill a larger arena. You could have sold more tickets."

"Correct, we could have. But I wanted this college crowd. It is the young people who will become fans. I wanted an intimate arena where the fans are very close to the action. They are the future of this business. You see, Mr. Tachigi, you might be the manager of the world champion, but I know my end of the business: promotion. We have a couple of competitors now because our product is so good, and Aaron Michaels is part of that future."

Katsuro didn't want to be lectured to, so he bowed and withdrew. The ring announcer spoke into the microphone as the college kids, who had come to watch the workouts, cheered. "Now for his workout, Carl Brennar, the contender."

Katsuro watched with interest. He usually didn't watch the other fighters, but he had come to realize it paid off to evaluate their strengths and weaknesses. The talent level of the pros was far greater than the National Team.

He took mental notes and caught sight of Gian as he entered the arena. He was alone. He never noticed the tall, slim black woman sitting in the back.

Brennar left the ring to some mild applause. Most of the students had come to see the world champion, Aaron Michaels. Aaron decided to give them a show. In a manner that reminded Catherine of a well-choreographed ballet, Aaron performed: shadow boxing, dropping to the mat, and simulating a real fight, where he fought an imaginary character that seemed all too real. The students applauded and whistled.

Katsuro said nothing as the show ended. Phillip Manley said, "That was a great show, Aaron. Another workout tomorrow and then the real fight. You ready, boy?" He patted the monstrous shoulders of his world champion.

The old man remained silent, turned, and walked toward the entrance of the arena. Then he saw her. Tall and elegant, she was standing in the aisle alone. He approached her. He looked up at her. "I want you to leave my son alone. You are hurting him. That dance was for you. It wasn't a real workout. He has changed. He needs to be focused on fighting, not some loathsome slut. Leave him alone, or you will destroy him." Katsuro walked past her and left the building.

Catherine refused to cry. *That dried up old man is evil. How dare he talk to me like that way. I love his son. I love the man he has tried to destroy.* She never told Aaron about that encounter, but she never forgot it. She knew Aaron would want to hurt the old man. That she couldn't stand. She also knew what that old man was capable of doing.

As he left the arena, there stood Teddy. Katsuro put his thumb in a downward motion and walked past him.

Teddy turned to the man standing next to him. He handed him an envelope. "Do it!"

CHAPTER THIRTY-FOUR

DEATH:
THE LOSS OF LOVE

During the evening after Aaron and Catherine finished dinner, Katsuro's voice shattered her. With his remarks engrained in her mind, she broke a vow she had made to herself. "I want this to be your last fight, Aaron. I want to marry you. I want to take care of you."

Aaron said nothing. They walked upstairs and closed the door. It was then he spoke as he grasped her shoulders. He whispered at first then his voice strengthened, "Catherine, I am only nineteen years old. I do not want to get married. I am too young and I'm not ready to leave them. Maybe soon, but not now. This was not a good time to bring this up again."

Catherine trembled. Katsuro's words gripped her again, "But I love you. I want to protect you. I need you and you need me."

Aaron tried to control his anger. He was tired of the subject and tired of being told what to do. He gritted his teeth and turned his back on his lover. His frustration came forth from those years of anger; and he lashed out at the one person in the world who loved him. "Leave me alone. Can't you see I'm too young, too young to get married. Love has nothing to do with it. I am just reaching the pinnacle of my career and it is the only thing I can do. I must do this. So leave me alone. Leave me alone!" His fist jammed into the nearest table.

Catherine stepped back, turned and ran into the bedroom. The door slammed shut. Aaron could hear the sobs. He shut his ears. He was tired, far too tired for this, far too tired for anything. He slumped onto the couch, closed his eyes and faded into his own world, detached from everything.

He awoke early, showered while Catherine slept, and then made his way to the arena. He had to be there by eleven. He left Catherine's ticket on the nightstand next to her purse. He was getting himself mentally ready and in the mood for his fight, detached from the reality of the night before. But something was bothering him and he couldn't figure it out. A knot in his stomach told him something was wrong.

The day passed, Gian never heard from Catherine. He went through his normal prefight routine. The afternoon fight was near.

An ESK official came in to check on Gian's lightweight gloves. He checked the tape, took a urine sample, and left. Katsuro rubbed him down and Gian listened to his music, still troubled.

Harry came down to usher his fighter down to the ring. Aaron climbed through the ropes, and he peered out into the audience. Catherine's seat was empty. That ache became more intense. The ring announcer sang out the name of the contestants, and they both approached the center of the ring for instructions.

Catherine's seat remained empty. Aaron felt different than he had ever felt before going into a fight. He was unable to concentrate. His mind was full of thoughts, instead of being empty enough to act without thinking. The bell rang for the fight to begin, and Hirohsu knew instantly his fighter was in trouble. When the bell sounded, the lights went down and Aaron could no longer see the seat where Catherine would have been sitting. *Where could she be? What happened to her? Why wasn't she here?*

Katsuro's worst fears were realized. Aaron had become attached to something besides fighting and it would cost him. Katsuro constantly yelled instructions. Aaron barely heard them. He didn't care. *Where was Catherine?*

The first of five three-minute rounds ended, and Aaron sat heavily. He tried to see into the audience, but the spotlight from the overhead lights blinded him. He knew she wasn't there. Katsuro splashed his face with a water soaked sponge. "You are not with it, *Juko*. Become who you really are, a great fighter. Don't let this nobody take your title."

Aaron really didn't hear the words. He was torn and scared.

The bell sounded and Katsuro pushed his fighter into the ring just as Teddy came to the corner. "Katsuro." He whispered his message and Katsuro paled.

Aaron fell into a leg lock, pushed Carl off him, and dropped a knee to Carl's stomach knocking the wind out of him. Carl scrambled to his feet and wrapped Aaron in a headlock. Carl dropped to his knees and took Aaron with him. Carl torqued his muscular right arm and ground his knuckles into Aaron's neck. The Champion slid his left hand and arm into the hold and snapped Carl's right arm back. The move was robotic.

Aaron tried to get to his feet. Carl drove him to the mat with an elbow to the kidney. The bell sounded.

Aaron staggered to his corner. Katsuro splashed his face again and sent a shock through his head as he passed smelling salts under his nose. "Aaron, listen to me. Something has happened. You must finish this fight very quickly. We need to leave right away, but not until you beat this guy. This is urgent!"

The knot in Aaron's stomach tightened until he felt a cramp. He never asked what the situation was. He could feel it.

"Take a deep breath, concentrate and finish him."

Aaron gathered himself well before the bell sounded and stood. He shook his head to clear it. Rather than reacting, he thought about the last few weeks and what Katsuro had taught him. Now was that time.

Aaron raced to the center of the ring and waited for Carl Brennar. Aaron sent a straight right foot into the inside of Carl's knee. The blow, unexpected, but deadly accurate, forced Carl to drop his hands slightly. Aaron sent a straight right hand into Carl's face. He stepped forward, and wrapped his arm around Carl's neck and drew him in close. He bulldogged Carl to the mat while he held the headlock.

Aaron rolled his massive arms tightly around the neck and slid his knuckles into Carl Brennar's neck. Aaron pressed the two sides of the carotid artery with a power drawn from desperation. Carl struggled as Aaron counted to twenty. That was the time it would take for the blood to stop circulating to Carl's brain, and he would enter twilight. The seconds passed in eons.

The referee raised Carl's arm to see if he was still conscious. When he found him unable to respond, he tapped Aaron to break his hold. Aaron released the hold, scampered to the ring's apron, and jumped from the ring just as the referee declared him the winner.

Katsuro ran up the aisle with Gian followed by Teddy. The trio ran by Phillip Manley without a word.

Teddy now led the way. "I have a taxi waiting for you. Miss Tyler is in the hospital. She is seriously hurt." The trio rode in desperate silence heading to the *Klinikum rechts der Isar der TU Munchen* in central Munich.

"What happened?" Gian asked, his voice slightly above a whisper.

Teddy answered, "We were just told she was in the hospital. Somebody at your hotel saw the accident and called the ambulance, and then sent word to us at the arena. I don't know."

The cab stopped, and Aaron flew out into the hospital. He ran calling her name, "Catherine, I'm coming. Where are you?"

A man wearing a smock grabbed his arm. Aaron, dressed in his robe and shorts and a pair of slippers said, "I am looking for my friend, Catherine Tyler. Do you know where she is?"

The man shook his head. "I speak English little. Catherine Tyler? In emergency." He pointed the way.

They burst through the door and into a small room where a doctor and nurse were leaning over a bed. A sheet covered the person. The man spoke German to the doctor. Catherine Tyler was all Aaron understood. The doctor pointed to the sheet. "Catherine Tyler!"

Aaron took a hold of the sheet. The doctor grabbed his arm, "No, No!" He put his hands over his eyes.

Aaron said, "I must see her!" He drew back the sheet and he stared in horror. The black skin was matted in blood. Her face was so battered and bloody it was unrecognizable. But he knew it was Catherine's smooth black skin, her delicate fingers (those that weren't coated in blood), and the crazy nail polish she liked to wear. It was her!

Aaron went into his own world. This was not real. It was only a dream. So he played the dream out. "What happened to her? How did this happen? How? Why is she dead?"

The doctors didn't answer. The policeman who had found the body and the ambulance crew that had brought the body to the hospital didn't know. Aaron wandered into the waiting room and called out, "Does anyone speak English and can tell me how she died? Catherine Tyler! How was she killed?"

A small man in a servant's uniform stood. "I can tell you. I saw it happen."

Aaron sat down next to the man, "Tell me!"

The man removed his hat, revealing a balding head and deep lines etched into his face. "I am the doorman at your hotel. The hotel told me to come and wait for you until you came." The bald-headed man gave a deep sigh. "When I saw Miss Tyler come out of the hotel entrance, I called for the attendant to bring her your rental car. While we waited for it, she told me she was going to see you fight at the arena. That is how I knew where you were. The attendant brought the car and parked it on the street right in front of the hotel. As she was stepping into the car on the street side, another car came hurtling down the street. As she approached the driver's side of the car, on the street side, she opened the door and was about to step into her car when the other car smashed into her and sent her body into the air. She screamed once and collapsed. The other car kept on going.

"When I got to her, her body was so mangled I almost didn't recognize her. The other attendant raced into the hotel and they called the ambulance and the police. She was dead when they arrived. She must have been killed instantly."

Aaron buried his head in his hands and felt Katsuro's hands around his shoulder. "Gian, I will take care of Catherine's body. I will arrange for the corpse to return to Los Angeles. I will take care of everything. You just stay here as long as you need to. I am so sorry!"

It was an act of kindness that Gian would never expect from Katsuro. He mechanically mumbled, "Thanks."

Aaron had often placed himself in a state of denial that anything around him was real. He could and did become detached from his real place and go into his own dream world. He trained himself to not feel pain, to deny it. But all that was physical pain—pain to the flesh, not to the heart. Since he had never loved before, never had anybody love him before, this new pain was harder to cope with. Only when he had killed Dog did he feel such anguish and anger, but that rage was focused on himself and his own inadequacies, his own lack of courage to say *No*. From that he had learned and gained courage. On several occasions, Katsuro had threatened to kill Dog or force Gian to kill his best friend. Gian's new strength, forged in iron, led him to say *No* despite the consequences.

Catherine loved him. He loved her. This sense of loss was unbearable. As much as Aaron tried to become detached from this reality, he failed. He could not overcome this loss of love. He never wept. That would have been too easy. He did not know what to do, so he did nothing but sit next to her body and stare. He was alone, as always.

When they finally took the body many hours later, he left the hospital, shrugging off Teddy's plea to help him, and walked back to the hotel. He knew he had to pack. They were going to Barcelona. He entered their vacant room and began emptying all the drawers of their clothes. He placed both suitcases on the bed.

When he opened his suitcase, he found an envelope addressed to him. The smell of her perfume on the paper jolted him back to a brief reality.

Dear Gian, As I sit here getting ready to leave to see you fight, I am thinking about what we talked about last night. I only want what is best for you. If you don't want to get married now, I can wait until you are ready. We will still be together. And if you need to fight and feel good about still fighting, then fight on. I want you to love me and love what you do. I know our trip to Barcelona will be the most romantic and wonderful vacation we have ever had together. I can't wait to hold you again, Love always, Catherine.

Aaron clutched the letter to his heart, laid down and his mind went black. *I want to die. I want to be with you, Catherine. I can't stand not being with you. Please, Catherine, come back to me. Why did you leave me? You know I love you. God, why did you go?*

There was a sharp knock at the door. "Come in!"

The waiter wheeled in a cart with several bottles and a glass next to a bucket of ice. "Thanks, just leave it there."

Aaron got up and poured himself a drink and swallowed it straight. He didn't want to feel the alcohol—he wanted to feel nothing. Within the hour, he passed out on the bed and the first relief of the day was his.

Katsuro walked into Aaron's hotel room with the bellhop, key in hand. "I will take care of him." Katsuro opened a thermos of Armenian coffee and poured a cup for Gian. He lifted his son's head and poured the coffee in his mouth. "Our plane is leaving with the body this evening, and I need you up and ready. Being drunk is not a solution to any problem."

With the help of hotel staff, Teddy dressed, fed, and readied Gian for the long, solitary journey home.

CHAPTER THIRTY-FIVE

LOST IN TIME

Los Angeles was in its usual June gloom, only it was happening in August. The city was shrouded in clouds, the sun peaking through only in the late afternoon. For Aaron, it was the same. His whole being was shrouded in a fog so dense he could not rise above it. For him there was no sun, no light, no thought, just the numb feeling that his life had ended.

He did not recall the funeral, except for Catherine's mother's words, "You know she often told me she really loved you, and she knew you loved her back. What more could she want?"

Aaron nodded and hugged the vision before him and returned to his own darkness.

On the third morning following his return to Los Angeles, he found himself awakening on the beach. Like a bum, he had no hope, no future. He wandered the streets with a bottle in his hand and a rip in his heart. No one knew where he was; not Katsuro, not Ted, not Anna—not even Aaron.

Two days later, he staggered back to his townhouse. He packed some clothes in a suitcase and drove north. It took him a week to get to San Francisco. At a liquor store, he bought some supplies, food, and drink, pulled out his credit card, paid his bill, and headed for a small motel along Van Ness. There he stayed, blinded by anger and liquor and a sense of loss too profound to understand.

A month passed.

* * *

The short, slightly stooped figure got out of the taxi in the motel parking lot. He asked the motel receptionist for the room of Gian Molina or Aaron Michaels. The man checked his roster after the stooped old man placed a wad of money in his hand. "Nope, nobody here by that name. Look for yourself."

The old man looked at the register. His finger went slowly along each name listed until he came upon the name he wanted. "Here he is. A. Tyler." The old man pulled out a picture. "Is this A. Tyler?"

"Yes. 207. Upstairs."

"Thanks. Key, please." The old man exchanged the key for a hundred-dollar bill.

The blinds were drawn in Room 207. The old man placed the key in the lock and slowly opened the door, not knowing what to expect. Gian lay across the bed, not stirring, drunk. Katsuro opened the blinds and sat in a chair next to the bed.

The sun blazed through the open blind and settled on the bed, striking Gian's face. The drunk laid his arm across his unshaven, dirty face and moaned.

"*Juko*, time to come back to life. Your life is not over. It is just beginning again."

Gian staggered up on his elbows. He really didn't see the face of his mentor, just a sunny blur. "Go away. I don't want you here. I hate you. I don't want to be part of you any more."

Katsuro went on. "*Juko*, you have a contract as a professional fighter. Obligations to fulfill. You have responsibilities. You need to get back in shape."

"Shit, man, go away!"

Katsuro slapped Gian hard across the face, "Don't swear at me. I'm not one of your friends. I am your father, your trainer, your conscience. Get over it!"

Gian scrambled up on the bed and stared at the old man until he came into focus. He sat with his knees drawn up to his chest, staring at the old man, looking for guidance in his non-existent world. "What do you really want?"

"For you to go on with your life. Deal with your responsibilities. Honor your contracts. That's it."

"I'm not coming home. I want to stay here in San Francisco."

Gian was surprised at his own words. For some strange reason he was actually glad to see the old man. Maybe his appearance had brought some sense of normalcy back to Gian's life.

"That's fine. I will find a place for you to live. I know of some good places to train. I will pay for those things. I only want you to get back in shape. It is time."

"How long has it been?" Gian asked having no concept of time.

"More than five weeks. Time lost cannot be regained."

Still curled up in a sitting fetal position, Gian scratched his matted hair. "How did you find me?"

"Credit cards are easy to trace. You used yours several times and just recently in San Francisco. I will be back later. Get yourself showered. God knows you need one. Shave and look presentable. Don't run away again. It is time to get back on track." Katsuro left Room 207, waved at his attendant waiting for him on the ground floor, and called a taxi. "North Point Street, Fisherman's Wharf. The Tuscan Inn."

* * *

Katsuro smiled, proud of himself for finding Gian. *Teddy, Gian has been gone too long, find him. Call your detective buddy and have him track him down.* Teddy, an attorney by training and sadist by nature, nodded to his father and made all the right calls. But it was Katsuro who found Gian when he opened his MasterCard bill.

What are these charges from San Francisco? Who? But he knew. He called Teddy, and the detective did the legwork. It certainly wasn't hard to track a man with Gian's massive features. Besides, the last motel he stayed at identified him as sleeping most of the time and not leaving his room. "The cleaning crew could never get in there. What a slob!" said the office clerk.

Teddy called Katsuro, and the old man flew up to the Bay area.

* * *

That afternoon, father and son walked the shrouded streets at Fisherman's Wharf. "That, Gian, is where you will be staying, the

Tuscan Inn. Come now, I'll introduce you to the owner of the Karate Club. That is where I have paid for you to train."

The pair walked briskly two blocks to Sutter and entered the Karate Club to meet Bruce Cabin, a slim, dark-skinned Asian with a quick smile. Bruce extended a fist to Gian and they touched knuckles. "I have heard about you, young man, world champion. They say you are real good. Want to do a little work today?"

Katsuro stood back and watched. Gian, who hadn't done anything since the fight in Germany against Carl Brennar, wasn't sure at first. But he was curious how much his lay off had taken out of him. "Sure. Why not?"

Gian changed in the large dressing room of the upscale club. The soft material of the *gi* felt good against his skin. He started stretching and working out on the bag until he felt ready to spar a few rounds. Since this had been his longest absence from training since the age of six, he was still not sure of himself.

Bruce volunteered to work with him. Bruce put on his gear and said, "I've never had the opportunity to work with a world champion before. It will be my privilege."

Aaron took to his corner and danced his private dance, starting to put himself in his own little fight world. Bruce came roaring out of his corner and lashed a wicked right to the Aaron's right kidney. Aaron pulled back. *What is he doing? This is a workout, not a fight.* Bruce left his feet and drove a powerful right foot into Aaron's stomach. The now-flabby waist absorbed the blow. Aaron caught a left foot smack into his cheek, drawing a bloody tear to his face.

Katsuro sat back and smiled.

A small crowd had gathered to watch the world champion and wound up cheering Bruce as he delivered a series of roundhouse rights to Aaron driving him back against the ropes.

Out of the corner of his eye, Aaron saw the sly smile on Katsuro's face. It was game time. As he bounced from the ropes, Bruce sent a left foot toward Aaron's chin but Aaron caught the foot before it delivered its blow and he threw the leg in a circle, spinning Bruce off balance. He hooked Bruce's right knee with his foot and sent the owner sprawling.

Instead of falling on Bruce, as Bruce might have expected and as Aaron had been trained to do, he sent an instep kick into the back of Bruce's right knee. Bruce flipped up in a spring-like motion, rising to both feet, but his injured right knee gave way. He fell back clutching it. Aaron set his knee onto Bruce's, driving the knee into the mat.

Aaron bent down, picked up the owner by his two legs and spun him through the air, dropping him in the corner where Katsuro sat. Aaron then thrust himself onto the fallen Bruce and wrapped him in a headlock. Aaron's large muscles pressed unerringly against the owner's neck until he lost consciousness.

"You can see, old man, I am still the World Champion. Tell Bruce to remember that."

Aaron went into the dressing room, showered, dressed and met Katsuro. "That, old man, was a bad idea."

Katsuro shook his head. "Bad idea for Bruce. Good idea for you. I wanted you to know you are still the best. Just a little rusty. Slow in grabbing opportunities. Call me when you want a real person to train you." Katsuro left without looking back. He hailed a cab and headed for the airport.

Gian never went back to the Karate Club. Instead he hitched a ride on a cable car, went to Chinatown, and looked for the seediest gym he could find. There he made his home. He left the Tuscan Inn, he rented an apartment in Chinatown, and stayed there for the next three months. Only a voice message from Micah got him thinking about his contractual obligations. "Get your butt back to L.A. Fight next week at the Olympic Auditorium. Micah IFF."

"Damn! L.A. here I come." Gian had been called home. Anger and a sense of deep loss continued to engulf him. His emotions were still bottled up. Beaten to never feel pain, never to acknowledge its presence, never to confront loss, never to love or feel loved, his total being had not yet dealt with this greatest of all losses.

*   *   *

Gian entered his townhouse. The musty smell of a home untouched in many months permeated the place. He had driven south from San Francisco, throwing himself into his normal detached state. Once again, everything was a blur. When he was a boy growing up in Japan, he always had Dog with him. He was never really alone. Now Dog was being housed with his grandfather near San Diego and had not been a part of his life for a few years.

The house was eerily quiet. He walked into his bedroom and opened the closet. His few clothes hung carefully and neatly. Next to his clothes he touched Catherine's clothes. He pressed a blouse against his face and inhaled her aroma. "Catherine, where are you? Why have you left me?" He began to tremble. It felt just like the time she left to seek a new employer.

"I'll be back, Gian. I promise, I'll be back!"

"Catherine, I need you. Please come back to me. Come back!"

Never cry, Gian. Crying is for when you are really hurt. You can stand the pain. Never cry!" Katsuro stood above him, the Shinai in his hand, *"If you cry, the Shinai will not stop!"*

"God, Catherine, I miss you!"

The *Shinai* pounded his back as he fell onto his bed, *"The Shinai will not stop whipping you if you cry!"* The *Shinai* lashed his back. For one of the few times since the age of six, tears welled up and burst forth. He never felt *The Shinai*, only the pain of loss. His emotions had conquered the power of the *Shinai*. The grieving for Catherine Tyler had begun.

Gian slept on and off that night. He clutched his tear-stained pillow and allowed the pain to seep from him.

* * *

Ted sprang from his crouching position like a tiger. "See that? That's how you show you are ready. Show your toughness."

The squatting teenager smiled a pimply grin, almost laughing. "That looked silly!"

"It only looks silly because you don't understand yet what it takes to be a winner." Ted was angry. *Teaching these damn teenagers with no sense of combat is frustrating.*

"Okay, Jay, go to the punching bag, and then take five."

"What's the matter, Ted? Find these kids a little tough to teach?"

Ted turned, ready to explode. "Aaron, God damn, man, good to see you." Ted's face grew sad, "I was so sorry to hear about Catherine. I know she meant a lot to you."

Aaron hugged his friend. "Thanks, dude. I really loved her. She was special."

"Are you back to stay?"

"Yeah, I guess so. I got a call from Micah over at IFF. He wants me back fighting."

"Under contract?"

"Under contract, right. How have you been? How's your mom doing?"

"We are both okay. Mom's been asking for you. Why don't you come over for dinner tonight? Mom would love to see you."

"Okay. Why not?"

"Say, I got a call from Madeline. You remember her? She was a friend of Catherine's. She was looking for you. Wanted to talk."

"Did she leave her number?"

"I have it at home; I'll give it to you tonight."

Aaron sat and talked to Anna and Ted well into the night. It made him feel good. Talking to Anna relieved much of his tension. And for the first time he cried in front of another person. Even growing up at six, he would crawl away from the *Shinai* and cry in a corner curled up to protect himself from the blows.

The tears flowed more easily as he talked, and the fear of the *Shinai* was removed, at least for the moment. They talked about Catherine and what she meant to Aaron.

He clutched the paper with Madeline's number on it. Aaron's life was about to change again.

CHAPTER THIRTY-SIX

MADELINE'S STORY

The phone rang several times. The voice was soft and withdrawn. "Madeline? Aaron! You don't sound very good."

"Oh, Aaron. Thanks for calling. I feel so bad for you. I know Catherine loved you. She told me. How are you doing?"

"I'm surviving. But you, what's going on?"

"Can we meet today? I just need to talk to you."

Madeline was a stout girl. Her legs were too heavy, her thighs a little too big, but Aaron remembered her as always having a broad smile and an infectious laugh. She laughed from her gut. But when he saw her that afternoon, she was much heavier, with a sullen face and sunken eyes, not the Madeline he remembered meeting many times with Catherine.

Aaron sipped a malted milk while he and Madeline talked. Madeline told her story.

"I lived near the UC campus. Even though I was a member of the Delta Delta Psi sorority, I didn't live at the house. It got too noisy and I couldn't study. So I took an apartment off Barrington Avenue with a couple of girls. I had one night class on Thursdays, plus I often stayed at the library to study late.

"Sometimes I would see this guy also studying in the library and occasionally, we would talk. I was in the library until it closed at eleven. He offered to walk me to my car in the underground parking lot. The lot was empty except for my car and his. As I went to reach for my car keys in my purse, he said to me, 'You know, you're a very pretty girl. Why don't we go out?'

"'Look, I don't have time to talk right now. It's getting late. Let's talk another time.' Suddenly, I felt frightened.

303

"'No, let's talk now.'

"He grabbed me and pinned me against my car. He ripped my keys from my hand and opened the front door. It happened so fast I couldn't really get my balance. He pulled open the back door and shoved me in. My skirt flared up and he was on me. He clawed my panties off.

"I started to scream. He pulled a knife and showed it to me. 'Don't make a sound. Just do as I say and you'll live.'

"He unzipped his pants, unbuckled his belt and pulled his pants off." 'Take my cock in your mouth. Suck or you die!' He waved his knife at my throat.

"I did him. I almost choked. I felt like I wanted to die. 'Turn around and get on your knees.' I was so scared for my life I just did as he wanted.

"Then he penetrated me. It hurt so bad! I was a virgin. I could hear his heavy breathing. And then he tried to stick it up my ass but I guess he had gone soft.

"He got out of the car. He told me, 'I'll let you live. Don't say a word to anyone. If you do, I will come and kill your family. I know where you live.'

"He left and went to his car. Then he called back to me, 'Remember, Madeline. I love you. I would never have sex with anyone I didn't love.' He laughed and drove off.

"I drove back to my apartment. When I got home, my roommates were studying. I guess I never looked at myself. My face was bruised and cut. I was bleeding from my vagina. They took me to the hospital. When I told the hospital what happened, they called campus police.

"Some nice woman cop took down my story. I told her who had raped me. He was arrested."

"What happened after that, Madeline?"

"He was out on bail and, of course, denied everything. He said he was at his fraternity all evening and had the witnesses to prove it. The trial was delayed several times because his lawyer was working on another case. He got sick. His mother became ill. Lots of excuses. The public prosecutor said it was the usual stall tactics, hoping I would withdraw my complaint and the case would pass out of existence.

"By that time I was seeing a psychiatrist. I stopped going to school. I ate too much. I woke every night with the same nightmare. I went on strong medication. My therapist thought the only way for me to get help was to have the case go to trial and have him sentenced.

"When the trial finally came, I was very nervous. I was very scared. He kept looking at me with those sorrowful eyes. Like, '*What are you doing to me?*' Some of his buddies testified he was at the fraternity house all night. It was my word against his.

"I had no corroborating witnesses to back my story. My therapist testified about what incredible terror I felt and that I had dropped out of school and couldn't function anymore.

"The jury came back with a decision of not guilty.

"A week after the acquittal it happened again." Madeline took a deep breath. "I couldn't believe it. One night he was in my parent's garage. 'I told you I knew where you lived. You shouldn't have told on me. That was bad for my reputation. Come on, let's go upstairs to your room. Let's take the back way. I know your parents are away for the weekend. Besides, you owe me.'

"He pulled a knife from his pocket.

"We went upstairs from the garage. He raped me again. I am so scared, Aaron. He says he will do it again if I tell anybody."

Aaron held her close. "Do you know where this guy lives, Madeline?"

"I got his address from the police file before the trial. He has graduated and lives in Hollywood."

That evening, with the rapist's picture in hand, Aaron Molina made a visit to see him. He watched him leave his apartment and walk to Hollywood Boulevard. He went into a strip bar, paid the entrance fee, and sat watching the girls strip. Aaron followed him and sat next to him at the bar. "You see any of them as good-looking as Madeline?" Aaron asked, his words dripping in acid.

"Who?"

"Bad acoustics! The girl you raped!"

The rapist squinted in the dark at the large figure before him. "I don't know who the fuck you are, but you got the wrong guy. Get outta my face."

Aaron clamped his huge hand over the guy's knee and squeezed. The guy started to scream, but Aaron clamped his hand over the rapist's mouth. "Never go near Madeline again. Never contact her again. If you do, you might live to regret it."

The rapist grabbed the released knee. "I got plenty of friends who are very tough. I can play real dirty. Wanna to see how?"

Aaron sneered. "You want to play it rough, you got it. You just made the second biggest mistake of your life."

Gian went to see Katsuro in his office. He told Katsuro the story Madeline had told him. Katsuro listened. When Gian was done, Katsuro asked, "What do you want me to do to him?"

"I'm not sure."

"Give me his address and I'll take care of this."

Gian felt relieved. He had backup.

The next night Ryuu and Teddy, along with three of their workers, drove quietly into Hollywood. They parked across the street from the rapist's apartment and waited. Using the picture Gian had given them, they saw the man get out of his car. They crossed the street quickly and walked up to him.

"If you make a sound, we will kill you right here. Just come with us quietly," Teddy whispered. The rapist cringed. His stomach turned. His faced bleached white.

"What the fuck . . . .." Teddy slammed a hard fist into his face. "Quiet!"

They shoved the rapist into their car and drove along the back streets of Hollywood until they came to a large, deserted garage. "Open the door," Teddy yelled to one of the workers.

The garage door slid open and the car drove into the abandoned building. The rapist, securely tied with duct tape, was boosted out of the car and hoisted onto a pulley, to which he was tied very securely. Teddy ripped the tape from his mouth.

In the corner of the garage stood a slightly stooped older man. The man pulled a picture from his briefcase. "You know this girl?"

The rapist looked at the picture. "No!" His voice shook with terror.

The old man took a nail gun from an assortment of tools hanging from the wall. "Did you know, Ryuu, a well-placed nail just behind the knee will cause all sorts of pain but never really leave a mark?"

"Really!" Ryuu grinned. He loved to inflict pain.

The rapist screamed. "No! What are you doing?"

The old man showed the rapist Madeline's picture again. "Do you know her?"

"Yes, yes . . . I know her! Now let me go! Please! Please!" His voice gave way. He began to sob.

The old man showed the rapist the picture again. "Did you rape her?"

The rapist sobbed. Ryuu placed the nail gun against the back of his knee and pulled the trigger. The nail entered the back of the knee. A small hole leaked blood. The rapist shouted in pain. "What did you do?"

"It's more important to talk about what you did. Did you rape her?"

"Yes! Yes! Yes! I raped her. For God sake, let me down. Please!" His body fell limp as he lost consciousness.

"Wake him up, Teddy."

With his fist wrapped in brass knuckles, Teddy sent a sharp right to the rapist's stomach. The rapist lurched forward, then his head rolled back. "Well, gentlemen, we have the right man. He is the rapist. Take him down." The workers released him from the pulley, all the while laughing, as they let him drop to the cement floor.

The rapist tried to stand but crumbled back to the floor, his knee in agony. Ryuu laughed aloud. "Maybe we should show him how Jesus suffered for the sins of others."

The rapist turned sheet white. "No! No! Don't!"

"Why not? You said you were a tough guy. You can handle a little bit of pain. It won't be as painful as raping that innocent girl."

The rapist tried to run but couldn't. He fell over. The nail in his kneecap sent shock waves through his body. The workers held him up against a piece of plywood.

"This is not really a cross, and I'm sure they didn't have plywood in JC's days, but here goes." Teddy smirked. He pulled back the trigger of the nail gun, released it, and sent a piece of cut shrapnel into the palm of the rapist's hand.

Ryuu slammed his fist into the rapist's face. "Here, let me!" A worker drove a kick into the man's groin. Each worker took a turn kicking the rapist in the groin.

Ryuu looked up at the man. "We are letting you live. If you ever come close to Madeline again, you will die in more pain than you could ever imagined was possible. This is just a sample."

The old man finished taking his pictures of the rapist as he was held up by the workers. "He passed out again. I want him awake when Gian comes. I know he will want to talk to his friend."

While they were waiting for Gian to get to the garage, Katsuro doctored up the rapist. He extracted the nail fragments that hadn't gone clear through the rapist's hand and knee. "Oh, my God!" The rapist wept.

Then the rapist heard a familiar voice at the entrance to the garage. Gian stood and surveyed the scene. "He admitted he raped Madeline," Ryuu said matter-of-factly.

Teddy pulled back the man's head. "Did you rape Madeline?"

In a voice barely audible, "Yes! I raped her."

For the first time he could remember, Gian was appalled at what he saw. "You shouldn't have done this. You have taken revenge for me. I'm sorry, I must leave."

Teddy didn't understand Gian. So he went on talking. "But he raped her. He raped your friend."

"Yes, I raped her!" The man gagged on his own blood.

"You want to shoot him full of nails, Gian?" Ryuu asked.

"No, Madeline wouldn't want me to." Gian realized they didn't understand him nor would they ever. He wasn't like them. So he went on. "But does he understand if he ever goes near her again what will happen to him? And if he says anything to anybody about what happened here, he will get another dose of this?"

"I do," the rapist said. "Please let me go!"

Katsuro finished wiping the blood from the rapist's mouth, checked the puncture wounds behind his knees and in his hand. "He's ready to go. Boys, take him home. I think we established justice here today. Gian, give us a ride home!"

On the way home everyone was silent. Gian was bursting with curiosity and revulsion. "Katsuro, why were you there with this guy? You didn't even know the girl who was raped."

"You had a problem to solve. You are family. We do for family."

It was that simple. *We do for family.*

Gian continued the drive in silence. He had no feeling of satisfaction, only disgust at what they had done. He knew, at that moment, he wasn't part of them. For that revelation he was glad.

The rapist's beating left a bitter taste in his mouth.

Nearly a year later, Madeline was doing well, she looked much better and was back in school. Gian and Madeline, who stayed in touch, were in the Westbrook mall when they spotted the rapist walking on the other side of the walkway. He spotted them and he ran. "Gian, why did he run? Is there something you haven't told me?"

"Trust me, Madeline. You know all you need to know. That man is part of your distant past and will never bother you again."

Madeline looked as if she wanted to ask more, but didn't. "Okay, thanks for whatever you did."

CHAPTER THIRTY-SEVEN

KATSURO'S LAST FIGHT

Aaron was back into his regular routine. Everything was the same, except he was usually angry. All the happiness and contentment he had felt with Catherine had ended. Life was not right for him. For love, Aaron substituted sex. He told every girl the same thing. "This is just for sex. I don't make any commitments. You want me? I am yours, for tonight. I date whomever I want, and you might not be my only girl. Take it or leave it."

When Aaron told this to Anna, she burst out laughing. "You've never laughed at me before. What did I say that was so funny?"

Anna patted him on the arm. "Sweetie, I'm not laughing at you. I'm laughing at your gall. To think you have girls falling for that line. I'm laughing at them and their stupidity."

Aaron turned serious. "But I tell them the truth. I only want sex and I don't care who I'm with."

"You're scared of loving somebody. Love is a gamble and sometimes you lose. Sometimes you do lose the one you love. Sometimes you gamble and win. Love will come your way again. Didn't it feel good while you were with Catherine?"

He bowed his head. "Really good. But there will never be another Catherine. She was too good."

Anna said, "Let me tell you something. There are many fish in the sea, many fish to fry. That special person will find you and you will find her. Give it time. Few good things in life rarely come easy."

Talking to Anna made Aaron feel better. He had never had anyone to talk to before. He really liked Anna. All this talking and being with caring people was new to Aaron. Sometimes he found it hard to enjoy. Anger still filled most of his days.

That anger was no more evident than when Aaron fought. "Disqualified. Aaron Michaels has been disqualified." The referee raised the hand of the big man with the ugly scar sliced across his face. Katsuro never said a word to Gian when he was disqualified. He secretly admired his aggressiveness. Katsuro sensed that Gian could now kill a man in self-defense. That was the position he wanted his champion to be in.

Gian settled into his old lifestyle that made him feel more comfortable; however, at the same time he felt conflicted. His frequent mood swings, periods of aggression, and his inability to care for anyone left him drained and indifferent.

It was during this time, conflicted by a loveless existence and his emotional outbursts, that Katsuro came to see him in the dojo. "*Juko*, I have watched you closely in your last few fights. You have almost reached the point of perfection, but you are not quite there yet."

Gian stopped his shadow boxing, leaned on the ropes and listened. He knew what Katsuro would say, he had heard it so many times. "Remember when you fought the street fighters in London at age fifteen and I asked you if you would or could kill your opponent?"

"Yes, I recall that and many other conversations."

Katsuro stood up, his stooped shoulders now thrust back. "Are you willing to kill another human being now?"

Gian just stood there and didn't answer.

"If your answer is 'No,' then you cannot be all you hope to be. Because, when you can't kill, you have feelings that are holding you back, like when that woman was around. Just her mere presence held you back. You cared about her, became attached to her emotionally, and that held you back."

Gian, who seldom ever heard Katsuro speak so much except when he wanted to make a point and set an example, marveled at the old man's dedication to his own thoughts.

At that second, Gian knew he could kill someone, and that shook him to his core. Had he turned into Katsuro?

Late afternoon that day Ryuu entered the dojo, whispered to Katsuro, and sat to watch Gian work out. "Enough, *Juko*. I want you to go with Ryuu. He is going to a dinner meeting with some business friends. It is time you learned more about business."

The Tachigi family business was widespread. It involved protection, loan sharking, and other fringe criminal activities. Today's lesson was very succinct: never cross a Tachigi.

*   *   *

The Korean presence in Los Angeles had grown significantly since Katsuro had gone into business. Most were hard-working people, well educated and industrious, but a radical few were from feudal families with ties to the Korean mafia. Some were into drug running, bringing their trade from the Far East and setting up shop in their new locale.

It wasn't the drug business that bothered Katsuro, since the Tachigi family had never dealt in drugs. It was, however, the Korean gangs' attempted takeover of Katsuro's businesses that riled him. It was the protection business, the money laundering, and the loan sharks that Katsuro saw as a threat to his well-established business of protecting local merchants from criminals.

*   *   *

The soft-spoken Korean, tapped Number One with his gold-crested cane and waved his oldest son to take a car filled with his henchmen into the Cuban Market. The entourage of Koreans entered the large market filled with shoppers. Most of them were Cubans looking for food cooked from their country's recipes. They looked forward to inhaling the fragrances of a country they did not dare to return to, and gabbing the warm day away.

The entourage moved swiftly to the rear of the market and into the owner's office. He was simply known as Mr. Smith. He liked the name since it was pure American. "I love America. Where else could a poor Cuban make such a good living selling Cuban food to Cubans?"

he told his family. The only thing he hated were the Japanese men who came to collect money each month for protecting his market.

When the Koreans came to see him, he did not understand the purpose of their visit. Their announcement was very simple. "You are now paying us to protect you. We are charging you less than the Japanese. Call me if you need anything. This is my cellphone number."

"I can't afford to pay twice for protection. They will be here on the first. I can't pay both."

Number One poked his finger into Mr. Smith's chest. "That is the luxury we give you. You don't pay them. We will take care of them and you."

"And if I don't pay you?"

"I will burn down your business. Boom, no more business. Not even your insurance will cover all that loss."

Mr. Smith trembled. When Ryuu had come in to offer his service to him, Ryuu had said he would cut off his fingers. *Now this guy will burn down my business.*

Mr. Smith pulled cash out of the drawer and gave it to Number One. "We'll be back. If the Japanese come to collect, you tell them we have taken over." When the Koreans left, Mr. Smith called Ryuu.

*   *   *

Ryuu sat upright and rigid as he drove the business' SUV to an upscale Japanese restaurant in Hollywood. Three muscle men sat in the rear of the vehicle. Nothing was said until they arrived at the restaurant. Ryuu called back to his henchmen, "Just do as I say. Laugh at the right time and look mean."

Gian smiled to himself. *These guys look mean without acting. They are all dunderheads,* as Katsuro called them. *"They have plenty of muscle between their ears."*

Gian was learning the Japanese code of conduct as it applied to Japanese people or a foreign adversary like the Koreans. The Tachigi family would not provoke them or show disrespect, but an Anglo could.

Once inside the restaurant, Gian felt the tension between the two families. Seated at one end of a long table, in the upper balcony of the restaurant, was the Tachigi family with their hired hoods, and seated at the opposite end were the Koreans with their goons.

Ryuu whispered to Gian, "See that guy with the crew cut and scar on his left cheek? He is called Number One. Sitting next to him is his father, the Korean bastard who is trying to muscle in on our protection business. I want you to do something that would show disrespect to Number One and provoke him into a fight."

"Why can't you do that?"

"Too many elements involved. Korean, Japanese, Chinese. You are Anglo. You can do it. You won't start a real war, just a small battle today."

Gian didn't care. He took an instant dislike to Number One. He seemed arrogant. He talked in clipped English and then switched to Korean. One of Katsuro's dunderheads understood Korean. He whispered to Ryuu, "They want to know why we are here."

Ryuu stood. "We asked you to come here to explain our business and why you may not get involved in it. It is our protection business and you are not welcome in it."

Number One laughed. "We are in the business because you should be sharing your good fortune. There is plenty to go around."

Gian stood and held his nose, "Something smells in here. I believe it's you guys, a Korean stink. It's awful!" Gian leered at the Koreans.

Ryuu's muscle guys laughed.

The Korean leaned over to Number One and whispered.

"Yeah, they smell like shit," agreed a muscle man.

Number One stood. "This is no place to have a fight. You want us to fight you, so you are insulting us. That will not work. I leave."

Number One got up and walked toward the kitchen. Gian got up and followed him. They passed a small empty kitchen where some pipes had been left exposed. Gian ducked into the small room, ripped a three-foot pipe from the wall and went after Number One.

Sensing Gian's presence, Number One turned just in time to see the very tall, muscular young man with a pipe clenched in his hand lean forward and drive the pipe across his ankle. With one shattering blow Gian broke the Korean's bone.

The cry of pain reverberated throughout the restaurant. Several Koreans rushed into the kitchen and crowded around Number One. "Get that bastard! He broke my ankle."

The word melee was the way the *Los Angeles Times* described the incident. Business is what Ryuu called it.

While the goons pummeled each other and Number One was having his ankle taped by the restaurant owner, Ryuu walked over to the Korean father and he bowed. "My father, Katsuro, sends his regrets that he could not be here personally to let you know of his displeasure. He says you will withdraw your business from our area and not return. Develop your own areas to do business. Not ours!" Ryuu bowed again, whistled to call off his men, and they left.

Ryuu drove the SUV while his men attended to some of their minor bruises. "And why was I invited to this shindig?" Gian asked. "Just because I am Anglo?"

"No! Because you need to see how business works. Never let anybody step on you, even if they are a small business. You let them have one foot in and before you know it they will try to take it all. Just like fighting. Never let a fighter in. Punish him; otherwise, he will gain confidence and think he can defeat you!"

The Koreans moved their business to another part of town.

* * *

Aaron did not sleep well. Nightmares pervaded his slumber. Sometimes he dreamed about growing up in Japan, and about the torture inflicted by Katsuro.

Aaron had dinner with Ted and Anna. As usual, Anna and Aaron talked. Anna was the only one, besides Catherine, to whom Aaron had ever talked about his upbringing.

Anna just listened. Sometimes she would offer advice, but she knew Aaron had to work out his past and not make it part of his future. A summer squall was tattooing the roof. Aaron looked up and listened. "Remind you of something, Aaron?" asked Anna.

"Yeah. It sure does."

"Do you want to tell me about it?"

"Why not? It's just another type of abuse I faced."

"I must have been six, maybe seven. I had already learned not to complain because the beatings became worse when I did. One day while I was shoveling snow, I said, 'It's cold out here.' A simple statement. Not a simple response. Katsuro led me into my bathroom and ordered me to take off my clothes and to fill the tub with snow. I walked outside naked, got a shovel full of snow, and emptied it into the bathtub. I walked back and forth until the tub was full. Then he ordered me to get in naked.

"'Stay there until I tell you to get out.' Meanwhile some of the grandchildren were directed to bring pails of ice to put in the tub. I sat in the tub, naked, in the freezing snow and ice and bitterly cold water. If I had gotten out too soon, he would have ordered me back in again and to start all over. He would tell me, 'This will make you tougher. Everything is in your mind. You can overcome anything if you believe you can. Anything you have to overcome is in your mind. You will make it.'"

"The rain reminds you of that?"

"Sure! The snow would turn to rain. No matter what the weather was we would workout before I went to school."

"What would you do?"

"We would have our routine in the morning; running, moving rocks, then boulders. That started when I was six. It started with small stones I had to carry from one end of the yard to the other. Then, I had to carry rocks, then boulders. I would dig deep holes where Katsuro would bury me alive. Then he would water the area with a hose to make it extra hard for me to dig my way out. He called it strength training."

"Did you ever get buried for more than a day, like that one time?"

"Only overnight one time. Somehow I managed to dig my way out. Ryuu pounded the dirt tight around me, that made the ground extra hard and impossible to dig out."

"Strength training?"

"Right. And, of course, there was always the *Shinai*. When all else failed, he would beat me with the *Shinai*."

"Is that part of your nightmares?"

"Always."

Anna put her arms around Aaron and drew him toward her. When she first hugged him the night they met, Aaron had let her arms engulf him. No one except Catherine had ever hugged him, never while he was growing up, never. So Aaron did not know what to do the first time.

While Anna held him, she said, "You can put your arms around me if you like, if that makes you feel better. It's okay!"

Aaron extended his arms slowly around Anna and drew her in close. They hugged. Aaron's mind went blank; he became detached. He didn't feel anything. His arms went soft. As soon as Anna felt his arms loosening, she whispered. "It's okay to hold someone, to hug someone. Just let it happen."

Aaron hugged her back. He felt her closeness, like the mother he wished he had had. He was brought back to the present by Anna's gentleness. He had never realized the simple act of a hug could be so powerful. Anna's hug felt good. Aaron hugging Anna felt right.

"Was that so bad? Did it feel okay?"

Aaron couldn't speak. He felt like crying but he didn't want to, so he just nodded yes.

"If and when you need to talk, I am here for you. Anytime, anywhere, just come over or call me. I am here to listen and give hugs." She saw the moisture in his eyes; she dotted them with her handkerchief. I know you weren't raised that way, but it's okay for a man to cry. In fact, it might make things clearer."

It was after that visit Aaron came full circle. He was no longer alone. He didn't have to face the future by himself. He could now share it with two people who cared about him. He felt very much at ease spending another evening with Anna and Ted.

"You said at dinner you wanted to tell me something. Are you still okay with that?"

Aaron drew in a long breath. "Are you okay to listen? What happened to me must be hard for you to hear."

"Not as hard as it was for you to endure."

"I told you about the time Katsuro strung me up and beat me within an inch of my life. Well, that wasn't the only time he did that. Many times, he would string me up to the pulley system from the punching bag, beat me with the *Shinai* and just let me hang there. And then he would preach: *'The human body will do anything you want it to do. All you have to do is ask it. Your mind can handle all things. Train your mind to handle the pain you think you will feel.'* And I would just hang.

"Sometimes his sons would come by and beat me. They would rarely say anything, just laugh as they whipped me. Then Katsuro would come back and take me down. He would rub me with that awful smelling stuff he used to heal my cuts. But much worse was when he would take very hot oil and pour it over my body and say, 'This will make your skin tougher.'"

"Hot oil?"

"Uh huh. It would burn something awful, especially on the cuts. But I would never cry out. I would never give him the satisfaction of hearing my pain. When it was all over, he would tell me to go back to my room. Somehow I managed to walk out of the dojo and then collapse to the ground in agony, but never in front of him. That would mean he won."

"Like the game you told me about?"

"Like that game!" Aaron took a deep breath and let out a long sigh.

"After we moved to Canyon Falls, he would lead me to the barbeque grill, light it, and add potash to the charcoal. When the coals were red hot, he would make me roll my hands in the burning coals. He would always say the same thing, *'It will make your hands tougher.'*"

Anna was horrified. Keeping her calm, she asked, "Did he do any of these things he made you do?"

"Katsuro? Sure. He would roll his hands in the coals. But his hands were real hard. Even well into his eighties he would do what I did. He would run every morning, lift rocks, dig holes and refill them, and run his hands through the red hot coals."

"You told me he buried you once for two days. Did he ever bury any of his other children?"

"No! Katsuro told me I was the only one of his children and grandchildren who never complained about anything. I could take it. Besides, I think this was a game with him, seeing if he could break me."

"So why didn't you cry out and tell him to stop?"

"Because if I did, he would have won the game. I would never let him win. The only time I told him I wouldn't do something is when he wanted me to kill my second Dog. When he wanted me to kill him for loving him too much, I told him no matter what you do to me, I would not kill Dog."

"And what did he say then?"

"He didn't say anything, he just walked away and forgot about it, I guess."

"And how do you feel now?"

Aaron didn't hesitate. "Tired. Very tired of everything that has gone on in my life."

Aaron was opening up. He felt comfortable talking to Anna. He realized talking made him feel better. "The game started when I was about ten. I began to understand completely. The *Shinai* was his primary weapon of torture. At first, when he beat me, I cried and pleaded with him to stop. He didn't. He lashed me until I stopped crying. Then he would stop, and say, *'Learn to take it. Your mind can control the pain. It will do what you want it to do.'*

"If I was on the ground when he was beating me, he would keep whipping me until I got up and walked away. So I learned not to yell out, not to cry, not to grovel, not to plead for him to stop. I learned to tolerate the pain and eventually even embrace it. I fell into a routine of work, beatings, and being berated and punished for anything he thought was good for me. Even though his thinking might have been irrational and convoluted, I played the game. But now, the game has become wearisome. It is time for me to stop and change my life."

"How would you do that?"

"I'm not sure. I really don't know."

Anna moved closer to him on the couch and held him. Aaron put his arms around her and held her, too. It felt so right. On a whim, Aaron asked, "Anna, can I call you Mom? I've never had a real Mom. I would like you to be the Mom I never had."

"Aaron, I would be honored to be your Mom." Anna cried. She had finally reached him. *God, this feels right!*

* * *

Katsuro and Aaron were in San Francisco at the National Kung Fu Tournament. During the event, they attended an important meeting with many other Grand Masters.

The Grand Masters talked about their various systems and techniques, strength holds, balance, each others' specific methods and practices, and also their strengths and weaknesses. As he always did, Katsuro bragged about his system. "*Akin Jitsu* is superior to any system. It has no weaknesses. None!"

Gian was in awe. These men were the greatest Grand Masters of the era. No fighter was better than any of them. None were more proficient. None were more knowledgeable. None were more savvy or skilled. These Grand Masters were all icons.

During the discussion voices were raised, tempers heated, and men raked each other over the coals. The Grand Masters protected their own system vociferously while they railed the other systems. None of them was more bellicose than ninety-year-old Katsuro Tachigi. He screamed at a gaping Grand Master as he challenged his system, "Not only is your system flawed, it is weak and easily overcome!"

The Grand Master, livid at being challenged by Katsuro, bellowed at the old man, the oldest of the Grand Masters, "If you weren't so damn old, I would beat you! I would prove to you that your smug superiority is not true!"

Katsuro stood, slowly. "My age has nothing to do with it. My system is better and I am willing to prove it. No matter my age, I will beat you." Katsuro banged on the table with the cane he now used. "Age makes no difference. I will beat your young ass."

The challenged Grand Master, a man in his early sixties, was furious at being called out. "Tomorrow, in the main building, we will fight." He pointed his finger at Katsuro and fumed, "Fucking old man."

The next day the two Grand Masters took to the mats in the center of the main floor of the Exhibition Center. Older fighters, seasoned veterans, novices, children and teens, professionals, they all stood captivated, eager to watch the two Grand Masters square off.

Fighters who were loosening up and preparing for combat stopped. Fight mats were deserted. The crowd of onlookers was hushed in whispered clusters as the two approached the middle of the mats.

Katsuro stood there. When the other Grand Master bowed, Katsuro did not bow in return. Katsuro did not even acknowledge him. Katsuro looked at Gian and said, "Call me."

Gian walked over to start the match. "Hands up!"

Katsuro stood without moving. The other Grand Master, thrown off by Katsuro's failure to follow protocol, skulked toward this older Grand Master.

Katsuro shifted his feet. He placed one foot in front of the other, his hands still at his side. The younger Grand Master continued to inch forward and gave Katsuro a shoulder fake. Katsuro still did not move. He just stood, eerily still. The buzz of the crowd was intense and echoed through the Center.

The sixty-year-old Grand Master launched the first blow. Only then did Katsuro move. He slid his right shoulder forward and with his right hand stiff hit the man with one shot to the sternum. Simultaneously he turned, shot a well-placed stiff hand into the man's neck, and followed it with an elbow into the other side of the neck.

The younger Grand Master fell flat onto his face, unconscious. Katsuro was done.

He pivoted and walked off the mat. He never looked back. The crowd stood in stunned silence. Katsuro walked over and wiped his face with a towel.

The blows didn't look hard to Gian. But they were perfectly placed. Pinpoint! *Your blows don't have to be hard, just accurate.*

That evening Gian talked to Katsuro. "That was incredible, Katsuro. He is a Grand Master, he is the best in his system. How . . .?"

"You, you, my son, know how. I have taught you what I know. The first blow, a blow to the sternum, is where all the nerves in the solar plexus lock endings; it essentially paralyzes someone if you hit them there. That blow in the area of the diaphragm makes it hard to breathe.

"The second shot is basically around the carotid artery. The muscle tissues swell, the neck spasms and the fighter drops, out cold. You do not have to hit someone hard, you just have to hit him accurately. Know where to turn a person off."

Gian now knew why that wooden figure was in the dojo. The wooden figure represented *that* Grand Master.

CHAPTER THIRTY-EIGHT

SEX

Aaron dated many girls after Catherine. Who they were and what they did is not important. Perhaps the story of Michelle is a perfect example of how Aaron handled his many relationships.

Michelle Fitzler was a petite, elegant girl. She was the daughter of a prominent physician and a nurse he married many years before. Brought up in Canyon Falls, she met Gian while he was jogging along the back trails, usually reserved for the resident horse set. Her mount, Pretty Boy, was a purebred stallion she had gotten on her sixteenth birthday.

She rode Pretty Boy every morning before school and each afternoon before she did her homework. She was in her senior year at California Academy, studying Japanese.

"Why in the world would you want to study Japanese when they offer

Spanish, French, and Russian?" her mother asked as she was signing Michelle's program card for the year.

"Let me list the reasons," offered Michelle. "I can pick up Spanish from the maid—too easy. French is irrelevant. The French have been irrelevant for many years. And Russia is no longer a power. So, Japanese is my choice."

Her exasperated mother took a deep breath, shook her head, and thought to herself that Michelle was a great student and should be mothered only when it made a real difference.

Pretty Boy was galloping easily along the winding path over the hills near her home. The trail meandered through grass-covered knolls, passing large oak trees and dried riverbeds. Occasionally rattlesnakes, when not in winter hibernation, made a sinister buzzing sound to scare both rider and horse.

Michelle first saw the huge figure loping along the dusty trail, racing full speed, and then stopping to shadow box, then run again. She thought to herself, *That guy is weird—running, stopping, dancing, and then running again. I wonder who he is. A new family moved in last week. Maybe they have a son.*

Pretty Boy was full of run. He sped along the narrow path not wanting to stop, so Michelle could not chat with the guy running. She pulled the reins back hard to slow her stallion, but today the horse was headstrong. As they approached the dancing figure, Pretty Boy let out a loud whinny and galloped right by the now-still figure.

"Sorry," shouted Michelle as Pretty Boy raced by, kicking up a torrent of dust.

Aaron swallowed the dust and coughed. "Sorry, shit!" Aaron was angry. He took off after the horse and rider, finally slowing down enough for Aaron to catch up. He reached high and dragged the petite figure from the horse.

Startled, Michelle screamed at the aggressive move. A giant pair of hands encircled her waist. Michelle wiggled, kicked her feet and flayed her arms. Pretty Boy lurched to a stop, turned his head, whinnied, and walked back to his mistress being held aloft.

"Put me down, you son-of-a-bitch. Damn it!" Michelle screamed, Pretty Boy neighed and Aaron glowered.

"Your damn horse tried to run me down. Ain't you got any control over that bastard?"

"Pretty Boy is not a bastard. He's my sweetheart." Michelle, held aloft, couldn't reach her steed.

Aaron, still holding Michelle, said, "You want to go up on the horse or down on the ground?"

Frustrated, Michelle screamed, "Just put me down, you big oaf."

"Big oaf? I've been called many things but never a big oaf." He dropped her onto the path.

"Shit! You could have been more gentle."

Aaron whirled and continued his run.

"Wait! Wait! Stop!"

Aaron stopped, turned around and yelled, "What do you want? You tried to run me down. I saved you from a runaway horse with no thanks from you. So what do you want?" Aaron was angry and Michele knew it.

Michelle looked at the hulk. She could not help but admire his rugged good looks and soulful eyes that never looked directly at her. "Thank you for rescuing me. I'm Michelle Fitzler. I haven't seen you around here before. Do you go to school here?"

Aaron took a close look at the girl standing before him. *She's pretty enough. I wonder if she fucks.* "I'm a UC graduate."

"I'm a senior," Michelle said. She just forgot to mention she went to California Academy. "Are you training or something?"

"Training. I'm a fighter."

Michelle lifted her eyebrows, "What kind of fighting?"

"Mixed martial arts." Gian noticed immediately the confused look on Michelle's face. "You've never heard of mixed martial arts, right?"

"Right! What is it?"

Aaron thought this girl might be pretty good in bed but was definitely not worldly. The thought hit him hard. "Why don't you come back to my place, and I'll show you what it is."

"Your place?"

"Sure, the Tachigi home."

"You live there?"

"I'm the son."

"That's a Japanese family. You're their son?"

"It's a long story."

"You read, write, and speak Japanese?"

"I was born speaking Japanese."

Michelle was giddy. "I'm learning to speak Japanese. Would you help me if I need help?"

Aaron knew his contact just got a lot closer. He wanted only one thing and he would do anything to get it. "Sure, I'll help you."

They exchanged numbers. Aaron jogged on thinking about Michelle in bed.

Michelle met Aaron late the next afternoon. The eighteen-year-old entered the Tachigi estate's back gate that exited to the horse path surrounding the ranch. Aaron knew nobody would be home for two days. Rita was visiting a relative and Katsuro was away on a business trip to San Diego. They left Aaron to watch the house.

Aaron was already dressed in his *gi*, the cloth wrapped around his body, his underwear snug, and his bare feet clean from the ritual bath. Michelle peered into the dojo. "Well, I'll be damned. This is really neat. So, what do you do?"

"I'll show you." Aaron went through a short version of his daily workout, striking a pose at the end, showing off his rippling abs as his *gi* came loose.

Michelle looked at the sweaty body and was turned on. His skin glistened from perspiration. She could feel the tenseness in her loins. She wasn't a virgin. She had had sex several times with her first boyfriend until she moved on to better pickings. But here was a real man.

Aaron let the *gi* unravel, revealing his underwear. "I wondered what men wore underneath their garments." She stared at the bulging muscles. All her other boyfriends had puny bodies. This body was solid and muscular. "You are quite well-developed."

Aaron slid out of his cloth. "Come over here. Do me a favor." He picked up a bottle of massage lotion. "When I lay on this massage table, will you rub my back? My muscles get sore."

Michelle smirked. "That's the first time I've heard that line. Haven't you got a better one?"

Aaron laughed, "Sure, you get undressed and I'll massage you."

Michelle laughed a silly laugh, "I'm sure you would like that better. What else you got?"

"Want to do a little boxing?"

"What do you mean?"

Aaron went to the punching bag and tattooed it with a steady rhythm of pounding fists. "Do you want to try that?"

"Sure." A game Michelle said. For the next two hours Aaron walked Michelle through all the different type of equipment in the dojo.

"Here, throw on this *gi*, and we'll practice some moves."

"What do I leave on?"

"Nothin' as far as I'm concerned. But your panties and bra would be okay."

Michelle undressed behind a screen and moved to the middle of the mat. "Now what?"

Gian gave the pretty teen a short lesson in martial arts, including a lesson in self-defense. "You can try this on anybody. Watch the three moves." Gian demonstrated the moves and ended by showing her the groin kick. "That move will stop any man but me."

"And what stops you?"

"Nothing. I'm impervious to pain."

Michelle repeated, "Impervious to pain? That's quite a statement."

Aaron stood with his legs apart. "Go ahead. Kick me! Kick me hard! Don't hold back."

"Are you sure?"

Aaron nodded.

Michelle sent a right foot into his groin. Aaron took the shot having detached himself from the pain, thereby feeling nothing.

"Damn, didn't that hurt you? It sure hurt my foot."

"Want me to rub it?"

They sat in the middle of the mat and Aaron rubbed the foot with massage lotion. Michelle lay back on the mat and went into ecstasy. Aaron kneaded her foot with the touch of a Master. "I've had many massages after a fight, but I've never given one after a fight."

"I'm a lucky girl. What do you do after the fights?"

"When I'm here, I go to the bath."

Michelle smiled. "Don't tell me you have a Japanese ritual bath in this house."

"We sure do. It's in the house next door. Do you want to see it?"

"Sure!"

"But there is one thing you must know. Nobody but the family has ever been in the bath. If you go there, you must follow the rules."

Michelle's stomach tightened. "What rules?"

"Well, you're studying Japanese. Have you studied the ritual bath?"

"Well, sort of . . .." Michelle hesitated. She shook her head. "Not really. Tell me." Michelle was suddenly getting excited. This was a real adventure.

"Before you get into the bath, you get naked. You cannot go in there with your clothes on. The bath is a place to cleanse your flesh and your soul. It is sacred."

"Uh oh. Naked?"

"Those are the rules."

"What else happens in there?"

"After you get naked, you totally wash off in the shower and then you go into the bath. The bath soaks away your sins and ills. If you have sinned, the bath will purify you."

"You shitting me?"

"No, I'm not shitting you."

"This will be your only chance ever to do this: your only chance to see a real ritual bath. It is rare that my parents are away like today, and all the servants are off."

Michelle stood up and thought about the words her father had often said to her: *Do what you can do when you can do it, for you never know when you'll be able to do it again.* Of course he always added, *But don't do anything I wouldn't approve of.*

"Okay, let's go. Your rules."

They ran across the yard. Pretty Boy, hitched to the fence in the back, munching on the plentiful grass, looked up, then went back to nibbling.

Entering the ritual bath, Michelle slipped off her *gi*. "The panties and bra, too," Aaron reminded her.

Michelle looked up at Aaron. "Unhook me."

Aaron slid his arms around the slim body of the teen and caressed her. "Not now. In the bath first before you get anything."

Michelle stared at the shower and the bath beyond. "Oh my God. This is incredible!"

"And you are the first outsider to ever see this place. You may never tell anybody you've been here. Right?"

"Right."

Gian was firm and erect. Seeing Michelle's body made him impossibly stiff. "Can't you keep that thing under control for now? Get it down!"

"There is only one way it goes down. You need to make it go down." Gian paused, then asked, "You on the pill?"

Michelle nodded yes.

They showered and entered the bath. Gian grabbed her, held her face up to him, and kissed her firmly. Her lips were quivering and eager, but he didn't really feel anything, just the urge for sex. She kissed him with her mouth open and tongue pressed deep into his mouth. There, Michelle and Gian found contentment and bathed away their sins for the next few hours.

*　　*　　*

"No, I don't know where she is. She left hours ago. She was going to see this boy Aaron; but I don't know where he lives. She should have been home by now." A worried Mrs. Fitzler said to her husband.

"Well, dear, I'm sure she's fine. Maybe she's just taking Japanese lessons from this boy."

*　　*　　*

Michelle sighed, "Is this the way they do it in Japan?"

Aaron kept a straight face. "It sure is."

Michelle dressed as she checked the time. "I'd like to see you again. When can I see you?"

Aaron held her face between his fingers. "Michelle, I don't want a woman to ask that question. I will call you when I want to. When a woman is with me, I dictate what we do. I don't ever get serious with a woman. I date who I want and see who I want. You want to see me again? Well, we'll see."

Michelle was flabbergasted. This was not what she expected. Her whole body shook in anger. She screamed at him, "You only wanted me for sex, didn't you? You don't care about me."

"Right, I don't care. You want sex with me again? Fine. If not, there are plenty of others out there." The smirk on Aaron's face enraged Michelle.

Michelle was furious. "You lured me here for sex and nothing else. You bastard! You . . . you bastard!"

She dressed, ran out of the bathhouse, stomped through the fence, jumped onto Pretty Boy, and galloped off. Her mind was sprouting short quick thoughts, each one about killing the bastard. She was trapped. She couldn't tell her parents, they would be furious. Her friends would mock her. Her friends probably would tell her she's stupid and got what she deserved, having sex with a stranger. *Damn him! Shit! They probably wouldn't even ask if he was cute or if it was any good. Damn!*

Four days later, Michelle called Aaron, her girlie voice high-pitched and squeaky. She really wanted to see him again. "I miss you, honey. Call me."

He never called her back. Too many fish in the sea. He was in command.

CHAPTER THIRTY-NINE

THE LAST HURRAH

He called him. It had been several weeks since Katsuro and Gian had talked, had seen each other, had any contact. The voice on the phone wasn't as strong as usual. The tone was more subdued. The manner was warmer and friendlier than Gian could remember, but it was the voice that upset Gian.

The voice haunted him. It was a voice of someone in distress, someone who needed to talk, a voice that said *please* without saying the actual word. Still, that voice sent a small quiver through Gian. He wasn't sure why. It just did.

They set the time for one the following afternoon. Katsuro was always punctual. He ran by an internal clock that never waivered. When there was a fight scheduled for seven in the evening, Katsuro was ready to go by three. *Must arrive early. Need time to get ready mentally, physically, and emotionally. Time to stretch. Time to relax. Time to prepare but not to think.*

Gian arrived at the Canyon Falls estate, pressed the automatic gate opener, and drove through the entrance. He parked the car in front of his old residence, stared at the edifice, and shivered as he remembered what had gone on in that building. Usually the old man would be there, waiting for him, wanting him to train to get ready. But Katsuro wasn't there.

Gian entered the Tachigi home and was greeted by three uncles. Actually, they were Katsuro's sons, not uncles at all, just called uncle out of respect, as taught by Katsuro. All three were large men by Japanese standards: Teddy, Tim, and Ryuu. "This way," Ryuu said waving his hand toward the family library.

The four entered. The old man was sitting in his favorite easy chair, staring out the window and watching a pair of blue jays bathing in a small birdbath.

"You three leave, now." He waved at his sons and they left without a word or a glance at Gian. "Did you bring your stuff?"

"It is in my workout bag in the trunk of the car. I'll get it."

Upon reentering the library the old man was still sitting in the same chair, reclining. He glanced up when Gian came through the door. "Dress, my son. One last lesson." Gian was startled at the word *last*. But he said nothing.

"Come on, one last lesson. I have to give you one more lesson." The voice was soft, almost timid. "One last lesson." Then it became melancholy.

Gian thought. *Whatever! If it will make him happy, I will do it.*

They went into the backyard. Piles of dirt remained in place from when Gian had dug the holes and had not replaced the dirt. Some large holes, still left open, were partially filled with scattered debris. These were the holes Katsuro had buried him in. Large tires stood leaning against the back fence, treads peeling. Boulders were scattered throughout the yard, leaving the lawn looking unkempt and menacing.

The old man leaned on his *Shinai.* Katsuro barked out the routines. He took a long look at his protégé. This wasn't the child he had raised. This wasn't the man-child who had become his world champion. This was a man. His son's body was streamlined. Narrow hips led up to a thick chest with rippling muscles, not only denoting strength but power, quickness, and an agility that few possessed.

His son's muscular legs were like chiseled indentions on a statue by Rodin. Every ounce of flesh bulged with muscles so taut and sleek that they looked like they would explode into action with lightning speed and deliver blows so destructive they could annihilate anyone faster than the blink of an eye.

This Greek God with a sculpted body is deadly. His abilities could be classified as lethal. Sitting ramrod straight with a gleam of satisfaction in what he had created, Katsuro called out the moves he wanted Gian to perform. Like none of his other sons, Gian was an artist. He was a poet in a *gi* just like his father, an artist for the world to see and admire and eventually appreciate.

Gian's art was still in its infancy, the learning curve on the upswing, and would surely grow as he developed into his full potential. Katsuro was stunned by and proud of the creature he had created.

One last time he wanted to see the swift movements he had choreographed so meticulously. As Katsuro called out the routine, Gian, the artist, became a Nijinsky—a Nureyev as he danced rhythmically, floating over the mats—a Baryshnikov whirling on his toes and catapulting into the air like a glider whisked away in the wind.

Only the other Grand Masters, men like Ehsan Shafia or Wudang or Yuan Yubao, would understand what Gian had done to reach this height of artistry reserved for the Grand Masters of this centuries-old craft.

Gian slid from one situs to another with the invisible wings of a seraph. His arms and legs snapped gracefully from one position to another as Katsuro called out the forms. The thrusts of Gian's legs exuded overwhelming power—the power to subdue any fighter. The force of his hands, accurate and timed perfectly, could shatter any human.

Watching Gian, Katsuro realized unequivocally that Gian could kill. He could and he would kill. Thus, he was that Grand Master Katsuro had always imagined he would be. Gian was *his* champion.

"Show me Kaj." Gian moved through his routines effortlessly. *This, old man, is what you want me to be. So watch and see what you get.* Gian wondered if this would really be the last time—just one last time.

"Show me Kaj." Gian moved through the routine easily. "Show me Dance." Gian slipped into the routine trying to impress his mentor.

Gian finished demonstrating each of the techniques to Katsuro. It took well over an hour. Katsuro sat with his *Shinai* across his lap, tapping it in rhythm with Gian's moves.

At the end Katsuro approached Gian, "Every Master chooses an identifying name. Why?"

Gian thought about the question, "To show who he is, what he thinks about himself. His place in time."

"I believe I am wise, a teacher, a translator of history. And you, my son, what about you?" Gian knew Katsuro's name was Wisdom.

"If I were to choose a name . . .." Gian went into deep thought. *Here I am talking to this man, the man who abused me, who never honored me, who wanted me only so I could be transformed into his image, and now he wants to have a serious discussion? Why?* Gian could only think of a name that would offend Katsuro.

Gian chose the Master of the Samurai. "I choose Ronin."

"Of course you do." Katsuro never paused at the blatant insult since Gian had never been a Samurai like his father. Startled at Katsuro's lack of response, Gian stood quietly as the old man went on. "Now I am going to give you a gift. I am going to give you your Grand Mastership. In every form of Martial Arts there is a recognized champion called the Grand Master. I was a Grand Master. My father was a Grand Master. There is nothing about the system my father didn't know and I don't know. And now you know everything. There are things that only Grand Masters teach other Grand Masters. I taught you things none of my children or grandchildren know, because they were not worthy. You are. This is your gift. I give it to you!"

"Your children, do they know what you are awarding me?"

"Yes, I told them. They do not like it, but they appreciate everything you went through to earn it. They never could have withstood what you did. They never could have survived everything I have given you."

Gian did not respond. He did not know what to say.

Katsuro continued, "I give you permission now to say whatever you want to me."

Gian withdrew into his quiet shell. He did not want to disrespect Katsuro, not after being honored with the title of Grand Master, a title no one else could ever have. "Thank you. It is an honor to speak to you." The words felt surreal and robotic.

Katsuro shifted in his chair as if he were uncomfortable, but he wasn't. He was finishing a job he started when Gian was three. This was the culmination of a string of well-orchestrated, well-planned events, based on his own life's experiences, all leading to Gian's world championship.

"Okay," he said, "you have talked, and now I'm going to talk." His voice held steady, even though the day had tired him like no other day. "You know you are special. You rise when you fall, You stand defiant even when you know you shouldn't. You have never failed because you are special. You were given guts I did not give you. I am sad because you have decided to live your life among people who will not allow you to be special. You have decided it is better to be mediocre, because you think that is what everyone will love about you. But they will not love you because you have excelled and succeeded. I love you for that." Katsuro paused, looking directly at his son. Then he lowered his eyes and went on. "But I hate you. I am proud of you, but you disgust me. I would have given anything to have your gifts. I would have given anything for one of my children to excel the way you excelled." The old man, short of breath, waited for a response. The response he got surprised him, yet pleased him.

"That's nice. I love you. But I hate you. Fuck you. All I ever wanted was for you to be proud of me. I did this so you would accept me." Gian glared at the old man. At that moment he hated him more than ever before. He finally heard the words he had waited all his life to hear, *I love you,* yet they felt like a yo-yo as Katsuro pulled his verbal strings.

Katsuro heard the words. They were what he had expected. That was Gian—defiant, contrary, needing to be in command. "What do you want from me? Did you want me to hug you and kiss you? Lick your wounds? Pat you on the head? You did a good job, but you failed. It did not matter what I did or said. *You* never broke. That was *you.* That wasn't me. It was *you* being defiant. Maybe if you had failed, maybe if you were weaker, maybe if you hadn't been you, your life would have been different. I would have raised you in a different way, been more nurturing and given you a life you *think* you would have wanted. But what did I do? I gave you a life that exploited how special you are. You are brilliant. You are strong. There are so many things you are—you cannot even grasp how special you are. You are special! You are very special!" His voice trailed off.

Gian wondered, *Is he really showing some emotion?*

After a momentary respite, Katsuro continued as the leader of the family, its monarch and the father. His voice was powerful once again. "And it is not important for you to have these people in your life, like that fucking woman who loved you, that black woman, and then your other family. It is an American family that will hold you back. I have done everything in my power to alter that path for you. Some day you will wake up. Then you will realize you have wasted your gift. That will be a sad day for you."

Gian just sat there and did not know how to respond. He was stunned by the ferocity of Katsuro's words. They baffled him.

"Were the words I love you hard to hear?" Katsuro rose slowly from his chair and walked over to Gian. He put his hand on Gian's head the way a father touches a son, the way a person who loves another touches him.

Then he slapped Gian's face. "There is not pleasure without pain, and love without hate. Everyday I watched you succeed, I hated you for it. At the same time, I loved you for it."

Gian looked at his father, who, in his own way, had finally said the words he had been waiting to hear all his life. Gian's voice was soft. "All I ever wanted was for you to love me. That's all I wanted. I didn't need anything else. I didn't need any of the other stuff, the abuse, the torture. All I ever wanted was for you to love me."

Katsuro sat down next to Gian and they both sat silently for a while, like two fighters fatigued from a battle.

Finally, Gian gathered his strength. "Because I choose to have different types of people in my life than you want for me doesn't mean it's wrong. I know the road ahead will be difficult because it will be a totally different kind of life from that in which I was raised. But I will live it well."

Katsuro, frail yet still filled with vigor, dug deep into his soul, pulled up his hidden passion for Gian, and said, "I have told you I love you, and that I sometimes hate you, but *you* have never been able to tell *them* what you have done, who you really are. You will never give them a glimpse of how dark you are. If you did, it would crush their image of you. Their perception of you."

Katsuro's face grew somber as he reached into the bowels of his mind for his darkest secrets. "Whatever evil you think I forced upon your life and took from you, and whomever you think I *have* taken from you, I have. I *have* taken from you." Hirohsu sat proudly. The darkness was out into an eternal light.

Gian was stunned. *What did he say? Did I hear right? Is he telling me, in his way? The bastard. He had somebody kill her. He took care of it. He had Catherine killed.*

Katsuro had chosen the one thing that could bring Gian back into his life. Katsuro's controlling demonic mind had miscalculated.

Gian was angry, but not at Katsuro. He was angry at himself because he didn't protect her. He should have known.

Gian rose slowly from his chair. He cocked his fist. His mind went blank for an instant; he shook his head to clear his thoughts. If he acted violently against his mentor, Gian would have become his mirror image. But if he walked away to live his life as he wanted, he would be free from his lifelong tyranny. He chose his words carefully.

"If I have become the person you actually raised, I would destroy you. I would take my revenge on you. But I am not that person." Gian unclenched his fist. At that moment he felt free. "I just want to be left alone. I want to find someone who will have a family with me. And as for you, leave me alone."

Katsuro struggled to his feet. He looked at the floor and then glanced at his son, "Then it is over. I know the rest don't want to have anything to do with you, so it's over. Done!"

Gian stepped past the old man and walked right out the door, finding himself in the backyard. Like a robot, he walked to the dojo. He entered the sanctuary and fixed his eyes on the punching bag and the pulley that controlled its range. He shut his eyes, but upon opening them he saw a six-year-old boy, his hands strapped to a dangling set of pulley ropes, his flesh burning from the sting of bamboo, and the hurtful words repeated so often for so many years: *"This will make you tough and teach you to feel no pain."*

He wheeled around and saw the child crawling to the exit, its skin dangling, shredded, with pulps of flesh from ruptured blood vessels. The child moved and stood next to Gian and disappeared into his skeleton. He was no longer that child, no longer the man-child. He was free.

Gian left his vision, left his child, and knew immediately what he must do. He walked back into the room where Katsuro had been just a few minutes before. It was there, leaning against the chair Katsuro had been sitting in—the *Shinai*. Gian picked it up and felt the smooth bamboo. How could one of nature's most important gifts dispense so much terror?

The old man, unseen by Gian, watched from behind a door that was slightly ajar. He watched his son place the bamboo under his arm and walk out with it, and then he smiled. *It really is his. He was raised with it. It is part of his past. Good luck, my son. I love you. Use it wisely, like I did.*

With the instrument of terror snugly under his arm, Gian strolled through their house knowing it would be his last time here. The others saw him, then glanced away without saying a word. He never acknowledged them either. Looking straight ahead, he reached the front door of their house, opened the latch and walked through the entrance leaving the front door open.

It was the first time and the only time in his life, he had ever entered or left their house by the front door.

Three days after his last meeing with *his* World Champion, Katsuro Tachigi died peacefully in his sleep, joining his beloved father—ending his final journey in this life.

CHAPTER FORTY

AT LONG LAST, LOVE

Shortly after Katsuro died, his wife Rita put their Canyon Falls home up for sale and moved back to Japan. A few family members stayed in Los Angeles to run the remaining family businesses. Margaret married her Chinese boyfriend and stayed in Los Angeles. Rita, the eldest daughter, moved to Santa Susana after her Chinese husband passed away.

As for Gian Aaron Molina, he spent the next sixteen months trying to find his own identity. He continued to fight, became a personal trainer, worked in several private gyms, and dated on his own terms. He rarely saw any member of the Tachigi family except for Rita, who had made it a point to contact him on a regular basis. Her message was always the same: "We want you to remain part of our family. We know the things that happened to you were unpleasant in many respects, but we don't want you to throw away your past." Anna became Aaron's surrogate mother. He wanted it that way, and so did she. Even when he did not need help sorting through his life, he would call her to say hello, especially when Richard, Anna's husband, passed away. Aaron spoke at his funeral, further strengthening the family bond that had been formed several years before. Aaron has remained a permanent member of Ted and Anna's life.

Aaron was working as a full-time personal trainer at an *Exercise for Life* fitness center. It was his way of meeting women or girls, depending on his taste at the moment. But Aaron had changed. If he had been a religious Catholic, which he wasn't, some would have called it an *epiphany*.

Anna sat next to Aaron and patted his knee. "Don't tell me this was your first birthday dinner!"

"No, but almost. Sometimes Margaret would come over and visit and bring me a dish of ice cream and remind me it was my birthday. That was it. No big deal."

"Was tonight a big deal? Did you like it?"

Aaron began to bounce gently on the couch—his body lifting off the cushions like a kid. "Yeah, I really did! It was great. Thanks!"

"We can't replace all those missed birthdays, but we certainly can make sure all future birthdays will be celebrated properly. And just to finish off this birthday properly, Ted and I have a present for you."

Ted, who was standing at the edge of the couch, took a wrapped box from underneath the sofa and handed it to Aaron, who ripped the paper off, opened the box, and saw the wristwatch. Aaron wiped away a tear.

"It tells heart rate and workout time, and it has an alarm for your class scheduling," Ted said.

"Outside of the time I was with Catherine, this is my first birthday present ever. Thanks so much."

It was at that moment Aaron knew he had reached a turning point in his life. "Oh my God! I do know what I want. I want somebody to celebrate all my birthdays with me for the rest of my life. I need that person and I *want* that life."

Anna did not say anything. She stood and hugged her son, the man who called her Mom.

* * *

It was nearing the ninth anniversary of Catherine's death. The memory was still strong but no longer overwhelming. He thought about her only a few times a month. Although he still had occasional nightmares and eruptions of anger, he knew now what he had been searching for all along, He wanted a family. He wanted children. He wanted a wife with whom he could share his life.

February 20, 2001

She walked into the *Exercise for Life* Center, wearing a maroon sweatshirt emblazoned with "USC" across her ample chest. She swiped her plastic registration card across an electronic device and walked into the gym. Her Vans paced evenly toward the early-morning yoga class.

She joined the many members of the club torturing their bodies at 6:30 a.m. The thirty-minute class ended and she felt her muscle soreness ease. She walked past an open door and stopped to watch an advanced aerobics class go through their paces. The class was filled despite its heavy-duty, advanced nature.

"Ready! Here we go. Step lively. We are increasing our cadence." Aaron wasn't happy about this part of his job. He had agreed to fill in if one of the instructors needed help or was sick but not when the gym had to fire an instructor for incompetence. But he did his job, and eyed the dancing boobs of those women who had not yet learned about the added support of sports bras.

She watched, noted the handsome face of the instructor, and went to a treadmill machine. She set the timer on the machine and became engrossed in a television show, an old *I Love Lucy* rerun.

Aaron toweled down after his workout class ended and checked his watch. He had become much more punctual since his last birthday. His client was also prompt.

The buzzer sounded and Ali's time was up on the treadmill. She threw her towel over her shoulder and walked toward the front desk. On her way she noticed a door slightly ajar. She stopped and peaked inside. It looked like a private workout room. The tall guy who had led the aerobics class was giving a lesson. She watched without meaning to. *That guy is really handsome.*

Ali turned and went back into the gym and took another treadmill time. She kept her eye on the private room door and waited. At the twenty-minute mark, a girl left the room followed by the large guy. They both went to the front desk, talked briefly, shook hands, and she left.

Ali stopped the treadmill and walked briskly to the front desk. The large guy was talking to an attendant, glancing at his watch every couple of minutes. Aaron's next client wasn't known for promptness.

Ali looked up at the big guy, "You give private lessons, right?"

Aaron looked down at the light-haired woman beside him and said, "Yes, I am a personal trainer."

Ali stammered, "I . . . I . . . I've never had a personal trainer before. What are your fees?"

Aaron said, "Why don't you come into my office and we'll talk."

Ali followed him and walked into his office. The name on the door was "Aaron Molina." They both sat. "What's your name and why do you think you need a personal trainer? What did you do in the gym today?"

Ali bit her bottom lip. "Ali. Today I worked out in a class and did the treadmill."

Aaron looked at the woman sitting in front of him. Gone were the thoughts about sex. *She's a nice-looking girl. I think I've seen her in here before.* So he asked, "How long have you been a member?"

"A few months."

"How long have you worked here?"

Aaron shrugged. "A few months."

"I don't think I've seen you here before."

"Hmmm! Maybe because I usually come in later. Today, I was filling in for an 'ex' instructor's class."

"Oh. I think I would like to have private lessons. How much are they?"

*   *   *

Ali made it a point to be at the gym during her lunch break the next day. Two weeks later she was sitting at a table, near the gym's snack bar, eating her sandwich. She saw Aaron and waved to him. "Come over. How about joining me?"

"Okay, I have a break for a few minutes. How are you?"

Ali glanced at Aaron's left hand. *No wedding ring.* "Doing well. I decided I can't afford those private lessons."

"That's okay. You don't really need them."

"Are there some days you don't work? Do you work at night? Are you ever free?'

Aaron smiled. "That's three questions. We usually allow no more than two."

Ali smiled back. "Okay then. I'll ask you one question. Why don't we go out on a date?"

Aaron had been asked out before, but not by a girl just to have a date and nothing else. Funny, he had no thoughts of anything but having a good time. "Sure. Why not? When?"

"Well, those were your two questions. How about Saturday night? You're off then, aren't you?"

"Two good questions. What time?"

Ali put her hand on Aaron's arm. "Since I'm asking you out, does that mean I have to pay for the dinner?"

"It should. But since I'm a Molina and chivalrous, I'll pay."

They exchanged phone numbers. Ali wondered if Aaron would be a keeper.

Ali talked about her family as they shared a plate of Mexican food at the Cantina. Aaron mentioned his father had passed away recently. He remembered Katsuro's words, *New families won't understand your past. They won't appreciate the gifts you have. They won't understand how special you are.* So Aaron became a very good listener until he knew he could trust Ali.

They drove back to Ali's house, where she lived with her parents. "They went out tonight. I think they will be home late. Do you want to come in?"

They sat on the couch together. His eyes fixed on her. He held her hand. On an impulse, he drew her near and kissed her full on the mouth. She kissed him back. And then he knew: her lips and mouth tasted just like he'd hoped they would.

They held each other. "I have to confess, I spied on you. I talked to a few people at the gym who said you seldom went out with a girl more than once; and if you did, it was on your terms. Love 'em and leave 'em. Is that true?"

Aaron was embarrassed. "True! I confess. That is true."

Ali touched his chest. "Do you want to see me again?"

"You know I do."

"Then it's on my terms. You date me and nobody else."

That seemed pretty easy to Aaron. Why not? He tried to kiss her again.

"Agreed? You date me and nobody else?"

"Agreed!" They kissed again, their lips melting into one. Aaron was finally at peace.

*   *   *

Two months later Anna called Ali in the middle of the night. "Ali, I know you have been seeing Aaron only for a short time, but I think he needs your help. Ted is with him now. Can you come to the hospital right away?"

While in the waiting room, Anna told Ali some of the stories about Aaron and his childhood Ali had never heard.

Anna held Ali as she cried. "He's getting better. I see he really is getting better. Between you and me, I am pretty sure he will make it."

*   *   *

Ali and Aaron were married and now have two beautiful daughters. They live in the San Fernando Valley, close to, but many light years away from Canyon Falls.

THE END

DEDICATION

I dedicate this book to my family and friends who played a major role in my life as it is today. I thank each of you for your love, support, and understanding.

To my wife's family: You are my wonderful, warm, and loving family, too. I hope you know how much I love and adore each one of you. Even though I know I can be challenging at times, you continue to open your hearts and arms to me, and I cherish the time we spend together. How fortunate I am to have become part of your family.

To my wonderful in-laws: I am a lucky man to have the kind of relationship with you most sons-in-law could only wish for. You have been more like parents than in-laws. Thank you for accepting me, opening your home and being so warm, understanding and loving. I have learned a great deal by observing you parent your children. I use many of the techniques I have learned from you with my own little ones. A million thanks are not enough but each one is given with much love.

To my wife's Aunt and Uncle: What can I say? Thank you for all you do seems so understated and lacks the depth of gratitude I feel toward you. I love you both more than I can express. You have been a loving and compassionate Aunt and Uncle; you have been understanding and supportive friends as well. You not only invited me in but you also made me feel like it was okay to take my shoes off and stick around. I love you both. I am grateful to you for including me as part of your family.

Ken and Cindy and family have been extraordinary, wonderful friends. You have been an important part of my life, guiding me and helping me to grow and reach my potential. Thank you so much.

Special thanks to Don Goodman for the thoughtful way you have told my story. At times, it was painful for me to recount some of the events of my life, but you were never judgmental and always asked insightful questions to probe deep into my past.

To my sister and my brother: Sis; you have always shown me the tenderness a big sister shows a little brother. Thanks to you, I learned sensitivity and gentleness and compassion. Bro, you are my big brother and my best buddy. Without you I would not know what "family" means. I was like a stray dog when you took me home. Everyone was inconvenienced by my presence; yet your family fed me and cared for me. Lucky for you guys I had had all my shots and was housebroken (kind of). To both of you, thank you for all you have done for me and given to me. I will be forever grateful. I love you and respect you more than you will ever know.

To my adopted Dad: I miss you terribly. I hope you knew how much I loved and admired you. You were the first man in my life I ever wanted to emulate. I will be a father to my little girls by following the example you set as a father to me. I intend to walk in your footsteps even though yours are awfully big shoes to fill.

<u>At three different times, when my life desperately needed a change in direction, a phenomenal woman appeared.</u>

Catherine: I know you will never read this book, but I thank you from the bottom of my heart for believing in me and showing me the way to a door that would change my life. You convinced me I deserved to reach that door and go through it to a life that would be very different and much better than the one I was living . . . Sadly, you never had the chance to walk me through that life changing door.

Anna, my adopted mom: You opened that door for me and pulled me through into a life I never imagined existed, never imagined I deserved or could ever have. For the first time in my life, I had a mother. You gave me love I had never had before. I will always need you and be grateful to you for your compassion, your love, your understanding, and all the lessons you taught me. To paraphrase

346

one of my favorite lessons learned: *Parents and children have a responsibility for each other, with the only reward being love. No matter what our life becomes and how crazy things get, the most important thing is to take the time to enjoy each other and celebrate the accomplishments of every member of your family. A mother looks at her children and feels nothing more than pride and equal amounts of unconditional love for all.* **You are my mom and I am your son.** You gave me my life and taught me how to live it. I will be indebted to you forever. I love you, Mom.

My loving wife, my best friend, the mother of my two beautiful little girls, you had the hardest job of all. You walked beside me through the door that led to a family of our own. A family I shall cherish and love forever. This is a life I never could have had without you. How blessed I am that you accepted me from the day we met. You accepted my background and my life as it was before we were a couple. You accepted my personality, which is sometimes unaffected by emotional involvement. Your mental toughness, tolerant loving nature, stoicism, beguiling charm, and unconditional love have kept me grounded and make me feel needed, wanted, and loved.

You calm me down and build me up. I could spend hours, days, weeks, or even years saying thank you, and it would never equal the gifts you have given me. My life has been like a staircase, each step a block of learning, both positive and negative, each step filled with persons and events leading to the top step, where you were waiting for me. I knew from the beginning you were the only one for me. You are my love. You are my life.

To my amazing and beautiful daughters: You have completed me as a person. I look at both of you and see all the things I want for you. I want to be every bit the father I never had. I want both of you to always remember I love you and you are the greatest gift I have ever received. I will strive my entire life to make sure you understand how much I love you and I will always be proud of both of you.

A final thought . . . long overdue . . . I thank the little boy inside me. Believe it or not, you are finally free. You can go out and play.

347

The world is waiting for us. Without you I would not be who I am today.

WE DID IT! WE ARE SAFE AND WE ARE LOVED!

—G.A. Molina

CPSIA information can be obtained at www.ICGtesting.com
Printed in the USA
BVOW032356251012

303912BV00003B/2/P